Love Overdue

PAMELA MORSI

Love Overdue

WITHDRAWN

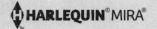

Recycling programs
for this product may
not exist in your area.

ISBN-13: 978-0-7783-1537-7

LOVE OVERDUE

Copyright © 2013 by Pamela Morsi

For questions and comments about the quality of this book, please contact us at CustomerService@Harlequin.com.

Printed in U.S.A.

www.Harlequin.com

For my cousins
Denise and Danny Max
who know a lot about wheat harvest
and even more about living happily-ever-after.

And for public librarians everywhere.
Bravely fighting on in the battle for
equality of information.

021.1 Library Relationships

Through the windshield of her aging Chevy hatchback, Dorothy gazed across the yellow poppy fields toward the Emerald City. Of course, the poppy fields were more accurately described as "amber waves of grain" and the visible tower on the distant horizon was a grain elevator rather than a wizard's dwelling, but she couldn't have felt more caught up in an unlikely fantasy. She was eager, excited, out of her comfort zone.

Dorothy Jarrow, D.J. to her friends, had been waiting for her chance since grad school. Six years is a short time, people assured her. A very short time, in an era of tight budgets and declining community commitment, for a public library administrator to find her own institution to manage. For most of her colleagues, simply maintaining employment was challenge enough. But inexplicably and sight unseen, D.J. had been plucked from her obscure job as collections assistant (aka gofer to the boss from Hell) and offered the position to head a tiny but thriving library system in Verdant, Kansas. It was as unlikely a scenario as a tornado trip to the Land of Oz.

"We're almost there, Dew," she told the small black terrier with his pink-and-black nose inching through the wires of the crate. "It's a clean slate in a brand-new life."

Three weeks ago, D.J. had never even heard of the place. Verdant, pronounced by the locals with the emphasis on the *dant,* had been simply another anonymous, inconspicuous, unremarkable small town. But after today, it would be home. A place D.J. had been searching for her whole life.

As she neared the town, she eased up on the gas pedal, forcing herself to maintain the pace of the speed limit. Not merely because all her worldly possessions were packed into a rental trailer she was towing behind her. But also, eagerness notwithstanding, small-town librarians were expected to be law-abiding, as well as sedate, slightly stuffy and incredibly sexless. D.J. was pretty certain she fit that bill perfectly.

She had dressed for the occasion in regulation gray, including low-heeled practical pumps, wearing her eyeglasses and with her dark brown hair neatly tamed and tied back at the nape of her neck.

"That part of Kansas is one of the most conservative places in the country," her former roommate, Terri, had pointed out.

"Then I should fit in very well," she'd answered.

There was a hesitation on the end of the phone line. "D.J., just be yourself," she advised.

Terri always said things like that. And D.J. always discounted such advice. It was all well and good for other people, like Terri, to follow her inclinations. But D.J. had found circumspection and reticence could be very comforting lifestyle choices.

However, none of the careful restraint she'd professed was in evidence as she reached the tiny town that was to become the center of her universe. She was almost giddy with excitement. Past the roadside gas stations, she immediately recognized the Brazier Grill. She'd seen it on Google Earth, of course. She'd been glued to the internet for days learning all she could about her new locale. And although officially there seemed to be nine commercial eating establishments, the Brazier was the only place in town that had an actual restaurant review (three stars). Beyond it were several metal buildings with business names like Avery Pipe, Gunther Fencing and Vern's Seed and Tractor.

D.J. slowed as she came to the small incline where the road crossed the collection of railroad tracks of the Burlington Northern & Santa Fe. Off to her left, the giant grain elevator loomed, casting a long afternoon shadow across the entrance to the main part of town.

This was where she was going to live. This was the community where she would plant her life. And she secretly vowed that the people who gave her this chance would never have cause to regret it.

Along the street she passed neat rows of houses, all vintage, well kept, many with porch swings, flowers in the yard, evidence of love and care.

"Plenty of places to run around here, Dew," she announced. "No more cramped apartment and crowded dog park for you."

The elegant arches of St. Luke's Methodist with its gothic spire reaching toward heaven seemed to divide the residential community from the commercial one. With angled parking and a spattering of traffic lights, D.J. thought downtown Verdant was adorably picturesque. The two-story brick and masonry buildings lined each side, some fancifully ornate and others stodgily square. On the second corner a triangular sign extended out over the sidewalk rather gaudily declaring itself the Ritz Theatre. The marquee read Movie Nights: Friday and Saturday.

D.J. spotted two banks, a hardware store, a bakery, appliance sales and a pharmacy. There was something called Flea Heaven in a building that still proudly proclaimed its earlier incarnation as Kress Five & Dime. She was glancing into the bright windows of the florist shop and nearly missed her turn. The library was on Government Street, just past the corner fire station, the 1960s turquoise city hall and the former territorial jail, still in use.

She pulled both car and tow into an empty parking spot right in front of the building and gazed at the gorgeous classical red brick with oversize concrete columns and a triangular pediment that drew the eye to the modest dome. D.J. sighed aloud. It was a Carnegie, of course. Andrew Carnegie, the billionaire philanthropist of the Gilded Age, had been a great believer in the power of the public library. He'd erected them everywhere, in every corner of the country. And this one, this one, D.J. was sure, had been built just for her.

"Perfect," she said aloud. "Perfect library, perfect town, perfect future. Way to go, Dorothy!"

She gathered up her self-congratulation and her purse and got out of the car. Though she wasn't actually starting her new job until tomorrow, D.J. just couldn't wait to see the place. She opened the back door and released Dew from his captivity. The little dog immediately raced to the patch of green lawn beneath a nearby tree and did a quick spritz before dutifully hurrying back for his leash. D.J. clipped the hook on his collar.

"Dogs do not belong in libraries," she reminded him. "I won't be long and I expect you to be good."

D.J. twisted the leash handle around the lowest limb of the tree. Dew had already spread out on the ground, happily decapitating a stick that he'd found.

D.J. climbed the steps, her heart pounding in anticipation. The opportunity had truly been out of the

blue. She'd been checking her email at lunch break and
there it was, an inquiry from her posted resume. The
first inquiry in the two years since it had been up. D.J.
had almost forgotten that it was there. And the email
was so incredible, so unexpected, she'd almost deleted
it as spam.

She'd committed the text to memory.

After examining your credentials, the members of the
board would like to offer you the position of Librarian
for Verdant Independent Regional Library. We have a
70,000 volume collection inclusive of the Main library
and two bookmobiles. You will be supervising four full-
time staff. Competitive salary, benefits. Housing provided. Please contact us immediately.

D.J. had read over it a dozen times before the words
sank in. She was being *hired*. No interview, no consid-
eration of other candidates, no nothing.

She had called to say "yes" before she even finished lunch. She'd given her notice less than an hour
later. And now she was here. Finally, finally here, D.J.
thought to herself. She had her own library in her own
town.

It took some strength to open the building's heavy
oversize door. That immediately had her wondering
about handicap access. Once inside the stuffy, airless
foyer, access became the least of her worries. The building was dark and worn, with the distinctive odor of
cellulose decay. The smell of old books could be wonderful, but the acids that eat up paper are as devastat-
ing to a library as a fire, and this place smelled rife
with them.

D.J. took a couple of steps inside, allowing her eyes
to become accustomed to the dim light. In the shelves to

her left she caught a glimpse of a man in the shadows, who immediately disappeared into the stacks.

The place was eerie, spooky, unwelcoming. Outside it had been all Andrew Carnegie. Inside it was all Tim Burton.

The main desk was a curved dais fronting a two-level, limited-access book collection behind wrought iron bars. The woman seated at the desk was a bit pudgy and probably fiftysomething, D.J. surmised. She was wearing a garish orange sweater that was easily the brightest thing in the room. And she was looking directly at D.J. Or, more accurately, she was glaring at her.

D.J. made a mental note to stress friendliness at her very first staff meeting. Leading by example, she put on a gracious smile as she stepped forward.

"Hello," she said quietly. "I'm Dorothy Jarrow, the new librarian."

Somewhere behind her a book slammed loudly closed. The unexpected sound in the hushed library made her jump. D.J. recovered herself quickly and offered another smile to the woman behind the desk.

"I know *exactly* who you are," the woman replied. Her tone was almost openly rude. She continued her task, which seemed to consist of putting address labels on postcards.

When the woman didn't volunteer her own name, D.J. requested it.

"I am Amelia Grundler," she declared with such adamancy that she obviously expected D.J. to know it. When she did not, the woman added, "I am the librarian."

D.J. managed not to drop her jaw on the floor, but her smile did waver. "I...I understood that the librarian had...died."

"Miss Popplewell died six years ago," Miss Grundler said. "But the old woman hadn't darkened the door to this place in more than a decade. All that time I've been here, the acting librarian. Now they go and hire some...some..." The woman was looking D.J. up and down. "Someone else," she finished.

"I see."

D.J. was mentally gathering up a strategy. New on the job was like being the new kid in school. It always took time to fit in, and more so when your presence was going to displace someone else. She could go with blaming the board, but she wasn't sure, as an outsider, if risking more dissention wasn't worse. Or she could beg for help, pointing out how much the woman's experience and expertise was needed. But at first glance, Amelia Grundler didn't seem to be the type to be won over by teamwork.

D.J. had just begun to consider option three, authoritarian threat, when the main door swung open letting in a broad shaft of light and a white-haired, middle-aged woman dressed in elegant purple pinstripes and a fluffy scarf of violet hues.

"Oh, it *is* you, it is you," the entrant said excitedly. "When I saw that moving trailer with the Texas license tag, I said, that's got to be our girl." She rushed forward and grabbed D.J. by the hand, as if they were dear friends. "But you shouldn't have come here first. I was expecting you at the house."

"I wanted to see the library."

"Not before you get settled in," the purple person corrected her. "Believe me, you'll get all the time you can bear in this dreary old place. I'm sure I do."

The woman waved away her surroundings with denunciation.

"But where are my manners! I haven't even introduced myself. I am, of course, Vivian Sanderson."

D.J. had spoken to the head of the library board on the phone. "It's nice to meet you in person."

"We are going to be such friends," the small woman predicted. "I'm also your landlady. Come, come. Let me get you out of this drab, dusty old place." The small powerhouse began herding D.J. toward the door.

D.J. made some effort to resist. After all, this so-called "drab, dusty old place" was her dream job, her future.

"I really wanted to tour the building," she argued.

Mrs. Sanderson tutted and shook her head. "Tomorrow is soon enough for that," she said. "This place has been here since dirt was the new thing and it will be exactly the same when hell freezes over. Besides, I'm sure your staff is not ready for you. They'll want to make their best first impression."

D.J. was already fairly certain that if Miss Grundler was any indication, her employees weren't going to be all that happy to see her at all.

The feisty woman had managed to steer her all the way to the door. She huffed a little as she tried to push it open. D.J. had no alternative but to assist.

"Goodbye, Amelia," Mrs. Sanderson said with a little wave toward the front desk. More loudly she directed a call toward the stacks. "Goodbye, James!"

Once outside in the sunlight, the woman paused to look D.J. over from head to toe. "Oh, yes, aren't you lovely," she said. "Taller than I expected, but rather prettier than your LinkedIn photo. Though gray is not your color, dear. Pink, I'm thinking, but not pastel, more a deep rose."

D.J. never wore pink, neither rose nor pastel, and she didn't intend to start.

"Mrs. Sanderson, I…"

"Oh, please, call me Viv, everybody does. And what should I call you? Dorothy? Dot? Dottie?"

D.J. would have expected the members of the library board to call her Ms. Jarrow.

"My friends call me D.J.," she heard herself saying.

"D.J." Viv tried it out on her tongue. "I like that. Very cheerful and peppy. Yes, let's definitely go with that."

Flashing a broad smile she began hurrying toward the street.

As they walked toward the car, Dew spotted them and began making excited circles in anticipation of being on the go once more.

"Is this your dog?"

"Yes."

Viv nodded. "He's not too large. I'm sure he'll be fine."

Fine for what, D.J. wasn't sure. She'd made it very clear to Mrs. Sanderson that she had a pet. She hoped that her "provided housing" would definitely accommodate that.

Viv's car, parked directly in front of D.J., was a Mini Cooper convertible in the exact same shade of purple as her suit.

D.J. gathered up Dew's leash and put him back inside his crate. She tossed the leash on the passenger seat beside her and she hurried to follow the older woman.

With the top of her convertible down, Mrs. Sanderson's scarf flapping in the breeze a la Isadora Duncan was hard to miss. And though the distance had several turns, which led to the edge of town and left streets for blacktop, her speedometer never got above twenty miles per hour.

When the purple Mini turned into the driveway of a gorgeous two-story Queen Anne, D.J. pulled in behind it with some trepidation. She had pictured her furnished housing as a second-floor walk-up in a taupe-colored stucco apartment complex. This place was not that. D.J. was fairly certain that the residence was Viv's own. The lavender paint color with eggplant trim was a dead giveaway.

Once Dew was let out, he immediately began exploring the front yard. D.J. stood by the car tentatively.

Mrs. Sanderson walked back to her and followed her gaze to look up proudly at the house. "What do you think?"

"This is your home," she said.

"Oh, yes, of course. And I am so happy to share it with you."

"I wouldn't want to intrude."

"Oh, good heavens, I need all the intrusion I can get," Viv said enthusiastically.

"But I…I'm not used to living with anyone." D.J. tried again.

"The upstairs apartment is completely private," Viv assured her. "There's a little second-floor deck off the back with a beautiful view at sunrise. And I'm as quiet as a mouse. Well, maybe not a mouse. But except for bridge club and Town Girls and Library Friends, the VFW Auxiliary…the Chamber of Commerce, but that's just once a quarter…the United Methodist Women and…other than that and the occasional friend or neighbor, nobody ever darkens my door."

"I'm not sure if it's the best thing, as librarian, for me to live with the head of the library board."

"Don't give it a thought," Viv responded. "In a town this small, keeping a respectful distance simply isn't possible. And remember, I'm providing the accommodation rent-free. With the sad little salary we pay, that will certainly help you save your pennies."

The woman did have a point, D.J. agreed. She was frugal by nature and with the money left to her by her parents, she'd paid off her student loans. Still, savings was always good. Besides, she intended to spend most of her time at the library. She could certainly sleep in the upstairs apartment of a well-connected local gadfly.

"Well then, I suppose I should unpack the car."

"I'll help," Viv volunteered. "I was going to ask my son to come by and carry your things up, but then I thought, 'why introduce them when she's all hot and sweaty.'"

041.4 Biographies in American English

Scott Sanderson glanced up to see Jeannie Brown standing at the narrow counter that served as the pharmacist's window at Sanderson Drug.

"Hi, how are you doing today?"

The thirtysomething woman blushed and shrugged. "I was going to be in town anyway and I thought... Well, I thought why don't I go by and get Mother's prescription while I'm here and...so here I am. I mean, I'm fine."

Scott smiled at her. "It'll just take me a minute."

"Oh, I hope it's not any trouble."

"No, of course not," he answered. "Look around, have a coffee. I'll bring it out to you."

She was blushing again. And he was smiling back.

Scott liked Jeannie. She was nice. She'd been nice in high school. Now, divorced with a couple of smart, well-behaved kids, she was even nicer. And she liked him. It was hard to mistake that. He should probably ask her out some time. He probably should. But he knew he never would.

Jeannie would make some guy a nice wife. But Scott had already tried that. He'd already settled for "nice." He'd married the nicest girl in town. And that had really not worked out for him. Next time, if there was to

be a next time, it was going to take something more
than nice to capture his attention.

He finished gathering up the final two scripts in
Dutch Porter's post-operative medication regimen
and then called his wife's name. The woman already
looked exhausted and her husband hadn't been home
for a whole day yet.

Scott went through all the medications, when they
were to be taken, alone or with food, and what to watch
out for.

Mrs. Porter was nodding, but he was fairly certain
that she wasn't hearing much of what he was saying.

He pulled out his business card from the holder at the
side of the window and stapled it to the top of the sack.

"My cell phone number is on here, you call me any-
time, night or day. This is complicated enough that I
expect you to have questions."

The woman immediately looked relieved. "Thank
you, Scott."

"Tell Dutch we expect him back in here lying to us
about fishing as soon as he's up to it."

She was smiling now, looking better. Dutch's health
was falling apart piece by piece. His wife, Cora, was
witness to that on a day-to-day basis. If he could give
her a break from that worry, even for only a minute or
two, he would. That was as powerful as any medicine
he had in the store.

As Mrs. Porter moved away, Scott glanced across the
room toward the long, marble-topped counter and the
soda fountain that had been a fixture in Sanderson Drug
since the day it opened in 1920. His great-grandfather
made more money as a soda jerk than he ever had as
a druggist. But he had loved crafting medicines. And
apparently that had been passed down all the way to

Scott, though what crafting was done these days didn't occur behind the pharmacist's window.

Jeannie was sitting at the fountain. She had her back turned to him, but he caught her stealing glances at him in the mirror. He pretended not to notice.

Quickly he clicked though the screens on the computer until he found her mom's regular monthly prescription. He clicked on BUY/PRINT that produced the label. Jeannie's mother was in the store every few days and could undoubtedly pick it up herself, but if anything were true about the citizens of Verdant, it was that logic and reason were not always the first choice as a guide to behavior.

Scott walked straight to the right bottle on the right shelf. He'd been working in this small, rigorously organized space practically since childhood. His father had been the pharmacist then, and he had trained Scott in the same way his own father had trained him. Every evening, every Saturday and every summer, Scott had worked in the pharmacy. It had never been considered that he might want to do anything else. In small towns, stores were simply passed down. But Scott enjoyed what he did, and he knew he was lucky in that. What if the family vocation had been septic tanks or mortuary service? It didn't bear thinking about.

He glanced up to see Jeannie looking at him again. He didn't make eye contact.

For Scott, living as a divorced man in Verdant meant there were two kinds of women to be avoided: single women *and* married ones. Or to put it another way, those who expected commitment and those who couldn't be bothered with it.

Scott had experience with both types.

He'd started dating Stephanie Rossiter his sophomore year in high school. Six years dating. A two-year engagement. The biggest, fanciest wedding that Verdant had ever seen. But the marriage was dead on arrival. Including the divorce's 60-day waiting period, they had been lawfully yoked together for exactly eight months.

Scott had hardly begun to recover when he found a shoulder to cry on in Eileen Holland. The wife of the proprietor of C&H Grain Elevator secretly amused herself with brief but thrilling affairs. She was discreet enough not to get caught, and savvy enough to pick men who wouldn't give her away. It would have been lying to say he hadn't enjoyed it. But there was an emptiness to it that he hadn't expected and that he hadn't been able to tolerate. Scott had been the one to bow out first. That was apparently an uncommon experience for Eileen and she hadn't liked it much. She hadn't spoken to him since, which was very hard to do in a town that size.

Scott poured a guesstimate into the pill tray and swept them across one-by-one with the quick precision of a man who had done this a million times. He was only off by one, which went back into the storage container. The month's supply went into a prescription bottle. He double-checked the label before affixing it to the front. Then he rang it up on the computer to be billed at the end of the month. Although city pharmacies wouldn't dream of distributing drugs on credit, most of his patients *expected* to run a tab.

He bagged it, stapled the bill to the front and carried it out to Jeannie.

She smiled up at him. A broad, friendly smile that was even more winning in the dark pink lipstick she was wearing. Jeannie looked great today. Big blue eyes and blond hair cut to frame her face. She'd gained a few pounds over the last few years, but she was more curvy than chubby, and Scott found her very attractive.

"Do you have time to take a break with me?" she asked.

He didn't want to give her hope, but he couldn't be rude.

"Sure," he answered, but instead of taking the seat beside her, he walked around the counter.

Paula, his fountain help, looked pleased.

"Well, great. I'll take this chance to make a trip to the Ladies,'" she announced.

The last thing Scott wanted was to be left alone, but he could hardly ask his employee *not* to go to the bathroom.

With a falsely cheerful smile, he drew himself half a glass of root beer with lots of ice and perched atop the cold box. He was immediately opposite Jeannie, but with twenty-two inches of solid rock between them.

"So what brings you to town?" he asked her.

It was an innocent enough question. It was probably asked in his store alone a dozen times a day. For those who lived and worked on the thousands of acres of surrounding wheat fields, a trip to town always had some purpose.

"I...I just came in to go to the gym."

Her hesitance made it sound like a lie. And Scott figured it probably was. She had on dressy jeans and a crisply pressed blouse. Her makeup was perfect and her hair completely straight except for the one blond curl that she kept nervously tucking behind her right ear.

They had been friends since high school. He hated that both of them now being single had to ruin that. In Verdant, however, the unmarried comprised a tiny segment of the population and there was constant pressure to dwindle the numbers. Most people wed high school sweethearts and never looked back. Both he and Jeannie had tried that without success. And they'd both found being back on the dating scene in their thirties to be dicey. They couldn't even see a movie together without raising speculation. And if they raised speculation and nothing came of it, that would be even worse— especially for Jeannie. For Scott, it would merely disappoint his mother. As a single man, he could still play the field and be admired for it. Old Mr. Paske was known as the Rest Home Romeo, and the townsfolk cheered him on. It was different for women, though. Misogyny was alive and well in the small town of Verdant. And any guy whose ambition was not to be a total jerk needed to remember that.

He searched his brain for some subject of conversation that might put her at ease.

"How are the kids?"

"Oh, they're great. Great."

"How's your wheat?"

"It's pretty good," she answered. "Browning up nicely. Dad hasn't checked the moisture content yet, but I suspect we're not more than ten days to two weeks from showtime."

Showtime was the local euphemism for harvest. Winter wheat was the lifeblood of the area, the foundation of the local economy. There were soybean fields, too, and more than a handful of oil and natural gas wells dotting the area. But it was wheat that paid the bills for everybody in this part of Kansas.

"What have you been up to?" Jeannie asked him.

Scott shrugged. "It's Verdant. Same headaches, same people."

"Well, not *all* the same people," Jeannie said. "The new librarian arrived today."

"Oh, yeah?"

"Suzy Granfeldt called me," Jeannie revealed. "She hasn't met her yet, but she said Miss Grundler hated her on sight."

"Miss Grundler hates everybody," Scott pointed out. "Sometimes even without seeing them."

Jeannie giggled. "True. So that's at least one thing in the librarian's favor. And then, of course everybody knows that your mom picked her. Your mom is so good about people. She wouldn't choose somebody we couldn't live with."

Scott wasn't so sure. A year ago he would have trusted his mother's judgment completely. But since his dad's death, she'd been different. He'd expected her to be grief-stricken and lost, and she had been for a while, but lately she was all motivated about something. He couldn't figure out what. And there was that crazy food thing. His mother, who was cooking for one, bought enough canned goods to feed a small army for months.

"It's probably good that Mom's getting more involved in the library," he told Jeannie.

"I'm sure the new librarian will be just what we need," she said. "Although honestly, why Viv thought we needed anybody remains kind of a mystery. I mean, we've gotten along fine forever. Now suddenly our sad little book collection requires a professional?"

"Maybe she hopes that people will actually *go* to the library," Scott suggested.

"Well, the kids still go," Jeannie pointed out. "They have to. But since I got my ereader, it's worth it to me to keep my distance."

He nodded. "I don't think you're alone in that. Every time I'm there, the place is like a tomb."

"A tomb to share with Miss Grundler."

"And James, don't forget James."

"Oh, yeah, James."

"Do you think there really is a James or is he just a figment of our imagination?"

Jeannie giggled. "Well, you can't prove it by me. I've hardly caught a glimpse of the guy since tenth grade."

The bell at the front door tinkled and Maureen Shultz, coughing into a handkerchief, arrived with a prescription for antibiotics.

As if she'd been listening from the door to the stockroom, Paula returned to the fountain immediately and kindly offered to make Maureen a cup of hot tea while she waited.

The woman might have been ill, but it apparently didn't hamper her hunger for gossip. As Scott filled the script he overheard the three women sharing what little they knew about the new librarian. No one had met her. No one had even seen her, except Scott's mom and Miss Grundler, but that didn't deter speculation. It seemed to stimulate it.

"She's moving into the upstairs apartment at Viv Sanderson's house," Maureen revealed.

Scott raised an eyebrow at that news. During his divorce, he'd made the upstairs into a separate retreat for himself to take away some of the sting of having to move home with his parents. Five years ago, when he'd bought his own place, he'd encouraged his parents to rent it. They hadn't been that interested. Once his mother became a widow, he'd renewed his urging, not wanting her alone at night in the big old house.

"I don't want a stranger living here," she'd stated

adamantly. "This has always been a family home. I'm not turning it into a boardinghouse."

Apparently she had changed her mind.

The discussion at the fountain continued. "What educated, professional woman in her right mind would want to bury herself in a town like Verdant?"

The question had come from Jeannie, who had lived in the community, apparently by choice, for her entire lifetime.

"A homely old maid, married to her cat?" Paula suggested.

Maureen disagreed. "Karl saw her photo on that website job application thing and said that she looks kind of pretty."

"I never heard of a pretty librarian in my life," Paula declared.

Jeannie giggled. "That's because you've always lived here and we've always had Miss Grundler."

"Well, if she's pretty and she's here, then she must be running away from something," Paula declared.

"Maybe so," Maureen agreed. "I'm sure we'll figure it out. It's as true as I live that when you set your future toward running away, your past will come to trip you up every time."

South Padre Island (Eight years earlier)

D.J. woke with a terrible taste in her mouth and a pounding headache. She must have slept in her contacts. Her eyes were burning so much she refused to open them. She was slightly sick to her stomach and her whole body hurt. The twinges in the muscles of her legs and thighs felt like they did the first day back at the gym. She groaned. She hated being ill and she almost never was, but she must be coming down with something. Some really crappy something.

She was sweaty and hot, with a big, breathing body pressed up beside her. Her roommate's dog must have sneaked into her bed again. She loved the big, goofy Labrador, but he should at least stay on his side of the mattress. Blindly she reached out to nudge him over.

"Ugh."

It was not a doglike reply, and at that very same instant she realized that the skin beneath her fingers was not a healthy pelt of fur, but an expanse of human flesh.

She sprang up like a jack-in-a-box, sitting rigidly in the bed, her eyes wide-open.

She was in a strange room, in a strange bed, with a strange man asleep beside her.

A wave of nausea swept over her, which she only

just managed to swallow as the flash of memories from the previous night came flooding back. Sun. Surf. An excess of suds.

Spring break.

Take a vacation from who you are, she'd told herself. Find out what it's like to be another woman. A crazy, sexy, wild woman. A woman who sleeps with strangers.

As she remembered it, remembered it all, her terror turned to horror and embarrassment. Humiliation tinged with desperation. What had she been thinking? Obviously, she'd not been thinking at all.

She had to get out of there. She couldn't face this man, this person who knew all about her body, but nothing about her.

Deliberately she tried to calm her breathing and engage her brain. She had to get away. And it was best to slip away unnoticed.

He had his head turned from her. That was good. She didn't need to see him to remember him. The way he'd touched her. The response he'd drawn from her. That was not forgettable. But she was determined that there would be not one more thing to remember.

She eyed him warily as she slowly, carefully peeled the bedcovers from her body. Beneath the tangle of sheets she was totally naked. That is, unless she counted some whisker burn and a love bite on the inside of her thigh.

She eased her right leg off the edge of the bed and rolled slightly trying to create the smallest impact possible on the mattress. She made it to her feet with minimal jostling, only to involuntarily gasp when her first step encountered something cold and wet and squishy. She glanced anxiously toward the man in the bed. When he didn't move, she breathed easier. Standing on one foot, she peeled the used condom from her heel. She looked around for a place to throw it and was grateful to locate some of her clothes strewn on the floor nearby. Well, not really *her* clothes. There was Terri's leather skirt. Heather's sequin-covered bikini top. And the five-inch turquoise Plexiglas heels that had been the gag gift for her birthday. Yesterday she'd turned 21. She was a full-fledged adult now. And apparently her first official adult act had been to behave like a very stupid kid.

She silently gathered her things and backed into the bathroom, keeping a cautious eye on the guy in the bed as she closed the door. On the vanity inside she found her borrowed evening bag and sighed in relief. Her wallet was there, as well as her keys, lipstick and mascara.

She turned to look at herself in the mirror. She would have laughed if it had been funny. She still had on plenty of makeup, at least twice as much as she normally wore. It was merely smeared in all the wrong places. She turned on a small stream of warm water and washed up with the one available cloth she found.

That made her feel a little better, but she needed to get away from here. Away from the stranger in that bed. Away from the craziness that she'd brought on herself. And she needed to do it now.

She slipped on her top and skirt. Where were her panties? They were not among her clutch of retrieved clothing, she realized. She would have to go without them.

She put on the shoes, but they were way too high for her and she felt wobbly. How could she have danced the night away and now not be able to stand? Regardless, they really made the short skirt seem even shorter and without underwear...

Barefoot again, she decided she could not leave without panties. She didn't know where she was or how far she'd have to walk to get to her own motel, and she didn't have the guts to make that trek going commando. Her panties were somewhere in that bedroom and she had to go back in there.

She gave herself a determined glance in the mirror before easing open the door and scoping out the room. There was his shirt, his shoes, his trousers, belt still attached. Something glimmered on the carpeting. She tiptoed over to it and picked it up. It was the belly chain he'd bought for her at that little hippy store next to the beach. It was broken, of course. The way they'd been tearing at each other's clothes, it had no chance of survival. It was cheap and shiny and never meant to last. Still, she stuffed it into her purse.

She stacked the shoes and purse on the table next to the front door, then moved stealthily around the bed that dominated the space. Slowly, methodically, she picked items up off the floor to see if anything was hidden beneath. She found boxer shorts, socks, a bar tab receipt and two more used condoms, but no ladies' underwear of any kind. She was working up the courage to check under the bed, when the occupant moaned.

She froze as he rolled over on his back. His face looked different in the daylight than in her foggy memory. She remembered how Terri had urged her to go for the beefy guy with the *World of Warcraft* tattoo. But somehow this guy's smile had won her over. He was not smiling now. His mouth was slightly open, his face unlined as if dreaming the dreams of the innocent. He had not seemed innocent last night. Last night he had been sexy, powerful, aggressive. Asleep he looked actually very ordinary. Last night he had been mature and sophisticated. This morning he looked young. And kind.

Young and kind? That was not at all how she wanted to remember him. In fact, she didn't want to remember him at all. Except perhaps as a cautionary tale. This was the type of mindless, naive indignity that a woman could bring upon herself when she doubted her own value. When she felt less than other women around her. When she felt incapable of engendering normal relationships. When she talked herself into believing that experience for the sake of experience was something to be desired.

D.J. was ashamed. She was embarrassed. She was remorseful. If she could make it out of this motel and back where she belonged, she promised herself to hold those three emotions tightly to her notion of self-respect and never let anything like this happen again.

It was then that she spotted the red lace panties she'd been searching for. He was wearing them like an arm-band on his right bicep At first she thought she would just have to let them go. But smoothing down the back of the short, short leather skirt changed her mind. She steeled herself for a long moment and then stepped forward and attempted to ease them down his arm. She made a few inches of progress, only to find difficulty negotiating around his elbow. Carefully, so carefully, she pulled at the handful of lace, watching it move around the sharp point of bone. And when it did, the elastic unexpectedly snapped back.

The man startled awake, his brown eyes wide-open. "Uh, hi."

She yanked the panties possessively and ran for the door.

"Hey, wait!" he called out.

She didn't. Before the door had even slammed shut, she was down the steps, racing across the parking lot and up the sidewalk of an unfamiliar street in an unfamiliar town, her purse and shoes in one hand, her panties in the other.

080. General Collections

The sunrise view from the apartment's second floor porch was really as nice as Viv had said it would be. And D.J. was up to see it, her cup full of coffee and her mind full of ideas. It was only six-thirty, but she was already showered, dressed and ready for her workday much earlier than she could ever go in.

The little porch was furnished with a small teak table and two chairs, as well as a comfy-looking glider beneath the roof overhang, which offered a fabulous view of sky and wheat fields as far as the eye could see. But D.J. was too excited to sit. Instead she paced. At her feet, and in solidarity she was sure, Dew marched right beside her.

"Hello! Hello up there."

D.J. heard the voice of her landlady and walked over to the railing to see her just below, near the entrance to the stairs.

"Good morning, Mrs. Sanderson."

"Viv, honey. You have to call me Viv. I heard you moving around and I made popovers. I hope you haven't already eaten."

"I don't really do breakfast," D.J. answered.

"Well, your first morning in town certainly calls for a celebration," Viv told her as she made her way up to the porch. "And I just love a relaxed morning visit."

D.J. had thought that the two were surely *visited out.*

Last night as she'd unloaded her possessions, Viv had seemed eager to help her unpack. Even after D.J. had very sternly refused the help, she'd come back a half hour later with dinner on a tray.

D.J. was too much of an introvert to find that comfortable. She hadn't shared living space since her best friend, Terri, got married. The idea of Mrs. Sanderson as constant companion was a nonstarter. No reason to even bother unpacking. She wouldn't be here that long.

And she was determined to be straight about that right up front, she decided as she got the woman a cup of coffee. By the time D.J. returned, Viv was already seated at the little teak table. Dew was perched with his front paws up on the chair wearing his I'm-too-cute-to-resist-me look. Mrs. Sanderson was trying to feed him a popover. He was dutifully sniffing at it, but showing no particular interest.

"He doesn't eat table food. He doesn't like it," D.J. told her, adding, "Get down, Dew."

The dog immediately complied.

"Do?" Viv chuckled. "Is that the puppy's name? As in do-do? You did say he's housebroken…"

"Absolutely," D.J. assured her. "It's actually Dew as in Dewey Decimal System. My friends always kid me that I'm 'married to the public library.' So I decided to name 'my only child' after his father."

D.J. patted her lap and her very well-behaved bundle of energy jumped up and took a seat.

"Mrs. Sanderson, I'd like you to formally introduce you to Melvil Dewey, Jr."

Viv laughed. "He is charming," she said. "My son, Scott, had a cocker spaniel when he was a boy. What do you do with him while you're a work?"

"Oh, he just hangs around the house. Typically I race home on my lunch break to walk him."

"No need to do that," Viv said. "I'm here anyway. I'd be happy to take him for a walk."

"Mrs. Sanderson," she began to protest. Then seeing the words forming on the woman's lips, she corrected herself. "Viv."

The landlady smiled, pleased.

"You don't need to do that. I know there will be lots to do at the library, but I can take care of my own dog."

"Of course you can," Viv said. "But I'm out walking every day anyway. I might as well take Mr. Dewey along with me. If only for my own protection." She added the last with a grin.

Dew rose up on his paws in D.J.'s lap and began wagging his tail as if he knew that he was the subject of attention.

"See," Viv pointed out. "He loves the idea!"

D.J. acquiesced with reluctance.

"I'll leave his leash by the back door," she said. "I guess you have a key to my apartment?"

Viv nodded and then directed her response to Dew. "We're going to be such friends, you and I."

D.J. carefully gathered up her thoughts. This woman was her landlady and, in a large sense, her boss. She was not a roommate or a best friend.

"Viv, I think I must be blunt about this," she said. "I am a very private person. I've been accustomed to living on my own. I don't mean to be unfriendly, but…"

"Oh, honey, I understand perfectly," Viv answered. "A woman definitely needs her own space. I was young myself once. And I have a daughter of my own."

"Do you?"

"Yes. She's my eldest. Married to a nice man and living in Kansas City. She teaches drama, of all things. I told her it was a vocation she's been cultivating since birth. No child was ever more dramatic about everything than my lovely Leanne. My husband John used to say it was like living with Norma Desmond. She came down the stairs every day 'looking for her close-up, Mr. DeMille.'"

D.J. felt herself being charmed by Viv's obvious delight in her children. Her own parents had never seemed to have any opinion on who she was or what she did. Viv spoke of her daughter with such warmth, it was almost as if their relationship had been by choice rather than a mere accident of fate.

"I'm sure it was…pleasant having someone so… artistic living in your home."

Viv nodded. "The way John and I saw it, our children balanced each other out. Leanne was edgy and imaginative and never saw a risk she wasn't willing to take, while Scott has been steady and responsible since the day he was born. I can always count on Scott. Come to think of it, there's not anyone who knows him who can't count on him. He's that kind of guy."

"Isn't that nice," D.J. said politely, resisting the urge to look at her watch.

"John and I worried that he might want to leave Verdant. Well, I guess the truth is we worried he might leave and we worried that he might not. The last thing we wanted was for him to feel trapped here with the business."

"The business?"

"We own the drugstore downtown. It's been in my husband's family since they were selling cigars to the Kiowas."

Viv laughed at her little joke. D.J. smiled.

"In the end, we were so glad that Scott stayed. Not everybody who grows up in a small town wants to live there forever."

"No, I suppose not," D.J. agreed.

"And after his divorce... I did mention that he's divorced?"

"Uh..."

"Well, he is. You might as well know that. It's a fact. It can't be helped. And it was a mess." Viv waved her hand in front of her face as if she could whisk it all away. "I suppose that sort of thing always is. I wouldn't know. We've never had a divorce in our family before. But infidelity..." Viv gave an exaggerated shrug of her shoulders. "What's a mother to do?"

D.J. gave no answer, but Mrs. Sanderson didn't appear to require one.

"I am just very grateful that he decided to stay. They say the only way to get past gossip in a small town is to avoid it completely or grow so old you've outlived it."

Viv sighed. "Oh, but now you'll be thinking you've moved into this hive of rumormongers," she said. "It is kind of that way. But mostly we're very chummy, you know. Everyone knows everyone. It's like a gigantic extended family. That can be very appealing. Although I'm sure it may be very different from your upbringing as an only child in a city neighborhood."

D.J. paused midsip of her coffee.

"How did you know I was an only child?"

Viv looked momentarily like a deer in headlights. "Didn't you mention it?"

"No, no, I don't think so."

"It must have been on your resume."

That was ridiculous. There was absolutely no personal information listed.

D.J. shook her head.

Viv shrugged. "Well, something must have made me think so." She gave a bright smile and then glanced at her watch. "Look at the time." Viv downed her coffee and rose to her feet. "I'd better get busy. Mr. Dewey, I will see you later. So much to do today."

That was supposed to be D.J.'s line.

By 7:30, she couldn't wait another minute. D.J. drove her car, empty trailer still attached, back the circuitous route she'd come toward the beautiful library on Government Street.

The small parking lot behind the building was completely empty. D.J. parked longwise, taking up three spaces but promised herself that she would find the place to turn in the trailer by midday.

There was an employees' entrance in the back. Hopeful, she gathered up her box of moving-in files and carried them to the doorway. As she neared the entrance, her eyes were drawn to the bicycle attached to the metal railing. Her first thought was simply that perhaps one of her employees biked to work. As she got a better look, she began to hope not. The very ordinary-looking, slightly rusted bicycle was attached to the railing with U-locks on both the front and back tires. A chain connected the two locks together and to another chain that wove in and out of the metal with padlocks attached every few inches. Two U-locks and half a dozen padlocks?

D.J. stopped to survey her surroundings. She couldn't imagine this place as a high crime zone. She could almost see the police station from the sidewalk. Still, she made a mental note to ask questions about security. The safety and property of both the employees and patrons were her responsibility, as well.

In contrast to the precautions for the rusty bicycle, the back door was open and D.J. was able to walk right in. The place appeared dark and deserted. She found the light switches to the right of the door and quickly illuminated the building's nonpublic workroom. There were boxes, book carts and tables spread with supplies. Here was where books were shipped and received, cataloged or repaired and made ready for lending. Although the nature of such work was chaos, the place appeared relatively neat. In the far corner there was a tiny break room space with a circular table, four chairs, a microwave and coffeemaker. D.J. immediately walked over and began going through the cabinets, locating what was needed to make coffee. She smiled to herself. Making sure the director had a hot cup of morning coffee when she arrived had been one of her tasks at D.J.'s last job. Now that *she* was the director, somebody should be bringing coffee to her.

She thought about the only employee that she knew and couldn't imagine Amelia Grundler performing such a duty.

As the hot brown liquid began dripping through the machine, D.J. ventured out into the public area. If it had been a dim and gloomy cave yesterday afternoon, it was even more so this morning. D.J. went behind the circulation desk and began switching on the lights. From the corner of her eye, a shadow moved through the stacks, startling her.

"Who's there?"

There was an almost eerie silence and then a book slammed shut loudly, startling her.

"Who is there?" Her voice was sterner as she repeated her question.

Silence again. Then from somewhere among the shelves of books a timid baritone voice answered.

"James."

D.J. remembered the name from the day before. Viv had called out a goodbye as they left.

She still didn't see him anywhere.

"I'm Ms. Jarrow, the new librarian," she announced in his general direction.

No answer.

"Why are you hiding in the stacks?"

She thought he was going to ignore that question as well, but after a moment there was a tentative reply.

"Working."

D.J. couldn't imagine what kind of work he could be doing alone and in the dark.

"Come out here so I can meet you," she said.

Another hesitation.

"No," he answered.

"No?"

D.J. walked in the direction of where she thought his voice was coming from. She turned down that row of books. He was not there. She went to the next aisle, and the next. She couldn't find him, though once she did sense a shadow moving just beyond her vision. Finally she stopped, annoyed.

"I'm not going to chase you down!"

"Okay."

"HEL-LO!" A voice called out from the back door. D.J. stepped out from between the shelves to see a young woman hurrying toward her.

"I thought you might be here," she said. "I came early just to meet you. I'm so excited!"

As if to illustrate that, she grabbed both of D.J.'s hands in her own and almost bounced with enthusiasm.

"Uh...hi," D.J. said.

"I'm Suzy, Suzy Newton— No, I mean Suzy Granfeldt. See, I'm so thrilled I can't even remember my own name!" She giggled delightedly. "I'm the girl from Bookmobile 2."

D.J. thought the term "girl" was being misused. Despite her clothes from the "juniors" department and bouncing ponytail, Suzy was at least as old as D.J. herself.

She continued to giggle. "Last night my phone just rang and rang. I'm suddenly Miss Most Popular. Everybody wants to talk to me because everyone wants to know about you. Getting a new person in town who's not like...married to one of us, is so unordinary. And it's almost like a TV drama having you come in and throw Miss Grundler out on her tuffet."

Another giggle escaped the small woman. D.J. was pretty sure that sound would get very old in a hurry.

"I'm not *throwing* anybody out. We're a small staff and we're going to need to work as a team."

Suzy's expression immediately changed to wide-eyed worship as she grasped D.J.'s hands once more. "I *love* being on a team," she stated with great drama. "I was on cheerleading squad for four years in high school. In my whole life so far, it's the thing I'm most proud of."

D.J. was sure the woman must be joking, but there was nothing in her expression beyond solemn sincerity. At a loss at how to respond, she was rescued by the arrival of the other bookmobile operator, a stoic man who also appeared about her own age. He was as big and quiet as Suzy was tiny and animated. He shook D.J.'s hand very formally and introduced himself as Amos Brigham.

"I haven't had a chance to look at the bookmobile

schedules," D.J. admitted to them. "But I am hoping
that you two have time for a short staff meeting this
morning before you head out."

"A staff meeting." Suzy repeated the phrase wistfully, as if it were some strange exotic vacation locale.
"We've never had a staff meeting."

"Miss Grundler typically leaves a note in our mailbox when she has something to say to us," Amos verified.

D.J. wanted to roll her eyes, but managed to maintain
professional decorum. "Notes in the mailbox are fine,
too," she weaseled slightly. "But staff meetings bring
in every voice and build team unity."

Suzy turned to Amos and informed him in a whisper. "We're on a *team* now."

No reaction showed on the man's face. Instead he
answered D.J.'s question. "I have to be in Hadeston by
ten o'clock."

That meant nothing to her.

"I'm loaded up, gassed up and ready to go," he continued. "So if we could get through the meeting in the
next half hour, I'd be okay."

"I'm in Elmira and Brushy this morning," Suzy piped
in, "but I can get there real easy. I wouldn't miss the
staff meeting for anything."

D.J. nodded. She glanced at her watch. Amelia Grundler had yet to show up, but perhaps it would be better
to have their first meeting together privately.

"Okay, let's get started," she said. "Shall we sit at
the table in the break area?"

"Did you want James at the meeting?" Amos asked.

"Of course," she answered and then turned toward
the shelves behind her. "James, I need you to attend the
staff meeting."

There was no immediate response, but a moment later a book slammed shut loudly.

"Maybe we'd better have it out here," Amos said. "That way he can hear what you're saying. He won't go to the break room if anyone is in there."

The idea of meeting in the middle of the dark, depressing space in front of the circulation desk wasn't going to enhance the quality of the meeting, but D.J. didn't argue when Amos began bringing chairs for them.

"James is an odd duck," he said to D.J. by way of explanation. "But he's a good worker."

Suzy was nodding with agreement. "You'll get used to that slamming-the-books-closed thing," she assured her. "The shelving he does is perfect. Every month or so, I ask him to do my bookmobile. I just tell him I need it and leave it unlocked. I never see him go in or come out, but the next day, the books will be absolutely perfect."

"He never takes a day off. He's never sick. He's been working here since he was a kid, really. They hired him on staff maybe thirty years ago."

"You'll never get three words out of him," Suzy explained. "But he's very dependable."

Having his co-workers defend him so adamantly, D.J. realized she was going to have to give the guy some latitude. Still, she worried.

"As long as he does his job and doesn't upset the patrons, I'm sure we'll get along fine," D.J. said, a little louder than necessary, expecting her words to carry into the most distant nooks and crannies of the building.

Suzy giggled again. "The patrons rarely even see him. And it really keeps the children out of the adult section. Going into the stacks is something only brave boys do on a dare."

D.J. wasn't sure that could be seen as a positive, but she decided to change the subject. She found the notes that she'd carefully written up as an agenda.

"Since we've all met," she began, "I won't need to introduce myself. I am very happy to be here in Verdant. I commend all of the staff on the work that you've been doing. And I am very motivated to work with you to ensure this library continues to be an asset to the community."

She glanced down to "Point 1" of her notes, but before she could make it, Suzy spoke up.

"So where did you grow up, where are you from?"

"Uh…Wichita," D.J. answered.

"I love Wichita," Suzy assured her. "What part of town?"

"College Hill."

"Oh, that's nice, I think." Suzy looked over at Amos for confirmation. "That's a nice area, right?"

Amos shrugged.

"It was lovely," D.J. replied shortly. "Now I wanted to talk to you…"

"Does your family still live there? In College Hill?"

"No, my parents died several years ago."

"Oh, my God! That's awful. What happened?"

"They were killed in a traffic accident," D.J. answered. "But this isn't what I wanted to talk about."

"Of course not," Suzy agreed. "You're obviously still grieving. When a tragedy occurs it can get stuck on you and it just goes on and on. It's called PSST or something. What is it, Amos?"

The other bookmobile driver did not respond. His face remained completely deadpan.

Suzy smiled at him apologetically. "Apparently some terrible things happened to him when he was deployed overseas," Suzy said, looking between him and D.J. "PFPC? What is it? We try never to talk about it."

Amos rose from his chair brusquely. "I've got to get on the road," he said as he moved away.

"I had to tell her," Suzy called after him. "Otherwise she wouldn't know."

But Amos kept going and didn't even look back. D.J. was stunned at the sudden ruin of her meeting.

Suzy leaned toward her slightly. "He was deployed with the National Guard and nobody really knows what happened. When he left he was just another happy-go-lucky guy, but he came back so…strange. He must have—"

"PTSD," D.J. interrupted before Suzy could get it wrong again. " And it's none of my business," she said sternly. "If Amos wants me to know something, Amos will tell me."

"Oh, right, sure," Suzy agreed. "So where did you go to high school?"

"What?"

"College Hill, that's like East High, right?"

"Yes. Uh…no. It is but I didn't go to high school there. I went to Hockaday in Dallas."

"Your family moved to Dallas?"

"No, it's a boarding school."

Suzy clasped her hands beneath her chin dramatically. "I read a book about a boarding school once!"

At that moment the door to the back room swung open so violently that it rocked all the way open to slam against the opposite wall. Suzy made a startled squeal and jumped to her feet. Amelia Grundler stood on the threshold, her expression grim, her brows furrowed in anger.

"It is 9:02 a.m. and the front door is not open!" she announced stridently.

A pale, wan figure emerged silently from the shelves, rushed to the front door and clicked open the lock before disappearing as abruptly as he'd appeared.

Miss Grundler glared at D.J. "Your first day in charge and you can't even open for business on time."

Suzy scurried out of the room with a quick, worried glance in their direction.

The woman was looking daggers at D.J., but she was not about to be intimidated on her first day.

"You're late, Amelia," she said. "And I'm afraid that we were forced to have our weekly staff meeting without you."

Amelia's eyes narrowed. Obviously, the woman was going to make things hard for D.J. She would be on eagle-eyed watch for any trouble, any error, any weakness, and she would use that against D.J. while she was on probation. Amelia was going to try to get her old job back any way she could. That was as clear as if she'd said it aloud. She didn't need to verbalize. D.J. could easily interpret the woman's body language, and it was saying something like, "I'll get you, my pretty. And your little dog, too."

102. Miscellany of Philosophy

Scott took his early-morning run along the banks of the small green brook that meandered along the west edge of his hometown and gave the community its name. The path was well worn by hikers, joggers, walkers and those in search of a good fishing spot. Scott had been up and down it so many times, in so many seasons, in every kind of weather, that he really no longer saw the stands of tall native grass or the hard, leathery fruit on the hedge apple tree. He didn't hear the throaty call of the meadowlark singing for his ladylove or the trickle of the water as it passed among the stepping-stones.

He had taken up running in high school to combat sexual frustration. He could never have imagined back then that at age thirty he'd still need it…and for the same reason. He felt like moaning aloud. Instead he picked up the pace.

Scott rounded the corner and at the fork in the path, took the incline that led around the edge of the nearby cemetery. A sturdy stone wall fronted the area, but on the side where he ran, no one had bothered to build one. There were no grazing cattle to get in and no sleep-walking ghosts to get out. Near the southeast corner, he spared a glance in the direction of his father's final resting place. Even now, more than a year later, the loss still ached. His dad had been a great man. Not in the sense of money or power. John Sanderson had been fair, trustworthy and hardworking. He was a man to be counted upon to step up and help. And it didn't matter to him if the need came from a neighbor or a stranger. He was honest, almost to a fault. And you could tell him anything and he'd never judge, never even bat an eye. He'd been the one person his son could speak to in confidence.

The worst thing about Kansas, his father had said on that long-ago morning when Scott had made his embarrassing confession, *is that with the exception of death or the weather, we grow up thinking everything bad that happens to us is somehow our own fault, even when it is not.*

That had turned out to be the truth. But the truth had not set him free.

At the blacktopped street, officially named Cottonwood Avenue, but known by everyone in town as Cemetery Road, he paused. To his right a path cut through a scraggle of overgrown milkweed to his parent's home. He needed to check in on his mother. It had been almost a week since he'd seen her and she wasn't the type to call and say she needed something. Then he remembered what Maureen had said about the new librarian rooming with her. That could be good. That could be very good.

Scott smiled as he turned north toward his own home. Verdant was already wide-awake and people would be making their way to the drugstore very soon. He'd have to stop by his mother's later on.

A half hour later, promptly opening the pharmacy doors, he was showered, groomed and appropriately dressed in his side-button shirt with the standing band collar. His name was embroidered on the pocket, but the style was strictly his dad's. While his colleagues wore white coats, scrubs or even their favorite golf shirt, at Sanderson Drug the uniform of the day was still stuck in the 1960s.

Scott was okay with that. The shirts were comfortable, incredibly inexpensive and looked amazingly formal. Medical compounds that spilled or splashed could be destructive to fabric. But he could throw his shirts in the wash or throw them away. That's how he defended his mode of dress to other pharmacists. To himself, he admitted that he didn't mind being a younger version of his dad. And he'd never seen change, merely for the sake of change, to be the equal to progress.

Coffee was still dripping through the machine when Amos Brigham showed up at the door. He had the haunted look he sometimes wore. He asked for coffee, but Scott was pretty sure a whiskey might have served him better. Amos didn't drink. That was probably a good thing.

As soon as he sat down at the counter, Scott poured each of them a cup and took a seat on a nearby stool.

Amos and Scott had been pals from childhood, best buddies in high school and college roommates. They had shared the best and worst of each other's lives. Physically, they couldn't have been more different. Amos was a big, beefy guy. His hair, clipped military style, was prematurely gray making him seem older than his years. And the aviator glasses couldn't completely hide the vacant-eyed expression that had been with him since he'd returned from Afghanistan.

"You don't look so good," Scott said.

Amos shrugged. "Some days I feel almost normal and then something stupid happens to drag me back in."

Scott nodded sympathetically. "You know, that prescription that Dr. Kim wrote is still active."

Amos sipped his coffee and then replied with a slight shake of his head. "The pills make me too sleepy to drive. Besides, depression medication is for people who are depressed for no reason."

There was some truth to that. Mood elevators could only prop up those suffering while natural healing took place. With Amos, however, the sad sense of disconnection lingered. And all his friends and neighbors could do was stand by and watch.

"I'm okay," Amos assured him. "I'm having almost as many good days as bad. And I keep putting one foot in front of the other. It's just new situations or new people, sometimes that can throw a wrench in it."

Scott listened. Scott nodded. He had no words of wisdom to offer the man, but he didn't need any. He was fairly certain that Amos had been given as much well-meant advice as a man could stomach.

Injured animals hide to nurse their wounds, Scott's dad had told him once. *Men sometimes have to do the same thing. But they tend to disappear inside themselves.* Scott's father had done a year of draftee duty stationed on a hospital ship off the coast of Vietnam. The experience had given him a keen eye for human behavior.

For some reason that the rest of them would probably never know, Amos Brigham had disappeared inside himself.

Scott thought it might be easier if the guy could see a light at the end of the tunnel, but he didn't say that. It was none of his business. He changed the subject. That was what a friend was supposed to do.

"So, did you meet the new librarian?"

Amos nodded and took a sip of coffee before answering. "I did. She's young. Late twenties, I'd guess, but she dresses older. Kind of going for that old maid look."

"I don't think we're supposed to say 'old maid' anymore," Scott pointed out. "The PC term is single working woman."

"She's definitely that. Stuffy business suit, gray on gray with her hair pulled back into a little bun like somebody's grandmother."

"Not my grandma," Scott said. "She always dressed in canary yellow."

"And your mother dresses in purple. I think it runs in the family."

Scott nodded acceptance. "That's why my dad and I have always worn white. So we won't clash with our womenfolk."

"Well, nobody is in danger of clashing with the new librarian. She dresses like a little sparrow. I guess she thinks she has to."

"Well, she's probably smart to, anyway," Scott said. "Remember Old Man Paske is on the library committee. That ancient reprobate would grope a bass fiddle."

Amos nodded. "Makes you wonder how often he's tried to pinch Amelia Grundler's fanny."

"Good God, Amos, are you trying to ruin my day, putting an image like that in my head."

He agreed. "It surely is more horror movie than porn flick."

Scott chuckled. "As long as I don't have to see it, that old coot is welcome to all the old maids he can manhandle. I just hope that this one is not as sour as what we already have."

Amos was thoughtful for a moment. "No, she doesn't

seem sour. She's cheerful, enthusiastic. And she's actually kind of cute."

"Really?"

Scott thought it was probably a very good sign that Amos could even notice the level of a woman's attractiveness.

"I'm not saying she's some stunner," he clarified. "Nice features, nice figure. She's nice-looking. Pretty enough to fit in with the other women. But not so pretty that they'd begin to worry about their husbands."

Scott grinned. "The perfect balance, then?"

"Maybe so. She may be just right for us. She seemed very matter-of-fact. And she was able to roll with the strangeness of James."

"Did you try to explain him to her?"

"There is no explanation for James," Amos answered. "If Amelia Grundler doesn't run her off," Amos concluded, "she just might make a go of it."

"Good," Scott said. "We can always use another pretty woman in town. Even one determined to look like an old maid."

Amos made a huff of disbelief and shook his head. "We have at least our share in this little burg," he said. "A single guy like you ought to notice that."

Scott shook his head. "I'm married to the store," he answered.

"That's total bull," Amos answered. "The right woman could make this town a heaven on earth."

"Does that mean the wrong woman could make it hell?"

Amos shrugged. "Didn't you already marry the wrong woman? You tell me."

"Maybe that's my problem," Scott said with a laugh. "Once burned, twice shy."

"It was the luck of the draw," Amos assured him. "You're older, wiser now. And the test driving can be important...as well as entertaining."

"*Test driving* wasn't that much of a help last time," Scott pointed out. "And I'm not sure how well this town would tolerate a lot of *test driving* among the populace."

Amos managed a genuine smile at that. "Couldn't you try to stir up a scandal," he suggested. "I'd see it as a personal favor. Otherwise the talk this summer will be nothing but wheat, wheat, wheat."

Scott grinned. "Todd Philpot was in here late yesterday on his way back from the elevator. His moisture content tested at twenty-two."

Amos nodded. Moisture content, the amount of water held within the grain was the scientific determinant for harvesting time. So many factors affected it and none of them were within the farmer's control.

"It's pretty dry out there this morning," Amos said. "But I saw some clouds bunching up out to the west. They'll bring in humidity if nothing else."

"And if they don't," Scott pointed out, teasing, "it'll be nothing but wheat, wheat, wheat."

"Now you're plainly being mean."

Scott laughed.

"I honestly look forward to the harvest," Amos said. "I simply prefer doing the work over talking about it." He finished his cup and stood to leave. "Speaking of work, that's my cue. I need to be in Hadeston by ten, so I'd better get on the road."

"Hmm, the road to Hadeston. Talk about your wheat, wheat, wheat."

129.9 Origin and Destiny of Individual Souls

Vivian Sanderson walked across the cemetery with the new librarian's dog trailing on a leash. She was pretty sure that dog walking wasn't allowed, but this was the only place she wanted to walk. And she figured if somebody called her on it, she could drag out her best "ditz" persona and claim total ignorance. She was utilizing "ditz" a lot lately. A fact her husband, John, wouldn't have been pleased about.

"Why should a bright, intelligent woman go around pretending that she's an idiot?" he'd asked her early on in their time together.

"The world is simply an easier place when people think you're too dumb to understand it," she explained. "When people see that you know what you're doing, they have no qualms about second-guessing or offering critique."

Still, because John hated it, through the years she'd tried to be more true to herself. But now...well, when a woman needed to hide her motives, it was always best to appear too stupid to have one.

Viv stopped at the most familiar tombstone and used the excuse of dust to run a loving hand across the top of the granite.

"Good morning, darling," she said. "I'm back with

the pruning shears for these moss roses. I knew I should have planted perennials, but I thought it might be a waste." With a hand on the stone, she dropped to her knees. "I brought someone with me." Glancing over at Dew she added, "I'm hoping he won't take it into his mind to poop on you."

The dog, apparently seeing her move to the ground as an invitation, hurried over, tail wagging, to sit right beside her. He rolled over on his back, offering his tummy for her attention.

"Silly mutt," she said. "I wasn't talking to you." Still, Viv obliged him with a belly scratch. Enough so that the dog's eyes closed in rapt appreciation and his right leg moved in concert, as if attached to her fingers with a string.

She couldn't keep from grinning. "He's not my dog," she assured the stone. "I'm just walking him." She urged the dog to his feet. She unhitched his leash and shooed him away. "Go! Play!" she ordered. "And try not to dig anybody up."

As if following her directive explicitly, Dew tucked his body low to the ground and began racing around the cemetery in large circles. Stopping suddenly to gaze at her before taking off again. It was almost as if he were daring her to chase him.

Viv laughed. "He's a funny little dog," she said. "And he seems smart, too. He belongs to the new librarian, of course. I nearly choked when she asked if a pet would be welcome in the accommodations. I'm too much like my mother, I suppose, but I've always believed that animals should be outside or in barns. Even that dog we got Scott lived in his doghouse or on the porch. It's like inviting dirt and fleas right into the living room! But I knew from the sound of her voice that if I said no pets she simply wouldn't have come."

Viv retrieved her scissors from her bag and began to deadhead the blossoms that were past their prime and trim up the leaves that were growing so well they threatened to obscure the name and dates chiseled into the granite.

"I guess it could be worse," Viv said. "She could have a big old cat. That's like buying a billboard to say, 'I'm an old maid!' A dog at least indicates that a woman still craves affection."

Trimming the moss rose was a two-minute task. She stretched it into five and then spent another five carefully cutting the grass that grew nearby with the precision of a haircutter. The fine-bladed bermuda had spread over the grave like a scab on a wound until the hard-packed earth beneath it was almost completely hidden. The memory, however, was still fresh for Viv. She had come here every day since her husband had been buried. She intended to keep doing that until she lay beside him again.

"His name is Dewey, Melvil Dewey," Viv continued, glancing over at the dog as he made mad dashes around and around. "That's kind of clever, don't you think? It shows some creativity and a bit of humor. I mean she could have called him Rover or Blackie. Anyway, she's certainly attractive enough and she seems to be smart, I just want her to be fun."

Perhaps hearing his name or simply tiring of his game of circles, the dog trotted over to sit beside her. He wormed his little fluffy head under her hand, almost forcing her to pat his head and rub him behind the ears.

"Remember the fun we used to have," she said wistfully to the carved granite. "That's what I want for

Scott. He's far too serious and responsible. I want him to have a life full of shared laughter and private jokes. I want him to have…what we had."

She continued to scratch the nape of Dew's neck as he perched his nose up on her knee.

"Remember sitting in all those Chamber of Commerce meetings where Baldo Schultz would make one of his crazy suggestions for turning Verdant into a tourist destination? You'd be sitting up there on the stage looking at him all respectful and serious. You could never meet my eyes, cause we both knew that you were about to bust out a big guffaw." Viv shook her head. "Oh, Lord, do you remember when he thought we should try a 'Welcome Aliens' sign, hoping that space creatures would make us some crop circles and drive more business onto Main Street?"

Viv began to chuckle and once she started, she couldn't stop. She was laughing until she was crying. And then she was simply crying. Her body began to quake with weeping, and she struggled to keep quiet as the grief welled up inside her. The tears, however, would not remain in her eyes. They ran in rivulets down her face as she bit on her lower lip in an attempt to hold them back.

Within the aching, painful silence of her mourning, a small noise penetrated. Beside her the little terrier whimpered sympathetically. Viv found the reality of that so startling that it caused the blackness enveloping her to momentarily recede.

The little dog sat beside her, his back straight, his big dark eyes gazing up at her soulfully. At first she dismissed the empathy she saw there as simply her imagination. But the sounds of distress were so obvi-

ously generated to reflect her own hurt, she could not
ignore them.

"Oh, no, puppy, it's all right. It's all right," she cooed.
"I'm sorry, I didn't mean to upset you."

She ran her fingers lovingly along the shiny curls of
his coat. "Nothing for you to be sad about. I'm so sorry.
I've tried to hide it. I've tried to hide it from everybody.
But I didn't even think to hide it from you."

The dog climbed into her lap and began licking at
the wetness still fresh on her cheeks. Viv had never allowed a dog so close to her and was initially startled
by the rough feel of his tiny tongue on her skin. But the
canine compassion, strangely, made her feel better. In
a moment she was smiling again.

"You are quite a clever little dog, Mr. Dewey," she
told him as she dragged a tissue from her pocket. "My
son sees me a couple of times a week and never sus-
pects a thing. But you figure me out in one morning's
walk. Well, I hope I can trust you to keep it to yourself." She laughed as Dew's face, now openmouthed,
seemed to be grinning at her, his tongue hanging out
slightly to one side. "I've got a plan for Scott, you see.
John is helping me. But it would be good to have you
on my side, as well."

Dew leaped to the grass directly in front of her. He
lowered his front paws and, with his hindquarters in
the air, he wagged his tail enthusiastically.

Viv took that as a yes.

140.4 Philosophical Schools of Thought

D.J. would not have said that her first day on the job was an unqualified success. The tour of her new domain revealed the dark, dismal catacomb of stacks, threadbare rugs in the children's section and a teen book collection so woefully out of date that the only vampire novel available was by Bram Stoker.

She found her office on the second floor of the barred enclosure, accessible only by a very narrow flight of spiral stairs. The desk was literally buried in the library's Books-By-Mail program. For those who because of age, disability or distance could not get to the main library or one of the bookmobiles, a delivery service utilizing the post office was a great idea. Unfortunately, a quick glance indicated that request fulfillment was apparently nobody's priority.

D.J. attempted to talk to Miss Grundler about it.

"I do it as the schedule permits," the woman answered, her tone superior and snide.

"It doesn't look as if the schedule has permitted much lately."

"The *schedule* is the second and fourth Thursdays," Miss Grundler replied. "Suzy is in-house those days and can man the circulation desk while I take care of the requests."

"Twice a month? You only take time for this twice a month?" D.J. was incredulous. "What about the days that Amos is not on the road. He could man the desk."

Miss Grundler sniffed. "Not very well," she said. "Besides, those are the days where I do interlibrary loan."

D.J. was unpleasantly surprised to hear that. An extra two weeks on a service that typically took a fair amount of time under the best of circumstances, seemed like not a "service" at all, but an excuse for one.

Deciding that priorities had to be a first priority, D.J. cleaned off her desk, moved enough books to give her a view of the activity downstairs and began making a map of what the library was attempting to provide and the route and personnel currently utilized to accomplish that.

Her progress, however, was repeatedly halted by visitors braving the narrow winding stairs to meet the new librarian. Marianna Tacomb, Nina Philpot, Claire Gleason, Helen Rossiter. The names began to blend together. D.J. smiled and smiled until she thought her face might break. Everyone seemed to want to know everything about her. She would have been happy to talk about the library, but her guests weren't actually patrons.

"I never come here," Claire Gleason said. "Who wants to waste time in this dusty old place?"

D.J. secretly ground her teeth as she did her best imitation of not being offended. But the library was becoming personal to her. She wanted the community to love it, but she reminded herself that a good relationship had to be mutual. The library needed to love its community.

Since Mrs. Sanderson had assured her that Dew had been out on a long walk, D.J. took the opportunity of her lunch break to return the moving trailer. Checking on the internet, she found the nearest rental location to be Vern's Feed & Tractor out on the highway.

A couple of guys unhitched her car, disconnected the brake lights and removed the temporary bumper hitch. Her paperwork was in order and it all seemed very straightforward.

"Hey there, you must be the new librarian." The low, modulated voice behind her seemed small and feminine, but when she turned, she found herself facing a hefty woman with a buzz cut and overalls.

D.J. held out her hand. "Hello. Yes, I'm the new librarian. Dorothy Jarrow."

She shook her hand and gave her a broad smile. "Vernice Milbank," she introduced herself. "Everybody calls me Vern."

D.J. recovered quickly enough not to make a fool of herself—when she'd heard about Vern's, she'd assumed she would be meeting a man. Though now that she'd met her, she could see the name suited the thickset, rather masculine-looking woman. "It's a pleasure to meet you."

"My sister, Nina, told me she was going to stop over and introduce herself this morning."

"Oh, yes. She did visit me."

"She takes the kids up there from time to time. I'm not much of a reader, myself. Can't sit still long enough to get through a book."

D.J. had heard that kind of thing many times before. "The library is not just about books anymore," she told Vern. "We loan out movies and music and games. Audiobooks. We provide online access. It's truly a 'something for everybody' institution."

Vern chuckled as if that were funny.

"So, how's your first day going?"

"Busy," D.J. answered.

"Yeah, I bet every knothead and numbskull in forty miles would be nosing into your business," she said. "But that's a small town for you. Best get used to it."

"Verdant seems like a lovely place," D.J. said. "I'm not really a city girl. I'm originally from Wichita."

Vern's brow furrowed. "Wichita's not some wide spot in the road. It's the biggest city in Kansas." She raised her hand up as if anticipating argument. "I know, I know. If you add up those Kansas City suburbs or claim any part of Missouri, you've got a much bigger metropolis. But that doesn't mean that Wichita hasn't grown faster than goat grass in a wheat field."

Vern appeared to love her own analogy and slapped her thigh in celebration of it.

"Verdant is surely no place for strangers," she warned. "You're going to be put under a microscope and everybody is going to have an opinion. I don't envy you and that's for dang sure."

D.J. thought that Vern was undoubtedly overstating the case, but being a woman with a rather masculine appearance in a small conservative town like this certainly might make one touchy about those…less precise about minding their own business.

D.J. thanked her for her concern.

"Lots of folks are going to be asking what you're doing here," Vern said. "They're going to make up stuff in their head about what might motivate you to come to Verdant."

"I'm *motivated* to improve your library system."

Vern nodded. "Which brings up the other question," she said. "What on earth motivated the library committee to show any interest in making improvements?

They haven't done a gall-darn thing in twenty years. Why now?"

Because it's high time, D.J. thought. But she didn't say that aloud. She knew from her own experience that libraries were usually the last taxpayer-funded institution to get support. It was hard to argue a book budget against overcrowded schools, hungry seniors and transportation for the disabled. Virtually the entire country had put libraries on hold as they waited for better economic times.

"Whatever the reason," D.J. said, "I'm very grateful and I'm up for the challenge."

Vern smiled thoughtfully. "Of course, there is always Stevie's theory."

"Stevie?"

"My partner," Vern explained. "She thinks Viv brought you here for Scott."

"I beg your pardon?"

"Viv Sanderson has had no luck finding the right girl to marry her son. Stevie thinks Viv has plotted to bring some new blood to town to see if she could tempt him toward the altar."

"Well, that person is certainly not me," D.J. assured her.

With a bit of careful maneuvering, D.J. managed to turn the subject of the conversation to more mundane matters. In a few moments she was able to plead much work on her desk and make an exit. Though her stomach growled in protest, she made the decision to get back to the library without bothering with the sandwich. She had a lot to do and she was eager to get to it. She hoped that the afternoon would not be as full of interruptions as the morning had been.

In fact, there were almost no interruptions at all.

Miss Grundler spent the entire afternoon sitting at the circulation desk and whispering on the telephone. A number of people came in, most of them looking up toward D.J.'s office, but after a discussion with Amelia, they left without climbing the stairs.

D.J. assumed that the woman was running interference for her. If so, the whole personnel-management thing might end up being easier than it first appeared. Feeling upbeat and encouraged, she made excellent progress on her operations map—until a little after four when Suzy returned from her bookmobile route. With barely a word past greeting, she came straight up the stairs and shut the door behind her.

"Did you have lunch today with Vern Milbank?" Suzy asked in a shocked whisper.

D.J. raised an eyebrow. "I saw her while I was on my lunch break," she clarified. "I was returning my moving trailer."

Suzy let out a long, relieved sigh and dropped into a nearby chair.

"I knew it was something like that," she said.

"Actually, I missed lunch completely," D.J. said, regretting having forgone the sandwich. "Is there some reason I shouldn't eat with her?"

"Miss Grundler is telling anyone who'll listen that on your first day in town, you met Vernice for lunch."

"So?"

"So Vernice is… Well, she's 'light in the loafers' as they say."

D.J. was pretty sure that "they" didn't use that phrase for lesbians, but she didn't bother to correct Suzy on that.

"We serve all the citizens of this community," D.J.

pointed out. "A public servant cannot be a respecter of persons."

"Huh?"

"We treat everyone equally," she clarified.

"Sure, of course," Suzy agreed. "But treating them and being them is two different things. Miss Grundler is making it sound like you had lunch with Vernice because you're old friends. Like you're one of them."

"Oh." D.J. would have smiled and shook her head if that had been only slightly more expected. Naturally Amelia would take the very first opportunity presented to her to try to make D.J. some kind of pariah.

"I know you're thinking that nobody would believe it, because you're pretty and feminine," Suzy said. "But Vernice's partner is, like, the most gorgeous woman in town. She was Autumn Queen in high school. She had the biggest wedding the town had ever seen and then dumped her husband for Vern. Honestly, a lot of people have never gotten over it."

Suzy's words were as dramatic as if she were speaking of some terrible tragedy.

"I'm sure it wasn't as bad as all that," D.J. reassured her.

"Well, it was pretty shocking," Suzy said. "And people in Verdant really, really don't like to be shocked."

Suzy's blue eyes were wide with concern.

"I'm sure that anyone new coming to the community will have a few rumors spread about her," D.J. said, reassuringly. "Once people get to know me, they won't be swayed by idle gossip."

"Oh, they will," Suzy insisted. "They will. Idle gossip is almost a sacred duty in this town. People love it. And they pass it on. And a lot of folks act upon it. There are people in town who never speak a word to Vern or her girlfriend. They'd cross the street to avoid them. And they grew up here, their families still live here. How would they be treated if they were outsiders?"

D.J. was pretty sure that they would not have fared well.

"We can't let that happen to you," Suzy pleaded. "You just can't get run out of town. Not when I've gotten so hopeful about things changing around here. You can't let Amelia win. And she will, if you're not careful."

"It's ridiculous to judge people by who they talk to," D.J. pointed out.

Suzy shrugged. "I guess small towns can be ridiculous places. I'm sure not smart enough to understand it," she said. "Maybe it's looking at the best in folks all the time sort of makes us eager to see the worst."

"Well, I intend to be the best librarian this community has ever imagined," D.J. declared. "This is my hometown now. I intend to embrace it. And I refuse to believe that I can be ruined by a bag full of gossipy lies. People are smarter than that."

Suzy didn't appear convinced. "We may not be as smart as you think. I was voted president of my senior class." She was all solemnity and concern. "I have such hope for you and the library and all of us," she said. "I don't know if I could bear having Amelia take that away."

"Don't worry. I'm not a woman who can be brought down easily."

For all that Suzy was silly and dramatic, she also made a good point. In order to make a success of running the library, D.J. had to earn and hold the support of the community. She knew she was up to the task. Though, admittedly, thinking about it made her tired. Or maybe she simply *was* tired, a reasonable reaction to the combination of restless sleep, first-day jitters and not a bite to eat since popovers for breakfast.

But her long day was not yet done. She'd accepted Mrs. Sanderson's invitation to dinner. It had sounded like a good idea when she'd agreed to it. But as she closed up for the night, she wanted nothing more than to soak in a tub of hot water and go to bed.

Still, she was hungry and there was nothing in her apartment to eat. So, dutifully, she showed up in Mrs. Sanderson's kitchen at six.

It wasn't a terrible sacrifice. Though certainly a bit pushy, Viv was also funny, vivacious and entertaining. D.J. leaned against the kitchen counter amid the fabulous smell of dinner cooking and sipped on a small glass of dry white wine.

Dew had completely made himself at home on the throw rug beneath the kitchen sink. Mrs. Sanderson was forced to step over the dog every couple of minutes.

D.J. was surprised when she set a small dish of food on the floor.

Dew sniffed at it, but moved away.

"He doesn't eat people food," D.J. reminded her.

"It's meat."

She shook her head. "Sorry, he doesn't have any interest in table scraps or really anything cooked, even roast beef."

Viv's tone was incredulous. "I've never even heard of a dog that wouldn't eat anything and everything."

D.J. shrugged. "I didn't *train* him to be like that. He's been picky since the day I got him."

The terrier perked up, wagged his tail against the floor and turned his head slightly, as if aware that he was the subject of the conversation.

Viv laughed at the sight. "He's certainly a very unique little fellow," she said.

"I really appreciate that you took him for a walk today," D.J. said. "Believe me, I don't expect you to do that. It's way too much trouble."

"Oh, it's fine," Viv assured her. "I kind of like having him underfoot, it keeps me on my toes."

The dining table was set for three and Viv confessed that she'd invited her son to join them.

D.J. clearly recalled Vern's suggestion that Viv was trying to fix her up. Well, the woman was welcome to try, but D.J. was sure there was little danger of it working out. Over her dating years, she'd been fixed up with friends, brothers, cousins and colleagues. The spark was never there. She almost regretted even knowing "the spark" existed.

When they heard the sound of a car door outside, Viv became almost giddy with excitement.

"That's going to be Scott," she said. "I know you two are going to be great friends."

D.J. nodded vaguely and pasted a benign but welcoming smile upon her lips as she turned to the back door.

"Hey, Mom," her son called out as he opened the screen.

The glare from the sun momentarily obscured his visage, revealing only a tall male stranger with broad shoulders and a white shirt. Then he stepped inside.

D.J.'s heart leaped for one instant before the blood drained from her face. The one man in the world that she *never* wanted to see again had just walked into the room as if he were right at home.

South Padre Island (Eight years earlier)

Three women, friends and roommates from college, stepped through the open doorway of the Naked Parrott. The place was crowded to the point of crazy and everyone there seemed young, loud and intoxicated.

It was exactly the atmosphere that D.J. wanted. Her brain was buzzing happily after a few drinks, and on the edges of her peripheral vision were teeny-tiny stars that seemed to appear and explode at irregular intervals. This was the third such joint on tonight's tour of beachside pickup bars. The evening was no longer young. And D.J. was determined to be likewise.

Beside her she heard Heather whisper, "Total meat market."

"Perfect."

The three young women had consumed several glasses of bubbly alcohol before they'd even left the motel room. It was D.J.'s birthday, and that was a cause for celebration after what had been a long spate of depressing and drear months. But bouts of laughter earlier in the night had eventually turned into tears of self-loathing, and finally to steely-eyed determination. D.J. had confessed, to the two women who knew her best, how much she lagged behind her contemporaries and how inadequate she felt. She'd admitted to feeling stuck, as though her life was on hold, still waiting to really get started. So with their can-do, problem-solving attitudes, plus an impressive amount of alcohol, they conspired to change all that tonight. It was time to take action.

"You don't have to do this," Terri pointed out as they hesitated at the front of the bar. "It's a crazy idea."

D.J. was unwilling to hear any last-minute voices of reason. "It's a crazy idea whose time has come," she said. "I'm twenty-one and I haven't been a teenager yet."

"This seems like a terrible place to become one."

At that moment, a girl at a nearby table wearing a cropped tee and bikini bottoms accidentally, or on purpose, poured beer down her chest, revealing her breasts in a way that was more exposed than actual nakedness.

The men around her laughed, cheered and applauded the behavior.

Terri efficiently guided them away from the scene.

"I could do something like that," D.J. suggested.

"You won't have to," she assured D.J. "You look good enough that setting your hair on fire won't be necessary to draw attention."

D.J. did look good. In fact, she looked amazing. Terri and Heather had made sure of that. The makeup alone had taken nearly a half hour, and a second bottle of champagne, to apply. Her typically ponytailed hair was not only hanging long and loose down her back, but Heather had sprayed in some shiny blond high-lights. She'd also loaned her "lucky" sequined bikini top. The glittery eye-catcher drew attention to D.J.'s not completely insubstantial assets. The leather skirt was Terri's idea.

"When all the other girls are in skimpy swimsuits,"

she'd said, "a skirt can be an advantage, especially if it is short enough."

The one D.J. was wearing couldn't have been much shorter. And the five-inch Plexiglas heels they'd gotten her as a birthday gift made her legs look a mile long.

"Those shoes definitely say 'Do me!' loud and clear," Terri told her. "If a guy can't read that, he's too stupid for you."

"It's the stupid ones I want to attract," D.J. said. "A smart guy would be able to see right through me."

"No worries there," Heather assured her. "On spring break, all the guys are stupid."

As they were weaving through the crowd of hot, sweaty bodies smelling of beer, seaweed and suntan oil, D.J. caught sight of herself in the mirrored wall behind the bar. If she'd not been standing between Heather and Terri, she'd never have recognized herself. That was good. That was very good. Tonight she was someone else. Dull, boring Dorothy Jarrow was back at school tonight, nose stuck in a book, undoubtedly. This sexy-looking stranger wouldn't dream of wasting her last night of spring break that way. This stranger was some ridiculous girl-gone-wild.

She knew she could act. She'd won a major role in the Hockaday/St. Mark's Fine Arts production of *Oklahoma*. Of course, it was her singing voice that won them over, but she'd been able to competently embody her character. She enjoyed acting, pretending to be someone else. And she could do that here, tonight, in this place.

With resolve, D.J. raised her chin and flashed a big, fake smile on her surroundings. If a woman was looking for a good time, half of the search was to act like she was having one.

Terri ushered them to the far side of the room where

a row of booths was raised two steps above the main floor, giving the occupants a clear view of all that was happening below. She went over to a group of four very drunk, slightly sunburned girls who were already seated in the choice booth.

"Which one of you is Jennifer?"

The four looked at each other stupidly.

"Nobody's Jennifer, I'm Ginny…"

"Oh, then it must have been you," Terri said. "There's a quartet of really hot guys outside that said they met you on the beach today. They're looking for you."

With a shriek of excitement, the young women vacated the booth, which Terri, Heather and D.J. immediately took over.

"I didn't see any hot guys outside," D.J. pointed out.

Terri grinned. "There are always hot guys outside somewhere. We need this perspective to find your Mr. Right."

"Not Mr. Right," Heather corrected her. "Mr. Right Now. Mr. Right Tonight. Mr. I-Know-How-To-Do-You-Right."

All three women fell into giggles.

They ordered drinks and surveyed the occupants of the bar.

"When it comes to plucking men out of a crowd, it's all about balance," Heather told her. "If you pick one who's in the middle of a tight testosterone group, you run the risk of being taken for granted or handed off. But if you go for the total loner boy, he could be, like, a Freddie Kruger or something."

"What?"

"Heather, you're going to scare her silly," Terri said. "Look, we're sticking close until you send us away. Don't go anywhere you don't want to go. Don't do anything you don't want to do. If you're feeling threatened or you simply change your mind, holler out a name and we're right beside you. Now let's check out your choices for Birthday Surprise from a nice safe distance."

It didn't take them long to get the measure of the men in the room, and each of the women had her own preferences.

"The dancing dude is the one," Heather announced. "Look at those moves. If he can make his body flex like that standing up, just think what he can do in the sack."

"She doesn't need an acrobat," Terri disagreed. "I like the gentle giant sitting at the bar."

Heather's brow furrowed. "He looks slightly biker to me. He's probably got his whole gang outside."

D.J. thought they both looked...well, pretty ordinary. She wasn't attracted to either of them. But this night wasn't really about attraction, it was about efficiency. She was ready to get past this last step into adulthood as simply and conveniently as possible.

"What about the guy with the 'hook 'em horns' in the chair near the dance floor?" Heather suggested. "He's big and quiet and not nearly as scary."

"He's quiet because he's about to pass out on the floor," Terri said. "She doesn't want somebody she has to sober up."

"Well, there's always the guy behind you," Heather said. "He's been nursing the same beer since we got here. And he's looking over the crowd just like we are. Maybe he's looking for you, D.J."

Terri and D.J., who were sitting across from Heather, slowly turned to get a look at the man in the booth behind them.

He was definitely hot, D.J. decided immediately. His Foo Fighters concert tee was stretched across very broad shoulders. He was muscled, but without the thick-neck look that some guys get. And he had a handsome face with strong, masculine features and neatly clipped sandy-brown hair. Totally gorgeous.

"Nice," Terri whispered beside her.

D.J. hoped that wasn't a word that defined him.

Although he was attractively tanned, a day at the beach meant a certain amount of redness in the cheeks of light-skinned visitors. There was none of that. He definitely hadn't spent the afternoon in sun and surf. He hadn't come on spring break for the beach. He'd come for the girls.

Just then he caught sight of her. Their eyes met. D.J. would have sworn that an actual spark of electricity passed between them. She had felt it. Then again, maybe it was another one of those exploding stars. Her initial reaction was to look away, but she didn't. She would not be cowed by her own uncertainty. Instead, she raised her chin and looked him over, unsmiling, assessing.

That brought his eyebrow up.

She held his gaze. That's what sexy, confident strangers did with men. They held the gaze. They held their own. And she was playing her role perfectly.

Then he smiled at her. It was a beautiful smile. Warm, welcoming and incredibly sexy.

"Oh, no," Terri said. "He's not the one."

"He might be," D.J. told her.

"Don't do it. He's probably an Eagle Scout."

"You're kidding, right," Heather said. "He's got serial killer written all over him."

"What?"

"That's exactly what they look like," she insisted. "They're always clean-looking, the boy-next-door type."

"You're crazy," D.J. told her.

"She is," Terri agreed. "But still, he's not the one for you. You're looking to get laid, not fall in love. This guy is one you could fall in love with."

D.J. thought about the spark. Terri was probably right.

"Look at the guy at the table right below us. Now he looks like a genuine guy. A little bit pudgy, but he'll work harder to make it good for you."

"Terri, he's got a *World of Warcraft* tattoo," Heather pointed out with derision.

"Well, at least it's not Dungeons & Dragons," Terri said.

Heather laughed. "The D&D tat is probably under his shirt."

D.J. hardly looked at the tattooed option. She glanced back behind her again. The guy in the booth was still looking at her. Still smiling. He seemed pretty comfortable. As if he knew exactly what he was doing. He probably made hookups six nights a week in places like this.

"Come on," Terri said, standing and pulling D.J. up beside her. "You can't really decide from this distance. Let's go dance."

Terri and Heather took turns hanging out with her on the dance floor, making the rounds, meeting the guys at the bar. D.J. completely threw herself into the new alter ego. She was a wild child, sexy through and through. Every moment was choreographed to portray the unrestrained, sultry and very available woman she wanted to be tonight. She even added a kind of Ado Annie east Texas twang to the performance, and it seemed as if the men around her were completely buying it. She was going to get her pick. She was going to get to choose. It was a heady sensation of power for a young woman who'd felt powerless for far too long.

She was catching her breath from a very athletic pairing with "dancing dude" when suddenly the hot guy she'd seen in the booth stepped in front of her. He filled the entirety of her vision until there was nothing except him.

"Oh…hi," she said, forgetting the fake drawl.

He was even taller than she'd thought, and his dark brown eyes looked down at her with warmth that seemed to penetrate her skin.

"I think you're going to have to dance with me," he said.

"Have to?" she replied with a smirk. "Why would I have to?"

"Because I came here to party with pretty girls," he answered. "And that's what I want to do. But you sparkle so brightly I can't even see anyone else."

"Sparkle?" she asked and then, realizing what he must be referring to, D.J. put her hands on her hips and deliberately pushed her bikini-covered breasts forward. "It's called sequins," she pointed out.

He smiled. "That, too."

She was almost paralyzed as he raised one long tanned finger to the spot where the ties for the halter top crossed her collarbone. Then, never touching her skin, he gently traced the direction of the strap down her chest all the way to the hollow of her cleavage.

The electricity was there again, but this time it was more like a lightning strike, and in places typically kept safe from that sort of thing.

"You don't need sequins," he said. "You sparkle from deep inside."

The bottom fell out of D.J.'s stomach. Her knees turned to Jell-O. She felt suddenly sober and didn't like it. She'd come so far, and she wasn't going to allow fear to back her down. Desperately, she clung to her sexy vamp persona. She tossed her hair and gave him her best impression of a worldly-wise grin.

"Be careful," she warned him. "If you get too close you might get glitter all over you."

His eyes narrowed with arousal, then he grinned and pulled her into his arms. "I'm willing to take my chances."

As a new song began, D.J. felt her hips moving to the beat. "I think *you're* going to have to dance with *me,*" she said. All around them people jumped and gyrated, when suddenly he brought his mouth down to hers. As their lips touched, the voltage zizzed through her, hot and quick and scorching. She kissed him back with all the expertise she could muster and with all the enthusiasm of the starving. The kiss was everything she'd ever imagined and more, so much more. She didn't want it to end, she didn't want to let it go. She persisted, making the most of the moment. It was exactly what she needed and she tried to make it last.

When they finally came up for air, she felt drunker than any champagne could make her.

"Wow." She felt more than heard him breathe the word against her temple.

She could have easily said the same, but why waste words? Instead, she edged closer to him, letting the desires of her body do all the talking. They swayed together to music that may as well have been in their heads.

"This is so what I've needed," he whispered. Her arms were wrapped around his neck. His hands low on her hips. She wiggled against him, encouraging free rein. A moan escaped from deep in his throat and she felt a brush of lips against her hair. Then he pulled away slightly, as if needing to put distance between them.

"You're incredible," he told her. "I don't want to scare you off by moving too fast."

She couldn't let him cool down. This was her night and there was no room for breathing space. D.J. smiled with all the enticement she could manage as she released him long enough to push his hands lower on her buttocks. "There is no such thing as 'too fast' for me right now."

He stopped dancing. "Let's get out of here."

152.2 Perception, Emotions & Drives

It was more than his mother's roast beef that had drawn Scott home for the evening. He told himself that it was important that he check out his mom's new tenant. And he was always up for a home-cooked meal. But he'd heard enough talk in town about the new librarian that he was as curious as anyone else. His mom's invitation simply made the introduction easier and more straight-forward.

Without bothering to knock, he opened the back-door screen and entered the bright, eat-in kitchen of his boyhood home.

He was surprised to be welcomed by the skittering sound of nails on tile. With only a couple of playful barks, an unexpected but enthusiastic ball of black fur rushed up to him, tail wagging and tongue hanging out.

"Well, hi there, puppy," he said, squatting down to punctuate his greeting with some neck scratching. The little dog was cute and friendly. Maybe that's why he was inside. As far back as Scott could remember, his mother had not allowed animals in the house. Even on the most bitter cold winter nights growing up, he'd had to sneak Blondie, his cocker spaniel, upstairs under his jacket. This terrier pranced around as if he owned the place.

He looked up to see his mother stirring something on the stove. Standing opposite her was a younger woman looking very much the librarian stereotype with her stiff expression, boring gray suit and hair bun.

"I assume this guy belongs to you," he said, rising to his feet. He crossed the room in two steps and offered his hand. "I'm Scott, the son. If I know my mom, she's already told you *way* too much stuff about me."

From the wide-eyed look on the woman's face, one would have thought that his mother had mistakenly given the impression that he was an ax-murderer.

Belatedly D.J. shook his outstretched hand. That was the moment when recognition sparked in him.

"Have we met somewhere?" he asked, looking at her more carefully.

Her cheeks seemed to flush slightly. "Huh?"

He took the two steps across the tile to plant a quick kiss on his mother's upturned cheek.

"This is D.J., our new librarian," his mom said. "She's renting your bachelor apartment."

"It's not my apartment, Mom. It's in your house."

"Yes, but everything about it reflects your personality."

Scott had merely tried to make himself comfortable while he was waiting to restart his life. He was pretty sure that if the apartment reflected anything, it was the numb loneliness that he'd tried to drive away by living there. However, he wasn't willing to reveal that.

Instead he turned his attention back to the attractive young woman in the room.

"You look so familiar," he said. "I'm thinking that we've met."

"Uh…" She still hadn't managed a proper sentence, and wore a deer-in-the-headlights expression.

"Did you grow up in western Kansas?"

"Wichita. I mean my parents lived in Wichita."

Scott shook his head. "I haven't spent much time there, though maybe I ran into you someplace."

"No, no I don't...I...."

"Are you a KU grad?" he asked. "I spent about six years eating pizza in Lawrence."

"Uh...no, no."

"She went to SMU," his mother piped in. "Summa cum laude. And graduate school at Vanderbilt."

"Wow, impressive," Scott said. "So you wouldn't have been hanging out among my scholastic shirkers group."

"Nonsense," Viv corrected. "Don't let him try to fool you, D.J. He was president of his Rho Chi chapter, that's the honor society for Pharmacy."

He shrugged. "She's my mom," he teased in sotto whisper. "Bragging about me is a way of life."

The woman didn't crack even the smallest smile. Instead she sucked down the rest of the wine in her glass.

"I did do some traveling to national meetings and such," Scott continued. "Maybe we ran into each other on neutral ground somewhere."

That suggestion was met with an immediate, forceful response.

"I'm sure I've never seen you before in my life."

The last part of her statement was definitive to the point of denial. Scott had to take her word for it. Perhaps she merely looked like someone he knew.

"Well, whatever. It's very nice to meet you today. And Mom's roast beef is just a bonus."

D.J. was still looking at him with an expression of near panic. He heard the rumor that Amelia Grundler was intent on spreading, that the new librarian was an old friend of Vern's, thereby suggesting that she might be a lesbian. Maybe that was the uncomfortable vibe he was picking up. Of course, picking up those vibes had never really been a skill of his.

"Scotty, get D.J. another glass of wine," his mother said. "And you two go in the living room and get acquainted."

His mother never called him "Scotty" anymore but he hoped, for the scared librarian's sake, that the diminutive made him seem less threatening. He had the distinct impression that she didn't want to get acquainted, but he obeyed his mom, pouring them both a cool glass of sauvignon blanc. He allowed her to lead the way to the front of the house. As he followed he had a strange sense of déjà vu concurrent with two weird disconnected impressions, sexy and not tall enough.

He puzzled this craziness in his own mind. Not tall enough? Tall had never been a prerequisite to sexy. And anyway, D.J. did not strike him as sexy—and that had nothing to do with her height. It was the genuine coldness that radiated from her.

She ignored the comfy sectional couch in order to seat herself on his mother's antique slipper chair. It was very low to the ground and, while beautiful, was not particularly comfortable. Scott sat down on the couch opposite and it was as if he towered over her.

Inexplicably, her face was an angry thundercloud.

Scott offered what he hoped was a conciliatory smile. Perhaps her first day on the job hadn't gone so well. And maybe dinner with his mother had been received as more obligation than invitation. Viv was open and generous and extroverted. It would never have occurred to her that her roast beef might be viewed as an ordeal to be survived. Being a public employee in a small town was tricky on lots of levels, but especially so as a command performance by a well-meaning member of the library committee. So he pasted a curious but neutral expression on his face and waited for her to direct the conversation.

D.J. said nothing, but was practically chugging her wine. At this rate, she'd be drunk by dinner.

That should loosen her up, at least, he thought.

As the silence lengthened, Scott took pity on them both and forged into the standby topic for uncomfortable conversants everywhere.

"There was lots of blue sky today," he said. "Absolutely gorgeous, although I'm sure the farmers would love another rain before we get too close to harvest."

She continued staring at him with an expression that suggested he'd just revealed an interest in dissecting kittens and serving up their livers with a nice Chianti.

He noticed her glass was now empty.

"Let me get you some more wine."

Scott escaped the living room silence, making his way to the refrigerator.

His mom looked up expectantly. "She's nice, isn't she?"

Scott didn't have the heart to disagree with her. "Yes, Mom, she's great."

"It's so much fun having a new person in town," she said. "I'm sure you two will have a lot in common."

That hope was not particularly realized over the next painfully slow hour and a half. He found that even the taste of his mother's cooking couldn't seem to lighten D.J.'s black mood. As his conversation appeared to be unwelcome, he used his mouth for chewing and allowed Mom to carry the bubbly chatter. She was an expert at that and it worked well enough, but he would not have described Ms. Jarrow as being particularly sociable.

While they chatted, he used the opportunity to observe this woman that his mother seemed over-the-moon about. She was medium height, slim enough, well groomed and orderly. That was the word that came to his mind. *Orderly.* The business suit was neat, barely tailored and adequately disguised any curves in her figure. Her hair was pulled up in a knot on the back of her head that was more functional than attractive. She was probably wearing makeup, he thought, but not enough that he was actually sure. And her eyeglasses were standard bookworm issue. She looked, he decided, exactly how a librarian was supposed to look, almost as if she'd come from central casting. But there was something oddly familiar about her that he couldn't seem to shake. She reminded Scott of somebody, but he couldn't quite put his finger on who it might be.

At least she'd switched to water when they sat down to the table. He'd begun to worry that the library committee had hired a lush, though despite the amount she'd drunk, she did appear coldly sober.

His mother was talking almost nonstop, mostly about him. This was, he imagined, not D.J.'s favorite subject, but she did manage to listen politely. Not once even did she cast a stray glance in his direction—which made it extremely easy for him to watch her.

She had very formal table manners. Neatly cutting her meat. Forking small, manageable pieces into her mouth. She was controlled. Scott added that word to his impression of the new librarian. *Orderly and controlled.*

"There are not that many young, single people in town," his mother was saying. "Scott will have to fill you in on what they do for entertainment."

When the interminable meal was finally over, she tried to help with cleanup.

"No, no, no," his mother insisted. "You're my guest. Besides I prefer cleaning things up myself. You two young people run along."

"Uh…well, I…" It was pretty clear that D.J. was grasping for an excuse.

"Scott, show D.J. the moonrise across the wheat fields. I'll bet she's never seen anything like it."

"I'm not sure when exactly…" he began.

"8:46 p.m.," his mother told them and then glanced at the kitchen clock. "Hurry up, I don't want her to miss it."

Scott felt he had no choice. He offered D.J. what he hoped to be a friendly, unthreatening smile though it felt stiff and uncomfortable. He gestured toward the door and then followed her out. He had to do what his mother expected of him tonight if he didn't want to hear about it for days afterward. But the woman couldn't have made it plainer that she'd taken an instant dislike to him. Maybe she simply didn't like men. Or maybe he reminded her of some jerk who shot spitballs at her in third grade, but he was not sure that moonrise gazing was going to make it any better.

Outside it was fully dark and except for the sprinkle of stars overhead there was nothing to illuminate the path to the east side of the house. There was a real possibility of walking into something or stepping into a gopher hole. The librarian's dog flitting around their footsteps only added to the problem.

Scott would have taken it slow, but D.J. marched ahead of him into the blackness as if pursued. Good manners dictated that he keep up. By the time they reached the side of the house where the vista of wheat filled the distance, his eyes began adjusting to the darkness. She stood mutely staring out over the field. Scott found a couple of lawn chairs, but she didn't sit, so he didn't, either.

The silence lengthened and he let it. There was something about being here in the dark with her that was unsettling. He felt sort of jumpy. Then he recognized that feeling as being turned on. He was here in the darkness with the unfriendly librarian and he was turned on.

Jeez, Scott, you have got to get out more, he warned himself. *If this keeps up, you'll be hitting on the mannequins in the store windows.*

And then, as if desire weren't an emotion bad enough to conjure up in this moment, he suddenly felt the familiar weight of loss and disappointment settle down upon him. Mostly he considered his life a good one, but it was not at all what he had planned. And sometimes he couldn't help but miss that dream, that fantasy that he'd expected to be true for him.

From the far edge of a distant stand of ripening grain, a full moon as big and bright as a Hollywood searchlight eased its way into the night sky.

Scott's throat tightened at the sight. He disguised his own sentiment with a forceful "Ahem."

"It's called the moon illusion," he announced, as if he were the authoritative voice-over in a celestial documentary. "For years scientists thought that the atmosphere or the curvature of the earth formed some sort of magnifier that made the moon appear so large on the horizon. But they've taken measurements to show that it actually appears exactly the same size when it's high in the sky. It's our brains that perceive it as being so much bigger."

"Yes, I know," D.J. said.

Her tone was too sharp, efficiently jerking Scott out of the gauzy musings. Mawkishness was not particularly manly. And apparently she was unmoved by lunar beauty. Made of sterner stuff than he himself.

She turned to him. "I've had a long day," she said. "Please thank Viv for a lovely dinner." With that, the woman turned and walked away with a forcefulness that could accurately be described as stomping off, leaving Scott alone with the wheat and the moon and his own confusion.

176.6 Ethics of Recreation & Leisure

Bolstered by coffee, D.J. arrived at work the next morning bleary-eyed. She had spent the night tossing and turning. She'd felt like pacing, but was afraid her downstairs landlady might hear...and might suspect.

For the zillionth time her brain screamed, *Why him? Why here?*

Like the Humphrey Bogart line from *Casablanca,* the unlikely coincidence was unwelcome.

She had been so shocked by the sight of Scott, she'd hardly been able to speak.

He was the *guy. That* guy. The hot guy.

Sometimes she'd almost been able to convince herself that the incident had never happened. And in those times when the memories were too vivid to be denied, like whenever she'd see the moon on the horizon, she'd shaken off her feelings with a water-under-the-bridge analogy. In the category of youthful mistakes, hers had been short-lived, relatively harmless and with minimum consequences. She'd accepted her lessons and her regrets and moved on.

Unfortunately, she'd unwittingly moved into her mistake's hometown, his backyard, his childhood bedroom.

D.J. groaned aloud as she climbed the circular stairs to her office.

"Our librarian sounds a little grumpy this morning."

Suzy was seated on the floor, books and papers all around her.

"What are you doing?"

"Sorting out all my monthly reports," she answered. "Amelia tells us all the time that bookmobiles are dinosaurs. I figure you're going to want to look at cost/service analysis and decide for yourself. So I thought I'd have it ready before you ask."

"Uh…great. Good idea," D.J. said, impressed at Suzy's initiative, though not necessarily prepared for it so early in the morning. "Try not to worry. A lot of libraries have given up on bookmobiles. But for some areas, there is nothing more appropriate."

Suzy sighed heavily. "I think that, too," she said. "I guess I just need the numbers to prove it. It's times like this that I wish I'd listened more in math class."

"If you can get the raw data together, I can help you with the interpretation."

"Would you? That's so sweet. I was really worried. I heard you were on the warpath about Books-By-Mail and I thought maybe you were for that program and maybe anti-bookmobile."

"The two are completely different," D.J. told her. "The services complement each other more than compete. And if anything is threatened, it's Books-By-Mail. With digital download lending, it's been made practically obsolete."

Carefully toeing her way around Suzy's paper piles, D.J. made it to her desk, which was inexplicably cluttered. She set her laptop bag on the chair, as it was the only space available.

"What's all this?"

"It was there when I came in," Suzy answered.

D.J.'s first, uncharitable thought was that Miss Grundler had been going through her desk and had left a bunch of evidence on top. When she looked closer, however, she saw that each book had a request neatly tucked inside.

"Did Amelia stay late?"

"She left before I did," Suzy said. "Aren't you the one who locked up?"

D.J. had been.

"She must have come back to work later," she told Suzy. "These are the Books-By-Mail requests. It looks like all of them. All caught up in one day."

"You're kidding? Grundler hates that stuff. I can't believe she'd work overtime to do it."

Suzy had risen to her feet and went to examine the books atop the desk.

"Oh, wow," she said.

"Oh, wow, what?" D.J. asked.

"It wasn't Amelia. It was James," she said, pointing out the messy handwriting on the slips. "He must really, really like you."

"I haven't really even met him," D.J. pointed out.

"Well, something made him spend time doing this."

"Maybe he's like you getting your statistics together," D.J. said. "He wanted to take the initiative on something. A quick way to impress the new librarian in charge."

Suzy shook her head. "James is not a 'take the initiative' kind of guy. He's, like…strange. What is the word they use? It sounds like artistic…"

"Artistic? You mean autistic?"

"That's it. Autistic not artistic. Duh. Sometimes talking to me is a brain-free zone." Suzy giggled. "James was, like, 'special' before 'special' was cool. But he knows every book in this library and can put his hand on anything in no time flat."

"Good qualities to have," D.J. agreed. "A lot of people with Asperger's Syndrome choose library science."

"Asperger's Syndrome?"

"High-functioning people on the autism spectrum. It's a different way of relating to the world, that can lend itself to be very good at some things that the rest of us are not that good at."

"Oh," Suzy said. "Well, I guess it's good to know that he's not just simply weird."

D.J. sighed. It would take some time to get used to the blunt way people spoke in this small town.

Focusing on the pile of books on her desk, she managed to get all of the requests into mailers and waiting for the postman by opening time. Amelia waltzed in five minutes late, a deliberate look on her face, as if to say "I dare you to do anything about it."

D.J. had already figured out what to do about it. She was seated in Amelia's chair at the circulation desk. And she made no move to relinquish her position. Miss Grundler had few options. She could go back into the shipping and receiving area. She could hang out in the break room. Or she could wander around aimlessly looking for something concrete to do.

D.J. chose the latter for her. From the bottom shelf, she handed the woman the library's ancient feather duster. Book dusting was the lowest form of library care. While actual janitorial work was contracted out, no commercial service would actually go through and swish the cobwebs from the uncirculated tomes.

Amelia looked at the duster as if it were a snake.

"I should take this opportunity to pull the Books-By-Mail requests," she said.

"All done," D.J. replied.

The woman frowned. "The night return?"

"James took care of it," she said. "Everything was checked in and reshelved before I showed up this morning."

Ms. Grundler took the duster, but she was clearly not happy about it.

D.J. savored her little victory in stoic silence. Winning over the reluctant staff member was not the same as scoring a few points against her, she reminded herself. She was still hopeful that Amelia would find a way and a reason to be part of the team.

Having downloaded the library's budget to her laptop, D.J. intended to spend any free time at circulation familiarizing herself with how much everything cost and how monies were currently being appropriated. This was the kind of thing that she considered herself very good at. But her sleepless night, coupled with the anxiety she was harboring about running into…him… made the figures in front of her as incomprehensible as a rune cipher. Fortunately, interaction with patrons was at least as important as comprehending financial resources. So she gave herself up to meeting, smiling and chatting with all those who came by for a look at the new librarian.

Books that had been overdue for years were being reunited with their fellow shelf sitters. Although five-cents-per-day fines were still technically enforced, D.J. magnanimously granted amnesty to every person she met. Getting the books back and getting people inside the building felt like victory enough. However, there did seem to be a lot more visiting than book browsing. She met a few more women-of-a-certain age. A number of harried housewives with toddlers in tow. The firemen from across the street. And the old grandpas that hung out at the barbershop.

"I can't see a dang thing inside this place," one older fellow confided. "I make a special trip out to the bookmobile to find my reading material. But I wanted to lay eyes on the new librarian and I have to say, I like the cut of your jib."

D.J. appreciated the compliment, but worried about the lighting. Giant rows of fluorescents hung from the ceiling at great expense, but somehow they couldn't overcome the atmosphere of shadowy gloom.

D.J. had only meant to usurp Amelia's place for a few minutes. But the entire morning zoomed by with her still sitting at the main desk. She handed it over as she announced she was leaving for her lunch break.

Miss Grundler's brow was drawn down on her face angrily, but her response was perfectly respectful.

"Of course. Go on with your schedule."

D.J. carried her laptop and the few notes that she'd made on the budget up the narrow circular stairs to her office. She dug out the lunch that Mrs. Sanderson had packed for her and spread it out on her desk.

"You don't need to do this," she'd told Viv that morning when she'd flagged D.J. down as she was getting in her car.

"Of course I don't need to. I want to," Viv had assured her. "And don't worry about Melvil Dewey today. He and I will take a nice walk down to the creek before he gets too warm."

She had wanted to nix that. Dew belonged to D.J. and he should be going on his walks with *her*. But while she was working, poor Dew had nothing to entertain him but a basket full of chew toys and the TV left on.

It was selfish to deny him a bit of extra companionship because she was feeling a little jealous.

But, *oh!* How she didn't want him getting attached to the mother of the hot guy.

D.J. bit into the meat loaf sandwich, hardly tasting it. She'd really thought she'd put that stupid, idiotic, temporary insanity of her twenty-first birthday well behind her.

But Scott was, without a doubt, *the* hot guy. And he was here.

For what felt like the millionth time, she shook her head. It was so hard to believe. Or maybe she should have expected it. The bad penny always shows up. Or as the chaplain at Hockaday might have said, "Be sure your sins will find you out."

The more D.J. thought about it, the angrier she became.

How dare he be from my new hometown!
Thank God he doesn't remember me.
How dare he not remember me!

She promptly lost her appetite, so she rewrapped her sandwich, stuffed it back into the brown paper bag and threw all of it in the trash.

She opened the budget file on her laptop, but the little lines and squares and numbers jumbled together and she couldn't make sense of it all. She began tapping her pencil nervously against the desk.

With a growl of annoyance at herself, she rose to her feet and began looking around for something more physically demanding. As she headed downstairs, the front door of the library opened and a very loud boisterous group of seniors came parading in. The group, here on a day trip from Pine Tree Nursing Home, apparently visited on a regular schedule. D.J. was obliged to open up the door to the library's nonpublic area to allow wheelchair access to the building.

She had a lot more experience with older people than most young women her age. Her parents had been in their mid-forties when she had inexplicably come into being, so D.J. was accustomed to the peculiar bluntness that seemed to come with old age. This group, however, seemed particularly cranky.

"I hate this place," one woman told her, punctuating her words with a stomp of her cane. "The bookmobile goes to the center where my sister lives. But because we live in town, it's as if we get penalized."

"But you have so many more books here in the main library," D.J. countered. "There is so much to choose from."

"Well, you can't choose if you can't see," she snapped. "This place is as dark as a cave. I have to select titles by feel."

The man beside her, one of the few males in the group, spoke up. "You should switch to reading biographies like I do. They're all shelved next to the windows."

"I want to read fiction," the woman told him. "I don't happen to like biographies."

The man chuckled. "I don't read them because I like them. I read them because I can see them."

He did have a point. The stacks were dark. And short of having everyone carry a flashlight, she wasn't sure how to brighten them up.

Instead she spent the afternoon doing one-on-one service. Questioning the Pine Tree patrons about their interests and then bringing them selections from the shelves. Many of the regulars had already read much of the collection. So by the time they began loading back on the bus to leave, huge piles of books were everywhere. Amelia ignored the mess, but that was okay with D.J. An introvert by nature, after a couple of hours of chatty human interaction, she welcomed the peace of sorting and shelving.

As she loaded up a cart, she thought again about the problem for those with low vision and what she might be able to do about it. Maybe instead of pulling particular books for the patrons after they arrived, she could set up a table with a sampling of things that might interest them. Of course, setting up a table was problematic, as well. The only real space was in the open area in front of the circulation desk. But the light was only marginally better. She remembered what the man had said about biographies. She noticed that most of them did have sun-damaged spines. Maybe there was a usable space next to the windows.

She walked around the ranges of shelves to the aisle area between the adult collection and the outside wall. A half dozen tall oversize windows were spaced at staggered intervals. The afternoon light poured through them. But there was neither sufficient depth for a square table nor length for a rectangular one. D.J. was disappointed. But at the same time, something niggled her brain. She stood staring at the wall for a long moment, trying to figure out what it was that stood out so strangely to her.

Behind her she heard a squeak of wheels and turned just in time to see the book cart she'd loaded disappear behind a range of shelves.

"James?"

The cart stopped moving but the guy didn't show himself. She hadn't so much as caught a shadow of him all day.

D.J. peeked around the corner. He was standing

there, but his head hung down, unwilling to meet her eyes.

"Are you going to put these up for me?" she asked.

"Yes."

"Thank you."

"Okay."

"And thank you for pulling all the Books-By-Mail requests this morning."

"Okay."

"Being new to the library, I'm going to need the help of everybody on the team," D.J. told him. If anything, his head hung lower, as if he wanted to make it disappear into his chest.

"You're part of my team, right?"

"Yes. Yes. Okay."

James was nodding rapidly, but his body language screamed *leave me alone!*

D.J. took pity on the guy and headed back to her office, but she was smiling. She *had* gotten three words out of him. That was surely progress.

210.4 Natural Theology

The long approach to Scott's place would have been called a road by most standards. Certainly the county that graded it considered it that. But since his was the only building on it, and it ended abruptly at the edge of the river beside his house, many folks in town thought of it as his driveway.

He kind of liked that. The imagery of it appealed to him in some way. As if a journey, his journey arrived at this home and saw no need to go any further.

The truth was, of course, that the county had simply not wanted or needed to spend money on another bridge across Verdant Creek. So the county road stopped abruptly and then picked up again a couple of miles farther west.

Friday was his afternoon off. He kept his cell phone close so that Paula could contact him in the case of an emergency prescription, but since he had to be open on Saturday, the busiest day of his week, he didn't begrudge himself the break.

Scott pulled into his usual parking place near the back door. Although he'd grown up in a house where locks were never used, he understood that leaving his house open could be abetting the worst impulses of the desperate or larcenous. Still, he was a trusting, rural guy at heart. He reached up above the door's metal light fixture to retrieve his key, clicked open the lock and then returned it to the magnet that kept it at least sight unseen to would-be thieves.

Inside he began peeling off his clothes immediately. He'd installed his washer and dryer in the mudroom. And living alone he found little need for the frills of domestic life like hampers and baskets. He put his laundry directly in the washer and when it filled up, he did the wash.

Naked, he made his way to the front bedroom. The eighty-year-old one-story farmhouse retained much of the dated, retro appearance enjoyed by the former occupants. Scott had updated the kitchen and painted the exterior, but the bedroom still sported wallpaper with the faded pastel pressed-petals design. It was girly. Undoubtedly decorated for the daughter of the house. But he preferred the morning sun shining through the windows. And a few pink-and-yellow flowers didn't threaten his masculinity.

In fact, a little less masculinity might be helpful. As he pulled on his jeans, he glanced toward his rumpled bed as if it were an enemy. The last few nights he had been plagued by dreams. He couldn't quite recall the erotic events involved, but he awakened achy and aching, hard as a rock.

"You need a girlfriend," he told his image in the mirror.

Immediately he thought of Jeannie Brown. She was lonely and she liked him. That had him halfway into her bed already. He doubted she was any great shakes in the sack, but someone was better than no one, right?

"Wrong," he answered his own premise. "Someone is *not* better than no one. Been there, done that, got the T-shirt."

The rhetorical tee was exactly the soft and nearly ragged one he pulled out of his chest-of-drawers, a reminder of some long-ago rock concert that he could barely recall. He dragged it over his head and tucked it in, more to get it out of his way than any need for neatness.

At least all those early-morning, sexually frustrated runs freed up his afternoon for less strenuous exercise.

On his way back through the house, he stopped at the fridge and drank a big slug of orange juice directly from the bottle. He wiped his mouth with the back of his hand. Both behaviors would have horrified his mother and disgusted his ex-wife. But if there was to be any consolation for the unplanned single life, it was that a man could be as uncivilized as he pleased.

At the back door he pulled on his muck boots and a broad-brimmed straw hat. He stepped outside and made his way across the bare patches and buffalo grass that he euphemistically described as his lawn. On the north side was the drain field for the septic system. The grass was far greener there, but somehow the source of that lushness did not encourage him to linger.

The south end of his acreage had been transformed into a garden.

He'd bought the property, still known around town as "the old Paske place" along with the surrounding three acres between the house and the creek bank. At the time, he'd had no real plans for the land. If he'd considered it at all, it was as a buffer between the privacy he needed and those friends, family and neighbors who lived nearby.

But it was more than that to him now. Scott gazed lovingly down the long rows of plants stalwartly growing out of the soil. The carrot tops looked pretty enough to put in a flower vase. The potato plants were already hardy and the peas appeared vividly green against the grayish-brown color of the Kansas soil.

From childhood, his parents had pressed him into service in the family garden. And like every rural teenager, he'd done his share of backbreaking farm labor. But he'd never really considered plants or cultivation as a hobby he'd ever care to pursue. Yet from the moment Scott had moved in, the need to plant something, to grow something, had been so strong in him he was unable to resist it.

He could only imagine that the genes of generations of dirt farmers were finally showing themselves. Scott had surprised himself. His parents had merely shrugged.

"What else would you do with all this good ground," his father had said.

What else, indeed?

That first year he'd thought to put in half a dozen tomato plants. Everyone knew that homegrown tomatoes were far superior to any bought in the store. But why go to the trouble of tomatoes without some cucumbers and radishes? Squash and gourds practically raised themselves. Broccoli, onions, sweet corn and salsify—every season his garden expanded its borders and its variety. This year he had even planned space for turnips and okra, two vegetables that he would never eat voluntarily.

There would always be people grateful to do that for him.

It was the growing that was important. The satisfaction of planning what needed to be done, doing what you were supposed to do and, with a lot of sunshine and the right amount of rain, seeing your efforts return a harvest of pride.

Scott walked carefully between the rows. Everything looked very good. Here and there he saw evidence of wildlife. He didn't mind sharing with the occasional rabbit, raccoon or possum. But he knew how easily a great garden could be overrun with pests. He walked over to the shed where he kept a spray bottle filled with diluted pepper sauce. He sprayed down all the cabbage. The water was always welcome. As for the hot pepper, it didn't deter the critters completely. But it did make them think twice about a casual salad at his expense.

Looking around his garden, Scott was reminded that no man is an island. Humans need fellow humans, but they also need plants. Whether it was God's great plan or nature's joke, the most evolved species on the earth was at the mercy of the food chain and its foundation of fruits and grains to sustain life.

Scott actually liked being a part of that. Gardening was a hobby. And he was pretty sure that a guy with no wife, no kids, no girlfriend and no social life needed hobbies.

The ruminations of his job always followed him home. And if he made no move to stop them, he'd spend his entire evening second-guessing his actions of the day and anticipating what might need to be done tomorrow or next week. His father had warned him to "leave the store at the store." His dad's philosophy was that the job and the home should be two different places and that it could be dangerous to allow them to mesh together.

You can run a business or a business can run you, Scott remembered him saying. *Work hard and smart every minute you're here. When you step outside, leave it all behind.*

That hadn't always been easy, and not just in the aftermath of his father's death.

Certainly it had been difficult to shoulder the extra stress of running the family business without his father's help or advice. But even before that. When he was still feeling the sting of his divorce. When he'd felt so unsure about what he'd wanted and so disappointed about facts he couldn't change. The temptation to hide in his job, to allow all his thoughts and emotions to become absorbed in the details of his career was hard to resist. It felt like virtue and it was quite possible to be completely self-righteous about it. But it was, he knew, only cowardice in disguise. If you weren't willing to face your life—all your life, including the rough parts—then you weren't truly living. You were just making a living.

He was startled from his thoughts by the excited yapping of a little dog. The sound came only seconds before the creature was barging into his onions.

"Hey! Get out of here," he said.

Knowing obedience was unlikely, Scott grabbed the small ball of black fur that was intent on trampling his stalks. He recognized the librarian's dog immediately.

"You're a long way from home for a guy with short legs," he told the pup.

Scott looked toward the house. He couldn't see all of his drive, but he certainly hadn't heard a car. He glanced in the other direction, toward the creek, to see his mother walking up the path. She was dressed in a kind of knitted pantsuit with heels more suited to one of her bridge parties than a nature trek.

"Good grief," he muttered to himself.

With the dog clutched under one arm, he walked down to meet her.

"You walked over here?" he asked her incredulously.

Viv was flushed and breathless. "It wasn't my intention," she said. "Mr. Dewey got a bit ahead of me and… and here we are."

Scott offered his free arm and she took it gratefully.

"You should have had him on a leash," he told her.

"Oh, I suppose so," she admitted. "But he's so happy when I let him wander free."

The thought, *who are you and what have you done with my real mother,* floated through Scott's head, but he didn't voice it. Instead he commented on the obvious.

"This is a really long walk for you, Mom. It's got to be close to three miles."

Viv's smile faked nonchalance. "I used to walk that far to and from school every day."

"Yeah, sure," Scott responded with skeptical sarcasm. "With little blood prints of your bare feet in the snow. They had school buses in the 1960s, Mom. It's an historical fact."

"Well, whatever," she replied. "I could use a drink of water."

As they neared the back door, Scott set the dog down. "If you run off, you'll be finding your own way home," he warned.

The happy critter, ears perked up and tongue hanging out, appeared oblivious to the threatening tone. And when Scott opened the back door for his mother, the dog charged in ahead of her.

Viv sat down with a grateful sigh in the first kitchen chair she reached in the windowed alcove that was Scott's breakfast nook. He poured her a glass of cold water from the refrigerator. As an afterthought, he filled a small bowl from the tap and set it on the floor.

His mother was enjoying the view. From this vantage she could see his small expanse of lawn, the neatness of his garden and the tree line in the distance along the edge of the creek.

"You've made this a really pretty place, Scotty," she told him as he seated himself across from her. "I should come out here more often."

"You are always welcome, Mom. But you know, if you're not going to drive, at least put on sensible shoes."

She chuckled. "Sometimes you remind me so much of your father. He never allowed himself to scold me. He'd just get exasperated."

"I don't remember a lot of exasperation on his part," Scott replied.

"Well, of course you don't. We always made a point of keeping what was between us, between us. There was no need to drag the kids into the normal ups and downs of married life."

"Who knew that you two could be secretive? I would have said you were perpetually blissful."

Viv laughed. "There is no such thing as perpetual bliss. If two people manage chronic bliss, that's probably the definition of a happy marriage."

"I wouldn't know."

Scott had meant the words to be light. He immediately saw the worry line that emerged in his mother's forehead.

"Kidding," he assured her.

She reached across the table to pat his hand. "One of these days, you'll find the right one, Scotty."

He smiled at her, but he didn't voice agreement. It might be cruel to get her hopes up.

"What did you think of our new librarian?" she asked. "Isn't our D.J. a lovely young woman?"

Scott managed not to roll his eyes. "I'm sure she's very nice," he said.

"Perhaps you should show her around this weekend," his mother said. "I'm sure it's difficult, being all alone in a new town."

He wasn't about to get trapped into that.

"Mom, she very likely has plans of her own already," he pointed out. "They say she's originally from Wichita. So she'll probably drive there to see friends and family on the weekend."

"She doesn't know anyone in Wichita," Viv stated. "She's an only child, her parents died several years ago. They were quite elderly and from what I gather, she grew up in boarding schools and summer camps. Her only ties are the ones she makes right here in Verdant."

"Well, it sounds like you two are becoming well acquainted," he said. "Honestly, she wasn't all that chatty when I talked to her."

His mother blushed. "Well, naturally, no one tells her life story the minute she meets someone. But a part of vetting a new employee is finding out about her life."

Scott raised an eyebrow at that. His mom's information didn't seem like the type to be acquired in a job interview.

"I need to get home," his mother said, abruptly changing the subject. "D.J. will be worried."

"Worried about you?"

"About Mr. Dewey, of course."

239.2 Apologetics & Polemics

D.J. arrived home a few moments after six. She had the first week down as Verdant's new librarian. It wasn't a total success, but she'd gotten a lot done and she felt well on her way to having a handle on the situation. She also had some ideas on how things could be improved. Still, she'd ended the week on a sour note. She'd lost her temper.

That was not good.

Being cool under pressure was the hallmark of a good administrator. And the more troublesome the employee, Amelia Grundler being the poster child, the more calm the demeanor one should maintain.

"Fail," D.J. said to herself aloud.

She parked her car and gathered up her computer and the notes and files she'd planned to work on after-hours. Her heart was barely in it, though. D.J. really wanted to go upstairs, heat up something in the microwave and spend the evening vegging in front of the TV. Things would surely look better in the morning.

Yet she just couldn't seem to shake the events of the day. It was bad enough that she'd blasted Amelia. It was worse that she'd done it in front of Amos and Suzy.

A smart boss would have stayed at the circulation desk and made her point clearly and firmly without raising her voice.

D.J. had virtually dragged the offending biddy into the back and then proceeded to go off on the woman like a crazy person. Worse, she really *felt* like a crazy person. She'd been so angry, so overwrought, she hadn't even realized she'd had an audience—but the truth was that it might not have even stopped her.

Amelia had touched a nerve. In the short term, D.J. had embarrassed herself and behaved inappropriately. But the long term was even worse. Now Amelia knew which button to push. And D.J. had no doubt that she'd make full use of that knowledge.

With weary steps, she climbed the stairs to her apartment. She was disappointed in herself. Not simply for her unseemly reaction, but for revisiting the seeds of it. She'd come a long way since those days of emptiness, those old insecurities. They shouldn't still have an impact on her actions.

Somehow, she thought, the hot guy shared some blame for this. If she'd been sleeping better, eating better, been less edgy, she would have maintained her rational composure. But worrying about him had her walking through the world on eggshells. And that had made her more vulnerable to her own demons.

She groaned as she opened her door. Maybe she should quit while she was ahead. Maybe Verdant was not the place where she could finally find a home. How could she build a life around Scott's faulty memory? She couldn't see herself reminding him of exactly what they'd done together, but she'd never been good at lying, either. And it was probably late to be developing the skill.

Inside her apartment, D.J. dumped her load of work and her purse on the kitchen table. She hung her suit jacket on the back of a chair and kicked off her shoes.

She unpinned her hair. Releasing the weight of the severe bun at the back of her head was such a relief. It was almost literally taking a weight off her shoulders.

She wandered through the apartment aimlessly. Her apartment. This place had nothing in common with the sterile, nondescript, cookie-cutter condo that she'd owned in the city. Even with its mess of unpacked boxes, she already liked this place better. It was beginning to feel like home.

The solid character of the old house extended into its refurnished rental. The living room had two nice windows on the south side. The bedroom was a good size and brightly lit, as well. The kitchen was small and galley style, but it did feature a cozy nook with a little table for two. Her favorite room, however, was the bath. The huge, old-fashioned room was tiled in basic black and white, complete with both an antique claw-foot tub and a very modern dual shower in a glass enclosure.

She looked longingly at the tub. A nice long soak might soothe the worst of the day's mistake.

Maybe after she and Dew had dinner.

Dew?

D.J. suddenly realized that her best friend, buddy, roommate and pet had inexplicably not met her at the door when she arrived. That simply never happened.

She called out the dog's name as she walked through the place. With no answering yip or telltale patter of paws on the hardwoods, she knew Dew was not at home.

Annoyed, she headed out the door, across the porch and down the steps. It *was* nice, she reminded herself, that Viv was taking Dew for his walk during the day. But she should return him to his own house, not take him into hers. D.J. knocked on Viv's door sharply.

Nothing.

She waited a minute and knocked again.

Beyond the landlady's back door was complete silence. D.J. peeked in through the glass panes. No one in the kitchen. Perhaps the woman was taking a nap. But Dew was no sound sleeper. If he were in there, he'd hear the knocks and be barking the house down.

Viv's lavender Mini was still parked in the driveway, though. It was late for the two of them to be gone. Then she spied Dew's leash draped over the porch railing. He was running loose?

"Just perfect," she complained.

Dew was a great dog, mostly obedient, and he would come when D.J. called him. But he hardly knew Viv. There was no telling what he might try. And how would the older lady keep up with him if he took it in his head to run off?

D.J. would have to go find them. But she couldn't do that barefoot. She hurried back up the stairs to get shoes, then decided it made more sense to put on some clothes more suited to a dog search than her business suit. She began pulling boxes open looking for jeans. The first thing she spotted were biking shorts she hadn't worn since her bicycle was stolen. In the upheaval of moving, those things buried at the bottom had worked their way to the top. D.J. didn't have the time or patience to search any further. Quickly she pulled on the knee-length, skintight spandex and the bright blue zip-neck jersey that went with them. She hopped the length of the apartment as she pulled on first one running shoe and then the other heading out the door.

She jerked her hair up into a ponytail as she made her way across her second-floor deck and down the steps. She knocked again at Viv's, just in case, before taking off with a loping stride down the driveway. The idea of

Dew getting lost was scary. Verdant was a brand-new place. Nothing would seem familiar. The town was not that large, but he was a small dog. And the surrounding wheat fields all looked alike. She had no idea what kind of wildlife might live out there, but she was sure that most of it would be unwelcoming to a terrier.

In the street, D.J. hesitated. Left or right? One way led to the center of the community. The other toward the path along the creek. Viv might have gone either way. As she stood there, indecisive, a familiar vehicle came into view.

A white minivan with Sanderson Drug Store painted on the side was hardly mistakable. It was the hot guy. Beside him, in the passenger seat, was Viv. Dew was on her lap, his head sticking out the window, mouth open, tongue hanging out, his fur and ears blowing in the wind.

In a cloud of Kansas dust, the van pulled to a stop beside her. D.J. immediately reached out to her happy, smiling dog.

"You found him," she said.

"Oh, Mr. Dewey was never lost," Viv assured her. "He and I went for a good long walk along the river path to see Scott. The exercise was good for both of us."

Dew seemed perfectly content to let D.J. stroke his fur and scratch his neck. He happily licked her hands, but he was in no hurry to relinquish his place in the car window. In fact, he squirmed for release when she pulled him into her arms.

"Thank you for walking him, Viv. But you really shouldn't try that without the leash. He might wander off and I don't know if he'd come when you call."

Viv seemed unconcerned. "Well, he didn't disappear and he's home now. No worries."

D.J. raised her eyebrow at that, but kept her opinion to herself.

She allowed her gaze to go beyond her dog and her landlady to the van's driver, not quite able to meet his eyes.

"Go ahead," she said, stepping back and allowed Scott to turn into the driveway and park near the back door.

She walked back toward the house, holding Dew in her arms until his wiggling moved to full-on writhe. As soon as she let the dog down he went running happily toward Viv getting out of the car.

D.J. followed more slowly. As she neared the older woman spoke.

"He is the smartest little dog I've ever seen."

D.J. nodded. "Terrier mixes can be very intelligent."

"And he loves riding with his head out the window."

D.J. pursed her lips together thoughtfully. It was very nice of Viv to hang out with Dew, but she needed to understand the ground rules.

"I don't let him do that," she said, firmly. "It's not safe. If you're going to transport him, you'll need to get his crate."

Viv laughed lightly. "I'm not actually *transporting* him, dear. We're just taking a little jaunt through town."

D.J. didn't want to be difficult about it, but she knew that she was right and that it was important.

"It's too dangerous, Mrs. Sanderson," she said. "You could be involved in a crash."

"In Verdant? Maybe if I were intoxicated and out on the highway," she said with a facetious chuckle. "We haven't had a major accident in town…why, in years."

D.J. shook her head. "In even the most minor fender-bender a loose animal in a car gets tossed around like a projectile. He needs to be in the crate at all times and the crate needs to be secured with the seat belt."

The older woman shrugged, but her smile didn't fade. "Oh well, then," she said. "He and I will stick to the walking paths. But it does seem a shame with life so short, to give up such a sweet, pleasurable activity for something as stodgy and illusive as safety."

It was in her mind to retort that safety was neither stodgy nor illusive, but the ability to form a sentence momentarily eluded her as Scott came around the front of the car looking gorgeous in simply jeans and a tee. This afternoon he was the exact same person she'd met in South Padre. He was even wearing the same shirt, she was surprised to remember. He might not recollect their night together, but her lower body tightened as if in muscle memory of it.

He joined the women, leaning languidly against the car's wheel well.

"So were you going out jogging?" Viv asked.

D.J. glanced down at her cycling clothes, debating how to explain that she'd been about to go searching for them.

"Scotty runs, too. I'm sure I told you that." Viv turned to her son, teasing. "He doesn't dress as well at it. He wears ratty old sweats from his college days."

"Compression pants are for the bicycle, Mom," Scott said, indicating D.J.'s clothing choice. "You don't really run in them."

"Oh, is that what they're called? It seems like you could run in them. You make the same moves on a bike as in a sprint."

He shook his head. "No, Mom. They're not good for that."

"I don't see why not."

"Not enough ventilation in the groin," Scott said with a smirk.

Viv laughed a bit too loudly and gave D.J. a conspiratorial glance. "Oh, my goodness! Maybe we girls don't have as much need for that as the gentlemen."

D.J. decided that the less said about that area of human anatomy the better. But she was having trouble thinking about anything else to say. Why did he have to look so good? She stuttered slightly, grasping at words to change the subject.

"So do you have plans for the weekend?" she blurted out suddenly. She'd directed the question at her landlady. To her horror, the woman turned to her son, as if to indicate that the inquiry was meant for him.

He immediately quit his leisurely pose. Standing straight, he looked unhappily surprised and uncomfortable.

"I, uh…I work on Saturdays."

D.J. nodded. "I intend to open up tomorrow, as well."

"The library doesn't have hours on the weekends," Viv told her.

"I want to change that," D.J. stated. "I think it's the best time for families. Lots of kids who need something to do."

"How will you staff it?" Viv asked. "I'm not sure the board will welcome taking on new employees."

"I'm going to do it myself," D.J. told her. "At least until we see how well the community responds. Public libraries don't typically keep bankers' hours. Nine to six is fine if you're retired or home with small children. But we need to make our services available to all our citizens."

She was surprised to see Scott was nodding. "Probably a good idea. Saturday is when the most people are in town. It's our busiest traffic day in the store."

"Exactly," D.J. said. "If we are going to breathe new life into the library, we're going to have to reach out to people who haven't been in the habit of thinking of us as a source of things they need."

"Well, if that's what you want to do, then that's fine," Viv said. "As I told you when you were hired, we're all excited to see what new ideas you can bring."

"Thank you."

Viv wasn't finished. "But all work and no play makes D.J. a dull girl, right? A dull librarian is what we've had for years. I was hoping you would change that."

"Oh, I will," D.J. assured her.

"Good," she said. "You can begin on Saturday night. I was telling Scott that showing you around, helping you meet some younger people is simply the neighborly thing to do."

"Well, I…"

"Isn't that what I said, Scott."

"Uh…yeah. You did."

"Wonderful." Viv turned back to D.J. "What time should he pick you up?"

302.7 Social Interaction

Saturday was as busy as Scott thought it would be. Harvest was quickly approaching and everyone in town wanted to be ready. Their prescriptions needed to be filled. Their first-aid boxes needed to be replenished. They needed particle masks and flashlight batteries. Sunscreen and corn plasters. All of which could be purchased at Sanderson Drug Store. Between harvest preparation and the accompanying camaraderie of old friends and fellow farm families, business was hectic.

There was excitement in the air this time of year. The typically staid and sedate inhabitants of Verdant were almost giddy with anticipation. Not that harvest was a carefree, happy-go-lucky adventure. Actually, it was a couple of weeks of hard, backbreaking work. But it was also the proud culmination of a year of effort and a radical change in the town's day-to-day routine. Plus, with a harvest as good as this year's was looking to be, the mood was easily upbeat.

As Scott counted pills, answered phone calls and waited on customers, he couldn't help but be drawn into the noise and bustle around him. Farmer after farmer came to drink coffee and report or comment on the results of their crops' moisture content. Even those who were only growing petunias in pots were eager for the latest word.

With all the activity, the morning flew by. Scott had Paula bring him back a sandwich when she went on her lunch break. He ate it seated on the cold box behind the counter, since all the seats in front were taken. Age, occupation, gender—none of it seemed to trump the solidarity of shared expectation and experience.

But it was not as if other concerns couldn't provoke interest.

Scott had just taken a hearty bite of his spicy egg salad from Gleason Sandwich Shop when one of his mother's friends, Edna Kievener, spoke.

"So I heard you've got a date with the new librarian."

The silence that followed that bombshell was deafening. Scott struggled to chew and swallow as movement in the room was frozen and every eye trained upon him.

"Not a date," he managed to get out with food still in his mouth.

He gulped down a swig of pop so he could speak.

"Mom asked me to show her around, introduce her to a few people, that sort of thing," he explained. "It's no big deal."

There were a lot of nods and some feigning of unconcern. But Scott didn't exactly see people going on about their business. Everyone was interested. Everyone was listening.

"Well, do you like her?" Mrs. Kievener asked.

"I…uh, I really don't know her," Scott replied, diplomatically.

"Viv likes her a lot," Edna informed everyone within earshot. "She says the girl is very charming."

"She's not exactly a *girl*," Nina Philpot pointed out.

Scott thought to himself that he wouldn't describe her as particularly charming, but it was not an opinion he would share.

"From all accounts she seems to be delightful," Edna replied.

"That's because we don't know much about her yet," Harvey Holland said. Harvey, the local big shot, if Verdant had one, was dressed today in bib overalls and a Feed Company hat. This close to harvest, it was good business to be seen as a man of the people.

At the end of the counter, Karl Langley, the deputy sheriff and the only law enforcement for this part of the county, nodded. "Until we do, we give people the benefit of the doubt. Besides, aren't librarians supposed to be a quiet kind of people."

Beside him, Suzy Grandfeldt, who clearly knew the librarian better than anyone in town, spoke up. "Well, she's no Marsha Milquetoast, if that what's you're thinking. Actually, she has a bit of a temper."

Suzy glanced down the counter toward Amos Brigham who was eating a banana split for lunch. Her co-worker nodded in verification.

"Really?" Nina asked.

The room was all ears, including Scott.

"Yesterday she raked Miss Grundler up one side and down the other." The words were spoken with pride and admiration.

Harvey whistled.

"Good heavens. What brought that about?" Edna asked.

Suzy leaned forward slightly as if revealing a confidence, although in current circumstances it was tantamount to putting up a billboard.

"It was about Ashley Turpin."

"Ashley Turpin? Julene's little girl?"

Suzy nodded.

"Julene doesn't finish her shift at the Brazier until

after the dinner rush," Amos explained. "My guess is that she doesn't have anybody to watch Ashley this summer, so the girl's been coming to the library every day."

"At closing she walks out to the restaurant to meet her mother," Suzy added. "I've offered to give her a ride, but she says she isn't allowed to get into other people's cars."

"That's a long walk for a little girl," Edna said with a voice of concern.

"She does it all the time," Harvey said. "All summer I spotted the kid coming or going."

Edna tutted with disapproval. "A parking lot on the highway isn't *my* idea of a child's playground."

Amos agreed. "She's better off in the library."

"But I don't think D.J. even knew where Ashley goes or why," Suzy said. "Miss Grundler doesn't like 'the library being used for babysitting.' And since we never see Ashley's mom, she was making sure that Ashley passed on the message."

"I see her point," Karl said. "The taxpayers shouldn't be paying for someone to watch the woman's kid."

"But the girl shouldn't have been dragged into it," Edna said. "Children are often the innocent victims of a parent's bad judgment."

"And it seems that our new librarian agrees with you," Nina pointed out.

Harvey chuckled. "It says something, too, that she was willing to take on Amelia Grundler. That's one female I'd be afraid to meet in a dark alley."

Edna gave the wealthy owner of the grain elevator a wry glance.

"And yet, much of the gossip that shows up in this

town seems to be centered around you, a woman and a dark alley."

That brought titters of laughter to the room. Harvey took it with a good-natured shrug.

"No, you people don't understand," Suzy protested. "Nobody has more fantasies of telling off Amelia Grundler than I do. And for this, she totally deserved it. But this was way over the top of my imaginings. D.J. was seriously on fire and, I'm telling you, Miss Grundler got burnt to an ash. Normally she's so sweet, but she was practically snarling. It was as if she thought the entire purpose of the library was to provide a refuge for lonely children. It's one thing to argue for the right thing, but this was something more personal, and she really let Amelia have it. Ask Amos if you don't believe me."

"Of course we believe you," Paula reassured her.

"She'd probably come to the end of her rope with Grundler," Nina said.

Edna agreed. "That woman could get on anyone's last nerve."

Scott nodded. He didn't have any trouble believing that D.J. had a temper. She'd disliked him on sight and she'd made no attempt to hide the fact.

He continued to think about her off and on through the day.

"Who is it that she looks like?" he asked the group. "The librarian, she reminds me of somebody. Who is it?"

There were shrugs all around. People were shaking heads.

"She just looks like herself to me," Suzy said.

Scott was sure that he knew her from somewhere. She was simply too familiar to him.

He was still wondering about it later as he got ready for their date.

"It's not a date," he said aloud to his reflection in the mirror. Two people who didn't really like each other but were forced to spend an evening together out of politeness—that definitely did not qualify as a date.

Still, he did consider wearing a tie. Dark blue to go with his blue striped shirt. On second thought, Scott decided against it. If he showed up in a tie, people would definitely talk. They would probably talk anyway, but there was no need to give them more ammunition.

He picked her up at exactly seven. She came outside just as he approached the steps to the upstairs deck, as if she'd been watching for him. She hadn't exactly dressed for the occasion. She was wearing the same kind of blue-gray business suit and sensible shoes that he'd seen her in the evening they'd met. The shapeless, bland clothing was in sharp contrast to his memory of her in those biking shorts. A narrow waist and generous booty were not typically things women liked to hide. But then, women didn't typically look at him as if he were a worm.

He smiled, hoping to appear more sociable. If anything, that seemed to evoke an even less gracious response.

"You don't really have to do this," she said. "I am perfectly capable of meeting people and introducing myself."

"Of course you are," he said, agreeably. "But Mom is right. It's always nice to have someone to run the introductions. And if you're anything like me, after a long work week, it's always tempting to curl up alone at home."

"I'm not anything like you," she stated with more

certainty than she could possibly have on such brief acquaintance.

Scott didn't argue.

"I thought we'd catch a movie. It's about the only thing there is to do in town, so it's what most people do."

"Fine," she answered.

As they walked to the car, his mother came out the back door. "You kids have fun," she called out.

He didn't think that was likely. Scott liked the image of D.J. standing up to Amelia Grundler. Running defense for a kid who probably had more than her share of things to be defensive about. It made him want to like her more. But the grumpy expression on her face suggested that she didn't share his sentiment.

"I won't be out late," she assured his mother, who only laughed.

"I wasn't worried about that. They pretty much roll up the town after ten o'clock," she said. "Besides, I'm going to go up and get Mr. Dewey to keep me company."

"Uh…he's in his crate," D.J. said.

"No worries. I'll bring him downstairs."

Scott still couldn't imagine why and how his mother had become attached to the dog. But he didn't question it. Instead he opened the door of the van for his date, before remembering that it wasn't a date and that D.J. might not appreciate such a gesture.

She didn't.

The Ritz on Main Street showed films old enough that you could stream them at home. But the popcorn was good and there were lots of people to see and meet. A family of five could have a night out together for twenty bucks. And farm families in town for the weekly grocery shopping had a reason to stay through the evening.

The popularity of the place was evident in the parking. Scott pulled into an angled space across the street and at the end of the block.

D.J. didn't require his assistance to get out of the passenger door. He made an effort to walk beside her down the sidewalk, although she did keep a couple of arms-lengths between them, as if he might suddenly grab her and she wanted to be prepared.

At the glassed-in ticket booth, a line of rowdy teenagers had formed. Young guys were acting silly in order to get the attention of young girls, who were giggling with appreciation.

They took a place behind them. Scott wondered if he had ever been that young. Technically he had, of course. But he had been a quiet, studious guy in his teens, working in the store every weekend and dating Stephanie. She had valued seriousness and maturity. So even back then, he'd behaved more like forty than fourteen.

"I suppose you do this every weekend."

He was shocked that the silent woman beside him had finally spoken. Maybe that was progress.

"No, not very often really."

"It seems like a lot of very young people. Lots of teenage girls, I guess."

"All ages, I promise," he said, offering another polite smile.

She didn't like that one much, either.

"It is nice that we still have the theater," he pointed out. "We're so far from the entertainment extras that most people take for granted. If we want to keep it available, we need to patronize it."

She nodded thoughtfully at that. "Yes, I suppose so."

In truth, Scott rarely ventured to the place. In some ways it held bad memories. It was in the Ritz Theater that he had first begun to suspect that maybe there was something strange about his relationship with Stephanie. If he'd acted upon his instinct then, everything afterward might have been a lot different.

D.J. was rifling around in her purse for something. The kids in front of them were buying tickets. One second before it was his turn to step up to the window, she found what she was looking for. She held up a twenty-dollar bill and attempted to hand it to him.

He simply stared at it, uncomprehending until finally realizing her intent.

"I've got this," he said.

She pushed the money toward him more forcefully. "There is no reason that you should pay my way."

"It's two bucks a person," he said. "You can buy the popcorn."

He pulled out his wallet and handed the appropriate amount to Christy Tacomb, the ticket seller, who was watching the exchange between them as avidly as a cub reporter at a house fire.

Scott hated provoking gossip. But at least everybody in town would soon know that the librarian, at least, didn't consider their night out to be a date.

He took the tickets that were handed to him, but he was so distracted that he forgot to mention the half inch of uneven flooring between the town's more recently relayered sidewalk and the old movie theater's 1920s black-and-white tile.

D.J. stumbled, and Scott reacted on instinct, wrapping a protective arm around her waist.

Touching her felt so familiar, so perfect, that his heart immediately caught in his throat. Other body organs were also affected.

304.3 Factors Affecting Social Behavior

D.J. could have happily choked Viv for the unwelcome suggestion of a Saturday night with the hot guy. After a difficult first week on the job, she would have been very content to unwind with a good book. Instead she was expected to smile and talk and be charming to the one person in the entire world that she most wanted to avoid. Scott had the knowledge and the power to make her a laughingstock to her new community. And perhaps the potential to get her run out of town.

"Okay, maybe the locals won't be coming after me with pitchforks. But I could be quietly let go, 'for the good of the community.'"

She poured out her worries to the only listener she could trust.

Melvil Dewey.

The little dog sat in rapt attention on her bedroom rug as she paced back and forth. Trying on everything in her closet and then discarding it on the bed. As she dressed and undressed and redressed, she ranted.

"If he remembers, I'm doomed. I'd never be able to look him in the eye. And you know he'd brag about it to every man in this town. Guys like him do exactly that sort of thing."

Dew made no comment.

"He simply can't remember. He can't. He's already said I look familiar to him. I've got to be careful what I wear, how I walk, how I talk. I can't do or say anything that might remind him."

Her tone was certain, but she was not.

"How can he *not* remember?" she asked the dog, incredulously. "It's so…so embarrassing to think that a moment that changed my life, *ruined* my life, would, for him, have been so…forgettable."

The word *forgettable* was voiced through clenched teeth. Dew cocked his head as if in question.

D.J. placed a steadying hand on her forehead as if her brain ached. "Okay. 'Ruined my life' is maybe a bit over-the-top," she admitted. "I had sex with a stranger. It was a dangerous, irresponsible thing to do. It's exactly the kind of dangerous, irresponsible thing that twenty-one-year-olds do all the time."

Dew offered no words of consolation.

"I was damned lucky that I didn't get pregnant or catch some disease."

Still, babies and STDs aside, D.J. had never imagined that the ramifications of one stupid night were going to echo through future relationships.

"If you could call my dysfunctional sex life 'having relationships,'" she complained. "I do better with a glass of wine and a dirty book."

Dew opened his mouth to pant, his little pink tongue hanging out to the side.

"Easy for you," D.J. told him. "You should thank me for having you neutered."

She tried on outfit after outfit. Every one of them either looked so nice it gave the wrong message. Or so casual D.J. was afraid it might make him recognize her. In desperation, she opted for her librarian disguise. She went with glasses and no eye makeup. But even that time saver barely had her ready when she heard his car in the driveway.

She quickly crated Dew and hurried out to meet her fate.

He was at the bottom of the stairs and the mere sight of him pissed her off. How dare he look like some harmless boy scout!

D.J. was so annoyed, she could barely offer a civil exchange with Viv when she asked to hang out with Dew. The woman was on the library board. D.J. needed her. And more than that, she liked her, too. But any crazy ideas that Viv had in her head about her son and D.J.... Well, the woman should give those up ASAP.

She knew she was acting like a prig. And that such behavior with someone who was supposed to be a virtual stranger was very suspicious. But she couldn't seem to stop herself.

He held open the door to the functional but ugly van. D.J. remembered vividly the sporty blue Mazda Scott had been driving in South Padre. Back then she'd refused to ride and they had walked, first through the funky shopping area and then along the moonlit beach. The walking should have sobered her up. But it had been almost as if his very nearness to her was intoxicating.

Tonight she was perfectly clearheaded.

She slid into the seat and sat, back straight and stiff as he walked around to the other side of the vehicle.

Scott made several attempts at polite conversation, but D.J. answered in monosyllables. It was not that she was afraid of revealing something that would connect her to South Padre. She'd been completely another person that night. She'd said almost nothing personal. Anything she *had* said had been a pack of lies. She had revealed nothing about who she really was.

And yet, part of her had to admit she'd revealed everything—everything that mattered, anyway. She'd deliberately stripped herself naked, body and soul.

She tried to keep her gaze focused directly ahead. But they kept drifting over to his hand on the steering wheel. The way his jean-covered knee was flexing as he operated the gas pedal. Under no circumstances would she look him in the eye. But looking him in the thigh wasn't exactly conducive to higher thoughts, either.

D.J. was exceptionally grateful when he finally parked the van and she could escape his too-near proximity. As they walked down the sidewalk, she kept her distance. Literally and figuratively.

She hated the way Scott moved. There was so much confidence and ease in his gait. As if every step he made would lead him to whatever he wanted. He was accustomed to getting his way, she could tell. Certainly getting his way with women. The player types always had their pick. There had undoubtedly been so many women who fell at his feet, begged for his touch, screamed in orgasmic pleasure that it was no wonder he couldn't recall when she had done exactly the same.

That thought really made her mad.

"I bet you do this every weekend."

He seemed surprised that she'd spoken. But not so surprised that he couldn't come up with a hasty denial.

Her first impulse was to not believe him. But as they stood behind a line of boisterous teens, she postulated that probably this was not a great adult pickup scene. She imagined that somewhere nearby, maybe out on the highway, there was a dark, seedy bar. Not even as nice as the Naked Parrott, where the local South Padre honeys got drunk, poured beer down the front of their shirts and let the hot guy take them home to screw.

But not her. Not again.

As they approached the ticket booth, she rifled through her purse for cash. She could not allow him to pay. She wanted him to be clear that she didn't think this was a date. And she didn't want to owe him anything.

He left her money hanging in the wind, suggesting that she could spend her share at the concession stand. Her stomach was so jittery, she couldn't eat a thing. Besides she would not be compelled to share anything with him, not even a bag of popcorn.

That thought was firmly in her mind when she tripped on the uneven floor beneath her and fell into his arms.

The same spark that had sizzled between them on that one night so long ago lit up again at his touch. His arms were so warm, so familiar, so welcome. She felt as if she belonged there. But she did not.

"Are you okay?" he asked, getting her back on her feet again.

"Yes, I'm fine. Fine."

She began brushing off her suit as if his touch could be discarded.

Their gazes met and his eyes narrowed intently. He couldn't be remembering. She couldn't let him.

"Let's go in," she said, heading in that direction without him. He rushed up to get the door. She didn't even bother to be annoyed at that. She needed to get into the darkness of the theater.

The lobby, however, was very well lit and thick with people. D.J. would have been happy to avoid them. But the proposed purpose of the evening was Scott making introductions. And he seemed determined to do that.

However, the aftereffects of falling into his arms still plagued her. The heart patter and gooseflesh added to her already fluttering stomach and the combination kept her brain from functioning normally. D.J. smiled, she nodded, she shook hands, but she couldn't hang on to one name long enough to commit it to memory.

Fortunately she didn't need to say much. After a polite acknowledgment of her personally and the existence of the library, the talk quickly changed to wheat.

Harvest time was almost upon them and it was apparent that the folks in Verdant looked forward to it as eagerly as kids to Christmas.

"The weather is going to be on our side this year, I'm thinking," a farmer perhaps a decade older than D.J. said. "We don't want a big rain, but a nice little one will help out nicely."

Beside her Scott shook his head. "I don't know that you're going to get it. It must be dry as a bone out there. Lots of static electricity in the air."

The farmer raised eyebrows in surprise and glanced toward his wife.

"I haven't noticed anything."

"The weather man on Channel 3 said humidity was moderate."

"The librarian here got a shock just skidding on the tiles in front of the building," Scott said, turning to D.J. for confirmation. "Right?"

"Mmm-hmm," she mumbled, attempting to look interested as a sinking pit of fear opened up in her midsection. "Would...would you excuse me for a moment?"

She didn't wait for a reply, but hurried toward the sign that said Restrooms. She'd hoped for an escape and a moment of solitude. Of course, neither was available. A half-dozen women milled around the ladies' room.

D.J. didn't want to talk to anybody. She deftly avoided eye contact and stepped into the first available stall. She threw back the bolt and then leaned against the door, mentally admonishing herself to get a grip.

Yes, the hot guy had more than his share of sexual magnetism. Yes, he still had the power to make electricity zing through her bloodstream. But no, she could not go that direction again.

She allowed herself a momentary fantasy that it was all different. That she'd just met him days ago. That he would fall for her, the real her, and there could be something incredible between them.

Her bubble burst as quickly as it had formed. The man was good in bed. That did not mean he would be good for her. In fact, she was nearly certain that he wouldn't be. She needed the boring, stodgy stability that a hot guy could never offer. If that came without the fireworks in the bedroom, then so be it.

The bathroom had finally gotten quiet. Gratefully, D.J. figured everyone had left. She flushed the toilet and opened the door.

The area wasn't completely empty. At the far end of the room a fortyish woman with a snappy, expensive-looking haircut was bent toward the mirror putting on lipstick. When their eyes met, D.J. gave her the slightest nod of acknowledgment before focusing intently upon washing her hands in the sink.

The woman put the lipstick into her purse, which she closed with an audible snap. She turned. D.J. kept washing her hands, expecting the woman to walk past her and out the door. Instead she moved to stand beside her.

"So I guess you're *it*."

D.J. looked directly at the woman. She was curvy

and attractive. Her clothes were well cut, obviously expensive and very chic for western Kansas.

"Uh…yes, I'm the new librarian."

The woman laughed lightly, but not really in a nice way.

"No, I meant you must be Scott's new sex buddy. I've been waiting to see what he might come up with after I dumped him." The woman looked D.J. up and down. "Quite honestly, I'm not that impressed. But, honey, you are welcome to him. For as long as it lasts."

The woman swept past D.J. before she could respond. Although D.J. had no response to give. The situation was exactly what she expected it to be. Scott was a player. He knew how to pick up women and then discard them like tissues. What she'd always believed had now been confirmed for her as truth. But that didn't stop her from being furious about it.

She quickly dabbed her wet hands with a paper towel and followed the woman out the door. She was already out of sight when D.J. made it down the hall. In the lobby, Scott stood waiting for her. He held a cardboard tray with two drinks and a bag of popcorn. His eyes were wide.

"From the look on your face, I guess Eileen said something to you," he suggested calmly.

"Eileen? Your ex-girlfriend? Why, yes, actually. She definitely has the wrong impression about us." D.J. could hear the snide tone in her own voice.

He shook his head. "Don't worry about it. Eileen's opinions are rarely anyone else's."

"I don't want anyone, including your ex, thinking that we have any kind of relationship at all."

"Absolutely," he agreed. "You've made your feelings very clear. So let's go watch a movie, meet a few more people and then we can make a point to steer clear of one another."

D.J. was briefly tempted to sock the man in the nose, but more out of embarrassment than anger. She knew she must seem unreasonably stuffy, but this was how it had to be. She would get through this evening. He would not recognize her. And forevermore she would stay as far away from the man as humanly possible.

The previews had started and the theater had been darkened by the time they'd made their way inside. One center aisle sloped down toward the screen. It wasn't as if she could get lost. But after her near fall at the front door, D.J. allowed Scott to lead the way.

The visibility of the carpeted runner beneath her feet varied with the brightness of the image on the screen. In near total darkness, Scott approached two empty seats on the aisle. When the trailer moved on to bright sands and surf against the beach, the faces around them became visible. D.J. spotted Vern, the woman from the Feed & Tractor store. Seated next to her was a small, slight, very pretty blonde.

The couple made startled eye contact with Scott. Who gave them only the very slightest of acknowledgment before moving three rows away to take a seat.

Oh great, D.J. thought to herself, *my onetime "sex buddy" is not only a liar and a player, he's a bigot, as well.*

306.5 Culture & Institutions

On her most recent trip to the grocery store, Viv had wandered down the pet food aisle, amazed at all the options. She'd wanted to buy a few dog biscuits for Mr. Dewey and ended up with a grocery cart full of interesting choices. There were fake steak strips and bacon made of vegetable meal, even pizza rolls. She'd made a couple more attempts to feed him scraps, but he'd turned up his little pink-and-black nose. If dog food was what he liked, at least she could find some of it that was a bit more unique. Viv had decided to buy some of all of it. That way she would find out which kind Mr. Dewey actually liked.

She'd stored the packages away in her extra under-the-stairs pantry. The shelves in there were loaded, but not as badly as the kitchen pantry or the cupboards.

With the little black fur ball at her heels, she rifled through the assorted bags and boxes.

"Why don't we try this one first. 'Chewy Bison Burger,'" she read aloud and then laughed. "Now this is an interesting choice for you. I can't imagine that any of your ancestors could bring down a buffalo in the wild."

Mr. Dewey, tail wagging appreciatively, hurriedly consumed what she gave him. Then he rose up on his hind legs effectively pleading for more.

"Look at you! Okay, one more. But I'm not going to

let you become a junk food junkie no matter how many tricks you can do."

As she put the bag of treats back on the shelf, she caught sight of something from the corner of her eye.

"Oh!" she exclaimed with excited delight. "We've got a live one here, Mr. Dewey."

From its place, crammed in a wide variety of fruit and vegetable items, Viv retrieved the misshapen can. She examined the bulging metal at the top with approval.

"Tomatoes," she said to Dewey. "I can always make something lovely with tomatoes."

She carried the can with her as she moved to the front of the house. Across the hallway from the living room she opened the door to the quiet, musty office that had been her husband's. The room was much as he had left it. Her daughter had done some straightening on the day of John's funeral. And Scott had been in and out several times getting papers from the filing cabinet. But Viv herself had not moved a thing.

She went to a narrow closet at the far end of the room and retrieved the key secreted above it on the doorjamb and used it to open the lock. Inside, a collection of fishing rods hung on the back wall. A half-dozen narrow shelves on the side held nets, reels and tackle boxes. As a young husband, her John had loved fishing, though as the children got older and the demands on his time got greater, he rarely took time from the drugstore for his hobby.

On the floor was the old-fashioned brown metal cooler that he'd used to transport his catch on hot summer days. She released the latch on the lid and opened it.

The dog, who'd trailed in behind her, was as interested in her discovery as she was herself. He plopped his front paws up on the edge and peered inside at what appeared to be a collection of misshapen and bulging cans of food.

"You keep your nose out of this, Mr. Dewey," Viv told him firmly. "This is not good for you. It'll make you sick."

The dog looked up at her expectantly, but she made no further explanation. She added the can of tomatoes to what was already inside the cooler and then closed the top, double-checking that it was secured.

"Come on, now," she told Dewey. "Nothing to see in here."

She closed the closet door and turned the key in the lock before secreting it once more on the doorjamb.

As they left the room, the phone rang.

Viv ignored the one on her husband's desk. Instead she continued on into the living room to answer the one next to the sofa.

"Hi, Mom," said a familiar female voice at the end of the line.

"Oh, Leanne, how are you, sweetie?"

The generic question was all her daughter needed to launch off into a play-by-play of her busy urban life. Viv settled in for a cozy chat. Dewey looked up at her expectantly, but waited until she offered wordless permission to jump up into her lap.

She stroked his fur and scratched his ears as she talked and listened.

Leanne always spoke as if her life was endless chaos. But Viv could see that she and her husband Jamie were happy and settled, each pursuing careers that they enjoyed.

"So how did it go with Ryan?" Leanne asked.

Viv tensed. It was a small movement, but enough that Dewey cocked his head to look up at her.

"Fine."

"I'm still dying of curiosity," Leanne said. "Ryan said it wasn't ethical to discuss investigations for his clients, even with family members."

"I simply had him look into something for me," Viv answered evasively.

"Is it about the drugstore? If somebody is robbing Scott blind, I need to know that."

"It's nothing about the store," Viv assured her. "It was personal business, I suppose you could say."

"Personal business? Really, Mother, what kind of 'personal business' could a sixty-two-year-old woman have with a private detective?"

Viv didn't reply.

"I've been racking my brain for weeks," Leanne said. "Could it be something about Dad? I mean that's what we see on TV when they hire these guys. It's how you catch a cheating husband in a cheap motel room with a bimbo."

"Your father was not particularly fond of cheap motels and he never looked twice at any bimbo."

"That's my thinking, too. But I thought you might be second-guessing yourself."

"No, of course not."

"Okay. Then were you taken in by some senior scam kind of thing?"

"What?"

"Lots of con men target women your age, especially widows," Leanne said. "You haven't been exchanging emails with any exiled Nigerian princes, right?"

Viv sighed heavily. "No, dear. No Nigerian princes."

"What about sweepstakes winning? They may say

you need to pay a portion back, but never wire money to anyone without talking to us."

"Of course I wouldn't."

"And if you get a phone call from a family member who says they are in trouble, call them back with the number *you* have for them."

"Honey, I am not being scammed, I promise," Viv told her. "Don't let your imagination run away with itself."

"Well, I'm your child, I worry about you."

"I'm the mother and it's my job to do the worrying."

"Not anymore," Leanne told her. "Once your kids are grown, you're allowed to stop."

"A mother only stops when she's dead," Viv stated with conviction.

"Whatever," her daughter said with a sigh. "But I would quit worrying if you would just tell me what's going on. I won't question or judge. But if you tell me, it will ease my mind. Unless it's about me…"

"It's not about you and it's none of your business."

"Have you told Scott?"

"It's none of his business, either."

"Okay, well at least you didn't tell him and leave me out."

"Of course not."

"Good. So it's not a scam. And it's not me and it's not Scott."

Viv kept completely quiet, not even taking a breath.

"If you're not going to tell me, I'll just have to spend more time guessing."

"Don't bother."

"I'm hoping I can wear you down," she said. "Anyway, Jamie and I are thinking about coming down there, either this weekend or the one after. Which is better?"

The hand that was petting Dew stopped abruptly in midmotion. The little dog who'd been luxuriating in the attention opened his eyes.

"This is not really a good time, Leanne."

"What do you mean?"

"Harvest is almost on us and you know how crazy everything gets around that time."

On the other end of the line, she heard Leanne chuckle. "Mom, I've been through my share of harvest times. I know it seems like it gets really busy and the traffic gets hectic. But we live in Kansas City. Jamie and I are immune to traffic and hectic."

"I…I don't think there will be any room," Viv told her. "With that many people in town, there are always people trying to crowd in."

"We can stay upstairs in the apartment."

"No, you can't. I rented it."

"Really? Well…that's great, Mom. So we'll stay in the guest room."

"No…no, I think someone will be using it, too."

"Who?"

"Uh…well, honey you know how it is at harvest, every room is at a premium."

There was a long silence on the other end of the line. Finally Leanne spoke. "So you're renting rooms in your house to augment your income. What the hell is going on? I'm calling Scott."

"Margery Leanne! You keep your nose out of it!" Viv told her sharply. "I told you it has nothing to do with money or the drugstore."

"Don't call me Margery and don't talk to me like I'm twelve," her daughter snapped back. "I'm thirty-two years old."

"Then it's high time that you learned to mind your own business."

Viv would have liked to slam down the phone and be done with the conversation, but *ladies* did not do that. And she had tried always to be a lady.

Dewey sat expectantly on her lap as if preparing for a joint escape through the back door. She rubbed his neck reassuringly as she modulated the tone in her voice.

"Leanne, honey, please don't make a mountain out of a molehill. Things are busy around here. I'm busy with my clubs and the library. I would love to see you and Jamie, but it would simply work out better for me if you came to visit around the end of the month."

Her daughter didn't sound completely mollified, but ultimately she did agree to wait until the wheat was in and day-to-day life back to normal. And when they finally said their goodbyes it was congenial if not completely back to normal.

As Viv hung up she uttered a sigh of great relief.

"Whew! That was close," she told Mr. Dewey.

324.4 The Political Process

D.J. had spent much of Sunday afternoon preparing for the weekly staff meeting on Monday morning. After the Friday fiasco, she felt very strongly that re-establishing herself as a calm, reasonable person with forward-looking plans and teamwork camaraderie was paramount. Miss Grundler had been looking for a weakness and in D.J.'s vehement defense of young Ashley Turpin, she'd certainly found it. D.J. needed to skew that bad experience into positive change for the library, and she was eager to do it.

She arrived at work an hour early, but she was not the first on the job. The rusted old bike that belonged to James was already thoroughly overchained to the railing. She wondered, not for the first time, if the guy actually lived in the building. She'd seen no evidence of that. No personal items anywhere. He hadn't left so much as a cracker in the break room. And he appeared never to leave the stack area. There wasn't even a chair in that section. So unless he was sleeping on bookshelves, he was upright and moving all the time.

D.J. smiled to herself at the image of sleeping in the library. She used to dream that she could do that. It had been her childhood fantasy. Going to the library and simply staying forever.

Perhaps she and James had more in common than she'd originally thought.

He was out of sight, of course, as she entered the darkened entry in front of the circulation desk. D.J. turned on the lights.

"How can you work the stacks in total darkness?" she asked the silence of the big room.

A long hesitation was followed by a tentative reply. "Miss Grundler doesn't want me running up the electric bill."

"But you can't see what you're doing," D.J. pointed out.

"I've…I've got a flashlight," he said, tentatively.

D.J. shook her head. "Flashlight shelf reading," she mumbled to herself, before adding more loudly, "James, you have my permission to turn on any or all of the lights that you need to do your work."

"Okay."

She turned to go and then changed her mind. "I'm going to the break room to make coffee," she said. "If you want us to have the staff meeting out here, I'd like to have a table and some chairs, please."

Without waiting for a reply, D.J. went back through the workroom to the little kitchen. It took her only a couple of minutes to put fresh coffee into the paper filter and pour the water through the machine. She'd already had a cup at home, but she decided to wait for the pot to give James time to do whatever he might do.

As she leaned against the counter, her mind began running down the meeting checklist. She wanted to make sure to praise what she saw and throw out new ideas for making it better. The copious notes she'd made left little necessity for her to actually remember. Still she attempted to focus very directly on her plans for the day. Allowing her thoughts to wander off in other directions was never a good idea. And the past couple of days provided two directions that she was specifically trying to avoid. There was the little girl who had caused her to so shockingly lose her temper on Friday. And there was her Saturday night with Scott.

D.J. considered herself some kind of an expert in compartmentalizing. It was undoubtedly a genetic trait. She'd shown early talent in boxing up every aspect of her life, careful never to taint any experience with another. Everything about life, the precious, the bitter, the uncertain, could be perfectly managed and excellently controlled if it was kept securely on its own. Home was home. School was school. Work was work. Although choosing librarianship as a career had certainly served to muddle the place she loved to be with the place she earned her living. Sometimes things spilled out of boxes.

It was the upheaval of change, new place, new people. That could cause old demons to crop up. Literally as well as figuratively.

Of course, it was probably unfair to categorize Scott as a demon. But he was not a nice person, she was convinced of that now. And worrying that he might remember her was certainly putting her through hell. Still, he was probably not the devil, though that would explain the quality of his bedroom skills.

"Box spilling over," she warned herself aloud.

Getting her cup, she "cheated" by pouring from the carafe before the pot was finished, but she managed not to spill a drop. By the time she returned to the circulation area, James had set up a table and four chairs.

"Thank you," she called out to the mass of shelving that separated her from the light of the windows.

D.J. made a quick trip up the spiral stairs to get a couple of things from her office and then lined up all her notes, files and her laptop at the head of the table. She decided to be already seated when her staff arrived. That way they could move straight to business almost instantaneously.

At least that seemed reasonable in theory. In actuality, it didn't go quite that way.

Suzy arrived first and with her own agenda items, none of which D.J. wanted to discuss.

"I am all totally squeeee!" she declared. "You went out Saturday night with Scott Sanderson!"

D.J. wasn't sure if her zeal stemmed from disbelief or disapproval.

"We saw a movie together," she clarified.

"I can't believe you had plans for a first date and didn't tell me," Suzy said as she seated herself in the chair on the right, leaning forward, chin on clasped hands as if in expectation of being told a fairy story.

D.J. barely managed not to sigh aloud. "It wasn't a date," she assured her. "And it wasn't planned."

"Spontaneous? Oh, spontaneous is the best kind of first date."

"Not a date," D.J. repeated. "Mrs. Sanderson asked him to show me around, introduce me to people. That's all."

"That's perfect," Suzy said, nodding. "Low-key, no pressure, men have no defense against that. Viv really does like you. And you know what they say, 'win the mother-in-law first.' It makes the long-term relationship so much easier."

D.J. could not believe that the term "mother-in-law" had actually been used in this conversation.

"There will be no long-term relationship," D.J. said.

"Now don't count yourself out," Suzy cautioned. "You are an attractive woman. And Scott goes for the quiet scholarly type."

"I doubt that. But it doesn't matter. I moved here to work, not meet men," D.J. explained.

"Of course that's not *your* reason," Suzy agreed. "But a lot of people are saying that Viv's whole new librarian plan had more to do with fixing up Scott than fixing up the library."

Suzy giggled delightedly at that.

D.J. felt slightly nauseated. She'd already been warned. But it didn't matter how many people thought it or who might want it, there would be nothing between them. In fact, she hoped never to catch sight of the man again.

"It was one movie," she explained calmly to her employee. "We have no interest in each other, nothing in common and we didn't hit it off. End of story."

"Oh." Suzy sounded genuinely deflated. She sat back in the chair, her expression confused. "So did you have a fight or something?"

"No, of course not. He's simply not my type."

The woman's expression went from puzzled to incredulous. "Scott is, like, one of the best-looking guys in town. And there are practically no single guys at all in Verdant."

"Then he shouldn't have any trouble finding someone else to date," D.J. said.

"He doesn't though," Suzy said. "He doesn't go out with anybody."

"I think you must be mistaken about that."

"Not likely," Suzy stated with sarcasm. "Dating in Verdant is like a spectator sport. The only thing that draws a bigger or more loyal audience is the high school basketball team. So if Scott had dated anyone, I would know it."

D.J. shook her head. "I ran into his ex in the ladies' room at the theater."

"His ex-wife? We were on cheerleading squad together. She's a sweetheart. Everybody loves her. But there are some things in marriage that can't be fixed. We all worry that it just broke Scott's heart."

"Broke Scott's heart? That's not the way I heard it. And I didn't meet his ex-wife, I met his ex-girlfriend."

"His ex-girlfriend?"

Apparently Suzy wasn't as in the know as she thought.

"Eileen," D.J. clarified.

Suzy's eyes got as big as saucers, but her voice shrunk down to a furtive whisper. "You met Eileen Holland? What made you think she was his ex-girlfriend?"

"She told me she was."

"O. M. G.!" Suzy declared, dragging each letter out dramatically. "There were lots of rumors, lots of speculation, but nobody knew for sure."

"So there," D.J. said. "Dating in Verdant may not be as public as you think."

"Oh, you don't understand," Suzy corrected her. "They weren't *dating*. Married people don't date. Eileen's husband is Bryce Holland. He and his dad own the grain elevator."

D.J. practically had to pick her jaw off the table and suddenly understood what all the whispering was all about.

"Bryce is like…like one of the richest guys in miles and miles. He knows everybody and has tons of influence on the library board," Suzy warned. "So whatever Eileen might have said to you. I'd forget that I ever heard it."

At that moment, Miss Grundler stepped in from the workroom. Suzy shot the woman a glance before telegraphing a further, unnecessary warning to D.J.

"Message received," D.J. replied grimly.

326.9 Enslavement & Emancipation

Scott awakened with an erection as big as Colorado, his bedcovers reminiscent of that topography. He groaned aloud as he recalled only glimpses of the dream that had stirred him. The sand, the surf and a flash of something shiny at a trim, tanned waist.

"Oh, Sparkle you're killing me," he said aloud.

He rolled out of bed and headed, eyes still half-closed, to his morning shower.

It was at the store an hour later, his hair still wet and his first cup of coffee only halfway finished, that the lightbulb at the back of his brain went off. "*That's* who she looks like," he said to himself with total disbelief. The snippy, stuck-up librarian had a passing resemblance to Scott's favorite dream girl.

"Un-effing-believable!"

He shook his head with incredulity. No two women could be any more different. His South Padre Sparkle was all spontaneity and sexiness. D.J., by contrast, seemed to be all planning and prudery.

Their date, which had not been a date, had only gone from bad to worse. What in the world had gotten into Eileen that after maintaining her silence for years, she would suddenly open up about their affair? And to a stranger, no less. Honestly, D.J. should have been flattered. Eileen had claws, for sure, but she rarely saw fit to do more than manicure them.

That incident was embarrassing, and he could understand how D.J. might be put off and resentful about being dragged into his stupid, now defunct relationship with a married woman. But she seemed even more angry by the end of the film than she had been at the time it had happened. That made no sense whatsoever. But then, very little of the librarian's attitude made sense to him.

He kept hearing people say how "nice" she was, how "sweet." Either the rest of town was completely off, or she'd decided simply to hate him.

The bell on the front door clanged and he turned to meet his first customer of the day, Amos Brigham.

"You got any more of that stuff," he asked, pointed to Scott's mug.

"I can probably share a swig or two," Scott said as he put a cup and saucer on the counter before retrieving the carafe from the warmer.

"So, are you running early this morning or planning to show up late?" Scott asked.

Amos shrugged as he took a seat at the counter. "We've got a staff meeting and it's sure to be a doozy. Amelia will be loaded for bear and I thought I might need some extra caffeine before the estrogen storm."

Scott chuckled.

"Hey, you don't know what it's like to be the lone man in a job full of women."

"I think I have a pretty good idea," Scott said. "I work with Paula every day in a business where I share ownership with my mother and sister."

"Yeah, maybe so."

"Besides, you're not the 'lone man.' There's James."

Amos managed a wry grin and shook his head. "You're right. I do have James."

"So drink up before we both have a misogyny attack."

Amos did as he was bid.

Scott poured himself another cup. He had things to do, but he couldn't resist the temptation to linger.

"I haven't seen Suzy yet this morning," Amos said. "So I don't have the gossip on your big date with our new librarian."

"It wasn't a date," Scott replied.

"Yeah, that's what you keep saying."

"Mom asked me to take her downtown and introduce her around. That was it."

Scott's tone was adamant. Amos's acknowledgment accepting.

"People seem to like her."

Scott agreed. "She was charming." To everybody but him. "Nice, but not in that fake, sugary way some women do."

Amos nodded.

"And you know around harvest every farmer in town has more words in his mouth than the entire rest of the year."

Amos laughed. "You speak the truth, bro. It's all the extra cash I make all year, and yet I get so tired of listening to the talk I wanna scream, 'so let's harvest it already!'"

"Amen," Scott agreed. "Max Schultz heard that Brandon Renny's crop is down to 12."

Amos nodded. "It's a little south, but it's getting close."

"Next thing that you know, we'll all be wishing that it was over."

Amos chuckled. "You know this town too well."

Scott nodded. "You should have seen the librarian's face while Max explained the finer points of measuring moisture content."

"Tough sale, huh?"

"No, she did pretty good. She was acting polite and looking interested. My own eyes were about to roll into the back of my head."

"Been there. Done that."

"T-shirt?"

"I played skins."

They joked together companionably as Scott poured Amos a second cup.

"Do you know what the rumor is about your date?" Amos asked.

"It wasn't a date," Scott replied automatically, but he was listening carefully. He really hoped that the confrontation between Eileen and D.J. had not been a public spectacle.

"They're saying that Viv brought her here just to fix her up with you," Amos said.

Scott released the breath he held, grateful for some secrets kept. "I hope you're wrong about that," he said. "I really hate disappointing my mom."

"You could do worse," Amos pointed out. "Her curves may not be much, but her face is pretty."

"There is nothing wrong with her figure," Scott corrected. "Have you gotten a good look at the booty on her?"

"Nope, can't say as I've noticed. But apparently you did."

"Bicycle shorts, tighter than skin. There is plenty of junk in that trunk and none of it needs to be jacked up or rounded off."

"Lucky you then," Amos said. "You should make a play for her."

Scott shook his head. "No, I don't think so."

"Are you going to live like a monk forever then?"

"Look who's talking," Scott replied. "Besides, if I were going to give romance another shot, I'd be much smarter to start with Jeannie Brown."

"Jeannie Brown? Is she dating again?"

"Well, she probably would be if somebody asked her," Scott answered. "Hey, we live in Verdant. Her choices are you, me or Old Man Paske. If you and I aren't picking up the slack, I don't think we can count on the coot in the nursing home."

Amos gave a slight grunt of humor.

"So I'll take Jeannie, you take the librarian and Paske is on his own."

"I can't take the librarian," Amos said.

"Why not?"

"Uh…because I like my job and she's my boss."

"Oh, right, I forgot that."

"I do kind of like her though," Amos said. "She's…I don't know, she's open, I guess."

"Open?"

"Yeah, she doesn't seem to have the kind of expectations everybody else does. She doesn't act like James is a weirdo. She doesn't talk to me like I'm…fragile."

Scott chuckled. "It's hard to imagine you as fragile," he pointed out to the burly man.

Amos slapped his rock-solid abs. "Delicate as glass," he declared with a grin. But then spoke more seriously. "That's how people treat me a lot. They're careful about what they say. Like I might go nuts and start taking hostages."

"They don't think that," Scott assured him. "I know they don't mean that."

"But they do think I've changed," Amos pointed out. "I have changed. And change is not so good in Verdant."

Scott could hardly argue the point. Living up to expectations had not been in the cards for him, either.

"D.J. is okay with people being whatever. That's what I mean by open," he said. "It's like she's not scared of the wounds, no matter how badly they're healed."

"That sounds like pretty high praise, Amos," Scott said. "Maybe a new job might be what the doctor ordered."

He shook his head. "Nope. It'll have to be you."

"It can't be me," Scott said. "She doesn't like me."

Amos's brow furrowed. "Why not?"

Scott shrugged. "Beats me. She detested me on sight. And it seems like the more she gets to know me, the worse it gets."

"Weird. Everybody likes you."

"I figure I remind her of some creep who jilted her or something."

"Yeah, maybe so," Amos agreed. "Didn't you think she reminded you of somebody?"

"Yeah. I finally figured out who."

"And?"

"She looks a little like this girl I went out with once, when I was back in grad school."

Scott gazed thoughtfully into his coffee cup.

"I see that smile."

"Huh."

"You thought about this old girlfriend and you couldn't help smiling," Amos said.

Scott shrugged and shook his head. "Sorry. Nice memories."

"I guess so. What happened to her?"

"Don't know. One minute she was there and then she was gone."

Amos's brow furrowed. "What do you mean by that? Didn't you look for her? Ask her friends?"

"I didn't know where to look for her," Scott admitted. "I didn't even know her name."

"You didn't know her name?" Amos repeated. "What kind of 'girlfriend' was this?"

"I met her on spring break."

Amos raised an eyebrow. "I never thought you were the 'spring break' kind of guy."

"I wasn't. You know I always came home and worked here in the store," he said. "But that one year I decided to go and see what it was all about."

"And?"

"And I met her." Scott hesitated a half minute before he continued. "You know the phrase, 'she rocked my world.'"

"Geez!"

"This woman literally rocked my world," Scott said. "It was like a sexual awakening that I had no clue about. Totally off the charts."

"Man, you're going to piss me off," Amos teased. "It was always my teenage fantasy to be seduced by a sexy older woman."

"She wasn't older," Scott said. "She was a college girl, younger than me, I think. But damn, she knew exactly what her body was for and how to use it. All these years later, and I still get worked up just remembering her."

Amos laughed. "Very inconvenient in your current bachelor state."

"Hey, it's not all that funny," Scott said. "Sometimes

I think it's almost sad. If it hadn't happened…if I hadn't known that it could be like that, I'd probably still be married to Stephanie."

"No," Amos said. "You two were never going to be happy together."

"But we probably would have been content to settle for what we had."

"And nobody's life would have been better for that."

333.3 Land Economics

The staff meeting was not going particularly well. The three women had sat uncomfortably together for what seemed like a lifetime before Amos showed up, not one minute early. Amelia Grundler was edgy, brittle and well prepared for battle. She had not taken well to her Friday afternoon reprimand, and she was looking for any opportunity for revenge. D.J. had expected that, but it didn't make her any happier about it.

D.J. had taken great care to provide positive feedback to the operation of the library in general and to each employee in particular. Fortunately, she didn't need to overly embellish, which might have made it all seem false. For what they were doing, D.J. felt that the institution was operating very well. But the vision was so small and the size of the community that received little or no benefit was so large, that taking on new challenges was going to be unavoidable.

Baby steps. She'd picked up on a couple of baby steps to implement. So after pumping everyone up and listening to their reports, she carefully broached what she'd anticipated to be the least controversial of the two.

But even that proved to be a good deal more contentious than she'd imagined.

"I realize that the furnishings in the reading room are antique. I agree that everything is quite beautiful and well made. But the room is gloomy and all that dark wood doesn't help."

"Maybe we could reupholster the cushions," Suzy suggested. "A nice fabric in a light color would brighten up the place a lot. And we wouldn't need to replace the furniture."

That was the kind of compromise D.J. had been hoping for.

Miss Grundler would have none of it. "One does not reupholster vintage leather with cheap cloth."

"If the leather is sick-poop green, I think you're allowed," Suzy replied.

Amelia's eyes bulged with fury that Suzy would dare to answer back. D.J. was pleased to see the younger woman undaunted by Amelia's typical display of dominance. Miss Grundler looked as if her head might explode.

"Those pieces were donated to this institution by Estes Milbank himself," she declared. "The family, indeed the whole community, would be scandalized to hear how cheaply you regard their largesse."

Suzy sputtered, her moment of self-confidence shaken. D.J. had no choice but to intervene.

"Thank you both," she said. "These are exactly the kind of ideas and concerns that I wish to take to the library board. This will, naturally be their decision, not ours."

Smiling all around, D.J. calmly but firmly moved on to another subject.

"I've been working up a plan for a new senior service model," she told them. "Based on our experience last week with the residents of Pine Tree."

Her proposal allowed for the busload of nursing home residents to remain in the hopefully better-lighted reading room area while the books were brought to them. "That's much too hands-on," Amelia stated flatly. "If people can't get around well enough to get their own books, then we can't be responsible."

"But we are, in part, responsible," D.J. pointed out. "Our stack area is very dark. Even I have trouble in that dim light. And James is carrying a flashlight. Right, James?"

There was an uncomfortable moment of silence before a disembodied voice answered. "Yes."

Amelia snorted. "If we do this for Pine Tree, everybody is going to expect it."

"Which is exactly what I want," D.J. said. "I'm actually hoping to lure some of the nursing homes that we're currently visiting with the bookmobiles into using their own transportation to come to the main library."

Amos shook his head. "Nobody's going to want to do that."

"Because it's too dark," D.J. said. "And the place is unwelcoming. But if we lighten it up and make it fun for them, perhaps we can change that."

"Why would we want to?" Suzy asked. "They like the bookmobile and I like going."

D.J. nodded. "But a lot of places are not being served at all. If we got more of the nearby facilities to come to us, then you'd have time to add some new stops that have growth potential. I'm sure both you and Amos could come up with some ideas about that."

Suzy nodded thoughtfully. Amos had an idea immediately come to mind.

"The kids from the high school that get dropped off at Batesville, a lot of them hang out there at the gas station for an hour or two every afternoon."

"They still have an elementary school in town," Suzy

explained to D.J. "But their older students have been coming to high school here for the last decade."

Amos nodded. "If we were parked there in the lot outside the gas station, just a couple of times a month, I think our YA stats would perk up considerably."

"That's what I'm talking about," D.J. said, "extending service to new populations."

"Plus the guy at the gas station might appreciate that the kids can occupy themselves in other ways besides shoplifting stale donuts."

Suzy giggled. "Donuts should only be eaten by people who have teenage appetites and metabolism."

"This does not deal with the problem!" Amelia stated harshly. "You can stop in Batesville or not, but you can't fill this library with needy nursing home residents."

"They are our patrons, Miss Grundler."

"We don't have the staff for that kind of one-on-one interaction," the pruney complainer continued. "Who is going to wait on them hand and foot? I'm not. So then, it must be you, *Librarian*. And I feel certain that the taxpayers of this district are not paying you to be a nursemaid. Opening Saturdays, babysitting abandoned children and now wasting valuable time on doddering old fools who wish to be spoon-fed light reading material."

D.J. managed not to take the bait, but she did swallow hard.

"Let's try it, shall we," she suggested. "I'll work with Pine Tree this week. And Suzy, perhaps you and Amos can discuss it with the managers of your current nursing home stops."

They both nodded, avoiding glances at Miss Grundler's face. D.J. could see in her peripheral vision that the woman was florid with anger.

"But we should probably hold off doing anything until after harvest," Amos said.

"Oh, sure," Suzy agreed readily.

Amos looked over at her, his expression sincere and without patronizing. "We're going to start cutting wheat in the next week for certain."

D.J. was aware that people in her adopted hometown did tend to drone on and on about gathering the local crop. But surely most would be able to manage a discussion on another subject.

"I want us to get started on this right away," she said.

"As soon as harvest is in," Amos agreed. "First thing when we get back."

"Get back? Get back from where?"

Miss Grundler gave a breathy sigh of exasperation. "The library will be closing for harvest!"

"What?"

"We close. Every year, we close."

"I didn't see anything on the calendar," D.J. pointed out.

"Because we never know exactly when it starts or when it ends. Whenever it does, we close."

"That doesn't make any sense," D.J. said.

Amelia Grundler gave a huge huff of disgust.

"Actually, Miss Jarrow, it makes perfect sense," Amos said. "Nobody has time to read. Almost nobody is even in town."

"I get it that's it's a very busy time for people," D.J. said. "Why would we not open the main library and run our regular bookmobile routes?"

"Well…" Amos began, as if he was hesitant to give her the bad news. "There will be so many heavy trucks and machinery on the roads, that it's a pretty dangerous idea to put the bookmobiles out there. Add to that the fact that you'll have to be the one driving them, 'cause Suzy and I are both commercial truck drivers. We're committed to haul grain. We always do."

Amelia seemed to take a certain dark pleasure in the turn of the conversation.

"And since you will be out risking damage to our bookmobile on narrow blacktop roads, the main library will have to be closed," she said. "I take my annual trip to my sister's home in Colorado Springs. She will be expecting me and I have no intention of cancelling."

D.J. sat there, completely stunned into silence. She had never heard of anything like this in her life. A library that closed its doors without notice to reopen at a time unspecified.

"I'll be here," a voice from the stacks said quietly.

D.J. almost laughed humorlessly, but managed to keep her decorum. "Thank you, James. I appreciate your help."

South Padre Island (Eight years earlier)

Scott had noticed her when she entered the booth next to his. At first he'd discounted her as too young. One of the girls with her seemed a little more his type. He'd always sort of secretly preferred brunettes and that sort of bleach-striped blond look reminded him of cheerleaders. And cheerleaders, of course, reminded him of Stephanie.

If he was really going to do this, he could not allow himself one thought of his girlfriend back home.

A few minutes later she turned to look at him. From that glance, there was no danger of thinking of anyone else. It was as if she glowed from the inside. It was as if there were a radiance within her, so desperate to escape that it lit her up like a firefly.

Scott had to remind himself to breathe.

She smiled at him. There was so much in that slight curve of her dark pink lips. She was confident, sophisticated, worldly, physical.

Scott smiled back in an uncharacteristic act of bravery.

She's out of your league, Scott, his inner voice warned him. *You're a naive farm boy with little experience and none of it good. You don't want to embarrass yourself.*

He chose to heed his fears and turned to concentrate on the dancers on the floor. That worked until she was down there with them. Scott couldn't take his eyes off her. She moved. She laughed. She flirted. And she was so sexy. Those long legs in those impossibly high heels, made that round butt in the tight black leather stand out like a sign blinking in neon. Do me! Do me!

He wanted to.

So, the inner voice prompted again, *are you going to sit up here alone or go down there and try to get what you came for, before somebody else snaps it up.*

He took a deep breath and then headed for the dance floor. He didn't look left or right, but walked straight up to her.

"Oh…hi," she said.

Her eyes were surprisingly shy. Shy, but at the same time audacious.

"I think you're going to have to dance with me," he said, almost daring her to reject him.

"Have to? Why would I have to?"

"Because you sparkle so brightly I can't even see anyone else."

"Sparkle?" She thrust her chest at him, taunting him with her barely covered breasts. "They're called sequins."

That definition of plastic shimmer didn't begin to explain the dazzle that she exuded.

He reached out to touch her then. Careful to only make contact with the flashy fabric rather than the flesh he feared might scald him. It was not an unfounded fear, he discovered. A fiery particle of static electricity visible charged between them. It was so strange and unexpected Scott could only remark, "You don't need sequins."

"Be careful," she teased him. "If you get too close you might get glitter all over you."

It was a dare he could not, would not, ignore. He pulled her brusquely into his arms. As loud music pulsed all round them, what passed for dancing between the two was more of a hot embrace. Her body simply melted into his. It was the sensation that he'd waited for all his life, but had never experienced. This was how it was meant to be between a man and a woman. She filled all of the hard angles in his past with a balm that was both soothing sweetness and sizzling heat.

Warnings went off in his head. *Don't move too fast! Don't expect so much! Don't scare her off!* All excellent advice gleaned over years of research, but he threw it out the window as he brought his mouth down to hers.

The touch of their lips brought the connection total.

It was never like this with…

His brain couldn't even complete the thought. This was kissing as he'd thought it should be and he knew now that he had never been kissed before.

When they finally parted, he missed the contact so starkly, that he clutched her more tightly against his chest. He lowered his hands on her hips and she didn't complain. He grasped her butt and lifted her slightly to press intimately against him. She moaned as if she liked it.

"This is so what I've needed," he said to himself as much as her. His words seemed to be welcome. She wrapped her arms around his neck and wiggled against him.

"Don't move too fast!" he warned himself again.

"There is no such thing as 'too fast' for me right now," she whispered to him in a tone so thick with sensuality he could have slathered it on with a butter knife.

"Let's get out of here."

Hand-in-hand, they were practically running for the exit.

Outside in the night air, Scott sobered slightly. His body was urging him to back this girl against the nearest wall and take exactly what she was offering. But he'd had functional before. He knew what that was like. He knew about that kind of release. Tonight he wanted more. He wanted everything. He glanced over at her. In the garish neon of the bar's flashing entrance, she looked even younger than she had inside.

"Are you twenty-one?" he asked her.

Surprisingly, she laughed. "Yesterday, I would have had to say no," she answered. "But this is my birthday."

"Happy birthday."

She stepped up closer to him, her eyes narrowing enticingly. "I think you should give me a present. I'm hoping for something a little hotter than candles on a cake."

She kissed him again and his body went into reverb over doing her standing up against the wall.

"Let's walk," he said, when their lips parted.

He took her hand and they started down the sidewalk. In fewer than ten paces, they stopped and kissed again.

Heart thumping, he clasped her hand once more and continued on down the avenue that led toward the beach.

The circuits in his brain appeared to be shorting out. He was incapable of coherent conversation. He heard himself saying, "You're hot. You're so hot."

His thoughts ranged from *Do her in the motel! Do her in the car! Do her on the beach!* To the even less coherent urgings of *Do her! Do her! Do her!* Scott kept trying to recall even one of *GQ*'s *Seven Steps to Siz-*

zling Sex or any advice from *The Performance Playbook* from *Men's Health Monthly.* He wanted to be anything but disappointing tonight. But he was completely on his own and the only help he could count on was his own sense that he wanted to make it good and make it last.

Conversation. Try conversation.

"I guess I should introduce myself. I'm…"

She reached up and set her fingers atop his lips. "We don't need names or histories. Let's just keep this exactly what it is."

Scott wasn't sure what that meant, but he loved the sound of her voice when she said it and the feel of her tongue on his after the words were gone.

They walked until they couldn't bear the absence of embrace. And then they embraced until it was necessary to walk in self defense. The crowds were thick and the music pouring out of cars and clubs and stores was loud. Drunken celebrants of both genders weaved to and fro. And other couples like themselves paused at irregular intervals for a fresh kiss or fleeting fondle.

A little cloud of smoke poured out of the door of the hippy shop. Scott might have walked right past, but in the window he spotted a headless mannequin wearing a peace symbol bikini thong and a dozen styles of nipple rings on her breasts.

He wrapped his arm around the waist of the gorgeous woman beside him and urged her inside.

"I want to buy you a birthday gift," he said.

He showed her the nipple ring, already imagining having her slip off her top to try it on. Scott watched her eyes widen. The naive expression contrasted sharply with the sophisticated hottie that he already knew her to be.

"It's a fake," he assured her, demonstrating the hinge

on one side. "I'm not asking you to get your nipple pierced."

There was so much relief in her expression that he wondered vaguely what other men *had* asked of her.

That was when he spotted the belly chain. The glittering rope of rhinestones and metals was more gold paint than gilt, but it shined in the fluorescent lighting. A tiny pink heart-shaped stone hung down like a tassel and drew the gaze to the sexy regions below.

"This looks like you," he told her.

"It's pretty," she agreed

"May we try it on?" he asked the hippy. He took the man's unconcerned shrug for permission.

Scott fiddled with the cheap latch before circling her waist with the chain. He secured the clasp and then lovingly ran his fingers along the metal, careful not to touch the warm, tanned flesh beneath it.

She stood so close to him that his hand trembled. Then she turned with a flirty sway to her hips and walked down the aisle and back modeling the potential acquisition.

Scott had not thought that she could be any sexier, but the cheap piece of chain hanging low on her waist somehow made his mouth go dry. The shimmering glint suited her. She truly did sparkle and he began to think of her that way, as if it were her name.

She came to stand immediately in front of him, cocking one hip to the side to give him a better look.

"I think you have to have this," Scott said.

She laughed. It was a great sound. Low and soft and full of warmth. It went straight to his heart.

"You don't have to buy me anything," she said.

"I want you to remember your twenty-first birthday," he replied.

He paid the hippy, who put a premium price on the tawdry piece of shiny. Not unusual in a tourist trap.

It was worth the cash when she gave him a wonderful thank-you kiss as the cashier counted out change.

Outside they continued down the street. Walking, laughing, kissing as her birthday gift winked at him in the streetlights.

By the time they reached the space where his car was parked, the teasing was being replaced by urgency. He perched her on the hood and spread her thighs so he could stand between them. The tiny black leather skirt slid up easily. And she had almost nothing on underneath it. That knowledge had him groaning aloud.

Her hand was on the back of his neck, her teeth nipping at the skin on his throat. He rubbed the taut bulge in his jeans against her intimately.

It wasn't close enough. He couldn't get close enough. He slipped an arm under her right knee and raised her leg to his shoulder. That was better. It was only when he heard a couple of frat boys cheering from the sidewalk, that he realized how crazy it had gotten.

This end of the street was not as busy and was less well lit, but he was still practically having sex in public. He'd never lost his cool so much in his life.

He stepped back and set her on her feet. Her legs were a little unsteady.

"This is my car," he said. "Get in."

He felt her pull away. "No, no. Not in a car."

Scott heard the trepidation in her voice. They were sobering up. That might not be a good thing.

"How about a birthday picnic on the beach?" he suggested.

He had a blanket in the trunk. They bought provisions in the corner store. He set his purchases on the counter. A huge magnum of cheap champagne, not truly chilled but a little bit cold. A pair of paper cups from the fountain. Not exactly crystal, but perfect for toasting. He had to pay as much as if they were actually filled with soda. A package of orange cream-filled cupcakes. And a box of birthday candles.

As the clerk totaled, his date tossed an item on top. Scott's mouth went dry at the sight of the flat square packages.

"I have condoms," he whispered.

She gave him a sexy smile and held her body in what was almost a pose. "These are glow-in-the-dark."

The clerk was grinning at her so lewdly it was all Scott could do not to punch the guy in the mouth.

"Great," he said to her. But managed to sneak the clerk a dark, dangerous scowl as he accepted his change.

Escaping the lights and the worst of the crowds, they made their way toward the sound of the surf slapping against the shore. In little over a block they crossed Gulf Boulevard and the sidewalk turned into a well-worn pathway. She leaned against him to remove her incredibly high heels as they walked up over the rise of the dunes to the vast expanse of white sand beach.

Their conversation was minimal. She'd made it clear that she didn't want to know anything about him. And although he was incredibly curious, he didn't want to threaten the mood with a twenty-questions interrogation. Besides, his brain kept replaying the image of those glow-in-the-dark condoms thrown on top of his purchases.

Scott spread out the blue-and-crimson blanket that he routinely carried to tailgate events upon an isolated spot in the sand. He popped the champagne and they toasted her twenty-first year. He put the birthday candles into the cupcakes, but the sea breeze made them nearly impossible to light.

They drank, they laughed, they kissed and stroked. The beach was not as public as the hood of his car. But it was not exactly privacy, either.

At one point a naked girl, laughing and shrieking, ran through the surf nearby with a jean-clad guy in hot pursuit.

Everything Scott had read about being a better lover, and he'd read virtually everything, had encouraged the need for taking it slow, doing plenty of chitchat amid sexy foreplay. This girl seemed all good with the fore-play, but he didn't get the sense she wanted him to take his time, to make it great. Her eagerness nearly routed his intent. He was here to test the skills he had and learn what he could. But the last thing that he wanted was the kind of failure he'd become accustomed to.

He loved kissing her. There was something about her mouth, the way she opened for him, the way she pulled him in. He'd never thought much about kissing. It was just something that a guy did. Something that girls liked. Stephanie had not particularly liked it. But then, Stephanie had never kissed like this.

A moan escaped the woman beneath him. She clearly did like it. And if Scott didn't hang on to his control a little better, he'd be banging her too fast, too soon.

He sat up. She made a tiny noise of complaint as he made an effort to control his breathing by staring off into the distance. He saw the shimmer out on the ho-rizon.

"Look, the moon is coming up."

He had seen it so many times across the wheat fields around his hometown. He had never viewed it across the water, but new experiences were what this night was all about.

At first she didn't seem that interested in sky gazing. But Scott encouraged it by positioning her between his thighs. This gave him two hands free to caress her. He freed her breasts from their glittery confinement of the bikini top and scooted her skirt up, so that it was not in the way of his exploration. He nipped at her throat and whispered into her ear.

She tried to turn to him, but he wouldn't let her.

"Watch the moon," he told her, as he gently rubbed one of her upright nipples between his thumb and finger. "Don't close your eyes. Watch."

Scott barely glanced at the sight himself. But he wanted this to be all her while he was still in control.

"It's so huge," she said.

He hoped she was referring to his aching erection that he pressed into the firm flesh of her booty. But in case she was not, he whispered astronomy facts in lieu of love words.

"It's called the moon illusion," he told her. "For a million years people thought that it was magnified somehow, that it really was bigger looking on the horizon than in the sky."

He slipped a hand inside the scarce bit of red lace that she was wearing for panties. Her sharp little gasp let him know when he'd found her clit.

"We think the moon looks larger, but it's not. It's an optical illusion."

He nipped the skin on her neck as he caressed her intimately. *It's not a doorbell,* he reminded himself from a quote from a magazine. *It's Aladdin's lamp.*

"It's just how we see things," he continued. "Not as

ordinary as they are, but as grand as we imagine them to be."

He was not looking at the bright silver orb arising from the edge of the sea, but at the woman in his arms. She was just as beautiful in moonlight as she had been in houselights. She was whimpering. And she couldn't seem to decide whether to clutch her thighs together to help his hand or spread them wider to give him more access.

Careful, careful, he admonished himself.

"That's it. That's it," he encouraged her.

The sounds she made were all new to him. They seemed hardly human and came from deep, deep inside her throat. She dug her heels into the sand. "You love it. You love it. Just let go."

As the moon burst free of the horizon, a cry of ecstasy came from her throat. Scott couldn't believe the clenching and grasping of flesh beneath his hand. He kept up the pressure until she was all done. When she collapsed in his arms, he cuddled her tenderly, feathered little kisses on her hair. He'd made it happen. He had done it. He wanted to shout it from the mountaintops. All his second-guessing and self-doubt had vanished in a flash. Or rather in a pulsing, vibrating clench. The questioning, the study, the effort, was all worth it. He had made her come. And female orgasm, it was the greatest. Totally spectacular. He loved it. The only thing better would be coming himself.

"Let's go."

"Huh?"

He retrieved her bikini top from the sand and began to dress her.

"Let's get out of here."

She looked up at him, suddenly almost scared and shy. "Are...are we done?"

He couldn't stop an incredulous laugh. "No, ma'am. I'm taking you to my room and I'm doing you until I'm dead."

She was up on her feet immediately. "What should I carry?"

349.2 Law of Specific Jurisdictions

The word came down that samples now being brought to the elevator were dry enough to cut, so from now until the wheat was threshed and in the silo it would be an uphill sprint with no relief. Farmers had to get their crop in before it rained or hailed or blew or… Really, there were plenty of opportunities for things to go wrong. Wheat was the bulk of the local livelihood and if it wasn't secured and stored soon, it could be disaster.

As usual, the phrase of reassurance was on everyone's lips: "Combines are on the way."

The combine harvester was invented in the nineteenth century for efficient, mechanized production of grain crops. It got its name from the three functions it provided. It could reap, thresh and winnow in a single process, reducing the time required for field labor and lessening the risk of a weather event amid the course of action.

The machines were expensive, though. Especially so when a farmer imagined parking and maintaining it idle for fifty weeks a year. So from the beginning there were farmers who bought the machinery and those who hired the use of it, the latter being by far the larger. Custom cutters moved across the wheat belt like a wave. Farm by farm, neighbor by neighbor, ever on the northward track as the fields matured.

And now that the wheat was ready, every sickle was sharpened, every vehicle gassed. Every eye was on the sky.

"Combines are on the way."

Scott nodded for the dozenth time he'd been informed.

"That's what I hear."

"You staying open?"

"I'll be in and out with my cell number on the door," he assured everyone. "Paula will be helping out at the elevator. And I'll have a quick coffee if you're passing through."

During harvest the functions of the town narrowed down to only two tasks: receive the grain and supply provisions.

The first resulted in a line of trucks forming on Main Street as they waited for a turn to unload.

The second meant ensuring everyone had food, gas, implements and a place to sleep. Typically a drugstore would not be a big provider of any of those necessities. But Sanderson Drug traditionally fed a grab-and-go breakfast to those who didn't have the time or the patience to stand in line at one of the local eating establishments.

There would be prescription emergencies, of course. But in the waiting game for the wheat to ready, most would have already updated their first-aid kits and gotten their tetanus booster.

That didn't stop anyone, however, from dropping in and sharing the nervous excitement that was more contagious than the summer sniffles.

Surprisingly, there was one person who showed up

that morning who seemed to have no interest in the activity going on around her. That was Scott's mother.

She breezed in as if she owned the place, which of course, she partly did. The little dog, now safely on a leash, trotted at her heels. She let herself into the dispensary to wash her hands in the sink.

"The dog shouldn't be back here, Mother."

She laughed as if it were a joke. "No worries. Mr. Dewey hasn't perfected the childproof caps yet."

Scott didn't laugh.

Viv turned off the water and pulled a paper towel.

"Don't give me that look," she told her son. "I invented that look and until you have children of your own, you're not authorized to use it."

Scott decided to change the subject. "So what are you and the dog up to today?" he asked.

"We already went by the cemetery to check for weeds. I decided to respace the annuals. That's how I got my hands dirty."

Scott didn't know how to respond to that. He almost blurted out, *so what did Dad have to say this morning.* Gossips had kindly let him in on Viv's habit of talking aloud at the gravesite as if it were typical to have a conversation with the deceased.

"I...uh, haven't been out there to visit since the day they set the headstone."

His mother smiled at him. "No reason that you should, Scotty," she said. "There is no one out there but the dead. And life is for the living."

That was a philosophy that was familiar to Scott. One that, in the past, he would have said was held by both his parents. With his mom lately, he hadn't been so sure.

"So," Viv said, eagerly. "Let's talk about something a lot more interesting."

"Like wheat harvest," Scott suggested. "That's all that passes for conversation in here today."

His mother frowned and shook her head. "I've seen harvests come and go for sixty years. What I want to know about is my son's big night out. How was your first date with our new librarian?"

"It was not a date, Mom," he said. "You asked me to take her to the movies and introduce her around. I did that. End of story."

His mother made a tsking sound. "That can't be the end of story," she said. "When you were seventeen or eighteen I accepted this secretiveness about your relationship. But your father was alive then to advise you. I feel like it's my responsibility to step into those shoes."

Scott resisted the impulse to roll his eyes. Instead he lowered his voice so that no one would overhear. "Earth to Viv Sanderson. Your son is a divorced man who is thirty years old. He doesn't need any motherly advice on his love life."

"Don't get cheeky with me," she warned.

"I apologize. But you deserved it," he replied. "Mom, I'm sure D.J. is a very nice lady, but we did not hit it off. We have nothing in common and she's not my type."

"That's ridiculous," she said. "She is exactly your type and you have almost everything in common."

"Well, that's news to me. Truth is, we didn't get far enough to find out. Something about me completely annoys her. And I haven't got the patience to put up with her crabbiness. So, sorry, Mom. If your plan was truly to fix us up, it failed."

"Well, you can't simply give up without giving it a fair trail," Viv said.

"I can give it up. In fact, I have given it up. And you should, too."

"You should ask her out again," Viv said. "One evening together doesn't tell anyone anything about the potential for a relationship."

"Not true. One evening can be plenty of time. Either the spark is there, or it's not. She and I together, the entire book of matches is soaking wet."

His mother set her jaw unhappily. But at least she retreated to the fountain counter where she chatted with other folks, listened to all the grain news and introduced the dog as if he were her own instead of a loaner.

She seemed at least in a better mood by the time she was leaving. Scott loved her and hated to disappoint her, but sometimes it couldn't be helped.

"You heading home?" he asked.

"No, stopping by the store," she told him. "There's something I need."

Scott visualized the shelves and shelves of canned goods practically bulging out of her house. She wouldn't need anything from the store for the rest of the decade. He did not say that, instead he smiled.

"Okay, well, bye."

"Yes, see you soon," she answered.

350.0 Public Administration

D.J. walked through the children's area. The open space there was a bit better than across the hallway, simply because the shorter shelves let more light into the room. It was late enough that most of the afternoon crowd had already headed home. But she spotted Ashley Turpin seated at one of the tables, her head bent intently on the book in her hands. D.J. felt the rush of empathy with the girl. A lot of people might have been surprised by that. Ashley was not the type of child that typically evoked fond feelings. She was a pudgy girl, though perhaps solid was a better description. She was tall for her age and with a very round, flat face, and hair that was a dull in-between color and grew as it grew without style or even much grooming. Both she and her clothes were clean, but the latter were ill-fitting and age inappropriate. All of these negatives could have been overcome, of course, with a winning smile and a warm personality. Ashley had neither.

D.J. walked over and squatted down to eye level with the girl.

"What are you reading?"

It was an ordinary librarian question, but Ashley's response was wary, as if her expectation was to be reprimanded. The girl's jaw tightened, but she didn't speak, guiltily she turned the book so D.J. could see the cover.

The YA title was way over an eight-year-old's suggested reading level. But D.J. believed those were more about ability than content. She had never limited herself to what others thought she should read. She would grant her patrons the same latitude.

"I loved that book," she told the girl.

The youngster's expression showed surprise and relief.

"I've read all the books that are my age," Ashley said, as if she'd been perfectly prepared to defend her choices.

D.J. nodded. "I know what you mean," she said. "I was already checking out the fifth-grade selections when my classmates were still bragging about trying chapter books."

The camaraderie clearly surprised the girl. Miss Grundler probably wasn't the only person who'd created an expectation of disapproval in this girl. But she hadn't helped, either. And Ashley needed this library more than most.

D.J. made a point of not making her reading choice more than it was.

"I hate interrupting a good story," she told her. "But I wanted to let you know that I'm going to keep the library open during the harvest. So tell your mom that I will be here and that you'll be very welcome to hang out with all your favorite books."

"Okay," Ashley said.

D.J. wanted to reach out to the girl. To give her a big hug and tell her, I know how you feel. I know why you're here. But of course, she did not. Instead she offered a calm smile and walked away.

That was a small difference that she could make in one life. As she made her way across the building and into the adult reading room, she tried to visualize what she could do for many others.

It wasn't going to be easy.

The area, crowded with old, heavy furniture, was cozy in a very bookish kind of way. Three sides featured eight-foot-high shelving lined with books. The fourth wall was half taken up by entrances to the public restrooms and half open to the marble-floored foyer. The purpose of the space was to be a welcoming encouragement to reading. But to D.J.'s eyes, it had more of the nineteenth-century stuffiness than modern usability. One almost expected the smell of expensive cigars and the clinking of sherry glasses.

For perhaps the thousandth time, D.J. examined the overhead lighting to see if there was any way to get it brighter in here. The weighty brass overhead fixtures had the incandescent bulbs replaced with CFLs. Maybe she could find some that delivered a higher intensity. Maybe there might even be halogens. She dismissed that idea as soon as she had it. They burned too hot and were probably a danger in a public building. A giant skylight would be fabulous. But the cost to make structural changes to an historic building wouldn't be cheap.

"Whatcha doing?"

The question came from Suzy. D.J. turned to see her standing just inside the entryway. From her clothing, a long skirt and Dr. Seuss tee, D.J. deduced that she'd been doing storytime today on the bookmobile. But she'd come in from her route a half hour ago and should have been headed home already.

D.J. smiled a bit more broadly than was necessary. "I'm just looking, thinking," she said.

D.J. knew that both Suzy and Amos were feeling a little uncomfortable about her reaction to their upcoming harvest break. It was an unexpected interruption in her plans. And made the work of the library seem unimportant. Something they would do only if nothing better was going on.

"You don't understand," Suzy had pleaded her case. "When the harvest is on, well Verdant might as well just roll up the streets. Everything is about wheat. And you're either a part of it or you have to get out of the way."

D.J. got it. But she didn't have to like it. Still, there was nothing she could do. So she decided the best course was to let it roll off her back. However, she was also determined that the time not be wasted. She would figure out some way to use the interruption for the betterment of the library.

"How was today's run?" D.J. asked.

"Oh, great. We had good numbers at all the stops. And I love my patrons. When the roads are dry, you won't hear any complaints from me."

"Did you inform everyone that you wouldn't be keeping up the route during the harvest?"

Suzy nodded. "Everybody already knew," she said. "But I made it official just like you said I should. The older folks and little kids were all stocking up. The rest of us will be too tired at the end of the day to read."

D.J. nodded as if she expected nothing else.

"Listen…I've got to ask you something…"

D.J. thought she recognized that hesitation. "Suzy, I'm not angry about you taking off to work on the harvest. I understand about that and you don't need to apologize about it again."

"Oh, I wasn't. I mean I would, if I thought that you wanted me to, but that's not what I was going to ask you about."

"Okay."

"Well, it's about Viv. Mrs. Sanderson."

"Uh…okay?" The last thing D.J. wanted to do was get involved in gossip about a member of her library board.

"Does she seem all right to you lately? She's not acting weird or anything?"

D.J. could have pointed out that "weird" is definitely in the eye of the beholder and she didn't know the woman well enough to make any kind of judgment. But instead she was adamant. "No, of course not."

Suzy nodded, as if in agreement. "Did you…did you ask her to buy something at the store for you?"

What a curious question. D.J. shook her head. She would never have presumed on her landlady.

"I mean, I know she's bought stuff for your dog," Suzy continued.

"She has?" D.J. was surprised. "I'm sure I haven't asked her to get me anything."

"Well…" Suzy hesitated. "You're sure you didn't ask her to buy any *personal* products for you?"

D.J. was certain. "No. Why?"

She moved closer and she lowered her voice. "You know Kimmi Morton? Her husband's parents own the IGA."

"Of course." D.J. had made a couple of trips to the grocery store and had made a point to meet everyone.

"Well, Kimmi's been worried about Viv for a while now. She buys too many canned goods."

D.J. remembered the stacks and stacks of stuff in the Sanderson house, but she didn't comment. In her estimation, if the community was now into pantry peeping, she wanted no part of it.

"The Mortons thought at first that she was maybe

storing up for winter, in case it's too snowy to get out. But she's buying way too much. And Kimmi saw her looking through the cans for the expiration dates. That made sense, if she were trying to buy the newest. But she was actually buying the oldest."

D.J. frowned. "That's odd."

"Very," Suzy agreed. "I mean if you're buying the oldest, it's because you want to use it right away. But if you already have twenty cans of corn, you're not going to use it in a hurry."

D.J. agreed. She also knew that twenty cans of corn was an understatement.

"So Kimmi told Scott about all the canned goods," Suzy went on. "But he already knew. He didn't know what was going on, but thought it had to do with the grief process."

"The grief process?"

"Yeah, her husband passed away like a year ago."

"Oh, I didn't know."

"It's kind of strange that she wouldn't mention it," Suzy pointed out. "Anyway, today she bought something even weirder and Kimmi doesn't want to tell Scott unless she has to."

"What did she buy?"

Suzy leaned forward, not two feet away from D.J. "She walked up to the checkout with the large economy box of super tampons."

That raised D.J.'s eyebrows.

"I know," Suzy agreed to D.J.'s unspoken disbelief. "Kimmi was sure that she's got to be sixty at least and definitely past it. When she verified it with her mother-in-law, Mrs. Morton said Viv had a hysterectomy about a decade ago."

Again, that was more information than your average

grocer knew about their patrons, but D.J. was getting used to the town's habit of oversharing. "So she must be buying them…for someone else…or something else…"

"Or she's going off her rocker," Suzy suggested.

"She seems sane to me," D.J. said.

"Somebody is going to have to tell Scott," Suzy said.

That seemed reasonable to D.J. She nodded agreement.

"Kimmi doesn't want to."

"Why not?"

"She says it looks funny for her to be monitoring what people are buying," Suzy said.

D.J. thought about that and offered a shrug. "Yes, I suppose she has a point." One of the big taboos of the public library was revealing what people were borrowing or searching on the internet. Such information wasn't even to be given to Homeland Security or the FBI, let alone a local gossip mill. The grocery store might not have the same legal expectation of privacy, but the ethics were exactly the same.

"She asked me to talk to him," Suzy said. "But how would I know what was going on, unless somebody told me. I'd hate for Viv to think people are talking about her. So I thought it might be better coming from you."

"Me?"

"Yeah, I mean it makes perfect sense. You live in the same house with Viv. And you and Scott are dating."

"We are not dating."

"Okay, but you had a date. You can obviously talk to him. And you're an outsider. Nobody would expect you to know what you can and can't say."

D.J. did not see the logic of that. "I hardly know either of them and, as for Scott, I know that I don't want to know him any more than I already do."

"My point exactly," Suzy said. "For you, it's no big deal. You don't care if he gets insulted, blames the messenger or holds a grudge for twenty years. You'd be fine with that."

"And you expect that's what he's likely to do."

"No, not really. I think if it were my momma, I'd want to know what other people are worrying about," Suzy said. "But the deal about how small towns work is that relationships exist on a razor's edge. We're supposed to love and care about each other. But the minute you get your nose a little too deep in somebody else's business, you get it chopped off. And that's a scar that you carry with you."

D.J. crossed her arms. "So you and Kimmi are opting out of any busybody danger and letting me stick my neck out."

Suzy didn't dispute the characterization.

"What about my reputation, my place in this community? It's my home now, too."

Suzy's expression was puzzled. "It's not like you're here forever," she said.

"What do you mean?"

"For sure you'll move on to a better job or a city with some social life," she said. "Nobody expects you to really stay here."

"I do," D.J. replied adamantly.

"Please talk to him."

"No."

"You have to."

"I don't."

"Yeah, you do. I already promised Kimmi that you would."

"What?"

"Please, I'll be your best friend."

"You sound like a second grader."

"You're right. And in this town I'm already your best friend. Please do this for me."

"No. I really can't, Suzy."

"Think about it. Think about poor Viv. I know you like her and wouldn't want anything bad to happen to her. Think about your own mother, you'd want to know if something was wrong."

The words brought a painful clutch to D.J.'s heart. She'd had sufficient practice in hiding her feelings. But she couldn't always hide them from herself. What her own mother had thought or did or struggled with would always be a mystery unsolved. D.J. did understand the ache to know.

"I can't promise," she said finally. "But I'll think about it."

"Yes!" Suzy pumped her fist in the air as if she'd scored a major coup. "I knew I could count on you."

374.6 Adult Education

Viv had never really spent any time with animals. It wasn't as if she disliked them. In all honesty, she never paid very much attention. In her busy life, where she helped run a business, parented two children and kept up civic work in the community, a pet had always seemed like one more chore.

Yet, to her complete surprise, she'd found Mr. Dewey to be a very welcome companion. They walked to the cemetery together every day now, and she let the little dog run wild while she talked to John. Mr. Dewey never ran far and when she was ready to leave, he was always there, happy and enthusiastic. Viv realized what a blessing that was. Leaving John every day was like losing him over and over again. She didn't want to leave him. She wanted to stay. And the allure of that had not faded with time, but had gotten stronger. It had become the goal that she was working toward.

She knelt at the grave, not even bothering with the excuse of weeding or planting. She was there for companionship. To share a conversation with the person that she loved best.

"I'm moving on to Plan B," she told the headstone. "I hate to do it. I never wanted to be one of those mamas that had to have everything to suit her. I guess that's who I've become. But extraordinary problems call for extraordinary solutions. Didn't some famous person say that?"

There was no answer from the chunk of polished granite.

"They're both being stubborn," Viv said. "He pretends that he's perfectly fine with things the way they are. And she disliked him on sight. But I'm sure I have to trust your judgment on this. I've always trusted you on matters of the heart. Do you remember when you told me we should get married?" She laughed at the memory. "You didn't *ask* me, you told me. You were so certain that you could make me happy. And you did."

She sighed heavily. "I'm not happy now," she said.

With determination, Viv firmed her jaw and her conviction. "What I've got to do is force them together. Like a rock in a river, nature will take its course and more quickly in a rainstorm."

She nodded to herself, reassured. "I know we're right about this, John. They just need the opportunity to discover each other. There's something about those two together that simply works. I'm sure about it."

Viv reached out to run her fingers tenderly along the carved out lettering in the stone.

"Together is one of my favorite words, you know."

The afternoon sun had warmed the dark granite. Viv needed that warmth. She needed it desperately.

She stretched out in the grass along the length of the grave. This was absolutely the closest she could get to him. But it wasn't close enough. She ran her hands along the stubby grass.

"I miss you," she whispered.

It was no good. He wasn't here. He wasn't listening. Why had he come that one time and then hadn't come back? Viv needed him. She needed to be with him.

The tears began spilling out of her eyes. Those on the left traveling across the bridge of her nose to rain down into the rivulets on her right cheek. She couldn't bear it. She couldn't bear the emptiness of it. It was as if her whole life had ceased to exist when John ceased to be a part of it.

Suddenly Mr. Dewey was there, panting his little doggie breaths and lapping up the salty tears on her cheeks. At first she pushed him away, but he came back even more enthusiastically.

"You silly pooch!" she scolded, but she couldn't keep from smiling. "I must look like an idiot to you. I certainly look like one to myself."

She scratched the happy dog behind the ears. Mr. Dewey had a big, satisfied smile on his face and his tongue lolling out the side of his mouth. It was hard for Viv to hang on to a pensive mood.

"You want to play, don't you? That's all you want to do. Play, play, play. Do you think I have nothing better to do?" She laughed aloud at her own question. "Okay, so you've got me on that one."

Reenergized, she got to her feet. The dog pranced happily along the path ahead of her as they headed toward home.

347.0 Civil Procedures

The arrival of the combines could have been heralded by a trumpet, but it honestly wasn't necessary. The sudden silence across town was heard as loudly as any announcement. After days of frantic energy, Main Street was drowsy, deserted. And Sanderson Drug was completely empty, except for the proprietor. Scott sat on one of the stools at the counter, putting together the grab-and-go breakfasts that he hoped to hand out the next morning. One fresh peach, a stick of beef jerky and a packaged cinnamon roll. At two bucks, it was the cheapest food in town. But it was a tradition in the store. The Sanderson Drug logo on the brown paper bags was as familiar to the hordes of harvest folk passing through as it was to the locals.

Scott had first performed this job when he was perhaps only six or seven. His father had given him the task, explaining how hungry the men would be and how disappointed if something were missing from the bag. Biting down on his lower lip, Scott had taken on the task with the seriousness and diligence that one could typically expect from children believing they shoulder adult responsibility.

Today he could do it by rote and allow his mind to wander. Perhaps because of the association with the task, he began to think about his dad. His father was a goodhearted, generous soul, who always had a word of advice for his only son.

"Listen to your mother. She's never on anybody's side but yours."

A worthwhile suggestion for a stubborn preschooler, who felt his mom and sister were tag-teaming him.

"Work hard, apply yourself in school. Your brain needs as much exercise as the rest of you."

An important concept for a twelve-year-old athlete who had vague aspirations of a career in the NBA.

"Marrying the right girl is the single most important ingredient for a happy life," he'd also said.

That had been more of a warning than a random bit of wisdom. Scott wished that he'd heeded it. But at the time he'd been listening to other voices.

"It's sin," she had said to him once after they'd slept together. "That's why it feels so wrong to me. Because I know it's a sin."

"Sin?" There had been incredulity in his tone and he made no attempt to hide it.

He had finally gotten Stephanie to come up to Lawrence to visit him. He'd spent the bulk of his coffee money on a nice bottle of wine, he'd lit up his little apartment with candles and strewn rose petals on the bed. He'd gotten on one knee and offered her a beautiful ring. Away from Verdant and all of the strictures there, he'd hoped it could be different between them, but it wasn't. Their relationship still felt tense, and their sex life was as uncomfortable as it had always been.

"You said 'yes.' Now we're engaged," Scott pointed out to her.

"But we're not married," Stephanie said. "So technically it's still sin."

She hadn't allowed him to completely undress her.

And the articles of clothing that he had managed so painstakingly to remove went back on in a rush of modesty.

"Stephanie, what is going on with you?" he asked. "The girl who made it through high school copying my homework and cheating off me in tests now has moral compunctions."

"That's different," she said. "You were going to have to learn the periodic table anyway. There's no reason for us both to know it."

She tossed her hair in that artless way that he'd always found so attractive. She was a truly beautiful woman. A natural corn-silk blonde with big blue eyes and a long, leggy figure.

"Maybe we should talk to somebody about this, a counselor or someone. Sex can be better than this."

"Oh really? So are you an expert on the subject?"

He didn't reply. He had no intention to confess, but Stephanie saw it in his face.

"You've been with somebody else!"

He didn't reply.

"My God! You've probably given me some disease."

"We're using condoms," he pointed out. "I would always use condoms."

"You *have* been with somebody else!" She stood angrily and began to pace the room. "Who was it? Some sorority skank? Some pharmacy student slut?"

"It's not important. She's not important. It was a one-night thing."

"Yeah, I've heard about the wild college lifestyle. Get some girl drunk and force yourself on her."

"I would never force myself on anyone."

"You force yourself on me all the time."

"What are you talking about? I have never made you do anything."

"You've made me do everything! Senior year and suddenly we have to have sex. I always said that I wanted to wait."

"But we didn't wait," Scott pointed out. "I just want it to be better for us. Better for you. That's why…that's why I went with that other girl. So I'd figure out how to make it better for you."

"It's better for me if there is a lot less of it!"

Scott slipped another peach into another grab-and-go breakfast bag and shook his head. That had been the moment when he should have realized as clearly as he did now that what he had with Stephanie would never resemble anything like what he'd discovered with a complete stranger down on South Padre.

"You could have saved yourself a lot of time and grief," he postulated aloud, "if you'd ended it then."

But he hadn't. Ever the optimist, he'd tried to make it work.

He'd since learned his lesson. Some relationships will simply never work. It was best to understand that up front. That way you don't end up with a messy, semi-public divorce. Or, in the case of Eileen, an ex-lover who holds a grudge.

Scott mentally reaffirmed his decision to steer clear of ill-fated entanglements. If his soul mate, his true love, the woman of his dreams happened to walk through his door, he'd make an exception.

He chuckled to himself at the unlikelihood of that.

The bell above the front entrance tinkled. Scott looked up to see the librarian stepping into his store. He was surprised. As grumpy as she was at the movies, he expected her to avoid him like the plague. Expectations could be wrong. But she didn't look particularly glad to be there.

His first thought was to make some snide remark. Then he reminded himself that just because she didn't like him, did not mean that he had to dislike her. Everybody in town seemed to believe that she was very nice. And his mother adored her and her silly dog. There was no reason in the world for him to reflect D.J.'s unreasonable negativity. So he put on his best businesslike demeanor and offered a mild smile.

"Hi. Can I help you with something?"

The question seemed to catch her off guard. She glanced around as if trying to recall what she wished to purchase.

"No, not really," she said finally. "I…I was taking a break and…most of the stores are closed."

Scott nodded. "The IGA and the sandwich shop are open. Food, gas stations and farm implements, that's about all anyone needs today."

She accepted his answer, but continued to look unhappy and ill at ease.

"What are you doing?" she asked as she surveyed his one-man production line.

"Putting together something for the harvesters," he answered. "Most of the businesses do something. It's less a money-making deal than a gesture of goodwill."

Her brow furrowed. "Does the library usually do something?"

"Uh, no. Not that I remember. I mean, what could the library do? It's hard to read a book while you're driving a truck."

"Audiobooks," she replied. "Maybe a free download."

Scott nodded. "For sure everybody out there has ear-buds in," he admitted.

"I'll try to work on that for next year," she said. "Thanks for the idea."

He shrugged. "It'd be fun to think of those gnarled old guys out there listening to *Wheat Farming for Dummies*."

"Perhaps we should suggest fiction," she said. "Willa Cather's *O Pioneers!* might be appropriate."

Scott smiled. "Or *One Hundred Years of Solitude*," he suggested.

"Ah, so you are a reader," she said.

He shrugged. "Self-defense. I grew up in western Kansas."

"Two words for you. Satellite TV."

"My mom and dad kept our house dish-free until I left for college."

"Smart parents."

"Maybe so. Have a seat," he offered, gesturing toward the empty stools at the counter. So far it was the most reasonable conversation he'd had with D.J. It was possible that a passing acquaintance could be built on that. "Would you like a cup of coffee? Or maybe on a hot day like this, an ice-cold pop?"

She raised her head and there was the slightest hint of a smile at the left corner of her mouth.

"I'd forgotten that we call it 'pop' here," she said. "My babysitter in Wichita used to call it that."

"I take it you've been living in the world of 'soda' for a long while now."

"Yes," she said as she took a seat. Scott walked behind the counter.

"Well, if you ask for a 'soda' at this counter," he teased, "you'll get a beautiful gigantic glass of flavored ice cream and seltzer water. I'd be happy to make you one. I'm an expert."

Something momentarily flashed through her expression but it was gone before he had a chance to interpret it.

"A pop will be fine," she said.

"I can make that special, too," he told her, hoping to coax the almost-smile back. "Chocolate Dr Pepper? Vanilla 7 Up? Cherry-coconut Coke?"

She shook her head. "I'll take a plain Pepsi, please. I know it's boring, but I like it."

He filled the glass with ice and carbonated beverage. "Boring can be good," he assured her. "Although we all know that sooner or later everybody's got to break out of the rut."

The weird look was back again as he set her drink in front of her. He had enough time to recognize it. Guarded. The librarian didn't trust him and was holding something back. He was vaguely curious about what and why, but not enough to press her on it.

Scott gave her a passive smile and moved to return to his bag-stuffing chore.

Surprisingly, she waylaid him.

"I have something I want to talk to you about," she said.

"Okay," he replied, cautiously.

He really hoped that she wasn't going to make some big explanation about why she looked at him like a loathsome worm. Scott figured that for the both of them, as well as the Verdant community at large, it was better for him not to notice how she looked at him and better for her not to comment upon it.

At that moment she looked as if she'd swallowed

something detestable, and he knew for sure it was not the refreshment in the glass in front of her.

"I need to talk to you about…about your mother," she said.

"My mother?"

"I'm sure that it's not my place to say…" she began.

Clearly a line that was only used when people were intending to speak up anyway.

"Your mother has been… I don't know if you're aware that your mother has been…has been behaving…"

D.J. was so obviously struggling with her words, Scott felt sympathetic.

"You think my mother has been behaving strangely," he offered.

She took his statement with a rush of gratitude. "Yes, yes, she has. I know that she's only recently widowed… and let me express how sorry I am for your loss, but some of the…the unusual things that she's doing…uh… concern me."

The subject was being wrenched out of her so painfully that it was excruciating to even listen. Scott was pretty sure he knew what this was about. His mother's machinations had been embarrassing to him, and he knew her and loved her. How much more humiliating must they be for the new librarian attempting to establish herself in the community to be swept up into a matchmaking scheme. He decided to put her out of her misery.

"Look," he said. "For sure my mom has been trying to fix the two of us up since the day that you got here. I know it's been kind of embarrassing. Uncomfortable for both of us. But you won't need to worry about it anymore. I had a talk with my mom and I made it clear to her today that she's really overstepped the bounds of good parenting. It is time for her to butt out of my life and yours. She's my mom. I love her and I try to please her. But on this, I put my foot down. You don't have to worry about it. Interference from her is over."

358.1 Other Specialized Warfare

Viv had the top down on the Mini. Mr. Dewey was standing up on the passenger seat, his little furry ears blowing in the wind. She glanced over at him with absolutely zero guilt. What was the use of having a convertible if one were going to be crated inside it?

Besides, when a pair was on a secret mission, an undercover battle offensive, a covert act of sabotage behind the lines, danger was an accepted part of the plan.

Viv turned down the road that led to her son's home on Verdant Creek near the edge of town. She pulled around to the back, parking the Mini as close to the kitchen door as possible, making sure that it was completely invisible to anyone who might for any reason pass on the road nearby.

She took a deep breath and then gazed at the eager pet beside her.

"If you're going to try to talk me out of this, now's the time," she told the dog.

He gazed up at her in silence.

"All right then."

She opened the driver's-side door and Mr. Dewey scampered out ahead of her. Viv retrieved a grocery bag from the floorboard.

The dog was waiting, his front paws up on the threshold. Viv set the bag on the step and began running her fingers along the upper doorjamb. When she discovered nothing, she continued along the sides. She picked up the mat. Nothing.

Viv took a step back. Surveying the area. Mr. Dewey watched her expectantly

"Don't think like a thief," she admonished herself. "Think like someone who never expects to be robbed." She looked over the space thoughtfully. "Close. Convenient. Hidden."

Her gaze stopped on the metal light fixture to the left of the entry. Stepping forward she ran her hands behind it, inside it and then up on the top.

"Bingo!"

She retrieved the key from its magnet and showed it to the dog.

"We're in," she told him.

Mr. Dewey wagged his tail excitedly and waited as she unlocked the dead bolt.

Viv hesitated just outside. "Are your feet dirty?" she asked her companion. "Little paw tracks on the floor will be a for-sure giveaway."

She picked the dog up and carefully wiped his pads and nails on her shirt before letting him into the house Carrying the grocery bag, Viv followed.

Her son's place was relatively clean. He was like his father in that. Order was more effective than chaos. And both perceived effectiveness as a moral imperative. That was one of the many traits they shared. Scott's heart, of course, was much more like her own. Devotion lingered beyond duty, beyond even death. Scott had made a commitment to Stephanie when he was little more than a boy. And despite its disappointments, he would have kept it forever. Viv understood that. In her own way, she felt exactly the same.

But Scott deserved a bigger life, a better life than the one bad luck and bad timing had left him with. Now, with some help, she was going to change that trajectory.

She walked into the bathroom. A wet towel lay on the floor and she resisted the temptation to hang it on the rack. She removed the box from the grocery bag and set it on the vanity next to the commode. The toilet seat was up. That's what you get with a man living alone.

Viv fumbled with the box lid and then pulled out the first long, slender item. She stripped off the paper, which she carefully deposited in her grocery bag. Then she plunged the contents of the small plastic tube into the toilet. A minute later a second tampon followed the first. Mr. Dewey, front paws on the edge of the bowl, watched her progress. Four were floating and expanding in the water when she spoke.

"We ready for the first flush?" she asked Mr. Dewey.

She took his nonresponse as an affirmation and pressed down on the lever that sent the wads of super-absorbent cotton on their way to the septic tank.

As soon as they were gone, she began opening more.

384.2 Communications

After a long, fruitless day at work, D.J. came home and put off dinner for the preferable hot soak in the bathtub. She pulled her hair up off her neck and lit a candle with the scent of seaside. Then she settled in to allow the steaming water to loosen all the muscles that she held so tight.

She loved the sound of the water running. It enveloped her in a kind of white noise silence that was familiar and safe. She had no illusions as to the origins of this particular pleasure. A million times during her childhood, at crazy times of the day or night, her mother would suddenly grab her from the dinner table, the television, homework or a good book and put her in the tub. At the time she hadn't really understood it. She had thought it had something to do with being a nice little girl, a clean little girl.

She understood it perfectly now. Her father had an explosive temper. And although he never lifted a hand to either of them, his words could stab as deeply as a knife. All too regularly he sliced his wife to pieces. The sound of running water could insulate a child from those cuts.

D.J.'s childhood, her teen years, her entire relationship with her parents, had been all about insulation, isolation. It was only as an adult that she'd realized that this had been their version of protection.

She closed her eyes and pushed the thought away. There was no changing the past. It simply had to be lived over. And if possible, forgotten completely.

From his napping spot on the bath mat, Dew suddenly perked up. D.J. watched as he jumped atop the clothes hamper and stretched himself tall to try to see out of the frosted glass window.

Mrs. Sanderson had driven off soon after D.J. got home and undoubtedly she'd returned. It seemed as if Dew was anxious to see her. D.J. admitted to herself a slight jealousy. Since coming to Verdant, Dew had become Viv's near-constant companion. And unlike those days when her arrival from work could send the dog into a tail-chasing fervor of excitement, his attitude lately was more in line with "Oh, yeah, you live around here, too."

Either the frosted glass discouraged him or he wasn't as interested as he'd thought. Dew returned to his spot on the rug, although he sat rather than lay.

The water was up to her shoulders and what was pouring in was no longer that hot. Utilizing her left foot, she was able to turn off the tap without giving up her reclined position.

Settling back, she closed her eyes once more, willing herself to relax.

She'd wasted an impressive amount of time at the library trying to jerry-rig more light into the building. She'd gotten a wild idea about mirrors. D.J. thought that she could install a line of mirrors to the upper molding next to the ceiling. If she got the correct angle, she could catch the light coming into the building on the other side of the shelves and reflect it down into the reading room. She figured and fiddled forever, until she was finally resigned to the fact that unless the mirrors could move, which they couldn't, it would only provide light for a very short period of time and that the reflected glare would as likely blind the readers or burn a hole in the furniture.

"Idiot," she whispered to herself.

She knew there had to be a way. It made her crazy that she couldn't think of it. There were wonderful libraries that had no natural light at all. She needed to figure out a way to run a ton of new fluorescents down the length of every shelving range…without having to rewire the entire electrical system to do it.

Dew jumped up again. This time he raced to the door and began scratching at it, as if he could open it himself.

"Dew, stop it!" she told him.

He glanced back at her, but continued to paw at it.

A minute later, D.J. heard someone on her deck, knocking.

"Oh, good grief."

Dew began making a yipping sound.

If she still lived in the city, D.J. would have been tempted to ignore it. But she didn't live there. She lived here, in Verdant. And the person most likely to be at her door was her landlady, a member of the library board.

Growling like an angry bear, D.J. hoisted herself out of the soothing bath water. The knocking persisted. D.J. grabbed a towel and opened the bathroom door just wide enough to holler.

"Coming!"

Dew pushed on through and hurried happily to the apartment entrance.

The thought that he was excited to see Viv after spending the entire day with her did not lighten D.J.'s gruff mood.

She wrapped the towel around herself, securing it in

place by tucking the loose end into her cleavage. Barefoot, she tramped along the hardwood floors to the deck entrance off the kitchen.

Without bothering a glance, D.J. threw open the door to greet Mrs. Sanderson, only to stare in gaping surprise at the hot guy standing there.

Momentarily he seemed to be as stunned into silence as she was herself.

"Oh geez, sorry. I didn't mean to get you out of the bath," he said.

That was the instant that D.J. remembered that she was wearing only a damp towel. She immediately flattened herself into the space behind the doorframe.

"Oh, my God, I thought you were your mother."

"Sorry," he repeated. "I'm…I'm looking for her, actually. Do you know where she is?"

"No."

"Did she mention where she might be heading?"

"No."

"Does she usually go out in the middle of the week?"

"No—I don't know. What do you want?"

"I… You wouldn't happen to know where she keeps a spare key to the house?"

"Why would I know that?"

"It used to be under the begonia pot, but I checked. There's nothing there," he said.

"I don't know."

"I've looked all around. Look, I don't want to bother you, but would you mind if I waited here on your deck?"

D.J. didn't care what he did, if he'd just let her close the door.

"Sure, that's fine," she said.

"Okay. You won't even know I'm here."

She doubted that. But she was grateful to get to shut the door. "Dew!"

He didn't come.

"Dew, come here, boy."

Her dog ignored her.

"Dew!"

Her pet gave one casual glance in her direction only a second before he jumped up on one of the deck seats and settled himself in, head resting on front paws.

"Go on back to your bath," Scott said. "The dog's okay out here with me."

D.J. had half a mind to go drag the traitor back into the house. But that would involve even more exposure than she'd already volunteered. Instead she offered a terse thank-you before gratefully shutting the door. She leaned her back against it for a long moment. Then, like a condemned criminal accepting her fate, she marched to her bedroom to face herself in the full-length mirror.

She'd held out secret hope that she was overreacting. That it would not be nearly as bad as she was imagining. Unfortunately, that hope was dashed. The damp green towel was only slightly over two feet wide. Not only was it low on her bosom, but it was high on her thighs, as well. And it clung vividly to all her curvy places. It was worse than being naked. Nudity was bold and daring and stark. Damp and skimpy was coquettish and risqué. The jerk probably thought she *wanted* to appear sexy.

She could have yowled in humiliation.

D.J. had no intention of returning to her bath. There would be no way that she could relax with him only a few feet away. The one thing that she wanted now was to be decently clothed.

She began rifling through the nearby boxes look-

ing for something to wear. She'd hung up her business
wear and conservative attire, but she still had not gotten around to unpacking her casual things since the
move. Summer heat was upon them, and of course all
the sweaters and gloves were still on top. She finally
located a pair of blue jeans. To that she added a sports
bra that smashed her breasts into near nothingness and
a T-shirt big enough for a linebacker. Even the sight
of her bare toes bothered her. She slipped on a pair of
ballet flats.

Once she was completely covered, she returned to the
full-length mirror and sighed. Better. Still she couldn't
quite throw off the embarrassment. And it didn't help
to remember that he had, after all, seen her completely
naked once upon a time.

She growled again.

Why was he here? What in the world was he doing
on her deck?

"Just behave normally," she counseled herself. "Do
what you would do. Pretend he's not even here and go
about your business."

It was good advice. But D.J. found that following
through with it was more difficult. She drained the
tub. Hung up her towel. Straightened the bathroom
and then the living room. She seated herself on the
couch, but she didn't stay there. She was too jumpy to
read. She couldn't even sit still enough to watch TV.
Finally she settled on getting something to eat. Unfortunately, her kitchen didn't present a lot of great options. In the fridge she stared at the freshly purchased
condiments, but there was no meat or vegetables of
any kind. She might have even opted for something
new, like perhaps a mustard and pickle sandwich. But
the cupboard revealed that there was no bread, either.

Ultimately she settled on the two things she did have, cheese and crackers.

Next to the cracker box was the bottle of wine her former co-workers had given her at her impromptu goodbye party. She pulled it down to the counter and noted, thankfully, that it was a twist top. She poured herself a small glass, assured that it would settle her nerves. Then she stood in the kitchen, sipping it, too nervous to eat.

"Oh, for cripes sake!" she complained eventually. "Get a grip, Dorothy. He's not going to out you as a spring break slut. He doesn't remember you, or he would have said something by now. You are a forgettable blur in his history of sexual conquests. He's one of the people in your community now. It's your job to be friendly while maintaining a professional distance. You can either do that or let him make you uncomfortable forever."

She wasn't willing to give him that much power. She raised her chin and faced her apprehensions straight on. "Time to put on your big girl panties."

The word *panties* conjured up the unwelcome image of red lace clinging to a masculine bicep, but D.J. pushed it back.

She put the wine, the plate of cheese and crackers and two glasses on a tray. Then she opened the door to the deck and carried it out.

Dew perked up to give her a happy, tongue-hanging-out smile. Scott immediately rose to his feet.

"Let me help you."

He took the tray and set it on the metal coffee table in front of the glider.

"You didn't need to do this," he pointed out.

D.J. shrugged. "We've both got to eat. All I've got is cheese and crackers."

"Sounds great. Besides, beggars can't be choosers. And I am so hungry I've been looking at your dog and licking my lips."

It was meant as a joke, but D.J. was too on edge to even laugh.

"Maybe you should have gotten something to eat before you came over," she said.

"I should have," he agreed. "But I was so ticked off, I couldn't even think about food."

"Ticked off?" she repeated.

He nodded. "I got home and my septic system was backed up."

D.J. made a vaguely sympathetic sound of support. She looked around for a place to sit. Dew did not appear predisposed to vacating the chair he occupied. The only seat available was the one next to Scott on the glider. Chin high, back straight, she sat down.

He didn't seem to notice her hesitation as he continued with his explanation.

"At first I thought that it was a clog in the kitchen sink. But it's some kind of serious blockage down the line."

D.J. knew nothing about plumbing, drains or sewers of any type for that matter, but sitting so near to Scott in the evening shadows, it seemed to be a safe, nonsexy topic for discussion.

"I'm not very familiar with septic systems," she said. "Does this sort of thing happen often?"

"It's *never* happened to me," he replied.

He poured himself a glass of the dark red wine and added more to hers, as well.

"I'm very careful about maintenance. And I had the sludge pumped last year."

She didn't know a thing about sludge pumping, but

she nodded and made supporting noises to keep the subject of conversation going.

"How do you think it happened?"

"I don't have any idea," he said. "It's the weirdest thing. I had zero problem when I left this morning. And this afternoon it was completely clogged. Not sluggish or slow, completely shut down."

D.J. sipped her wine and grasped at an appropriate reply.

"Bad luck," she said finally. "Do you call a plumber for that? I guess you couldn't get one to come out this evening?"

"I won't be able to get anybody to look at it until the harvest is done," he said with a heavy sigh. "Everybody who does that work is sitting in a combine, on a tractor or the driver's seat of a truck. Anything other than what is out in the wheat fields is going to have to wait."

D.J. was getting used to that explanation.

"So I'm out of my house," he continued. "And with no place to go. Every spare bed and motel room in town has a harvester in it. I've come here to throw myself on the mercy of my mother. And now she's not even home."

D.J. took another sip of wine as she mentally cursed the fates. It was uncomfortable enough to be in the same town with him, now she was going to have to be in the same house.

"I wonder where she is," he pondered. "She always tells me that she doesn't like to drive at night."

"She didn't say anything to me," D.J. clarified once more. "She simply got in her car and drove off."

She glanced at the strong, masculine curve of his jaw in the shadows as he shook his head.

"Pretty strange thing for her to do," he concluded.

D.J. was immediately reminded of what Suzy had

asked her to convey to Scott. His mother's odd behavior was being noticed by people in town. As bright and vibrant as she was, Viv appeared to be having some mental lapses that her neighbors found worrying. Sharing that concern with her son was at the very bottom of a long list of things that D.J. didn't want to do. She'd already tried once. She'd made a deliberate trip to the drugstore to confront him with the facts as stated to her by Suzy, who'd gotten them from Kimmi. She was totally geared up to spill it out, but Scott had misunderstood the direction of the conversation and sent it spinning into the two of them. Their relationship, or the lack of it, was the last thing that D.J. had any interest in discussing. She'd practically run from the building in fear.

But now she was on her on turf. Fortified with self-talk and alcohol, she might not get a better time. D.J. chose her words carefully.

"Your mother seems to be…preoccupied. Or maybe distracted is a better word. When she goes shopping, she's buying a lot of…a lot of unexpected things."

She was wondering if she'd have the guts to talk about the inappropriateness of an aging senior purchasing feminine hygiene products.

She heard him sigh heavily. "I am worried about her," he said. "I'm sure it's connected somehow to my dad's death."

D.J. nodded. "I'm sure it's been hard for her. And hard for you, too."

"Thanks," Scott said. "He and I were really close. And I miss him every day, but Mom… Jeez, I don't know what's going on. She and Dad had such a bond between them…a real bond, you know? The kind that the rest of us all wish that we could have. They enjoyed each other. Never seemed to get bored with mundane conversations. They liked being in the same room together. They had all these shared smiles and private jokes." He shook his head. "I grew up thinking all marriages were like that. I didn't discover how wrong I was until I had my own."

Scott gave a light chuckle in self-derision.

There was a flash of a smile in her direction that caused an unwanted clutch in D.J.'s heart.

"My parents shared everything," he went on. "My sister and I used to say that we only had to confess things once. Everything I ever said to one of them, the other could repeat back to me word for word. They were truly two halves of something very special, very complete."

He turned to look at her again, looking slightly sheepish, and shrugged as if to discount his own words. "People probably always think this about their parents."

D.J. could have reassured him that if "people" included her, then he was very wrong about that.

"I don't know what the weird purchases are about," Scott went on. "At first I thought she was simply lonely and had no place to go but the grocery store. But she's actually so busy with community organizations, she has some kind of get-together nearly every day."

D.J. remembered how full Viv's calendar tended to be.

"Then I decided that it was some kind of depression reaction. She felt this emptiness that she was mistakenly trying to fill with food."

"I guess that could happen," D.J. said.

"But that doesn't jive with her eating habits."

D.J. agreed. It also gave no explanation for the tampons.

"So now I'm kind of hoping it's a shopping addiction," he said. "For some people, when they feel low, they spend money and that temporarily makes them feel better."

D.J. had heard about that sort of thing, of course. But the sufferers she'd heard about always seemed to be young fashionistas with shoe fantasies.

"Do you really think so?" she asked.

He shrugged. "I don't know. I'm not that way. And Mom never has been, either. But grief changes things." Scott hedged quickly. "I know I'm not telling you anything you don't already know. Mom told me that you've lost both your parents."

"Yes."

"I can't even imagine how hard that must be," he said. "It must be a terrible feeling of being lost and adrift. Truly on your own for the first time."

"I've always been on my own," D.J. blurted out. She immediately wished that she could call the words back.

Scott didn't seem to take the words amiss.

"That can be a good thing, too," he said. "It fosters self-reliance and independence. Qualities to have if you're running a business or a civic institution."

"Yes, absolutely," she agreed. She'd made the same argument herself many times. Somehow it was not comforting that he'd come to that conclusion on his own. "And I believe it makes me a better leader not to have the distractions that a busy family structure can bring."

Beside her, he chuckled. "You know, I tell myself the exact same thing. I hope that it's been more of a comfort to you than it has been for me."

D.J.'s first instinct was to assure him that it was. But for some reason, she dealt with the question honestly.

"No, not particularly."

He seemed to appreciate that.

"So I guess it's fair to say there is no calf-eyed sweetheart pining away for you back home?"

"No. There's not even a back home, really. I haven't lived in Wichita since I was a kid. I went away to school."

"But you must have gone back for summers and holidays."

"Actually, no. I went to camps and visited with friends. My parents weren't really into family things."

"I can certainly visualize a lot of positives in that scenario," he teased. "You *have* met my mother."

D.J. laughed. "I'm actually a fan of your mother," she said. "And Dew is positively crazy about her. He's a great judge of character."

"And a good companion in a lonely life," he suggested.

"I don't have a lonely life," she disputed firmly.

"Sorry. I guess I should have said a solitary life."

That was a little better, she thought. "I like to think of it as being independent. I've moved from place to place, it seems like forever," she said. "But I'm here now. And I'm really eager to settle down and call a place home. I think—hope—that Verdant will be that for me."

"This town certainly needs you," he said. "And I don't mean simply as a librarian. We're getting so tired of talking to the same people all the time."

"I'm hoping to be around here long enough that everyone has a chance to be thoroughly sick of me," D.J. joked.

"You'll need to take up a unique hobby for that," he teased. "Competitive hog calling or collecting misshaped lima beans."

D.J. tutted dramatically and shook her head. "When you choose librarianship for a career, you don't need a weird hobby."

387.45 Space Transportation

Scott moaned as he rolled over in the bed. He hit his head on the corner of the nightstand and awakened fully with a curse on his lips. He sat up, put his feet on the floor and rubbed his injury. He was in his mother's guest room. The pink-and-mauve floral patterns were the height of his mom's fashion sense in the 1980s. They lingered on in the guest room because the fabrics were "perfectly good." The double bed, however, was to Scott's mind a little bit small.

But sleep was beginning to seriously elude him these days. And waking up with a hard-on every morning was like going through adolescence all over.

He'd dreamed about the girl with the sparkle once more. That woman was going to kill him. Groaning, he rose to his feet and stumbled into the bathroom. He turned on the shower and when steam was beginning to pour out around the narrow Plexiglas door, he stepped inside. The shower in his own house was big, roomy and produced a wide waterfall overhead. This one in the guest room was a cramped prefab model. Even the shower that Scott had put in the upstairs apartment was better. There was no other choice. The one in his parents' master had been replaced by a walk-in tub that was needed to care for his father.

Still the water was wonderfully hot and flowing

down the drain as it should, which was more than he could say for his own place. He had no reason to complain. Besides he still had his sparkle girl in the back of his brain.

He needed this and he didn't even try to talk himself out of it. He let the spray cascade down his chest as he took himself in hand and, with narrowed eyes, gazed not at his surroundings but into the past.

He was in South Padre and she was on top of him. The moonlight streamed in from the windows, illuminated her naked breasts, which bounced enticingly near his face. Those wonderful, animal, guttural sounds were escaping from her mouth again. And her warm, wet muscles clenched, clenched, clenched around him as if she were going to devour his body with her own. From some primitive instinct, without thought, only need, he grasped her under the knee and spun her in place. She shrieked in appreciation. And now he had that big, sexy booty right in front of him. He bit down hard on his lip to keep from exploding as he toyed with her a moment or two before slipping his fingers inside her. She was riding even faster. Clenching even tighter. She'd screamed the doors down last time. This time he'd make her peel off the wallpaper. He loved her gorgeous ass. It was a perfect, perfect ass. And he loved the shiny bit of bling he'd bought her. The belly chain hung low on her hips and the tiny pink glass heart dangled daringly between the muscles of her cheeks. It seemed to be begging for his attention, so with his last semicoherent thought he grasped the chain and used it to propel himself deeply inside her.

The chain snapped as they reached climax together.

Wallpaper. History.

Scott collapsed against the shower tiles. Loose-limbed and totally relaxed. He'd been masturbating on the same memories for eight years. Married, divorced, dating or sneaking around, it was always his Sparkle that he imagined. It was that one perfect night of sexual bliss, the memory of which overtook the most inviting reality. And the fantasies that evolved from that night surely didn't live up to the experience that it was.

He smiled languidly as he imagined her again. He imagined her coming to him now. To this narrow shower stall in his mother's guest bath. Confident and sexy. As eager and desperate for release as he was himself. He pictured her in his mind's eye. Not naked, but provocatively covered. Smelling of sea and surf, her hair slightly damp and dark, her glistening naked body barely wrapped in a towel of green. Her bosom invitingly one tug from being exposed. And the hot, familiar region between her thighs almost quivering for his touch.

"Mmm," he said aloud, as he lowered his lids to more easily peruse his vision.

Only a second later, his eyes popped open in shock. He was imagining the librarian.

"What in the hell!" he cursed aloud. He immediately reached for the temperature control and turned it all the way to cold. A high-pitched yelp thankfully took all the pizzazz out of his daydream. He left the shower and began drying off.

Okay, D.J. looked a little like his dream girl. But she wasn't that girl. That girl... That girl was his. And D.J. didn't even like him. They didn't look that much alike, he assured himself. He began to picture the young woman from the beach in his memory once more. To his horror, her face had been replaced by D.J.'s.

No. No. He didn't want that. He couldn't lose the

memory of that one sweet night. He wouldn't let it happen. But the more he tried to picture her, the more the face of the librarian intruded.

He nicked himself twice while shaving. That did not add any lightness to his mood. He hurriedly dressed for work, even knowing that it was way too early.

He grabbed his phone and his laptop off their chargers and headed out the door.

His mother was puttering around the kitchen, the smell of coffee redolent in the air.

"Good morning, Scotty," she said cheerfully. "What would you like me to fix you for breakfast? Pancakes?"

He shook his head. "Nothing. I'm not hungry."

"Nonsense. You're always hungry and you love pancakes."

"Not today, Mom. I need to get to the store."

She laughed. "That's ridiculous. Nobody's even awake yet."

She was right, of course. The combines would not cut the wheat while it was still damp with dew. The harvesting wouldn't begin until mid to late morning. And then they'd keep at it late into the night. With the workers getting to bed in the wee hours, nobody would want anything before nine.

But he still wasn't hungry.

"Maybe some coffee," he said.

"Help yourself," she answered brightly. "I am in the mood for some blueberry pancakes and not just because they're your favorite. I'm fixing them anyway, if you want some."

He sighed. He knew his mother was lonely, and having him here undoubtedly spurred a kind of holiday mood. All he wanted to do was get away. But being a good son meant not always doing what he wanted to do.

"You know, Mom, I'd love a couple."

"Great. Why don't you help me."

Scott found himself quickly swept into egg beating, flour sifting and baking powder measuring.

She was heating up the griddle, when the telephone rang. It was a big, wall-mount version from a bygone era that hung at the end of the counter.

"Hel-lo!" he heard her say cheerily into the receiver.

A moment later the tone was completely different.

"Shit."

Scott's head came up. Although the word was a common one, his mother never used it. Or at least she never used it in front of him.

"I'll be there in ten minutes, Karl." she promised the caller. As soon as she hung up, she turned to Scott.

"Dutch Porter shot himself in the head this morning."

Scott repeated his mother's initial reaction.

"What happened?"

"While Cora was taking a shower, he muffled the sound with a pillow so she wouldn't hear it."

"As if she wasn't going to be the one to find him," he said, with a heavy sigh. "Poor Mrs. Porter."

His mother agreed. "It's the height of selfishness," she said. "If you're going to take yourself out, you at least owe it to your family to make it look like it was natural causes."

Scott would have said that you owe it to your family *not* to take yourself out, but they didn't have time to delve into a discussion.

"Let me get dressed," she said, hurrying toward the bedroom. "Go upstairs and ask D.J. for Mr. Dewey. I'm going to take him with me."

"You're taking a dog to a suicide?"

"Pets can be a great comfort in times of trouble," she said before disappearing down the hallway.

Scott stood staring after her for a long moment before shaking his head. He turned the fire off under the griddle and took another fortifying swig of coffee before heading out the back door.

The morning was still. Not even the slightest breeze rustled the trees. Perfect harvest weather. He wondered how anyone could kill themselves on such a beautiful day. But then, with life so very short and very precious, he couldn't imagine how anyone could kill themselves at all.

He climbed the stairs to the upper deck. A flash of memory of D.J. in only a towel added caution to the moment. Last night he'd not expected her to be unclothed. This early in the morning, he certainly did. He knocked on her door and then turned his back to face the distant fields.

The door opened and the little dog hurried out to jump excitedly around his heels.

"You want something?"

A loaded question, but not enough to add any levity to the moment. He turned. She was not, as he expected, tousled from sleep and in a skimpy robe. She was fully dressed in a modest skirt and blouse, eyeglasses in place, her hair and makeup perfect.

"Hi," he said. "My mom is leaving and she'd like to take your dog with her."

"Okay, sure. What's going on?"

"Actually…there's been kind of a local tragedy," he answered somberly. "One of our old guys, Dutch Porter, has been pretty sick for a while now. It looks like he killed himself this morning."

"Suicide? Are you sure?"

"Bullet to the head."

"Oh, how horrible!"

Scott nodded. "The deputy sheriff is over there now, Mom is going to sit with the guy's widow. She thinks the dog might help."

"Of course, of course. Anything that we can do."

At that moment, he heard Viv coming out the back door.

The little dog did not wait for permission. He went bolting down the stairs ahead of Scott and D.J.

His mother looked as put together on short notice as she did when she spent hours in the effort. She hooked the leash on Mr. Dewey's collar.

"Call me if I can do anything," Scott said when he'd reached his mom.

"Thank you, Scotty," she said. "In situations like this, there is really not anything that any of us can do." His mother then looked past him toward the stairs. "It's just across town. I'm not going to bother to crate him this morning."

She didn't sound as if she'd been asking permission, but behind him, D.J. nodded assent.

They watched as Viv and Melvil Dewey got into the Mini. His mother turned the vehicle around and headed out to the street. Scott turned to look at D.J.

"Thanks for letting Mom do that," he said. "I think she's forgotten that the dog belongs to you."

"Some days I think he's forgotten it, too," she answered.

They smiled at each other for a moment.

"I...uh...I guess I'd better get on to work," she said.

"It's way too early to go in," Scott told her. "Would you like some pancakes?"

"No, but thanks."

"Seriously, the batter is already made and if we don't eat them, I'll have to throw it out."

"I don't usually eat much in the morning."

"Breakfast in wheat country is a big deal," he told her. "You wouldn't want some rumor to get around that you start your morning with some jam on a cardboard rice cake."

He almost detected a smile. "I could probably drink more coffee," she said.

"Come inside," he said, gesturing toward his mother's back door. "We've got a big pot brewed."

He held the door for her and she complied. He showed her to a seat at the breakfast bar and then placed a steaming cup of coffee in front of her.

"You have to try my blueberry pancakes."

"Please don't go to any trouble."

"It's already fixed," he said. "I'm going to have to cook it anyway. They're really good, I promise. And I always keep my promises to beautiful women."

Scott had meant it as a joke, but her chin came up and there was a wariness about her. He wasn't sure if it was about promises or his use of the term "beautiful." He decided to avoid both and concentrate on pancakes.

Once the griddle was sufficiently heated, he poured four large circles of batter on it. He rifled through a cluttered drawer for the spatula. Once he had it in hand, the quiet in the room, the only sound being the ticking clock, loomed a bit large. He flayed for a safe subject of conversation.

"You know…uh, pancake is another regional variation word, like soda and pop."

"Really," she responded. There was no sense of great interest on her part, but she obviously felt weighed by the silence as much as he did.

"When I was a kid, both my parents called them hot cakes," he said. "And there are parts of Kansas where they use the term flapjacks or worse, slapjacks."

He glanced toward her with a little smile. She mirrored it with an equally meager grin.

"Now everybody calls them pancakes."

The batter on the griddle was now completely covered with big wide bubbles. He slid the spatula under one and expertly flipped it. The other three turned as easily.

"Television got rid of a lot of regionalisms," he continued. "Especially television advertising. If you had a national chain of restaurants that sold pancakes, you couldn't change the name for every locale that called them something different."

"I suppose not," she agreed.

"Yeah, International House of Flapjacks just doesn't have the same ring to it."

"IHOF," she said. "That's not an acronym that makes you want to stop by."

Scott dished up the distinctive breakfast and set the plates on the breakfast bar. He put the jug of maple syrup between them and poured them both another cup of coffee before taking a seat.

"These are really good," D.J. said. She was mumbling through a mouthful of food, which not only implied truthfulness, but somehow endeared her to Scott. She seemed more like a real woman than the starchy librarian who generally disliked him.

"It's my favorite breakfast," he said. "I used to beg Mom to fix it for me all the time. Her way out was to teach me how to make them for myself."

D.J. gave him a bit of a smile. "That seems like a smart fix."

Scott nodded. "That's one of the interesting things about my mother," he said. "She's never really had what most people would consider a job. She worked on her father's farm and then in her husband's store. She never got paid a wage in either place. But she would have made one heck of a CEO. When she sees something that needs initiating or fixing or changing, she never sighs about it. She takes action."

"That makes sense," D.J. said. "Like hiring me. Most people in town were content to leave the library like it was. But she saw the potential to make it better."

"Right," Scott agreed.

D.J. forked another bite of breakfast. "She brought me here to be a solution to a problem."

Scott nodded, though he was pretty sure his mother's need for a solution had very little to do with the library at all.

390.1 Customs, Etiquette & Folklore

The library seemed big and dark and empty. D.J. sighed aloud. It was nearly noon and no one had even walked through the doorway. Not even little Ashley had shown up today. What James found to do in the stacks was a mystery. She knew he was there, but there wasn't so much as a footfall to give evidence of that.

D.J. sat at the circulation desk with her laptop. She'd pulled up all the planning files. She'd looked through the bookmobile routes. She'd fiddled with the acquisitions budget. She'd revised next fall's afterschool program. She'd crossed all the *t's* and dotted all the *i's* on her new proposal for a seniors' service initiative. But the truth was, to her mind, if she couldn't figure out a way to make the main building more welcoming, the usefulness of the library would always be stunted.

She'd spent hours on the internet looking at renovations of Carnegie buildings. Although Carnegie libraries were all unique, many were similar since the designs were created by a handful of architects through the years. She found more than a dozen that shared some elements with Verdant. But none of them had the narrow, oddly spaced floor-to-ceiling windows that she was cursed with. Typically, because electric illumination had still been in its early, less efficient stages, great care had been taken to utilize the value of natural light.

But not here, where the rooms were dark, gloomy, closed off.

"The place is beginning to sound like your parents," she murmured to herself in a private joke.

Death, any death, always seemed to bring them to mind. She didn't want to spend her day thinking about that, but wasn't inclined to distract herself with rumination over her wet towel episode from the night before. She closed her eyes and shook her head as the memory assailed her. So much for maintaining professional distance.

Thankfully, he'd not made any snide or suggestive comments. That's more what she had expected. Actually, after their conversation, it seemed as if he was nicer than she'd thought. And he made very good pancakes.

But she needed to stay wary. He might not remember her, but she did remember him. He was a player. He knew his way around a woman's body. He did things to her that she'd never even read in books.

Best not think about that, she cautioned herself. Stick to the facts. He'd been in South Padre picking up girls when he had somebody he was supposed to be engaged to waiting back home. He'd gone ahead with the wedding and then been caught cheating shortly afterward. Since then he'd been the hot guy in town, having affairs with married women.

"What a turd," she whispered to herself aloud. "Remember that. He's a turd."

Still, he could be sweet. And he made pancakes.

That's how he lures stupid women in, she reminded herself sharply. He makes them think that he's smart and funny and kind. And he has amazing sex with them, so that nobody else ever quite measures up. And then… and then…what? And then he's still a turd and there is no fixing that!

D.J. slammed her laptop closed resoundingly. And then sitting there with nothing else to do, she quietly opened it again. She was web searching for ways to add light to old buildings when the front door opened and a long shaft of it streamed across the vestibule toward the circulation desk.

A woman came inside and, spotting D.J., walked directly toward her. The lithely trim little blonde had a spring in her step and a broad smile across her pretty face.

D.J recognized her as the woman with Vern at the movie theater.

She was wearing a frothy summer dress and carried a basket covered by a cloth. The whole effect put D J. in mind of Little Bo Peep.

"Hi," she said, taking the initiative to greet the visitor. "You must be Stevie, Vern's…" The terms *lover, partner* and *roommate* occurred to D.J. But for some reason she went with, "Vern's friend." Maybe the small-town mind-set was rubbing off on her, she worried.

Stevie laughed. It was a very sweet, and almost girlish sound. She seemed small and sweet and precious. That thought surprised D.J. Precious was for children and puppies, but something about Stevie evoked the same feeling.

"I'm Vern's wife, actually," she said. "We got married in Iowa three years ago." Her tone was cheerfully matter-of-fact. "A lot of people in Verdant aren't onboard with that. But if I don't mind, it doesn't matter."

D.J. recalled Scott's reaction to discovering them

seated in the row at the movie theater. Stevie probably dealt with those minor slights on a near-constant basis.

"So I guess I should call you Mrs. Milbank."

She giggled. "Well, not if you want me to answer. I've been so eager to meet you. And I think we can start off on a first-name basis."

"Okay, then I'm D.J."

"Vern thinks I'm going to like you a lot. And she's almost never wrong."

"Good," D.J. said.

Stevie glanced around the drab, deserted building. "Are you all alone in here?" she asked.

D.J. cocked her head toward the stacks. "Except for James."

The woman turned in that direction. "Hello James!" she called out.

There was no answer. D.J. was surprised at that. "Maybe he stepped out," she said.

Stevie shook her head and leaned closer. "James doesn't like me," she said.

D.J. was surprised. She had never heard anyone say anything about James having an opinion about anyone.

"It's okay," she quickly reassured her. "I earned it. When I was in high school, I kind of went out of my way to make fun of him."

D.J. couldn't quite imagine it. Stevie seemed so kind and genuine.

"James was odd," she said, by way of explanation. "And the one thing I hated most in the world back then was oddness." She smiled a perfectly, gleaming bright smile. The kind that film actresses and beauty pageant contestants would kill for. "Curious, considering how *oddly* I turned out."

Her laughter was full of self-deprecation.

"I've always been a bit odd myself," D.J. said, and then quickly clarified. "I don't mean... I'm not...well..."

Stevie offered another dazzling smile. "You're straight."

"Yes. Odd, but in a straight way."

Stevie held up the basket she carried. "I brought cookies," she said. "I always take food to the people in the truck line. I had some left, so I thought I'd bring some to you."

"That is so nice."

She gave a cheery laugh and shrugged. "Odd people need to eat, too."

D.J. joined her in the humor. She took a bite of one of the almost perfectly round cookies that Stevie sat in front of her and discovered that not only was Stevie one of the most physically beautiful women D.J. had ever seen, she was also an exceptional baker.

"This is great. I think this is the most fabulous cookie I've ever eaten."

"My mother was convinced that clear skin and housewifely accomplishments would help me catch an excellent husband." She offered a little girly giggle. "Well, I suppose it did."

"So, you call Vern your husband?"

"Oh, no. Vern's my wife. I'm her wife. It's a gender thing."

D.J. nodded, but decided to change the subject rather than belabor the point.

"So what's a truck line?" she asked.

"Oh, the combines load the wheat into trucks that carry it to the grain elevator," she said. "So we've got a lot of trucks coming in and they're all headed to the same place. Sometimes they have to line up to wait their turn."

"Oh."

"The drivers are stuck there. So we have a few porta-potties available and those of us in town take turns showing up with goodies."

D.J. remembered the conversation she'd had with Scott.

"So is this what the drugstore does with its bags of peaches and beef jerky?"

"I don't really know what they do at the drugstore these days," she said. "But in the past mostly people would stop by there to get the grab-and-go bags. They know that they're there. It's sort of a tradition. Taking sandwiches or sweets directly to the line is more impromptu. It's a way that those of us who are stuck here in town can get in on the action."

D.J. nodded.

"And I thought today would be good, because so many people are going to be in town talking about the whole Dutch Porter incident."

D.J. nodded solemnly. "Yes, when a tragedy like this happens, gossips everywhere go into overdrive."

Stevie's blue eyes widened a bit as if the negative nature of pointed conversation had never really occurred to her.

"Oh, I guess you're right. Everybody will be eager for all the details. But it's more than just tattling. Dutch and Cora have six grown kids and a least a dozen grandchildren. They also have brothers and sisters and in-laws and cousins. There's probably a hundred people in town who consider themselves relatives."

D.J. hadn't thought of that. She'd pictured the house as empty and the widow as alone.

"Is Mrs. Sanderson a relative? She hurried over there first thing this morning."

Stevie shook her head. "No, Viv is just the kind of woman that always gets called in a crisis. She knows what to say and what to do. The community counts on her for that."

"Yeah, she does seem like a solidly good person," D.J. said.

Stevie nodded. "I think so, too. She has always been nice to me, even after I came out with Vern."

"I'm sure that she understood that you had to be true to yourself," she said.

The Bo Peep blonde was momentarily thoughtful. "I think you're right. I think she and John both understood that. But they were also shocked and angered."

D.J. privately mused that being "shocked and angered" at somebody's sexual orientation was exactly the kind of thing that gave rural Kansans their unfairly rigid reputation.

"I need to get back to the store," Stevie said. "This is our busiest time of year. Any implement on any machine could need replacing. And if we don't have it in stock, we have to locate it and Vern must go and get it."

"Well, it was lovely to finally meet you," D.J. said.

"You, too," she agreed

She unloaded the contents of her basket and then called out in the direction of the stacks. "They're homemade cookies. Oatmeal and peanut butter. And I'm leaving them right here at the edge of the desk for you, James."

Again there was no response.

Stevie gave D.J. a rolling-eyes expression before whispering. "Isn't that just like a man. Even long after you know you're forgiven, he'll still hold a grudge."

392.5 Human Life Cycle & Domestic Life

The drugstore during harvest always had a few customers in early morning. But the morning of Dutch's death was downright busy. The man had lived in Verdant his entire life. Everyone knew him. He wasn't universally loved, but he was respected. And in death, petty grievances always showed themselves to be petty.

The question of why, which so often haunted the survivors left behind, was not on this occasion difficult to deduce. The whole town knew that Dutch was quite ill. He'd been a gregarious and social guy, who'd spent his retirement days "shooting the bull" with those he called his "fellow local yokels." Once a large, imposing man with athletic prowess in his youth and working strength well into old age, the past year of health crisis had been tough.

"I think it's harder for a sturdy man to deal with infirmity than those of us who're more accustomed to it," Earl Tacomb said.

Earl had dealt with asthma and diabetes for twenty years or more. And although they were the same age, most would not have taken bets that Earl would be around for Dutch's funeral.

With a dozen people crowded around the counter,

Scott tried to make sure that everyone was served, but without any sense of rush to the solemn occasion.

The facts were gleaned from a half-dozen sources.

"Dutch always kept a pistol in the bedside table."

"His wife thought he was a little better the past day or two."

"The Rossiters next door didn't hear the shot, but they heard Cora screaming."

"They had to break into the house, she was too hysterical to unlock the door."

"Langley said it was definitely no accident."

"Cora was still in her bathrobe."

"The whole right side of his face was gone."

"There was blood and brains splashed all over the bedroom."

Scott didn't want any more of the details. But he understood that they had to be spoken. Whether it was a car wreck or a child drowning in the creek, people needed to try to make sense out of those things that were senseless.

So soon after his father's death, Scott was inured to the reality that even death from disease or old age felt senseless. He preferred not to be reminded. The whole senseless thing evoked reaction. He wanted to lash out at someone, something. But he'd figured out quickly that it was as good as air boxing. And blows that couldn't be landed gave no relief.

How must D.J. feel? She had lost two parents. Was the arithmetic applicable? Did she feel twice as bad? Perhaps there was a top level of bad and one couldn't go further. Or maybe it was infinitely worse than losing one parent. Scott could hardly allow his mind to touch on the idea of losing his mother, as well. He sincerely hoped that he would be a lot older, a lot wiser and a lot stronger before anything like that happened.

But life had a way of coming up with some dreadful surprises. Dutch Porter was certainly evidence of that.

The news had spread like wildfire. And with the dew still on the grain, groups of those not immediately connected to the family congregated to shake their heads and philosophize.

"This would have been the first harvest he'd missed since we were kids," Earl said. "You know that must have gnawed at him fiercely."

"If he even knew it was going on," Scott said. "He was on a lot of medication. He wouldn't have been thinking too clearly."

"Dutch would have felt it in his bones," Earl insisted.

Bob Gleason agreed. "They've scheduled the funeral at eight o'clock in the morning, so they can have him in the ground before noon."

"That sure seems like a rush," Maureen Schultz said. "Though I suppose there is no help for it."

"And no reason not to," Nina Philpot said. "When something like this happens, well…the less he's eulogized the better."

Jeannie Brown sat at the counter, stirring milk into her coffee. "I know he must have been in tremendous pain," she said. "But his timing was so bad."

"Or his timing was great," Amos said as he wedged himself into the seat beside her. "If you're planning on doing something that is going to hurt other people, you'd want those people to be as busy and distracted as possible."

"You could have a point there," Maureen said.

Nina shook her head. "I don't think so," she said.

"When people kill themselves, the wants and needs and feelings of other people don't even enter into it."

"You sound really sure about that," Jeannie said.

"And it's pretty harsh," Amos pointed out.

Nina shrugged. "That's how I see it," she said. "Suicide is a selfish act."

"But you know he did try to spare his wife," Maureen said. "He did wait until she was in the shower. So she didn't see it. And he muffled it with a pillow, so she didn't hear it."

"To spare her?" Nina asked. "Or to prevent her from stopping him? Who was going to find him? Who is going to have that horrible image in her head for the rest of her life?"

That somber truth had everyone nodding.

"I guess you've got the right about that," Bob said. "He wasn't thinking it through."

"Or maybe not all the way through," Amos admitted. "But I do think that…people can…can contemplate suicide unselfishly. That sometimes they can see their continued existence as so…so flawed that it would be better for everyone if they were no longer around."

Jeannie spoke thoughtfully. "It might be even more than that," she said. "We've all had times that were… well, so low. Maybe even that low. But we're still here. Why is that?"

"Because *we're* not selfish," Nina stated, as if to prove her point.

"Maybe not you," Jeannie said. "But I am seriously out for me."

Everyone chuckled lightly. Most would have testified that Jeannie didn't have a greedy bone in her body.

"Proof of my selfishness is evidenced in the fact that

I'm still here," she said. "Choosing to live in the face of…whatever…is a selfish choice."

"So then suicide is unselfish?" Amos asked her.

Jeannie shook her head. "No, I think it's not that, either. It's about your head getting so messed up that you can't see straight. You don't know up from down, day from night, wrong from right."

"Are you saying Dutch was off his rocker?" Earl asked. "'Cause I spoke to him just three days ago and he was sound as a bell."

"You don't have to be running-naked-in-the-street crazy to have a moment of insanity," Jeannie said. "I guess you could even call it a temporary insanity or maybe a compartmentalized one. In that moment, maybe just a brief moment, you act on instincts that lead you in the wrong direction."

Nina and Earl were both shaking their heads. Maureen was nodding. Bob was sipping his coffee thoughtfully. And Scott was silently contemplating her point.

Amos spoke up. "You're exactly right, Jeannie," he said. "I've known guys in the service who committed suicide and it seemed to me that they weren't a lot different than the rest of us. Their troubles weren't bigger. Their connections to their families weren't more tenuous. It was just like a kind of blurred reality overrode their better judgment. And no one recognized it, so no one could stop it."

"That's a bit easier to swallow than him being a lunatic," Earl said.

"I still think you're being too kind," Nina told him. "I blame Dutch for his own actions. It's a horrible thing to do."

"Well, it is horrible for his family," Jeannie said. "I certainly agree with that. For the rest of us, well, we are going to miss him. And we'll miss him as much now as a year from now."

"That's truth," Bob agreed.

Maureen was even more conciliatory. "The important thing is to remember his life, not how it ended."

There were solemn nods all around.

"Still," Jeannie said. "It's going to create some rough days out in the field, shorthanded. Half of our crew are members of the Porter family." Her words were punctuated with a tired sigh. "See, didn't I tell you I'm a selfish person?"

Beside her Amos offered a broad grin. The most genuine smile Scott had seen on the man's face in a very long time.

"Don't worry, Jeannie," Amos said. "You still got me."

She laughed lightly. "There's not that much that you and I can do," she said.

He tutted teasingly. "Now you're not only selfish, but your memory is failing. Have you forgotten the Homecoming Dance committee?"

Jeannie moaned aloud dramatically. "I've tried to put that nightmare behind me for fifteen years."

"Eight people on the committee," Amos explained. "And the day of the dance, six of them weasel out of doing the decorations."

"I twisted crepe paper into mums until my hands were raw."

The two laughed companionably. "We were both late for our dates."

"I was so tired that evening, that I didn't bother to put on makeup."

"I drove my date down by the creek to park and fell asleep in the car."

"She probably thought you were the perfect gentleman."

"No, I think she'd already figured out that I was an idiot."

It was a warm exchange of remembrance of time gone by.

"It was a tough day, but we did get it done," Jeannie said.

Amos nodded. "The two of us, there's not much we can't accomplish."

"You'd better hope so," Earl said. "There's a lot of wheat out there to get."

By ten-thirty, the drugstore had cleared out. The grab-and-go breakfasts were all gone and Scott was alone with his thoughts. The hours dragged by without anyone stopping by, without the phone even ringing.

He decided to close up a half hour early. But he was locking up the door even fifteen minutes before that. He headed to his mother's house with the intent of changing clothes. His garden probably needed water and he could check on his house, see if the septic system had healed itself as suddenly and mysteriously as it had gone on the blink.

Scott arrived at his childhood home to find his mother's car still gone, but D.J.'s vehicle was in the driveway. He imagined that the library must be even deader than the drugstore.

Good for her, he thought. Taking the initiative to close up and go home. Everybody in town had heard how hard-nosed she'd been about keeping the place open. It was to her credit that she could moderate her stance. There were too many people who had to dig in their heels to prove themselves right.

He let himself in the back door. The house was very

quiet and empty. Scott was reminded of his thoughts earlier in the day about D.J. losing both her parents. Considering it made him kind of queasy. Everyone would eventually pass away, of course. And it was natural, he supposed, to expect that his mother would likely die before he would. But he didn't want her to go now. Not now before he'd found someone, before she could see him start a family.

That thought caught him up.

What had got him thinking that he would find someone? He had deliberately given up on that possibility. Better to be alone than be with the wrong person. That was right. Scott was sure that was totally right. Maybe being back in the old home place was giving him flashbacks of the guy he once had been.

He was shaking his head as he went down the hall toward the guest room. A knock on the back entrance halted his progress and turned him around. In the kitchen, he could see D.J. through the window glass.

"Hi," he said as he opened the door.

She turned around. In her arms she held a cut-glass bowl filled with small red orbs in a sauce that smelled fabulous.

"The pancakes were no big deal. I hope you're not reciprocating."

"What? Oh, no," she said. "This is for…the Porter family."

"Oh, right, of course."

"That's what people do, isn't it?" she asked. "They bring food to the house. Even if they don't know you that well, they bring stuff."

"Yeah, I guess they do."

She glanced down at her offering. "It's watermelon salad," she said. "Isn't that what people bring? A meat dish, a dessert or a salad. I have to choose salad because it's about the only thing that I know how to fix. I'm a cooking school dropout."

"I'm sure it will be very appreciated," Scott told her. "There's probably fifty people just in the immediate family. Some of them coming from out of town. Everyone will need to eat."

She nodded. "So I wanted to take this, but I don't actually know where they live."

"Oh, of course you don't. They live on the other side of town, near... Wait. I'll take you."

"You don't have to do that."

"I know I don't have to. I want to. And that way you won't spill your dish."

He retrieved his phone and keys, made sure his shirt was tucked in and put on a jacket to show some respect before hurrying out to let D.J. into the van.

He held the salad while she got into the seat and buckled up. Then she carried it in her lap as he drove.

Scott felt it incumbent upon himself to keep up a shallow, unthreatening conversation. They had reached some sort of peace and he did not want D.J. to retreat into the avid dislike she'd met him with. Lighthearted chatter, however, did not come easily considering the errand they were on.

"You would have liked Dutch," he told her. "And he would have probably become a regular library visitor."

"Oh, he liked to read?"

Scott shook his head. "I doubt he ever read more than the *Farm Journal,*" he said. "But Dutch could never resist the company of pretty girls."

D.J. gave an incredulous chuckle. "I don't really think I qualify as a pretty girl."

"That's the way Dutch would have said it," Scott told her. "Anyone under fifty he probably viewed as a girl."

And, of course, D.J. was beautiful rather than pretty, Scott thought to himself. She had that ethereal quality that made her seem to glow from the inside.

Wait. That was Sparkle. This was D.J. He was getting confused again.

393.4 Death Customs

D.J. had wanted to turn Scott down when he said he would accompany her to the Porters' home. But as she walked up to the front porch, she found herself surprisingly grateful to have him by her side. And not simply because he carried the watermelon salad. Her hands trembled and her throat ached. She felt as if she might burst into tears. She could definitely not do that. She absolutely could not, would not, cry in front of strangers and over the death of a man that she'd never met.

The foursquare clapboard house was surrounded by beautifully tended flowerbeds. While everything looked to be in good shape, there was a lived-in feeling about the place. This was somebody's home. Where a family lived and loved each other and made memories together. Today's memories were going to be very sad. But they would not be the only ones to recall.

The door was open and D.J. saw a familiar face through the screen. Suzy invited them in.

"Good to see you, good to see you," she said, hugging them both as if they were old friends.

D.J. replied the same, surprising herself by the truth of that statement.

"You're part of the family?" she asked.

"My father-in-law is a Porter on his mother's side,"

Suzy explained. "The joke is, of course, that makes him an actual Dutch Uncle."

It wasn't much of a joke, D.J. thought.

Once inside the door, Suzy directed them to the dining table, which was spread with a wide variety of food. Much more than D.J. remembered from her parents' funeral. But then, there were a lot more people to feed here. She found a place for her bowl. Scott inched over the surrounding dishes so that she could fit it in.

That chore accomplished, D.J. would have been happy to leave. But instead she was pulled into a round of greeting people and making appropriate comments.

"I'm so sorry for your loss."

From her own experience, she knew that sound and tone was all they might be hearing.

She would have thought that a stranger in their midst at such a time might not be that welcome. She recalled being exhausted by the new faces surrounding her in her parents' home. But surprisingly everyone seemed eager to be introduced. And Scott obliged with the honors. Polite inquiries about her life, her accommodations, her plans for the future fueled the conversation.

She began to realize that as the new person, she was giving them an excuse to talk about something else. Think about something else. She let them do that. Grief and loss had to be experienced. It was unavoidable. But that did not mean that distraction wasn't allowed. She was honored to provide one. It was, in its own way, more of a gift than the watermelon salad.

Slowly, person by person, she made her way through the house. Sometimes Scott was right at her elbow. And at others he was half a room away. But she was very aware of him. Aware of how respectfully he treated everyone. Aware of how genuinely sympathetic he could be without fawning. Aware of how his eyes followed her every time she glanced in his direction.

In the front parlor she spotted her dog. Dew sat on an overstuffed chintz couch, wedged between Viv on his right and the deceased's widow on his left. Mrs. Porter was absently patting the top of Dew's head. It was not the way that Dew liked it. Even as a puppy he's always preferred having her dig her fingernails into the thick fur behind his ears. If D.J. had been petting him that way, he would have shaken her hand off. But stoically the little dog sat, chin up, his focus on the hollow-eyed woman. He offered one quick glance in D.J.'s direction as if to acknowledge, *I know that you're here, but I am too busy for you right now.*

Also sitting on the couch, Viv looked a million miles away.

D.J. felt a hand on the small of her back. Scott had come up beside her and was urging her forward.

The women looked up at her.

"Mrs. Porter," he said. "This is Dorothy Jarrow, she's our new librarian."

"Oh, hello."

D.J. clasped the cold, bony hand that she offered. "So sorry for your loss."

"This is your dog, right?"

Mrs. Porter glanced toward Viv for verification. She nodded.

"Yes," D.J. concurred.

"He's such a sweet little creature," she said, continuing to pat him. "He's not caused one bit of trouble."

"I'm so glad," D.J. said. She looked over at Viv. "I can take him home now, if you like."

Viv shook her head. "I'll bring him later."

D.J. gave one last look at Mrs. Porter, petting Dew before moving away.

Scott stayed at her side and leaned down slightly to whisper, "Are you ready to get out of here?"

D.J. nodded.

Calmly, without any appearance of haste, Scott got them across the room. Suzy was manning the door again.

"Thanks for coming," she said.

You're welcome seemed like a weird response, so D.J. simply smiled.

"I can't wait to get back to work," Suzy told her. "Driving these nasty old trucks sure makes me miss my bookmobile."

"Good. Sometimes it does take comparison to make us recognize what we've got."

"True," Suzy agreed and then leaned forward to speak more privately. "And if you look around at all the potbellied snoozers in this room, you'd realize that you're on the arm of the hunkiest hayseed in town."

D.J. gave her a stern shake of the head. "It's not a date, it's a condolence call."

Suzy looked unconvinced. "It's never a date with you, is it?"

D.J. had no comment.

Finally outside in the open air, she felt as if she could breathe again. She felt such a jittery sense of being constrained, of needing to break out. She didn't quite comprehend her restlessness, but it was real. Beside her, Scott said nothing. When they reached the van, he opened the door and she got inside. He walked around to the driver's side and got behind the wheel.

Instead of turning around and heading into town, he drove farther out into the countryside. It occurred to D.J. to question their destination. But the silence between them seemed strangely comfortable. As if somehow they had transcended the need to make shallow conversation.

On both sides of the narrow dirt road wheat grew tall and hearty. He made a couple of right turns and then a switchback left before pulling off toward the side and turning off the engine.

"Come on," he said as he opened his door.

Why he wanted to stop in the middle of nowhere, she wasn't sure. But D.J. got out of the van and followed him as he simply walked into the waist-high wheat of the field.

She stopped at the edge of the crop, unsure. He didn't even glance back. After a moment's hesitation and with some trepidation, she stepped into the field. Her shoes were not the best for agri-tramping. And it was not that easy to walk among the tall blond stalks. Mostly she kept her eyes on where she was putting her feet. Scott stopped up ahead of her and she had hopes of catching up with him, asking what they were doing. But when she looked up again he had disappeared. She hurried faster to where she had last seen him, but there was no one there. She looked all around, but in every direction there was nothing but wheat, wheat and more wheat. The sense of aloneness was almost overwhelming.

"Scott?" she called out.

"I'm here," he answered, not far from where she stood. "Duck down. Have a seat."

D.J. lowered herself to the ground. It was a strange sensation to have the world close in so tightly around her, but without any sense of claustrophobia. Above her was the purple sky of a sunset evening and all around her the welcoming embrace of tall grass.

"Amazing, huh," she heard him say.

"Yeah. Why do I think this was some game you played as a kid?" she asked.

"If you're thinking hide-and-seek, I did do some of that, but not out here. The wheat fields were never as much a playground as a getaway. Someplace where I could be on my own."

D.J. nodded to herself. She understood that. "I used to fantasize about building a tree house."

He laughed lightly. "Not a lot of tree houses in this part of the world," he pointed out. "In a landscape as open as Kansas, sometimes you need a place to hide."

As she sat there, D.J. began to appreciate her own bit of isolation even more. And having him far enough away that she was on her own, but close enough that he could talk to her, seemed just about perfect.

"It's about perspective, I think. This must be what it feels like to be a rabbit or a field mouse," he said. "Safe in every direction, except one. And I comfort myself that it's always good for the soul to look up."

"Yes," D.J. agreed.

They remained there. Separate but together as the light began to fade.

"It was hard being at the Porters'," he said.

D.J. murmured an agreement.

"I know that I'm there to be a comfort to them in their loss," he said. "But my own grief keeps raring up at me. Most of the time, I'm okay. When something like this happens, it's like all that hurt is fresh again."

"Yes," D.J. agreed. "It was like that for me, too. At least you have the excuse of time. Your family is still in mourning. My parents died ten years ago."

"But to lose both. I can't even imagine it. I don't want to imagine it," he said. "I worry so much about my mom. I don't think that I expected that. I thought that when Dad died, our relationship would continue as it always had. But there is this urgency about protecting her. Keeping her healthy and safe."

"Maybe you're trying to pick up where your father left off," D.J. suggested.

"Yeah, that could be it," he said. "Or it could be the fearfulness of 'who will I matter to' once she's gone. Mainly no one."

"You'll always matter to people," D.J. assured him. "To friends and the people of the community."

"But will what I do matter?" he asked. "So much of my life I've spent trying to make my parents proud of me. Wanting to prove to them that I learned the lessons they taught me. If they're not here, then who do I do it for?"

"For yourself," she answered.

"Yeah, I guess it has to be that way," he said. "Was it like that for you? Did you protect your remaining parent when the first one was gone?"

"No," she said. "They died together. Car accident."

"God. That's crap," he said. "At least with my dad's illness we could see what was happening. I had a chance to say goodbye."

"No goodbyes for me," D.J. said.

"And I'm the one whining," Scott said. "Sorry. Nothing like getting all wimpy in the wheat field."

"No, I...I think you have a right to whine. I do, too, but not in the same way. You had a real relationship with your father and you miss that. I had, well, basically no relationship with my parents and now I know that I never will," she said.

"So you didn't get along?"

"We got along fine," she answered. "They didn't get

along with each other very well, but they both seemed okay with me. They just weren't that interested."

"Maybe it seemed that way."

"No, it was that way," she told him with complete certainty. "Neither of them bonded with me, somehow. I used to speculate about it a lot. They were both in their mid-forties when I was born and I thought, maybe they couldn't make the transition between being a childless couple to being parents."

"I guess that could happen," Scott said.

"Other times I thought there was no room for me in the relationship that they had," she said. "My parents argued all the time. Among other people they could be smart and witty and interesting, but together they were always in battle, always looking for a weakness to exploit, always raising the level of insult and one-upmanship just a little bit higher."

"That must have been terrible."

"For me," D.J. said. "But for them? They must have loved it, because they stayed in it. I used to daydream about them getting a divorce. No such luck."

D.J. couldn't believe that she was sharing this. She couldn't believe that she was sharing it with him. She hadn't spoken of it. Not to her friends at school, not to her priest, not to anyone. But somehow in the anonymity of this wheat field, she couldn't stop.

"I guess my favorite rationalization is that maybe they didn't know how to be a family. Never once did I ever meet or even hear about any relatives. All those cousins and uncles and in-laws at the Porter house, at my parents' funeral there was one family member. Me."

She sighed heavily, gazing up from within the safety and concealment of the wheat all around her.

"That's your *favorite* excuse?" Scott asked. "I hate to hear the one you like the least."

She hesitated only an instant before she replied, surprising them both with her candor.

"That I am unlovable," she answered. "That there is something lacking in me that kept them at arm's length."

There was the sound of tramping through the wheat and then he was sitting there beside her. He wasn't too close. He didn't intrude upon her space. But he was there. Inches away. As if near enough to catch a fall. And far enough to allow standing on her own.

The darkness of the field, the towering height of the wheat created a space with only the two of them. It was intimate. No longer solitary. But they had forgotten that they needed that.

"I'm guessing your dad didn't have a lot of great advice for you."

"No, beyond 'do well in school,' I don't recall anything."

"Okay, so let me share what I think was the wisest words my father ever told me."

"Okay."

"Not every bad thing that happens to you is your fault."

"No, of course not," she agreed easily.

"Wait, don't just accept that truth. Own it. I think that's the key," Scott said. "Once you own it, then you're free to let the doubts go."

They sat staring at each other across the enclosed space for a long moment.

"That's pretty wise," she said.

"My father was a wise man," he said. "I hope to be one someday, too."

"That's an admirable goal. Do you think you'll get there?"

Scott shrugged. "Well, I wouldn't say that I'm much of a prodigy."

D.J. found his easy self-deprecation to be charming. There was no sense of false humility. There was an honesty and uncritical acceptance that was somehow winning. He was as easy to laugh with as he was to confide in.

"I've always been a bit of a late bloomer myself," she admitted.

"You've come to the right place for that," he told her. "In Verdant we like to take our time."

"Yeah," she replied. "It's one of the things I like about the place."

"Do you?"

"Yes."

"Good," he said. "Very good. I…I've been hoping that you'll stick around."

At that moment, D.J. couldn't imagine anyplace she'd rather be.

They sat together in silence watching the stars gather above them.

He did not move one inch closer in the quiet solitude. There was a safety in his presence that was both welcome and familiar. D.J. knew that feeling, but couldn't quite place it. It wasn't sexual. It was something else. Something that she had yearned for, but didn't quite understand. Secretly she was wishing this respite would never end. But as the world continued spinning, it did.

"We should probably go," he said, finally.

"Yes, I guess so."

They stood up and the world was totally different. The wheat was an onyx sea, ever moving in shadow.

Above it the heavens were illuminated with the wink of stars and planets, the Milky Way like a giant streak of glimmer slashing across the sky.

She was standing right next to him, awed by the beauty of the night sky and their tiny, tiny place in it. It seemed perfectly natural that he leaned down to gently press his lips to her temple. It wasn't a kiss really, it was a consolation.

"Take my hand," he said.

D.J. could see nothing as he unerringly led her through the darkened grain to the edge of the field.

398.5 Folklore

It was late when Viv finally left the Porters'. As she walked to her car, Mr. Dewey took the opportunity to relieve himself in the grass.

"You did really well," she told the dog. "I don't know how you know what people need. But you were exactly right for Cora today. What in the world was Dutch thinking? Did he tell himself that Cora would believe he'd gotten the pistol out to clean it? Ridiculous." She sighed heavily. "Or maybe he didn't care what Cora thought. That's even worse, of course."

She opened the door to the Mini Cooper and Mr. Dewey scampered inside. He took his perch on the passenger seat, his front paws on the armrest so that his ears could blow in the wind.

Viv got inside and started up the engine. She backed out into the street and turned toward town, but she didn't want to go home. There was nothing at home but an empty house and a plethora of canned goods. She began driving aimlessly up one street and down another. At the intersection with the highway she paused to allow a succession of three eighteen-wheelers loaded with grain to pass.

It occurred to her that a tired senior, unaccustomed to night driving and exhausted from a long day at the side of a grieving friend, might reasonably have forgotten to stop at an intersection and been run down by the trucks that were, after all, speeding along.

But, no. While being T-boned by a semi could be very bad, it was not guaranteed to be fatal. And what of the truck driver? She didn't know who it was or what might happen to them. And certainly Mr. Dewey would not fare well uncrated in a crash. D.J. would prove to be absolutely right about that.

No, her current plan had been arrived at carefully. And it was the best solution.

Once the road was clear, she crossed into the west side of town, where she wound her way without ever turning down the street toward her home. She finally pulled to a stop where her jaunts so often ended, the parking lot of the cemetery. When she turned off her headlights, the darkened landscape revealed nothing. She sat there, gazing out across the fenced area. She wanted to see something. Anything. A wisp of vapor. A translucent specter. An inhuman apparition. There was nothing. A deserted patch of ground where the bodies of people she knew and loved now lay lifeless.

"Food for worms," she quoted.

Mr. Dewey suddenly jumped in her lap, grabbing attention.

"So what are you up to?" she asked the dog. "Are you getting sick of coming to this place, too?"

She laughed as the animal, who had to be at least as tired as she was, perked into animation. She scratched him lovingly behind the ears. "I wonder if your mama will bring you here to see me? Probably not. I won't really be here, you see. I'll be up in heaven with John. My life here, it doesn't really work for me without him."

She looked down at the cheery, upbeat little dog face. "But I will miss you when I go."

She looked out the windshield one more time and sighed heavily. The phrase *move along, nothing to see here,* filtered through her brain, causing her to chuckle wryly.

"All right, I suppose we can go home now," she told Mr. Dewey. "I don't guess there is much chance that we'll catch your mama and my son *in flagrante delicto.* Should I speak plain English? I want them screwing each other's brains out. That's what young, healthy people who are obviously made for each other should do. But those two are slow to get the message."

Her tone changed to a whiney mimic.

"They've been hurt. They don't want to make a mistake." Viv gave a huff of disgust. "Life is way too short to hesitate when reaching for happiness."

401.2 Language Theory

Perspective. D.J. awakened early the next morning with the word in her head. It hung with her as she groggily sipped her first cup of coffee. She tried to push it back. She was sure it was all about the previous evening. It was about being in the wheat field. It was all about Scott. It was all about speaking unguarded and discovering that the earth didn't shatter and neither did she. She'd simply gained a new perspective.

Dew was as drowsy and bleary-eyed as she was herself. As his meal from the previous night remained untouched, D.J. highly suspected that Viv was overfeeding him on doggy treats. At least she knew that he wasn't gorging on table scraps.

In the shower with the hot water splashing down on her face, she allowed herself a little bit of nostalgic memory. Scott had been there for her and sympathized with her in a way that was not at all sexy. It had made her feel safe. It had made her feel whole. It had warmed her, satisfied her in a way that sex never did. Quickly, she was forced to correct herself. Sex *almost* never did. Sex with him. Sex with Scott. That had been different.

"You were different," she said to herself amidst the hot steam. "The difference wasn't him. It was you."

Perspective. There it was again.

Out of the shower, she dried off, smeared her face

with moisturizer and began brushing her teeth. Deliberately she pushed Scott out of her mind. Forcing concentration to her workday ahead and the problems ahead. Still the word continued to reverberate in the back of her thoughts like a chorus to a jingle that gets stuck in your brain.

She was staring at the blue-and-white bristles scrubbing across her lower molars when suddenly the image of the library's long, skinny windows, spaced at three-foot intervals popped up.

"Oh, my God! We've got the wrong perspective!"

D.J. was dressed in fifteen minutes flat. Forsaking her business suit for jeans and a T-shirt, with her hair pulled back in a ponytail, she headed for the library.

She was out so early, she expected deserted streets. But the small business district was alive with people. There was the bustle of getting breakfast out of the way and vehicles gassed up and a thousand chores done before the fields were ready. Added to that, for many, was the early-morning funeral service and respectful homage to the dead. The traffic crawled on Main Street, causing her to grit her teeth in impatience.

When D.J. finally pulled her car into her parking space, she was grateful to see that the rusty old bicycle was securely chained to the railing.

"Bless you, James," she muttered.

It was heartening to know that no matter how early she arrived, he would always be here first. She hurried inside, not even stopping to make the coffee.

"James! James!"

She walked around the stacks to the aisle in front of the windows.

"What an idiot!" she said aloud.

"Sorry."

The word was offered as apology and the timid, defeated voice came from the bookshelves.

"What? No, not you, James. Me. I'm the idiot. Me, and every other librarian who's ever looked at this place since the day that it opened. The shelving is going the wrong way."

She saw him peeking out at her from behind the books. Not quite ready to confront her in the open.

"The windows were designed like this so that the shelves should run between them, not perpendicular. It's *so* obvious. It's like some Escher Figure-Ground thing. It looks like a fish until you see the face and then you can't see anything else."

"I don't see a fish," James said quietly.

She laughed as if his words were meant as a joke.

"This is going to be so great," she said. "It's going to change…it's going to change everything about this place."

D.J. looked again at the windows and then at the long rows of shelving loaded with books. Everything was neat and tidy and in perfect order. But it was all in the wrong place. Every volume would have to be taken down and reshelved later.

"Okay, James," she said. "This is what we're going to need to do. We're going to have to empty the entire stack area and take up all the shelving ranges. They're undoubtedly bolted to the floors, so there will likely be some holes to patch. And the patina on the floor will be a bit mismatched. But it will be worth it. We'll turn the ranges 90 degrees, bolt them back to the floor and then put the books back on them."

His eyes were as wide as saucers. He looked as if she'd just suggested slitting him open and spreading his entrails around the room. Her suggestion was clearly encouraging panic.

"Oh, no, we can't do that," he said. "We can't do that. We…we can't do that."

"Of course we can," she assured him. "It'll take a little time and some elbow grease, but we will do it."

"Uh-uh, no, no, no," he replied. "Can't do that. No, uh-uh, no, no."

Clearly the threat to his perfectly organized stack area loomed large to him.

"It's okay, James," she told him. "It's not like we're going to start just piling books up and throwing things around. I'll come up with a plan. We'll…we'll maintain order. I promise. The books will be fine. Moving will all be very orderly."

"Oh, no," he said. "No, no, no, no."

D.J. was too excited about her plan. Too buoyed by her discovery to allow his negativity to dissuade her.

She went up to her office and found the tape measure. She brought it back downstairs and with a cheery hum on her lips, she heard the slamming of a book. As she walked across the floor, she heard another. She ignored the noise and began taking the dimensions of everything.

"James, would you like to hold one end of this?" she asked as she attempted to measure the length of the shelving range.

He made no response. She could hear him moving about and the explosive sound of book closing continued to go off at intervals, but he chose not to answer.

D.J. shrugged it off. She managed to hook the tape measure on her own and get the accurate length.

Definitely she wanted to institute the change in the stack area first, she decided. It was the space most desperate. What she wished she could do was take every volume, shelf and stick of furniture out of the room and then lay it out all at one time. Begin again. Clean slate. That was not possible or realistic. She would work around the constraints that she had. She would have to rearrange the sections of the building separately and utilize the other areas for staging. The stacks would be the most onerous task. It might be perfect to get that done during harvest, while the library was basically empty. If she could move really quickly, if she could get James to help her, if they worked day and night, it all seemed like a very good, very possible idea.

Once D.J. found some graph paper to model the room and its furnishings, she noticed a growing increase in book slamming within the dark confines of the stack shelving. On a routine day, she would hear James slam a book closed two or three times. They weren't even open for business yet and he'd done many times that number of loud, rifle-shot closures.

Also, uncharacteristically, James was making his presence felt. Typically, he moved about like a ghost. Not so this morning. D.J. could hear him pacing up and back among the shelves. He was muttering to himself and only stopped for another book slam.

"James, are you all right?" she called out.

There was no answer.

She went to the stacks to confront him directly, but he avoided her. As soon as she was in the same aisle, he rushed around the corner. And when she went to that corner, he was around the next. She would never succeed in chasing him down. So she attempted to reason with him.

"If we turn the book shelves to run east and west, then the light from the windows can illuminate the space between them. It's how it was meant to be, I'm sure. Somebody simply messed up when they first laid out the interior. It'll be better. You'll be able to see without a flashlight. The biographies won't get all sun-damaged and faded."

Her explanation was no help. If anything, it seemed to make it worse.

Maybe he needed to get used to the idea, she thought. He needed to think it through himself and come up with the same conclusion that she had.

She went back to her seat at the circulation desk and her graph-paper planning. But it was impossible to get anything done with all the tension emanating from the far side of the room.

"It's going to be fine, James. It's all going to be fine."

Muttering stopped. *POW!* Book slammed.

D.J. tried to ignore it, but she was concerned. He was very agitated and her attempts at reassurance weren't working. What would he be like when she actually attempted the move?

"James? Talk to me, James."

Pacing. Muttering. No reply.

Maybe he was now as angry with her as he had been with Stevie. But at least with Stevie, he had been quietly silent. His uncharacteristic behavior was a little bit scary.

D.J. wished Suzy were there. Or Amos. Someone who knew James better. Who knew what to do. Who to call. Surely James had parents or people who were responsible for him. How come she didn't know those people? Who could she ask?

At that moment the phone rang. She picked it up.

"Verdant Public Library."

There was a moment of hesitation on the other end of the line.

"Hello," she said, more sharply. The last thing she needed was a crank call from a heavy breather.

"Hi." She recognized Scott's voice.

"Oh, hi."

"I don't want to bother you," he began. "But I saw how you rushed out of here this morning and I thought… well, I worried that… Is everything okay?"

"Everything is fine," she answered optimistically as almost force of habit. "Except that it's not. James is…" She lowered her voice and shaded the phone's mouthpiece with her hand. "James is acting weird. Who should I call? Who takes care of him? His parents?"

"His parents are dead," Scott told her. "What's he doing?"

"He's pacing in the stacks, muttering to himself and slamming books closed."

"Let me ask my mom," he said. "I'll call you right back."

D.J. was amazed at how comforting she found that reassurance. She remembered how he'd held her last night. How she'd been able to trust him with her fear. She trusted him now.

He did not call back, however. He showed up. Fewer than five minutes after she'd hung up the phone. Scott and Viv came walking in through the library's front door. Both were dressed in respectful black.

D.J. felt her heart leap at the sight of Scott in a suit. She was right the first moment she'd seen him. The man was totally gorgeous.

"Oh, I'm sorry. I forgot about the funeral," D.J. said.

She had definitely caught them on their way to the service.

"It's okay," Viv reassured her. "We've got time."

At that instant the muttering momentarily ceased, followed by a book slam. Both Viv and Scott startled. D.J. had grown accustomed to it already.

"What happened to set him off like this?" she asked.

"I realized that I needed to change the library around," D.J. said, not wanting to delve deep into detail. "He told me not to. And I guess that my ignoring him made him quit talking to me. He started muttered and pacing."

"He's stimming," Viv said.

"Stimming?"

"It's a slang term for self-stimulation. Lots of people with different kinds of brain challenges do it. They focus on some repetitive behavior when they get anxious. It's a way to comfort themselves."

"I don't want to upset him," D.J. said. "I just want to make the library better."

"I know," Viv told her. "Let me try to talk to him."

"Do you want me to go with you?" Scott asked.

She shook her head. "He's not dangerous. He's stressed."

D.J. watched Viv enter the stack area without the least trepidation. The muttering became louder and the pacing was hurried enough to be running. There were three loud book closings before things began to level off.

D.J. couldn't hear what Viv was saying, but the tone of her voice was quiet, unruffled. Finally she heard the rough baritone of James. He was now conversing rather than muttering.

"Don't worry," Scott told her. "James will be fine."

D.J. nodded. "Viv will be, too."

He smiled at her. "So what brought this on? Did you

wake up this morning and say, 'I think I'll change the library around.'"

"Pretty much," she answered. "I realized that if the shelving wasn't perpendicular to the windows, we'd get a lot more light in here."

Scott surveyed the building in one visual sweep.

"I think it's always been this way," he pointed out.

She nodded. "And it's always been wrong. The day they installed the stacks, somebody made a mistake. Nobody questioned it. Everybody got used to it. Now, all these years later, it takes somebody from the outside to notice the error."

"Somebody from the outside?" he asked, facetiously. "No, that can't be right, D.J. You're one of our hometown girls. Only a genuine Verdanter would sit out in a wheat field on a summer night."

She liked the joke. She liked the smile.

Viv stepped out of the stacks and returned to the circulation desk.

"I think he'll be all right for now," she said. "It's a lot for him to take in. You realize he's lived most of his life in this building."

D.J. nodded. "That must be why he's so pale."

"I promised him that you wouldn't do anything today."

"Okay."

"And I said that you'd keep him informed of the plans. That you wouldn't be doing anything without warning."

Viv's tone was pleasant, but her intent was firm. D.J. was the librarian. But James had a say in the library's future, as well.

"I can absolutely do that," D.J. assured her. "I was so excited and eager this morning, it probably was pretty scary to watch. A move like this does require planning. And maybe the harvest is not the best time to make it happen."

"Harvest is probably the best time," Scott said. "I mean, you don't have as many people to help you. But you don't have to close the place down, either."

D.J. nodded. "Yeah, that was kind of what I was thinking this morning. But I was expecting to have James onboard. I was expecting for him to help me."

Viv smiled and patted her on the arm. "Then you need to remember to include him." She turned to Scott and tapped the face of her wristwatch. "It's never good to be late to a funeral. People will think we're part of the family."

In Verdant, there was probably no danger of that, but Scott did escort her out.

418.8 Applied Linguistics; Structural Usage

Dutch Porter's funeral was as sad and sorrowful as such occasions tended to be. It also felt rushed. And although much effort was made by the funeral director and those in attendance to negate that sense, it persisted.

Outside the church at the four-way stop on Main Street the air brakes of the grain trucks could be heard. They were headed through town and out into the fields. Life went on. Jobs were done. The world kept turning. And the truth of that invaded the seclusion of sorrow within the building.

Scott had liked Dutch. He'd been a hard worker, fine parent and excellent citizen. It seemed wrong that his life should get such short shrift because of one bad decision at the end. Or perhaps even natural causes during harvest resulted in a hasty eulogy. It wasn't until Scott noted the jitters in his own legs that he realized he was as antsy as everyone else.

With a final benediction, the body was loaded into the hearse and Scott and his mother followed the procession to the cemetery. Most people had taken that opportunity to disappear. At the graveside it was mostly the immediate family. The VFW was in attendance to acknowledge Dutch's service in the jungles of Viet Nam.

They played a CD version of "Taps" as they folded the flag atop his casket.

Finally, it was over. Except, of course, it wasn't. His mother needed to talk to everyone, interact as if she was tacit hostess of a garden party in this garden of stones.

Scott wandered over to his father's grave. He found it easily, though he hadn't been there since the headstone was laid. His mother had planted little dark pink flowers at the head and lined the rectangle with chalky white rock. Scott was pretty sure that was against the rules. But he also recalled her panic that first morning after the burial, afraid she might not remember where it was, that she might lose him.

Scott closed his eyes as if that could shut out the memory of the pain of those first days.

Suddenly she was there at his side and he smiled down at her.

"The flowers look good, Mom," he said.

She nodded. "The heat has been hard on them, but I try to water every day."

He hated that. He hated that she came here every day. He hated that she kept such a lonely vigil by herself.

"Maybe after the harvest is done, we could…we could all come out here and you and I can…I don't know. Leanne and Jamie would come. Should we do something? Some kind of ceremony?"

She looked up at him and smiled.

"No," his mother answered. "There is nothing else to be done. But thank you. You are a good son, Scott. I don't always remember to tell you that, but I want you to know. To always know, whether I tell you or not."

"Thanks Mom," he said. "I'll remind you of that next time you get pissed off at me."

"A lady may get annoyed, but she never gets…p.o.'d," she told him.

He let her drop him off to get his van. She went on to the Porters' home, where she intended to be of help if needed.

Scott changed into more casual clothes and drove to the store. He'd left his cell number on the door, but he hadn't gotten so much as a text from anyone. Main Street was deserted once more. He was too antsy to sit inside and do nothing all afternoon. So he left his sign up and drove on by.

There were a number of trucks lined up near the grain elevator. Unloading was a two-step process. Each truck was driven onto the scales for total tonnage. Then the wheat was dumped into the pit area, where cuplike conveyers scooped it up and moved it into storage silos. Once empty, the truck was weighed again. Because of the incendiary properties of airborne grain dust, the operators as well as the truck drivers took extra precautions to avoid the dangers of explosion that even the most up-to-date ventilation technology couldn't completely prevent.

Scott spotted Amos in the line, leaning indolently against the wheel well of a heavily loaded vehicle.

With a quick glance in the rearview mirror to make sure that there was no traffic coming behind him, Scott pulled to a stop in the middle of the road.

"Hey, shirker, what's up?" he called out.

Amos pressed one foot against the tire to push himself into a standing position and walked toward the van.

Scott noted that he was better dressed than might be expected for a wheat hauler. Even for a workday, he looked more slicked up that usual. Although he hadn't seen him, Scott assumed that meant he'd been to Dutch's funeral and said as much.

"No," Amos replied. "I couldn't really go. There was so much grain to be cut, and most of the Browns' crew were among the family. So I stayed out there to help. I was running the cart until the truck got full."

Scott nodded. "How long have you been in line?"

"Not long, twenty minutes maybe," he answered. "I'd say it's going pretty fast, but that would probably jinx it."

Scott grinned at the typically pessimistic viewpoint of his friend.

"With that attitude, I guess there's no use asking if you're making progress with Jeannie."

Amos actually blushed. "I did say, 'Do you want to grab a sandwich sometime?'"

"And?"

"She said, 'Sure.' But, she was probably being polite."

"Yeah," Scott agreed sarcastically. "Women are always agreeing to stuff they don't mean. Especially Jeannie, which is why she's still with her ex, right? And since you are asking women to eat with you basically all the time, she probably thought exactly nothing of the invitation."

Amos lowered his chin to eyeball Scott more effectively. "You mock me? The crazy vet guy is getting ridiculed by the sad sack whose wife had to find sexual satisfaction elsewhere."

Scott laughed. "If I don't mock you, who will?"

"Right back at ya."

The line of trucks moved, Amos waved off and Scott headed down the road. He seriously hoped that Amos and Jeannie could find something together. What had happened to Amos in service to his country couldn't be changed. But if he could move beyond it, find his share of happiness, that would be good.

"Take your own advice, Sanderson," he admonished aloud.

The librarian was warming to him a little bit. D.J. The name, or the nick of it, suited her. It was strange how he'd thought she looked like his Sparkle girl. She actually looked nothing like her. Or at least he didn't think that she did. As he tried to conjure up the woman from the beach so many years ago, he could no longer recall her face.

The face had not been one of her important parts, he reminded himself jokingly.

Scott drove out to his house. He parked the van in the drive and walked around to the backyard. His garden had missed him. He picked snap beans until his hands were so full he needed a pail. There was broccoli and cauliflower, as well. And from the looks of the tops on his root crops, the potatoes and beets were going to be ready to dig soon. What had been a lovely cabbage had been partially ripped out of the ground by an unwelcome wildlife visitor, but it couldn't be helped.

He carried his vegetable plunder to the back step and uncoiled the hose and turned on the outside tap. He took his time, watering thoroughly as his mind wandered where it would.

Where his mind mostly wanted to wander was back to D.J. He pictured her as he'd seen her earlier. Efficient and businesslike behind the circulation desk. The image made him smile.

He recalled the conversation of the previous evening. Their childhoods had been in such sharp contrast. Scott had been sustained and sheltered and sometimes nearly suffocated by the love of his parents. D.J. had been an unwelcome third wheel sent rolling off on her own at the earliest possible moment.

Scott had the best of that deal. He was certain. But all that early independence and self-reliance gave her a natural sense of confidence that was not typical of a lot of people in their twenties. He'd been working in the drugstore for most of his life. But he missed his father on-the-job even more than at home and wished he were around to talk things over.

D.J. had come to a town she'd never seen, where she didn't know a soul and stepped into a situation that had problems set in place for years. And she'd never flinched. He admired that.

"I bet *she* never studied sex in a book," he murmured to himself.

He quickly reproved himself. Best not to put D.J. and sex in the same thought. He found her incredibly attractive. But she was just beginning to accept him as a friend. If he went all masher on her, they'd be back to square one in a hurry.

When he finished watering he unlocked the back door and let himself inside. He'd left all the windows open to prevent any buildup of sewer gases. So far, everything seemed to be fine.

In case a plumbing miracle had occurred as unexpectedly as the plumbing disaster, he ran water in the sink. It took about five minutes before the water began to back up. The clog was still there, and it was very far down the pipe. For sure they'd be digging up the backyard.

In the bedroom he pulled out more clean shirts to take to his mother's. He was headed back through the house when the phone rang. He slung the clothes over the back of a kitchen chair before picking up the receiver.

"There you are!" the voice on the other end of the line announced in a fashion that was almost accusatory. "I've been calling the drugstore all morning with no answer."

"Hey sis," he replied. "You know, out in the country here we've got this new technology thing. We call it a cell phone. You can call the number and it rings right in my pocket."

"Very funny."

"It even has the cool texting feature where you can type in a message and the words fly through the air to find me."

"Stick with the drug dealing," she quipped. "You'll never make it as a comedian."

He chuckled. "I don't know, lots of strange stuff passing for comedy these days."

"I wouldn't know," Leanne answered. "My life is no laughing matter. Why aren't you at work?"

"Harvest," he answered. "And we had a funeral this morning. I didn't even open."

"Who died?"

Scott went into a short version of Dutch Porter's last days. His sister was sympathetic. She, too, remembered the older man. And had actually dated one of his sons a couple of times in high school. The two chatted companionably for several minutes, laughing as they remembered stories from the past.

"So when are you coming this way?" Scott asked her. "I sort of miss you, in a disinterested, kid brother kind of way."

"We were going to come this weekend, but Mom said no," she answered.

"You're kidding, right. Our mom? The same mom we've always had?"

"The very one," Leanne answered. "She said somebody was going to be staying in the guest room for harvest."

"Really? I didn't hear anything about that. And, actually, I'm staying there."

"You're staying at Mom's?"

"Uh-huh, I've got some snafu with my septic system. With everybody out in the fields, there's nobody to look at it this week."

"Well, good. I mean, bad for you, good for me. I'm glad you're staying with Mom. I'm a little worried about her."

"Oh, yeah?"

"She's being way too secretive these days. Surely you've noticed."

The only thing Scott had noticed was the excess of canned goods.

"Yeah, maybe, I guess," he answered, vaguely.

"Do you know about the private detective?"

"Private detective?"

"Mom asked Jamie to recommend a private detective. And he did! I could have killed him. I said, 'Why didn't you make her tell you what it was for?' and he said, 'Because it wasn't any of my business.' It's one of the things that drives me crazy about him."

"Absolutely," Scott said. "Integrity can be so inconvenient."

"Oh, shut up! You know you're as curious as I am."

In that, his sister was completely right.

440.0 Romance Languages

D.J. spent the whole afternoon working on her floor plan for the stacks. She must have been extremely intent on her job, because she didn't notice Ashley Turpin until the girl spoke.

"What are you doing?"

The pudgy, flat-faced little girl was wearing very baggy shorts and a pink T-shirt with the image of a unicorn. The shirt was both undersize and faded, but there was nothing lacking in the curiosity of the bright brown eyes.

"I'm drawing a picture of the library," she explained.

"Can I see?"

D.J. nodded and motioned to Ashley to come around the desk.

The little girl obeyed, but with the trepidation and reverence of one being beckoned into a secret, magical kingdom. Trolls might lurk anywhere.

"What do you think?" D.J. asked, showing off the precise, scaled graph paper layout.

Ashley looked at it for a long moment. "Well," she said finally. "The lines are very straight, but...it's not very pretty."

D.J. laughed. "You're right, it isn't. But it represents something that will be very beautiful."

The girl eyed her questioningly.

"You see these rectangles here on the edge," D.J. said, pointing to them. "These are the windows on the side of the building. By moving the shelving in this direction, the light from those windows can actually flow down the aisles, all the way to the vestibule."

Ashley's brow furrowed. "What's a vesta-pewl?"

"Vestibule. It's this area right in front of us."

The girl was surprised. "The light from the windows will come all the way down here?"

D.J. nodded. "Yes, I think in the morning, it will."

"That'll look good with the pink and white floor."

D.J. smiled. "Yes, I think it will look very nice with the marble."

"Maybe you should add that to your picture," Ashley suggested.

D.J. looked at her meticulously accurate representation. She didn't think it needed anything.

"Sometimes color helps," Ashley told her. "It helps other people see what you see."

The diagram was mostly for her own benefit. But the memory of repeated book slamming suddenly rang in her ears.

"I don't know that I really have time to add color to it," she hedged.

"Oh." The little sound was full of disappointment and resignation. As if a million ideas she'd come up with in her life had been rejected just as easily.

"I think it's an excellent suggestion," D.J. assured her. "Very much worth doing. But I need to get busy on laying out the aspects of the move, which is very complicated."

Ashley nodded thoughtfully. "I've got my crayons," she told her. "I could do it for you."

D.J. looked into the hopefully expectant little face

and saw, as she always had, herself. The lonely excess baggage of life plan that wasn't quite working out. She was transported back to those early days among the books of the children's department at Wichita Public Library where the encouraging whispers of the librarians were the only voices of approval that she ever heard. D.J. had to pass that forward.

"Go get your crayons," she told her.

As the girl scurried off, D.J. looked at her perfect, clear-cut, accurate rendering with a sigh. Then she hurried to the copy machine. At least if Ashley ruined it completely, she'd have a backup.

"I need to be able to read all these numbers," she explained, pointing out the measurements that she'd made. "Maybe you could color around them."

"Sure, no problem," Ashley told her.

D.J.'s expectation was that the little girl would be as haphazard in her illustration as she was in her personal hygiene and grooming. In that she was completely wrong. The child was careful and capable. And she was also curious about the process that D.J. was putting together.

"This is my master plan," D.J. explained. "It's kind of like a flow chart."

Ashley's expression indicated the concept of "flow chart" was a new one.

"It's the actions that we'll need to take to get from where we are now, to where we will be in the picture you're coloring."

"Okay," the girl replied, vaguely. "But don't you just take the books off and turn the shelves and put them back on?"

"Well, we could do that," D.J. told her. "But it would be very disruptive. Being able to locate the books we have quickly and efficiently is, in many ways, the whole underlying basis of librarianship. And book locations are not based on the books themselves, but to their relationship to the books around them. When a book comes off the shelf, the only way we know where it goes back, is what books are around it."

"Don't the numbers and letters on the back tell you that?"

"They help us," D.J. said. "They explain the relationship of one book to others. But if all the books are in a pile willy-nilly, there is nothing to tell us which book goes on which shelf. It could take months of trial and error and endless shifting to get everything back in order again."

Ashley seemed to be satisfied with that explanation. And D.J. would have left it there, if she had not heard, or perhaps merely sensed, a presence in the shelving range nearby. James was there. He was listening.

She kept her speech at a conversational volume, but she was careful to keep her chin up, so that none of her words would be missed.

"For each shelf in the stacks, I am assigning two numbers. One number is for the physical shelf. So we can know where it is now and where it will be after the move."

Ashley nodded.

"The second number is for the contents of that particular shelf. That same group of books will sit together in the new configuration, but on a different physical shelf, that we can point to before we've even removed one volume. While the shelves are moved, each set of books will be together vertically in the reading room with its number. So we can know where the books are every moment and get them back to where they are supposed to be with the least disruption possible."

Ashley seemed perfectly agreeable to that. D.J. could only hope that James would ultimately feel the same.

By closing time, D.J. had made a sizable dent in completing the flow chart. Ashley, on the other hand, finished her coloring. And D.J. was forced to admit that it looked surprisingly better. The rich browns of the library's oak shelves contrasted very nicely with the yellow light that flooded in through the windows. And Ashley had continued it down the aisles to cast a creamy, almost butter, color upon the pink-and-white marble in front of the circulation desk. All of her measurements and calculations were easily readable and the paper did simply look prettier.

"This looks great," D.J. told her. "You did a wonderful job. I am so proud of you."

Ashley beamed under the praise. Then seemed almost embarrassed at accepting it. Assuring D.J. that, "It was coloring. Even babies can do coloring."

"No baby could do this. It takes an artist's eye. I don't have that. And I appreciate the loan of yours. Thank you."

The girl liked that. "You're welcome."

"It's late, why don't I give you a ride down to the Brazier."

For an instant she looked delighted, but then her expression turned to worry. "I am not allowed to accept rides," she said. "It's my mom's biggest rule. Just because our town isn't full of strangers, doesn't mean that bad things can't happen to little girls."

D.J. was sure that Ashley's mom was right. Lonely little girls on their own would always be easy prey for someone. At least her own parents had the financial resources to pay someone else to keep her safe.

"Why don't we call her and ask permission," she suggested. "That way, even if she says no, she'll realize that you are running late and she won't worry."

Ashley agreed to that. And when her mother agreed to let her ride with the librarian, one would have thought from her reaction that the little Chevy hatchback was an amusement park and an ice-cream sundae rolled into one.

While the girl excitedly gathered up her things, D.J. considered the work she'd spread out upon the circulation desk. Her first thought was to take it all home with her and work on it that evening. See if she could get it done. But getting the plan done was not going to be worth a lot if she could get no one to help her implement it.

She left all of it sitting out on the desk, with the painstakingly illustrated future layout sitting right on top. She crossed her fingers for luck. She was going to need it.

D.J. locked the front door, turned out the lights and let herself and Ashley out the service entrance. The girl was so excited about the car, D.J. was worried she would be disappointed with the small, unimpressive vehicle.

"It is so cool," Ashley said. "It's like a kiddie car. Most of the guys my mom dates drive trucks. My grandparents have a car. I get to ride in it sometimes, but it's really big. And it kind of smells like old people." She wrinkled up her nose derisively. "Your car smells… like a dog."

D.J. wasn't sure that was better, but she laughed.

"I do have a dog."

"What's his name?"

"Melvil Dewey, Jr."

The girl stared at her blankly.

"I call him Dew."

The trip through town was completely taken up with questions about the dog. Where did she get him? What did he like to do? Where did he sleep? What did he like to eat?

Once all her questions were answered, Ashley gave a sigh of pure longing.

"I've always wanted to have a dog," she said.

"You should ask your mother," D.J. told her.

"I have…like a million times. She says, I'd 'better make enough money to feed myself before I take on feeding something else.'"

D.J. shrugged. "Well, she probably has a point. My parents said something similar to me once. So now I'm grown up and I work hard and support myself and I can have any dog that I want. And I wanted Dew."

Ashley nodded. "It's sure a long time before I grow up," she said.

"But the time won't be wasted," D.J. pointed out. "You can read about dogs, learn about the different breeds and how to train them. Decide what characteristics are important to you. As artistic as you are, you could put together your own notebooks of dogs you find interesting."

The girl considered it. "I'm not sure my drawing is good enough."

"Then trace the images out of one of our books," D.J. said. "I already know that you can bring a picture to life with color."

Slowly a smile crept across the girl's face. "I can, can't I?"

"You absolutely can," D.J. agreed.

The parking lot at the Brazier was overflowing. And there was a line of customers waiting outside.

"You can drive around and let me off at the back," Ashley suggested.

D.J. carefully edged through the narrow passage between cars at angle. At the back of the building her progress was stopped completely by a recognizable van.

"Thanks, D.J. I had a great day!" Ashley told her as she grabbed up her backpack and headed into the building. The girl nearly ran into Scott who was exiting, carrying a large cardboard box.

The minute he caught sight of her, D.J. was gifted with that amazing hot-guy smile. She deliberately tamped down her reaction, but the truth was, she liked it.

He stowed his load in the van and then slid the side door closed. He walked toward her and she assumed he was circling to the driver's seat. Maybe he was. But first, he walked straight back to her.

He put his forearm atop the car and leaned toward the window.

"Just get off work?"

"Yeah, I closed up maybe ten minutes ago."

"Have you got any plans for the evening?"

"Plans?"

His mother wasn't here to foist some fake date upon them. If he asked her out, if she agreed, that would be something real.

"I…I have some work to do," she lied.

"Can it wait? I'm taking dinner out to the Browns' crew," he said. "I thought maybe you could help me. It would be good for you to see the harvest process up close. And good for the library if people see you have an interest in it."

"Uh…sure. That sounds great."

"Okay. We'll run by Mom's house. You can leave your car and change your clothes."

He gave her a smile and a wave as he headed to his van. D.J. resisted the impulse to slap herself on the forehead and settled for silently cursing herself as an idiot. She was already attracted to the guy. Despite his oblivion, they had a history. They were getting way too friendly, way too easy with each other. Last night she had let him get way too close. Not like a lover, but still she'd felt his lips on her skin. That was dangerous stuff.

Typical of a practiced player—soften a woman up, catch her off guard.

The practiced-player warning rang hollow even in her own brain. He may have been a player back in the day. He may have cheated on his wife. He may have had affairs with married women. But there was something about him now that was genuine.

People could change, couldn't they?

The answer to that rhetorical question had always been, no, they cannot. Her parents never changed. She, herself, had never changed. It was her experience that you either accept people the way that they are, or you move on down the road.

But this was the end of the road for her. Verdant was going to be the place that was her own. Her hometown.

They reached the driveway to her place and she pulled into a space in the back. Viv was not home. She got her case from the backseat. Scott was already turning the van around.

"It'll just take me a minute," she promised.

"Jeans, not shorts," he told her. "And put on some real shoes. I don't expect you've got barn boots, but something sturdy."

Nodding, she hurried up the stairs. It was exciting. What an adventure! She imagined that her reaction was about as silly as Ashley's had been about a ride in her car, but she was okay with that.

499.9 Other Languages Not Specified

Scott tried to assure himself that it was merely coincidence that he'd run into D.J. It was purely a chance meeting. No way he could have imagined that she would be at the Brazier. But the fact was that he'd already imagined her going with him, that he'd already worked up the scenario in his mind when he'd called Amos to volunteer, that she'd shown up so opportunely only proved that heaven might well be on his side in this.

He lazed against his van, letting the house shade him from the heat of late afternoon. Having both a mother and a sister, he had no expectations that a change of clothes could happen quickly. The dog came trotting down the stairs eager to take a quick pee in the back-yard grass, then, grabbing his dirty tennis ball, he hurried to Scott in hopes to play. Obligingly, Scott threw it for him several times. He liked the dog. And he was pleased at how attached his mother had become to the little guy. Maybe he should consider getting her a pet for her birthday.

As his thoughts rambled in that direction, he was surprised to hear the sound of her footfalls coming down the stairs, not more than five minutes after she went up. With a whistle she got Dewey back up to the apartment.

"Sorry," she said immediately. "My stuff is in such a

disaster. If you can believe it, I really haven't unpacked yet." She hurried to the passenger door and climbed in. "Amazingly the hiking boots, which I never wear, were in plain sight. But I've got a half dozen different jeans and I didn't think I'd ever locate one pair."

She was smiling brightly. Looking very young and cute, he thought. *Cute* was probably not a word that a librarian, or really any professional woman, would likely consider a compliment. But in her SMU T-shirt, with her hair pulled back in a ponytail, Scott thought she looked totally, unequivocally cute. He couldn't keep himself from grinning at her.

"Why would you have time to unpack?" he agreed. "I'm sure there is a lot to do, settling into your new job."

"Well, there is that," she admitted. "But honestly, at first I was thinking I wouldn't stay in your mother's house one day longer than necessary. But as it turns out, I love the apartment. It's so cozy...so homey."

"Thanks," Scott said, feeling a bit more pleased than was reasonable. "I made it that way on purpose. I'm a homey sort of guy."

"Well," she replied, "that's better than being a homely sort of guy, I suppose."

It was an attempt at humor, he told himself, not really a compliment. Scott wasn't particularly vain about his looks. But he did kind of want her to like them, so he let himself feel a little pleased with her comment.

"So how'd it go with James this afternoon?"

"Better. A little better, at least," she said. "I've worked up some plans and left them in plain sight for him to look over. I'm hoping that seeing it all laid out will help him prepare before we actually start moving anything. I guess if I come in tomorrow and they're ripped to shreds, I'll know he's still not onboard."

"Did you make copies?"

She nodded.

"It's hard to change," she admitted. "Even for people without his kind of challenges, it's hard. We all get so comfortable with even crappy things, we find it hard to give them up."

As she spoke the words, Scott was reminded of his long, unsatisfactory relationship with Stephanie. Long after all evidence that things could ever really work out for them, he'd clutched at straws that somehow, some way it would all be fine.

Scott paused at the stop sign before turning onto the highway out of town. "If you know this is the right thing to do," he said. "Then waiting for everyone or even anyone to get onboard may be a waste of time."

"Well, your mother said to give James a chance to be a part of it," D.J. replied. "So I'm going to really try to do that. I'm sure for most people in Verdant, James is as much a part of the library as any of the books on the shelf."

He *so* liked that about her. He liked that she was willing to accommodate the town characters and put up with all their assorted local quirks. She didn't want to just come in and change everything, do things her way. She wanted what was best for the library and the town. His mother had been right about her. He didn't know how she was right, but she was.

They reached the outskirts of town. In every direction, as far as the eye could see, wheat stood weary and ready in the field. To the right, on the far edge of the horizon, a long line of irrigation equipment edged the area like a trim of lace. Its current idleness was a welcome rest from the active, demanding role that it had played in nurturing the bounty around it.

"I'm excited," D.J. admitted a little breathlessly.

Her enthusiasm was contagious.

"So," he asked, in a voice that mimicked a documentary voice-over. "Are you ready to do your part to bring in the winter wheat from the bread basket of the nation, the economic engine of the American heartland?"

She laughed. The sound of it made the bottom drop out of his stomach like a thrill ride, which then settled solidly in his crotch. Who could have imagined that the librarian could have such a sexy laugh? Why hadn't he noticed it before? But he had. He knew that he'd heard it before.

With her eyes forward and her elbow propped in the window, she looked eager for the challenge, ready to face anything. He had thought her beautiful last night, so full of self-honesty and vulnerability. But she was even more so now, brimming with vitality and spirit.

She turned to catch him looking at her and gave him a big smile. "Okay, I have a question," she said.

"Of course you do," Scott said, feigning gravitas. "Novices to harvest always have questions. And librarians have the most questions of all."

"We surely do," D.J. confirmed. "And typically we look up the answers ourselves. But I'm hoping that in your lifetime on the plains you've gleaned enough facts to save me from having to pull up a search engine on my phone."

"Search not for a search engine. Although I can declare myself no agri-sage, as a longtime observer of these dirt dabblers, I will answer every farming fact I know."

His silly, stilted language seemed to amuse her.

"Thank you for your help, Wise One," she teased.

"Now tell me, why do you call this 'winter wheat' when it's hot enough to fry eggs on the dashboard."

"I suppose you're thinking it's because farmers are such contrary people," he said.

"That never crossed my mind."

"See, you're one of us already. Blind to each other's faults."

"Yes, I suppose so. Except for yours, which I see quite clearly."

"What? That's not possible. You've been living with my mother for weeks now. And that woman's mantra is that I am a *perfect* son."

"Unfortunately for you, she's not the only one who brought up your name."

It was all said in fun, just joking. But as soon as the words were out in the air, they were there. And she looked as surprised at uttering them as he was in having them spoken. He recalled D.J. as he'd seen her returning to the movie theater lobby, her face pale and her eyes furious. And there was nobody to blame but himself.

Scott cleared his throat. "You're thinking about Eileen," he said calmly, seriously.

The uneasy silence between them filled the vehicle before she was finally able to respond. "It's completely none of my business. Please forget that I ever mentioned it."

"No, no," he said, quickly. "I should explain about Eileen."

She waited as he unsuccessfully attempted to collect his thoughts. He grasped his rationale like will-o'-the-wisps. All of his motivations sounded like excuses. Yes, he'd been lonely. Certainly he was hurting. Yes, he'd had something to prove. But why that woman, why that relationship? Because it was available. Because it was there.

With a sigh of defeat he told her the truth, "I have no explanation about Eileen."

"You certainly don't owe me one."

"I know I don't. But I at least owe one to myself and I don't have it. It was a mistake. A very stupid, regrettable mistake. I'm grateful and lucky that it didn't cause any permanent repercussions."

"No permanent repercussions?" she repeated.

"Except for involving and embarrassing you, no, not much. There were rumors, of course. Eileen's husband either never heard them or didn't care."

Her brow furrowed. "What about your marriage? That seems like a fairly permanent repercussion."

"Oh, I was already divorced," he assured her quickly. "I never even looked twice at Eileen while I was still married."

Scott thought his words would make his actions look at least a little bit better. But in fact, the expression on her face showed even more disappointment than before. Her chin came up slightly as she focused her attention on the road ahead.

He wasn't sure what more he could say. It *really* wasn't any of her business. It happened years ago. He was single and the woman was willing. But it had been a self-destructive behavior and one that had shaken his self-respect. That was why he broke it off.

But he couldn't explain that to D.J. There was just too much to explain. It was way too long and far too complicated. And they were not even exactly quite dating.

So after driving along in silence for another mile, he turned left, heading up the section line toward their destination and picked up the subject that they'd left behind.

"They call it 'winter wheat' because it's planted right before the ground freezes. Then it lays there under the soil until spring. Then it sprouts out of the ground and grows to maturity by the middle of summer..."

631.2 Agriculture: Techniques, Equipment

The prospect of getting a look at the harvest up close had made D.J. uncharacteristically effusive. She tried to put the brakes on her enthusiasm, but she couldn't seem to manage it. It was like skipping school. She was leaving the everyday and headed to where the action was happening. It felt as if she'd been asked to the prom. Of course, the outfit was significantly different. But the look on Scott's face was appreciative enough that no wrist mum was required.

The lighthearted and chatty conversation as they left town was welcome. D.J. was thankful to be an introvert and very able to tolerate long periods by herself. But when enthused with a new project, like the library move, it was always so great to have another party who was interested enough to listen. She delightedly rattled on as they made their way through the narrow streets and neat lawns of town, across the bridge that straddled the swath of wooded green and into the golden fields that stretched on and on.

The scenery was compelling, but again and again her eyes were drawn back to the interior of the utilitarian van and the man at her side. She really liked him like this. Loose and friendly, with the glint of sun in his hair. She'd liked him last night, too. Last night, in the quiet, intimate darkness of the wheat, she'd felt safe and comforted. And that was so soothing.

But in the full light of day, he was more sexy than soothing. He was funny. And the banter was easy, almost flirty. He didn't mind talking about her. And he was amusingly unassuming when he talked about himself. But he also had no reticence in discussing other things entirely. D.J. simply enjoyed the conversation. She felt completely friendly and so relaxed. All the way up to the moment she put her foot in it.

"It's none of my business. Forget that I ever mentioned it."

But of course, that was impossible.

D.J. did give him some credit for not throwing up a wall of excuses. He'd thoughtlessly slept with the woman and regretted it. Everybody makes mistakes. D.J. truly understood that. She'd made a very, very similar mistake. Of course, the kicker for her was that she'd made it with him.

"I'm just grateful and lucky there weren't any permanent consequences."

D.J. felt her jaw drop. "What about your marriage? That seems like a fairly permanent repercussion," she corrected.

"Oh, I was already divorced," he assured her quickly. "I never even looked twice at Eileen while I was still married."

He said the words as if they represented a virtue. She heard from the mouth of his own mother that he'd been cheating. So if it wasn't with Eileen, then it was somebody else. Some other regrettable, forgettable, woman… just like herself.

Sadness tightened her throat.

Get a grip! she scolded herself. *You knew from the*

beginning that he's a player. It didn't bother you then.
Stop letting it bother you now.

Deliberately she turned her focus back to the landscape. There was an awkward couple of moments
between them, but eventually they went back to conversation that was more appropriate for casual acquain-
tances.

Chatting took a backseat to her interest when the
Browns' work-in-progress came into view. Somehow
the image that D.J. had pictured in her head was a big
wide field with a small cutting machine scurrying
around it, perhaps like a push mower doing the grass
at Arrowhead Stadium. In fact, the wheat was alive with
giant vehicles. In the distance, the combines were lined
up on a slight diagonal, three vehicles across. Tractors
pulling giant carts darted in and out among them. Next
to the road, two semitrucks waited.

Scott pulled over beneath a row of identically sized
trees growing at the fence line. They'd been planted
during the dustbowl to protect the field from soil ero-
sion. Today they provided the only shade on a hot summer day.

Scott and D.J. got out of the van. She stood next
to the front of the vehicle. Shading her eyes with her
hands, she watched the roar of machinery in the distance that was headed their way.

He opened the sliding door on the side of the van and
pulled one of the cardboard boxes filled with meals in
greasy white bags nearer to the edge. Then he eased
forward a huge multicolored ice chest.

"Do you need me to help?" she asked him.

"No, hungry people are usually pretty good at fend-
ing for themselves."

D.J. nodded.

"Look, here comes Jeannie. Maybe she'll give you a tour."

D.J. looked around, but didn't see a woman anywhere.

"She's on the tractor, pulling the bank-out wagon," he clarified.

At least D.J. knew what a tractor was. And one nearby had just brought a big cart of wheat alongside one of the trucks. Behind the tinted windshield of the tractor, the driver's gender was indistinguishable.

D.J. felt a surprising hand upon her waist and Scott stepped up beside her.

"Come on, I'll introduce you."

A large pipe on the side of the tractor's cart was being raised. A lot of care was being taken to get it a particular height and angle. After a couple of shouts back and forth with the tractor driver and the men standing around the truck, everybody seemed satisfied with the position.

There was one instant of complete silence followed by a pealing whine that quickly rolled into a solid roar.

D.J. startled.

To her surprise, the arm went even more protectively around her waist.

"The auger on that thing is pretty noisy," Scott admitted.

Getting closer didn't make it any quieter. The driver was inside the tractor cab, her attention focused upon the spigot of wheat now flowing from the load in her cart into the transport of the semi.

"Hi, Jeannie!" Scott hollered, punctuating his words with a full arm wave.

She turned to return the greeting.

D.J. noted that Scott kept his left arm at the small of

her back. She wasn't likely to fall in her hiking boots, so she wasn't sure what that was about. And she wasn't the only one who noticed. But at least the woman didn't look jealous or angry.

Eagerly she climbed down from the tractor cab, pulling her gloves off as she walked toward them.

"You're the new librarian, huh?" she hollered over the din. "I'm Jeannie."

D.J. took the young woman's hand.

Jeannie was wearing jeans and a baggy sun-protection shirt. Her blond ponytail was poking through the back opening above the feed cap's Velcro closure.

"It's great to meet you," D.J. yelled in response, over the continued roar of the unloading auger. "I've heard lots about you."

There was lots of nodding and smiling among the three of them, but it was far too noisy for any real conversation.

The three stood closely together. Scott leaned forward. "Looks like you're coming toward the end," he said.

Jeannie nodded. "I'm not sure we'll get it done tonight. But tomorrow for sure," she said. "Two of the combines already moved to the next job."

Her words seemed to make sense to Scott.

Jeannie leaned closer to D.J. for a clarification. "We contract with custom cutters."

D.J. had no idea what that meant, but she nodded. The circumstances did not lend themselves to long explanations.

Even more abruptly than it began, the roar ceased. The tractor engine was still running, but it was a healthy purr by comparison. The suddenly more reasonable noise level gave D.J. an inexplicable desire to laugh.

When Jeannie and Scott actually did, she was happy to join in.

"So it's even nicer to meet you when we don't have to scream at each other," Jeannie said.

D.J. agreed.

"We brought food from the Brazier," Scott said. "Do you want to get something to eat while it's still hot?"

"No, I'll wait," she answered, before turning to D.J. "Would you like to go out with me? See the action up close."

"Yeah, I would," D.J. said.

Jeannie nodded "We'll be back," she said to Scott.

D.J. shot him a quick look. He waved her on.

"But save us some dinner," Jeannie added. "Working women get hungry."

D.J. followed her to what she would have thought of as the driver's side of the tractor. There were four ladderlike steps up to the door of the cab.

"Follow me," Jeannie told her.

D.J. mimicked the other woman's use of the rail. Inside the cab was cool and relatively roomy. The operator's chair was in the middle of the space, with screens and levers and a million buttons in the area to the right of it.

Jeannie offered her a much smaller flip-down seat just inside the door.

"Buckle up," Jeannie cautioned. "I'm not about to turn this thing over, but safety has to be big if I'm taking on a civilian."

Snapped in, D.J. anticipated a bumpy ride across the field. It was a lot smoother than she would have imagined.

"So this thing we're pulling is called a grain cart

or a bank-out wagon," Jeannie explained. "We use it to transfer the wheat from the combine to the trucks."

D.J. noticed that they didn't drive straight across the field to the combines, but followed a sidelined route.

"If the cutting is close to the road or the ground is really good, we can just go straight into the truck. But you can see that having a bunch of semitrailers out here in the field would not be the best thing."

D.J. could certainly believe that. With no specific path or trail, the tractor went through highs and lows that would have challenged a bigger, heavier vehicle.

Jeannie drove the tractor with confidence, as if she were on a paved road headed to the supermarket in her family car.

"So I guess you've been doing this all your life," D.J. said.

"Not really," Jeannie answered, giving her a smile. "My parents were, well they *are,* big believers in gender-based division of labor. There's men's work and women's work. And everybody should stick to their own."

"But you didn't agree."

Jeannie shrugged. "I did. I did for years. For me, harvest meant cooking and cleaning up. It was like serving a huge holiday meal three times a day. And all of the pots and pans and dishes associated with that."

"Ugh."

Jeannie nodded. "I always wanted to be out here where everything was happening. But instead of a nice air-conditioned tractor, I was sweating next to a hot stove."

She joked as she said the words, but D.J. could hear the truthfulness behind them.

"What changed?"

"Lots of things," she admitted. "These days we rely

more on hired labor. Those contracts don't include furnished meals. There is a much larger availability of fast food, restaurants and cafes. Workers are not going to go hungry. And then, I changed a lot of things for myself."

For a moment D.J. thought Jeannie was not going to elaborate and she was not about to pry. But surprisingly, she continued.

"When I got divorced, I was pretty raw," she admitted. "I didn't know what to believe in anymore. I started looking at everything in my life and asking, is there a reason why I'm doing this, beyond other people expecting it?"

Jeannie shrugged. "Sometimes really good things come from very bad ones," she said. "I realized that what mattered to me was my kids and my self-respect. If it didn't threaten either of those, I could pretty much do what I wanted."

It seemed like a relatively simple philosophy, but D.J. could tell that it had been hard-won.

As they approached the combines, the noise inside the cab got too much for casual conversation. The huge cutting machines loomed above them as Jeannie brought her tractor right alongside. The two vehicles went along side-by-side for a couple of moments.

"I have to get my speed a perfect match for the combine," she hollered out to D.J. "A couple of mph can mess things up completely. And you don't want to even know what happens if I were to clip the cutting wheel."

D.J. had no idea what she meant, but she did note that the combine continued to cut through the field as if nothing else was going on. But its big orange pipe began moving upward to hang over the cart they pulled. Jeannie glanced repeatedly in the rearview mirror, but mostly she was concentrating on her pace and the ground in front of her. D.J. watched as the grain began to pour into the cart. The sound was near deafening as the steady stream of wheat piled up.

"How's it look?" Jeannie called out.

"Amazing," D.J. answered.

Out the back window, she could watch the big green wagon slowly fill as the two vehicles stayed perfectly in sync. Like two dancers, perfectly matched, they continued side-by-side along the ups and downs of the field.

Abruptly, the flow ceased as if someone had turned off the tap. The combine's auger pipe slowly moved back into place and once it was clear, Jeannie gave a little honk and wave. The tractor's pace slowed immediately. As the combine moved on and away, Jeannie made a wide-angle turn and headed back toward the area where they had come.

As the noisy cutting receded in the distance, D.J. spoke. "I can't believe the combines don't even stop to load the carts."

"Sometimes they have to," Jeannie said. "If the cart driver is inexperienced or the ground is too rough. But it does save time if they can off-load while the cutting continues."

"Well, you were great," D.J. assured her.

"Thanks," she said. "The combine holds about 350 gallons of diesel. If they only have to stop to fill up, the work goes a whole lot faster."

"Yeah, I guess so."

"Of course, nothing ever goes that smooth," Jeannie said. "It's life, after all, so there is always some breakdown or screw-up or an equipment failure. But while things are working, you try to keep them working. And when problems come up, well, I try really hard not to be the one who's caused the mess."

D.J. laughed.

"Listen, I wanted to ask you something…"

There was clearly hesitation in Jeannie's voice.

"Sure," D.J. answered.

"When we were introduced you said you'd heard a lot about me." Jeannie's brow was furrowed. "Was that from Scott or…or Amos?"

D.J. pondered the question for a few seconds. Her words had been more a nicety than a statement of fact. From Jeannie's expression, however, the inquiry was serious.

"Honestly, I think the person who's said the most to me about you would be Suzy."

She seemed momentarily stunned, before bursting into laughter. "Of course it would be Suzy," she said. "I should have realized that. Duh. You guys work together and she can't shut up if her life depended on it."

"She's never said anything bad about you," D.J. assured her.

"No, of course not. I guess I was wondering…well, I was wondering about the guys."

"The guys?"

"Yeah, I mean, well, the last couple of days I've been thinking that maybe Amos is interested in me."

"Really?"

"Yeah, at first I thought, it's crazy, right? I guess we've all grown so used to the idea that Amos…that Amos can't feel like that anymore. That he doesn't get interested, but maybe he does."

"What about you?" D.J. asked. "Are you *interested* in him?"

Jeannie shot her a funny face with tongue out and eyes crossed. "Who knows?" she answered. "I'm so horny these days that anything in pants looks good to me. But I have to think about my kids first."

"Amos seems to like kids," D.J. pointed out.

"He does," Jeannie said. "Anyway, I need to take it slow. Although I'd love to jump his bones."

D.J. feigned a sigh. "It's too bad you can't do both."

"I would if I didn't have kids," Jeannie told her. "I was such a goody-two-shoes in high school. The only girl in class having less sex than me was Stevie Rossiter and even that's questionable now, 'cause nobody really knows when she and Vern became a couple."

"Well, don't look to me for advice," D.J. said. "I was the last virgin among all my friends."

Jeannie smiled at her. "I bet you waited for somebody special."

D.J. felt herself blushing. "No, I waited to make a fool of myself."

Jeannie laughed. "Love does make fools of us all."

D.J. would have corrected her assumption. It had not been love. She would have disabused her of that notion completely. But they'd arrived at the area where the semi was waiting. Jeannie had work to do. And that necessitated that D.J. keep her recollections and rationalizations to herself.

636.6 Animal Husbandry

Viv made her way home from the Porters' when she couldn't bear to stay a moment longer. Cora had held up well all through the funeral. But afterward, she had come apart. She was so very lonely. And so very angry.

Viv understood that. If anyone could sympathize with the hollow unfairness of having to continue on without the most important person in your life beside you, she could. But it annoyed her more than she was willing to admit that Cora completely refused to see Dutch's side of it. Certainly it was a bad choice on his part to end it so dramatically. Gunshot wounds were so messy. And there was almost no room for doubt that it was a deliberate act. Viv did fault him for that. But his motives were altruistic.

That thought stopped her. She recognized it as a lie. There was an altruistic component to it, of course. He hadn't wanted to burden his wife, physically and emotionally. He hadn't wanted his children to watch him slowly fade away. He hadn't wanted the costs of caring for him to soak up all the nest egg that he'd put by.

Those things were undoubtedly true. But Viv was honest enough with herself to recognize that wasn't all of it. A once vital, healthy man did not want to spend the last years of his life in and out of the hospital like a revolving door. He was exhausted with taking medi-

cation and sick of spending his days watching television. He saw absolutely nothing good on his horizon.
For all the years he'd lived, he'd made his own way, followed his own path. Been responsible for himself. His
life had gone out of his control. And this final act had
given him that control back.

She unlocked the back door and went inside her
home. It was dark and empty. She had not expected
otherwise. With any luck at all, Scott would be out making a move on his lovely librarian.

If only those two would get on with it!

But even as she could see her plan coming to fruition,
she felt alone. Only she could see the whole picture.
Only she understood how well it was all working out.

That's why people write suicide notes, she thought
to herself. It wasn't merely an explanation to those left
behind. There was a need to share the process, vent the
successes and setbacks. This was one of the biggest de-
cisions she'd ever faced and the only one that did not
allow for talking it out with friends or family.

Suddenly, she did not want to be in this empty house
by herself. She picked up her purse, but there was no
place to go. The whole town was in on the harvest. She
couldn't so much as scare up a bingo game.

She set her purse back down and dragged her keys
out. Poor Mr. Dewey was probably bored to death in
his prison cage. She went outside, climbed the stairs to
the apartment and let herself inside. The dog was enthusiastic about getting let out of the crate and eagerly
followed Viv back down to her own home.

"The truth is, Mr. Dewey," she told him. "You're
about the only friend I have on this deal. And the only
reason I can talk to you about it is that I know you won't
be spreading the story around."

She went to the storage beneath the old stairs and dug out a couple of puppy treats for her friend.

"It's not like I came up with this all on my own," she told the dog. "I guess I was starting to think that my life was over. And I really find the whole 'new life' thing just exhausting. But I couldn't leave Scott. Leanne has her career and her husband, but Scott…well, he only has his disappointments."

Mr. Dewey quickly gobbled down the pieces of fake steak that she'd given him and trotted after her as she headed for the living room.

Viv seated herself on the couch. Mr. Dewey jumped up to take a seat beside her. Typically, he would have relaxed into a nice cozy ball that encouraged her to pet him. Tonight, however, he sat up, looking at her expectantly as if he knew that her need to talk was greater than his need for a rubdown.

"So I would have never considered it," she explained. "Before I had the dream."

Viv eased back into the cushions of the couch, reveling in her memory.

"You know, I've never been one of those people who believe in visits from the afterlife," she said. "I'm a pragmatic Presbyterian. If you're alive you're here. If you're dead, you're not. And that's the end of it. No ghosts, no séances, no messages from the other side."

Mr. Dewey's silence was tacit agreement.

"But then about five months ago, I had this dream. I was walking through the grocery store and who did I run into? John." Viv laughed delightedly at her own remembrance. "I almost didn't recognize him. It wasn't John, sick John, dying John. It was my John when we were young. He still had all his hair and it was as ginger as it had been in high school. He was standing so tall and he looked so healthy." Viv sighed heavily. "I was so glad to see him and I talked to him and he talked to me. But, damn it, I can't remember anything that we said." She shook her head in disgust. "Except that he told me that Scott needed the new librarian and that I would know her when I saw her."

Viv reached out to Mr. Dewey, scratching him behind the ears. "That's where you come in," she said. "I looked through a hundred resumes on the Library Association website but the minute I saw D.J., I just knew."

The dog shook his head in reaction to the scratching but then immediately came back for more.

"Not that I relied on intuition completely," Viv continued. "After that disaster with Scott's marriage, I hardly trust my own judgment. So I hired a private detective."

She took Mr. Dewey's face in both her hands and bent forward to go nose to nose with him to speak in baby-talk fashion.

"Yes, I set a gumshoe on your mama's trail. Yes, I did. I really did."

Viv set back and spoke more conversationally. "I felt like I had to. She might have been involved with someone else or whatever. Anyway, she got a clean bill of health. Even better, she has the kind of lonely past that a man like Scott could do a lot to heal. I'm truly happy for both of them."

Mr. Dewey had settled into her lap, but continued to look at her with eyes that were almost sad.

"I'm happy for them," she repeated. "And I wish they would get on with it, so I could be happy for myself. I want to be young and strong and in the arms of John again."

642.2 Meals and Table Service

Once Jeannie had off-loaded her bank-out wagon, she and D.J. climbed out of the tractor and she offered her vehicle to another driver.

"I'm going to eat a quick bite, if you can catch a load for me."

Together the two women walked over to the van. There were several people standing around eating, but the two that captured D.J.'s attention were leaning against the front fender. One was rough and stocky. The other was long and lean and heart-stopping handsome, but they were both smiling.

D.J. felt a pang of regret so strong it was corporeal. If only she had met him first in this place. If only she had met him now. If only his past was a mystery to be forgotten. If only her own were free of the cynicism and disappointment that she couldn't shake.

Amos held up a sack he'd stowed on the bumper. "I saved one for you, Jeannie," he said. "This crew descends on anything edible like a swarm of locusts. And you're looking so slim these days, I worry that you might pass out from hunger."

D.J. was pretty sure that the curvy blonde would not, on her best day, think of herself as "slim," but she accepted his statement as if it were a kind of awkward compliment.

"Uh, thanks," she said.

She took the bag from him, blushing. The bright color in her cheeks was a match to that on Amos's neck. It was obvious that the two were nervously, tentatively trying out the idea of a twosome.

D.J. was hopeful for them. Deliberately, she moved to stand on the far side of Scott, giving the couple as much space as the area allowed.

Scott telegraphed his agreement on the couple before giving D.J. a feigned little frown.

"Sorry," he said. "I know you went for a ride around the field, but the actual food is for the working people."

"Okay," she answered. "I'm good."

"Oh, well if you've been *very good...*"

From behind his back he pulled out a greasy bundle wrapped in white paper. "I did manage to get hold of one burger," he said. "But we'll have to share."

Jeannie was already diving into hers. "Mmm, this... good," she related with her mouth full. "Don't pass it up."

Scott unwrapped the sandwich and held it up to her. "Do you trust me to divide it up, or do you want the honors?"

Some evil sprite must have taken over her brain, either that or the crazy persona last seen on a beach in Texas.

D.J. leaned forward and took a giant greasy bite. Hot meat, sour pickles, the crunch of lettuce and tomato, the tang of mustard. She took it all in and licked her lips.

Scott's eyes were wide.

"Mmm, Jeannie's right. It is good."

D.J. expected him to take a bite out of his side. To her surprise he turned the burger and put his mouth exactly on the spot where hers had been. She almost choked. His eyes never left hers as he sank his teeth into it.

Her stomach was now completely full of butterflies. No room at all for even the slightest nibble. But when he held the burger toward her again, she knew it was a challenge. If she demurred, that was the end of it.

Reasonably, she should want that to be the end of it. Her tummy continued to flutter. Her heart was pounding. And the memory of what this man could do with his lips caused her skin to tingle.

Be Dorothy the librarian, her sensible mind warned her. *Plain, boring Dorothy will be completely safe from him.*

But plain Dorothy faded into obscurity as the wanton creature from the beach began a series of tiny, toothy nibbles upon the place where his mouth had been. She closed her eyes as her only attempt to hide. When she opened them, he was looking straight at her and there was no mistaking what was in his own. The burger disappeared from between them, but his gaze never wavered. He was looking at her as if he'd kissed her already. She trembled. She knew she should look away. But she could not.

"So, D.J., how was your tractor ride?"

The question came from Amos and was startling, as she'd completely forgotten that they were not alone. She physically and emotionally took a step back.

"Oh, it was great. Jeannie was great. And it was so exciting to be out there next to that giant combine. Wow."

Amos nodded. "Yeah, it's pretty cool," he agreed. "From the time we're little boys, guys are always crazy for giant vehicles. But it's surprising how many women love the whole big machine thing."

As soon as the words were out, Amos obviously recognized the unwitting double entendre. He opened his mouth to try to pull the comment back, but was struck speechless.

A full half minute of embarrassed silence dropped down on the group like a heavy blanket. Amos looked like a deer in the headlights. D.J. couldn't even sneak a glance at Scott.

Suddenly Jeannie broke the spell with a big guffaw. "That's the truth, Amos. Us gals are always game for a big machine. Right, D.J.?"

She could feel the flame in her cheeks, but she pushed through it.

"Right," she said. "You know how we women think, size matters."

Everybody ended up laughing. D.J. counted it a plus that Jeannie had been so quick to jump in for Amos. He needed somebody to be in his corner. And a woman who could do that in little things, might be handy to have around in more rugged occasions.

The foursome continued to chat and eat for several minutes. Scott mentioned D.J.'s plans for rearranging the library and responding to their interest, relayed far more about the project than probably anybody but her would ever want to know.

"It makes me kind of eager to get back," Amos said.

"Anything that would make the place seem less like a dungeon has to be an improvement," Jeannie agreed. "It's so bleak inside, tearing it down would have been my first option."

"Oh, but I love that building," D.J. said. "It has the potential to be very special. You'll see. It's going to be wonderful."

"Well, if you're excited, we're excited," Amos said.

D.J. watched the blush blossom in Jeannie's cheeks again. She clearly liked being fifty percent of Amos's "we."

When the semi Amos was driving was ready to be loaded, he reluctantly begged off. Jeannie's tractor returned, as well. And then it was D.J. and Scott, standing alone, together.

He exchanged pleasantries with other people that passed and introduced D.J. to a few folks, including Jeannie's dad. But when the food was all gone and the work proceeding at its typical breakneck pace, it was time to go.

They gathered up the trash and stowed it in the back of the van before climbing in their seats.

"Thanks for bringing me out here," D.J. told him. "It's pretty cool."

He smiled that wonderful, hot guy smile at her. "If you're planning to be a part of this community," he said, "this has to be the place that you start. Wheat is the heart of who we are. At least for now."

"For now?"

Scott nodded. "Even out on the prairies, the world changes," he said. "We've got more natural gas drilling every day. And even the driest of dryland cultivation requires water. With the droughts of the last few years and the prospect of climate change, lots of farmers have been looking at their hold card. Half of this topsoil blew away in the dustbowl. We know what the weather can do. There are no guarantees."

D.J. thought about that as she surveyed the landscape outside the vehicle.

"It's hard to imagine the countryside without the wheat."

Scott agreed. "Sometimes it's hard to remember that

much of it had never seen a plow until a hundred and fifty years ago. Things change. We have to, too. We can't cling to the past, even if we wanted to."

That was true. But it was hard.

"I guess it's like the stacks in the library," she said. "I'm sure that rearranging is going to be the best thing that's ever happened to the place, but the mere upheaval of it is so upsetting to James."

"Yeah," Scott said. "I sometimes think of James as like the magnified version of the rest of us. We fault him for freaking about relocating shelves. But when the normal routines of our own lives get disrupted, we feel totally justified in flipping out."

D.J. lowered her chin to frown at him. "I can't imagine you flipping out. You seem so cool. So in control of everything."

He laughed. "Me?"

"Absolutely," she said. "You're like George Clooney walking around Vegas getting ready to rob the casino."

His jaw dropped. "You've got to be kidding, right?"

"You have that confidence," she answered. "Like you've got everything under control."

"I'm in control of nothing," he said. "You're the one with the professional demeanor. You've got everything marked and cataloged. No errors allowed."

"I wish!"

"Do you?" he asked. "My dad used to tell me that my mistakes were more important than my successes. The longer things go right, the less you learn. It's the screw-ups that teach and mold character."

"He sounds like he might be right."

"I think he was," Scott said and then added with a grin. "And he lived long enough to get to watch me screw up a number of times."

D.J. found herself laughing with him. She wondered how she could feel so relaxed. He was *the* hot guy and he was sitting mere inches away from her.

The afternoon sun was pouring in through the passenger window, so she was forced to turn her head in his direction. She watched his facial expressions as he talked to her. Noted the self-assured movement of his body as he drove.

Those perfect teeth between generous lips. Masculine shoulders. Lean, muscled arms. She sneaked a glance at his jean-covered thighs.

Don't look at his crotch! she warned herself.

She didn't need to look, she remembered it all too well.

Her insides were beset with butterflies. And little flashes of unexpected recall of that night long ago when he put his hands there or he put his lips where.

D.J. sat up straighter and hung an elbow out the passenger window. It was a comfortable position that offered the extra advantage of pouring cool outside air onto her flushed face.

She thought about their shared snack and imagined that the taste of it had been, in part, the taste of him. D.J. tried to keep her eyes forward as she was swamped with unwelcome sexual longing.

You're boring Dorothy. Be boring Dorothy, she admonished herself for the second time that day. But even boring Dorothy couldn't quite forget the things they had done and how it had felt.

She sneaked one more quick, guilty glance at him. This time their eyes met. And for an instant, there was something…something totally familiar that she would have sworn she'd never seen.

Suddenly he slammed down on the brake and the

van skidded slightly in the ruts of the dirt road. The momentum thrust D.J. forward and then back into her seat. Scott unhooked his seat belt and leaned toward her.

"I have to do this," he said, one instant before his lips came down upon her own.

His mouth was firm but tender and the kiss fit to her perfectly, exactly as she remembered. How did he do that? That slight, slight tug that seemed to pull away all her inhibitions. She moaned against him. And that response allowed him to deepen the kiss. The sensuousness spread like hot molasses down her throat, across her breasts, along her ribs and between her thighs. It was the desire of the love-starved. Eight long years she had needed this touch, this man. He was here in her arms now. She wanted him. She wanted all of him and she wanted it desperately. She didn't remember wrapping her arms around his neck, but became vaguely aware of her fingers buried in his hair. The texture and feel so familiar, yet so long withheld from her.

I need you! I want you! her brain was screaming at him. But she was not about to deter her tongue from its current pursuit to something as mundane as speech. She ran her hand up his jean-clad thigh to ask the question she didn't put into words. She found her answer, thick and hard and undisguisable even in thick denim.

She tried to press forward, to move against him.

She was restrained by her seat belt. The van must know, even if she didn't, that she was headed into a possible destruction.

Their lips parted.

"Wow," he whispered against her cheek. "That was good."

"Yeah," she agreed.

"That didn't feel like a first kiss."

Danger alerts finally sounded in D.J.'s brain.

"I don't know what you mean."

"I feel like I've kissed you a million times and it was always like that."

The click as he released her seat belt drowned out the noise of warning in her head. He pulled her into his arms and onto his lap. D.J. made no effort to resist. In truth, she allowed herself to revel in the taste of him, the feel of his skin, the trail of his hands upon her. From deep in his throat sounds of pleasure roiled up and boiled over. It heightened her urgency, but he was not in any rush. He took his time, as if kissing was not a signpost on the path to pleasure, but a pleasure all of its own.

He was just so good at it. And when she held her mouth against his, she was good at it, too.

His lips left hers and began a journey along her jawline to her ear and then down the length of her throat. At first he gave her only hot little pecks, but then he began to offer tiny nips of her skin that sizzled through her. That long-ago night of passion suddenly seemed like yesterday and the vivid memories of what he could do with his tongue and his teeth. She wanted his mouth on her ankles. She wanted his mouth on her spine. She wanted his mouth on her breasts. She wanted his mouth between her thighs.

She moaned aloud with the desire of it and tugged up her T-shirt to try to get his attention. She would have torn off her bra, but he didn't give her time. He slid a hand between her legs from the back and raised her up. Allowing him both a close encounter with some steaming denim and her nipples at lip level. He bit her through her bra. Her cry had nothing to do with pain. She was desperate, desperate to have him. He seemed determined to take his time. She both loved it and could hardly bear it.

"I want you. I want you," she pleaded.

She didn't know if he heard. At that moment the loud trumpet of a semitruck's air horn blared at them.

He cursed, glancing into the rearview mirror.

He practically tossed her into the passenger seat, before slipping the gearshift into low and moving the van to the edge of the road.

D.J. was pulling her shirt down over the damp cups of her bra as the truck passed, Amos at the wheel.

"He didn't see anything," Scott assured her. He kept his eyes forward, apparently concentrating on the dust left in the truck's wake. "Nothing to worry about. He didn't see a thing."

D.J. could hardly get her mind around worrying if they'd been seen. Sexual need still zizzed through her body like electricity. And the aching emptiness inside her was almost painful. It took a couple of moments for the inappropriateness of her situation became clear. She had been practically humping a man in the middle of a farm road. So much for the well-behaved, professional librarian.

She realized that Scott was attempting to regain his composure. She determined to do the same.

"He didn't see anything," Scott repeated. "I'm sure he didn't see anything."

"No," D.J. agreed. "There was nothing really to see. It was a kiss, nothing more."

"Right."

A buzzing sound erupted in Scott's pocket. He dug out his cell phone.

"It's a text from Amos."

D.J. met his eyes before he held it out for her to read.

Get a room!

D.J. stared at the words on the phone for one long moment, her brain racing with a million things to say or to do. Finally, unexpectedly, a small giggle bubbled up from inside her and she laughed.

After a few shocked seconds, Scott did, too.

657.4 Accounting

Kissing D.J. had been pretty spectacular. After the untimely interruption of the semi, Scott had been torn between pulling her back into his arms or offering a sincere apology. Ultimately, he chose neither path. She was so embarrassed she couldn't meet his eyes. But she hadn't slapped his face or burst into tears. Both of which might be possible reactions. She had laughed. The uptight librarian had laughed.

Scott had wanted to kiss her. He'd wanted to kiss her for a long time. And the sight of her out in the sunlight, looking so approachable and relaxed, had been encouraging enough. But the burger biting, that had been too sexy to be ignored.

"She couldn't have meant it that way," he muttered to himself the next morning as he made his way to work.

He'd gotten up early thinking he might follow his mother's example and invite D.J. for breakfast. Even before seven, her car was already gone. Scott reassured himself that she wasn't hiding from him, she was simply hurrying to get started at the library.

Still, he worried. What must she think? He did not come on to women like that. Maybe it was his easygoing nature or those teenage years with Stephanie as his girlfriend, but he was never really aggressive. Even in his affair with Eileen, he'd let her make the first move.

Except for his one-nighter in South Padre, he'd never really chosen to call the shots. That night he'd been completely intent on proving himself by pleasing her. He'd put them both through their paces. He'd snapped his fingers and she'd toed the mark. Roll over. Sit up and beg. Everything but play dead.

At that memory, Scott let out a long whistle through his lips. That was totally what last night had been about. D.J. reminded him of Sparkle. Holding her, kissing her, it had brought back all those feelings. In fact, D.J. was lucky Amos had come by when he did. A few more minutes and Scott might have had her bent over in the back of the van.

Now that was a pleasant thought to start his morning.

Scott unlocked the drugstore and barely got the lights on before Suzy Grandfeldt showed up.

"So, is it true?" she asked, eagerly.

"Is what true?"

"The hottest new romance in town," she said, almost giggling with delight.

Scott wanted to groan aloud. Amos was supposed to be his best friend. Why on earth would he spread gossip about him? And to Suzy. It would have been more discreet to take out a radio ad.

"I don't know what you're talking about," Scott said firmly.

"Oh, come on. You're bound to know something. Earl said the two are practically in each other's pockets. Every time he's stuck waiting for his truck to load, she's jumping off her tractor to whisper something in his ear."

"Oh, you mean Amos and Jeannie."

"Well, who else could I mean?" Suzy asked. "So come on, give. I need information."

"I don't know anything that you don't know," Scott

assured her. "They do seem to be friendly. But they've known each other forever."

"Friendly?" She made a sound of disgust at the word. "They'd better up their game if they're stuck at that. Honestly, I'd practically given up on Amos. He just seemed like he'd never snap out of it. And Jeannie always seemed to have her sights set on you."

"Me?" Scott pretended complete ignorance.

"Ridiculous, right," Suzy agreed, too readily he thought. "That could never work."

"Still, Amos has suffered a lot," he told her. "There are losses in life that you just don't 'snap out of.'"

"Of course, there are," Suzy said. "Look at you, still wounded after all these years. But I was thinking that Amos had no heart left inside him at all. If Jeannie's found it, everybody in town will want to know."

As if making sure that all were informed were a noble quest, Suzy continued to sit drinking coffee at the counter all morning, spreading the word to every person who came in.

Ultimately, Scott got so worried that he went back into the pharmacy and called Amos to warn him. He'd already heard.

"It's not bad, really," he assured Scott. "I do think Jeannie is interested. But if she's not, this gives her an opportunity to push back against the rumors without either of us risking a friendship."

"I'm not sure stuff works that way," Scott told him.

"Yeah, well not all of us can strip down the librarian at the side of the road."

"I…we… Nothing happened."

"Well, sorry to hear that. Next time maybe you shouldn't make your move on a public road."

"Look, you manage Jeannie on your own. I was giving you a heads up, that's all."

"A heads up?" he answered. "I guess that's a good description of you yesterday, huh?"

"Amos…" There was warning in Scott's tone.

His friend laughed. "Hey, you'll get no grief from me. I'm all for it. And here's my free advice. Don't back off. D.J. could be very good for you."

"You don't know what you're talking about."

"Oh, yeah? I know more than you think. I only caught a glimpse inside that steamed-up van but you two weren't playing Keep Away. I've been on dozens of double dates with you and Stephanie where the only game going on in the backseat was Parcheesi. I know the difference."

Slowly the drugstore cleared out as workers headed back to the fields. Scott filled a few prescriptions and waited on customers looking for antihistamines and cough suppressants. Grain dust was in the air and even within a closed cab, those who were susceptible were getting the itchy throats and runny noses that were a part of the season.

By midafternoon, everyone had cleared out and there was almost nothing left to do. Scott found himself pacing back and forth like a caged animal. He knew exactly where he wanted to be and it was not alone within the premises of Sanderson Drug.

With the previous day as a template, he transferred the business phone to his cell and left the number on the front door as he locked it. He drove down the street and around the corner toward Verdant Public Library. For all he knew, James could be having another meltdown. And even if he wasn't, the two of them couldn't move that library by themselves. D.J. might need him.

The word had come to mind innocuously, but there was something lusty in the thought of her needs.

With that thought haunting him, Scott parked the van and made his way from the gleaming sunshine of blue-sky summer into the dark, gloomy gray library. But the darkest, most depressing of buildings could be brightened by the sight of his librarian.

To Scott's surprise, however, the circulation desk was being manned by a homely eight-year-old who had her nose in a book.

"Hi, you must be Ashley."

The girl's eyes narrowed warily. "What do you want?" she asked.

Scott wasn't sure he was ready to state that. Fortunately, he didn't have to. At that moment, D.J. appeared from within the stacks.

"Hi," she said. He noticed the blush in her cheeks. He wanted to grab her and kiss all that shyness away.

"I came to see if I could help," he told her instead. "Is everything still a go?"

As if on cue, somewhere deep in the shelving a book slammed shut abruptly.

"I think we're on track," she answered, more loudly than was strictly necessary. "James has added some improvements to the plan. It's such a help to have someone onboard with such a thorough knowledge of the collection."

Scott knew that her words weren't meant for him, but he was happy to play her foil. Or whatever role she might want to give him.

"I'm here and I'm yours," he told her. "Tell me what I can do."

"Serious?"

"Absolutely."

"Okay, what I'm doing is assigning a number to every range, every shelf and to every set of books on each shelf. So that we can get them from where they are, to where they need to be in two moves."

Scott, who was accustomed to strict organization in his own place of work, quickly caught on to what she had in mind and, using the plan that she'd laid out, helped get the numbers where they needed to be. It was more busy than mind-boggling as the two of them worked together. He watched her relax into it as she had at the harvest. D.J. clearly enjoyed what she did and was excited about what she hoped could be accomplished.

The tasks he was given did not require collaboration, but he managed to make every possible excuse to pose a question, discuss a problem or simply pass by her in the aisle. It was fun working together. He knew he was seeing her at her best. And he was grateful that she could see him on a turf that was unthreatening.

And he was glad he was there to help. James might be tacitly onboard with the change, but he was not lifting a finger to effect it. He was slamming books on a relatively frequent basis and scurrying out of sight whenever Scott came around the corner.

Ashley, on the other hand, was apparently having a glorious time at the circulation desk, charged with checking out books and answering the telephone. Since no one came in and the phone didn't ring, she was able to devote herself completely to reading, and to do it in the most comfortable chair in the building.

When Scott's stomach began to growl, he remembered that he'd not bothered with lunch. But he ignored the fact, unwilling to give up the pleasure of being in D.J.'s company even for a few minutes. He worked on.

attaching the numbers to the front of the left-most volume on each shelf.

The time passed very quickly and it wasn't until Ashley announced that she was leaving that either of them realized how late it had gotten.

"You must be getting very tired of this," she said to him.

"I think, if I just keep at it another few minutes, I can get this part done," he answered.

He knew he'd said the right thing. The two of them worked on until nearly dark. By the time the last tag was in place, it seemed as if even James had given up and gone home.

"I can't believe we got all this done," D.J. said. "I planned on at least two days for this part of it."

"I think we *have* been working on this for at least two days," Scott answered, teasing. "I'm hungry enough that it may have been a week."

"I'm hungry, too," she answered. "But mostly I just want to go home and soak in the bath."

Scott was tempted to ask if he could help with that, too. Wisely, he refrained from flirty repartee.

"I've got an idea," he told her instead. "Why don't you go have your nice, long soak and I will cook supper for you."

"I couldn't let you do that."

"I want to."

"But you've already volunteered way too many hours."

"And I'm hungry. I'm going to eat anyway, so why shouldn't I feed us both?" he said. "Besides, somebody has got to cook all that food that my mother is collecting."

She tried again to refuse, but fortunately she was too

tired to put up much of a fight. She locked up and he followed her back to the house.

He got caught by the train at the railroad crossing and spent his waiting moments second-guessing himself. He shouldn't push too hard. She probably really needed some time away from him. He remembered how Stephanie needed space, needed to be alone. But D.J. wasn't Stephanie. And with Stephanie, he'd found their apart time to be welcome. There was nothing welcoming about not being with D.J.

He was sure the farm gods were smiling down on him when he arrived at his mother's house to see the combines working off in the distance.

Scott went in the back door. His mother was in the sitting area watching TV, the little black dog in her lap.

"I'm fixing dinner for D.J.," he announced, fully expecting to be forced to play twenty questions.

"That's a lovely idea," she said.

He began pulling the produce from his own garden out of the refrigerator before adding, "We're going to eat upstairs on the deck."

"It's a perfect night for it," she replied. "Perfect."

662.5 Explosives, Fuels Technology

D.J. loved her bath. She loved a long soak in the tub. It was her oasis from everything in the world outside. She discovered that upon this occasion, however, even in gloriously hot water, she was simply too skittery to sit still.

She quickly scrubbed the workday from her skin. But when she leaned back to relax, the events of the last few days crowded into her thoughts. Scott. Everything seemed to be about Scott. She so appreciated his help in the library. James was coming around, but he would never be a great right hand. Scott took on whatever mundane task she needed with almost as much enthusiasm for the end result as she had herself.

She liked his company. He was funny and cheerful. He'd been the friend she'd needed amid the anonymity of the wheat hideout when she'd blurted out her family secrets. He'd been the helping hand so welcome today at the library. And yesterday...yesterday he had been the lover that she remembered from her night of insanity in South Padre. She closed her eyes and groaned aloud at that. She wasn't sure if she was complaining about almost having a repeat or about having it interrupted.

What must he think of her?

He probably didn't think anything. He was probably used to women losing self-control in his arms. That wasn't what he said, of course. He talked as if he were the one channeling his inner skank persona.

He could really kiss. He could really, really do... everything. With sad but faithful recall, she compared the fumbling, embarrassing, unsatisfying sex she'd had with guys who might have otherwise been reasonable partners for her. Scott knew what he was doing and, despite her better judgment, she wanted him doing her.

"Why not?" she asked herself. "Why not?"

She didn't verbalize her answers, but she didn't need to. This was not some forgettable night in a place where no one knew her. This was the farming hamlet that she wanted to claim as her hometown. Scott was not a nameless stranger with a big penis, a great technique and a wealth of sensually practical experience. He was a member of her community and she was going to have to interact and converse with him for maybe twenty years. All the reasons that she didn't want him to remember their beach adventure paled in comparison to what it would be like for them to try to sneak an affair under the noses of the entire Verdant population. Not to mention the man's mother was her landlady, on her library board and lived downstairs!

"Impossible," she declared adamantly. "Not going to happen."

Yet she found that she could not stay lolling in the tub when she needed time to dress and do her hair and put on makeup.

She still hadn't sorted through all the clothes in boxes and she completely blamed that for the reason that she chose to wear a spaghetti-strapped cami and flirty summer skirt with a flared hem. She slipped on a pair of dangerously high-heeled sandals and checked her image in the mirror. She was momentarily pleased, before remembering why she'd never worn the outfit. She'd bought it enthusiastically during a shopping trip. But once back home she'd realized that it made her look young and pretty and…well, vulnerable. She never risked even the appearance of weakness. But Scott had already seen that side of her. She'd confessed her fears, her helplessness. He hadn't used that exposure to undermine her. He hadn't sought any advantage at all. He'd simply stayed beside her until she could be strong again.

She closed her eyes and took a deep breath. She couldn't stand here pretending he was something he wasn't. He was a player, intent upon playing her. She knew that about him, from the evidence she'd seen with her own eyes and the experience she'd felt from his own arms. Still, she trusted him. That was crazy. But sometimes crazy just felt right.

By the time she heard the tapping on the back door, her makeup was perfect and her hair sleekly groomed and she was wearing her contact lenses. One word demonstrated the complete worth of the effort.

"Wow!" he said.

D.J. resisted the temptation to simply fall into his embrace.

"I thought we'd eat out here on your deck, so we can watch the combines."

"Combines?"

He nodded. "They're cutting the fields behind the house."

"Tonight?"

"Yeah," he said. "It's pretty neat to watch."

Scott had covered the little table with a good tablecloth and set out a lovely dinner revealed in candlelight.

"It's not exactly a gourmet meal," he warned her.

"The chicken was leftover from my mom. But the veggies I picked yesterday from my own garden. Personally, I'm hungry enough to eat a dirt sandwich, and I thought you might feel the same."

"Famished," she agreed.

And although she would have thought she was too nervous to eat much. She found herself enthusiastically consuming both the food offered and the chilled white wine that he poured into her glass. They ate together casually, congenially. There was a surprising lack of the nervous energy that she'd felt getting ready. D.J. tried to rationalize its sudden disappearance, but there was no explanation for it, beyond the fact that sitting across from Scott felt as comfortable as the anticipation had been exciting.

"Your dog is downstairs, of course," he said. "He and Mom are watching TV. She said to tell you that she's invited him for a sleepover."

D.J. laughed. "Those two have really become a team. It's strange that I've gotten so used to Dew being with her."

Scott nodded. "We may have to find her a pet of her own before she takes complete custody of yours."

D.J. had never liked men who presumed a relationship by using the word *we*, but somehow it felt appropriate tonight. It felt appropriate with Scott. She held up her glass and he filled it for her.

Out in the distance, far enough away that the sound was muted, she could see the lights from the combines, the tractors, the trucks moving slowly through the field.

"Have you noticed how often we seem to be gazing across empty space?" she asked him.

"It's a Kansas thing," he answered. "With grain i

every direction, it's important to keep your eye on the horizon."

"Hey, I've already been lost with you in a wheat field," she said. "You seemed to find your way out easy enough, even after dark."

He chuckled lightly. "You know, I'm thinking that inviting you to stare off into the distance as an entertainment does come off as kind of weird," he said.

"No...it really is beautiful," she admitted. "When you think about it, much of the great art in the world is landscape painting. Seeing beauty in the form of countryside scenery must be something very elemental to the human heart."

He was looking at her so intently, as if he could see past all her posing, all her defenses. He smiled that wonderful woman-melting smile before lightly clicking her glass.

"You are definitely a fabulous addition to our hometown."

D.J. felt herself blushing. It was a silly, little half compliment but somehow it pleased her way too much. Deliberately she changed the subject to the vehicles working overtime in the distance.

"I never really knew that harvesting went on even after dark," she said.

Scott nodded. "They'll keep it up to midnight or beyond," he said. "The combines are so sophisticated, they have onboard moisture detection that will let them know as soon as the grain gets too damp for optimal cutting."

"I love how, except for an occasional shadow on the horizon, or the flash of one vehicle upon another, you don't really see the big machines, just the lights on the path in front of them cutting the wheat."

"That's probably a great metaphor for the people in

Verdant," he said. "It's easy to see what we do every day. What we manage to get done. But when it comes to who we actually are and what kind of loads we're lugging around, that's not so visible."

D.J. smiled at him. "You sound like a philosopher."

He chuckled. "Probably the wine talking," he said. "Although, after a man has spent a long workday slapping sticky-notes to library shelves, he can get a bit philosophical."

"I hope I've remembered to say thank you."

"Yes, I believe you did," he told her. "Although I am kind of hoping I might get another reward later. Maybe another one of those kisses we tried out yesterday."

She felt a flutter of anticipation quiver across her skin.

"Yes, well, we could probably manage it," she answered.

Within the circle of candlelight, she watched that slow smile broaden across his face.

"Then that's something to look forward to," he said

D.J. thought so, too.

They took time finishing their meal. He didn't appear to be in any hurry. And she tried deliberately not to be

Finally he refilled their glasses and suggested that they carry them to the glider.

D.J. was happy to comply. Although once in the closer confines, the nerves were back. A little shiver crept up her spine.

"Are you cold?" he asked.

That was not too likely in the hottest part of a Kansas summer, but D.J. voiced no reluctance when he scooted next to her and wrapped an arm around her shoulders

"I could get a blanket," he suggested.

"No, this is fine."

And it was. The warmth of his nearness calmed the butterflies in her stomach. Intellectually she knew that sitting together like this could be dangerous. But instead of wariness, his proximity made her feel surprisingly safe. She felt herself relaxing against him, strangely unwilling to listen to the wiser voices shouting warnings in her head.

They watched the flicker of lights out in the field.

"We seem to be gazing out at a distance again," she said.

"Kansas landscape," he replied. "It lures you in. If you live in the middle of the city, you wouldn't spend your evening gazing at the building across the street."

"Only if you're a gumshoe P.I. on a stakeout."

He turned his head to grin at her. "The new librarian must be reading too many fiction potboilers."

She laughed. "Likely," she agreed. "I'm probably reading too much and you're spending too much time staring at wheat."

"Could be," he admitted. "But the truth is, all I really want to look at is you."

His words made the fluttering inside her commence once more.

His face was so close she could feel his breath on her skin. Surely he would kiss her. Now was the time to kiss her. But he hesitated. And she did, too.

Determinedly she focused her attention on the lights in the field.

"So, in the long-ago days when you worked in the harvest, did you ever do the night shift?"

"Of course," he said, moving away from her slightly. "The day simply turns into night and you keep working as long as the work goes on."

"So it feels the same."

"No, it's actually very different," he told her. "There's an aloneness about being out there. Well, I'm sure you felt it when we went out into the wheat the other night. Even with all the other workers nearby and the noise of the equipment, there is some kind of deep solitude about night in the fields. It's very elemental."

D.J. nodded. "I can see that," she said.

"Sometimes I think about the families who settled here, my great-grandparents and their parents. Before there were cars and phones and people you could call on in emergencies a half hour away. Most of these farms were a man and a woman alone in the middle of nowhere. With only as many kids as they could raise to help them. They didn't see another person for weeks at a time."

"I bet it was hell on earth if they didn't get along," D.J. said.

Scott nodded. "I guess so. But I think it also forced people to resolve their differences. To make the best of what might not be the perfect situation."

"Some situations simply have no 'best' to them."

"You're right about that," he said. "That's what I didn't realize when I got married."

D.J. felt her defenses piling up into place. She didn't want to hear his excuses for adultery. Cheaters could always come up with rationalizations, but she wasn't interested in listening to them.

"Family secret," he said, grinning again. "My parents *had* to get married."

"Huh?" D.J. was surprised at his direction.

"True. I heard it at school when I was six years old. I wasn't even sure where babies came from and Dougie Morton taunted me that my parents had been *bad*."

"Good grief."

"I told you about gossip in this town. A favorite pastime for young and old."

"So what did you do?"

"I punched him in the mouth," Scott answered. "I got sent home for fighting and my father wanted to know why."

"Did you tell him?"

Scott nodded. "I think that was when I first realized that my dad could be trusted with the truth. That he was never going to be angry or disappointed with me if I was straight with him."

"What did he say?"

"Not really too much," Scott answered. "Maybe about as much as he thought I could comprehend. He said that he and Mom had loved each other since childhood and that they'd always planned to get married, but when they found out that Mom was going to have Leanne, they got married sooner."

"Factual."

"Right," Scott agreed. "I think he was trying not to excuse their behavior and say to me, 'hey, it's okay to get your girlfriend pregnant,' while still conveying to me that the things we do have consequences."

"Hmm."

"Unfortunately, I kind of got the wrong end of the lesson," Scott said. "I thought that it meant that even if things don't turn out like you'd planned, you could make the best of them and everything would be fine."

"Doesn't always work that way."

"No it doesn't," he said. "Even before my ex-wife and I married, I already knew that we had some serious problems. But I felt like…like I'd made a commitment to her and that if I honored that commitment, everything would turn out fine."

"But it didn't."

"No," he answered. "No, it didn't." Then after only an instant of hesitation he changed his mind. "Yes," he said. "Yes, in fact, everything worked out great. I am happily divorced. She is happily with somebody else. And now I'm single and on this glider with a woman I find incredibly attractive and I still think I might get a kiss for all the backbreaking labor I did for her this afternoon."

D.J. knew with complete certainty that she should plead exhaustion and walk away from him right there. She didn't. Instead she lied to herself that she could keep it to little more than a peck on the lips. Touching him didn't have to turn into the sex-crazed insanity of a van stopped in the middle of the road. Or two strangers on a moonlit beach.

682.7 Small Forge Work (Blacksmithing)

The only light in the family room emanated from the television screen. Viv absentmindedly stroked the dog on her lap as she watched a sitcom with humor that seemed to her to be more pathetic than funny. The bursts of canned laughter were the only evidence of where the jokes were supposed to be. She sighed heavily.

"Those two don't deserve to be married," she told Mr. Dewey. "It's hard to imagine how such unlikely people would ever get together."

The dog made no comment. He was content as long as the petting continued.

Viv continued to watch, even as she shook her head and clucked her tongue.

"I'll never understand why, in all these shows, the men are always so ugly and stupid while the women are always smart and pretty," she said. "I've lived a long time and I'll tell you, it's rare to see that kind of pair-up in the natural world."

Mr. Dewey continued to voice no opinion.

"Maybe they're thinking that the smart men don't get their heads turned by pretty women."

Viv chuckled as she scratched the dog behind the

ears and then held his face in her hands. "No, that's definitely not it."

Mr. Dewey's tongue darted out for friendly licks.

"With any luck at all, your pretty mommy is turning the head of my smart son at this very minute. That's what I'm hoping at least."

Viv muted the sound on the TV, as if she couldn't bear the inane dialog another moment.

"Don't worry," she told the dog. "If anybody can make D.J. happy, I think it would be my Scott. He has so much to offer the right woman." She sighed. "Unfortunately, he's spent most of his life offering it to the wrong ones."

Mr. Dewey rolled over upon his back, offering the opportunity to scratch his belly.

Viv chuckled. "Yes, I see. You are definitely the type of fellow that goes after what he wants."

She complied, digging her fingernails deep into the curly black coat. Mr. Dewey's eyes closed in ecstasy and his tongue lolled out the side of his mouth. Viv couldn't keep herself from smiling at the simple, expressive little creature that she had grown so fond of. She kept up the rubdown until her arms grew weary. Mr. Dewey had the good manners not to whine for more. Instead he rolled over onto his paws and looked up at her expectantly as if ready for any task she might give him.

Viv had no jobs for the canine to accomplish. There were no sticks to be fetched. No ropes to be tugged upon. No intruders to be barked at. So she let him do for her what he'd grown accustomed to doing. She let him be her listener.

"My Scott has grown up to be a very good man," she told him. "I'm very proud of him. I think he'll be good to you, too. He always loved that little dog he had.

And if he loves D.J., he has to love her dog, right?" She smiled down into the dog's big, trusting eyes.

"In some ways, he's a lot like me," she told him. "We both have a tendency to take dramatic action when we see something that needs to change. But there is a lot of John in him, as well. He and his father were so close."

She smiled bleakly. "I know how deeply he feels that loss. I truly hate to wound him again. But if he's got D.J. to put a smile on his face, he'll be fine."

Viv looked at the dog for confirmation, but she didn't get it.

Absently, she picked up the remote and began flipping through channels. There were news shows, game shows, reality series and rerun movies.

"Nothing interesting on tonight," she told the dog. "That shouldn't really be a surprise. I've lost interest. That's typical. It's what the lovely hospice lady told me about the dying process. People lose interest in the world as they are letting it go."

The animal's big dark eyes showed such a level of concern that she actually chuckled at the idea that he might understand her words.

"I haven't lost interest in you, Mr. Dewey," she assured him. "At least not so much that I can't find you one of those treats that you like."

In her house shoes, she shuffled over to the pantry and sifted through until she found the dog treats. Mr. Dewey was appreciative, scarfing down both treats he was given within two bites, and then continued to follow her around as she wandered aimlessly through the house.

Finally when she took a seat behind the desk in her husband's office, the dog sat at her feet, looking up anxiously.

"I know you're not still hungry," she said to him. "What is it you want from me? Explanation?" Viv sighed heavily. "The way I'm going about it is about avoiding explanations."

The dog continued to look up at her expectantly.

"Did I ever tell you how John and I met?" she asked. "Well, we didn't. We never met. We knew each other as far back as I can remember. My world never existed before he was in it."

The dog settled in on the floor, laying his head upon his front paws, with his eyes still focused in her direction.

"I didn't love him all that time," she said. "But he was a friend. He was actually my best friend until I got to school and found out that girls were supposed to pick another girl as best friend." She shook her head. "What a waste of time that was! But it was probably for the best. If we'd stayed in each other's pockets all through grade school, we might have been unable to fall in love. We might have felt more like siblings. And that truly would have been a great loss."

Viv sighed heavily and then gazed down at the little dog staring up at her.

"I have never been one to brag about my marriage," she told him. "People don't want to know that. Folks are eager to hear all about a man's bad habits or his foibles. They're happy when you make complaints that he works too hard or doesn't work hard enough. He either fails to do anything spontaneously romantic or he wastes good money on nonsense like cards and flowers. The world wants to know how dissatisfied everyone is. But the minute you claim to be completely happy, people either get annoyed or they try to convince you that you're in denial."

She tutted, shaking her head.

"Well Mr. Dewey, since you can't understand a word I'm saying anyway, and you're an extremely patient listener, let me tell you, I had a fantastic marriage. I loved and respected John every day that we were together. He was the one person I could say anything to. And he never failed to be on my side to root for me and celebrate with me. We could laugh together for hours over stuff that other people would have just thought silly. Every minute we were together, we had a good time. And the hours we were apart, I'd try to remember everything that happened, so I could share it with him."

She lovingly ran her hands along the arms of his desk chair.

"Oh, I'm not saying we didn't have an argument or two throughout the years," she said. "Mostly when serious things came up, we agreed on them. We trusted each other's judgment. And neither of us had much of a temper. But when we did get into a spat, his face would get so red it looked like it might explode. And I'd get mad and grit my teeth at him, like a crazed animal. We'd both end up laughing at how ridiculous we looked."

She chuckled at the memory. Then slowly the humor faded away.

"Our life belonged to the two of us. I can't continue it by myself. And the only person I can even talk to, the only one who wouldn't be bored to tears with the nonsense I need to say, is a little dog."

She glanced down to Mr. Dewey once more. He sat up, his tiny tail wagging in positive enthusiasm.

"Don't worry," she told him. "As soon as I can get those two upstairs on their way to happily-ever-after, I'll stop talking your floppy ears off."

700.6 Arts & Recreation

The combines had come right up to the edge of the property before they'd quit for the night. D.J. and Scott hadn't minded the noise. In fact, he wasn't sure he'd even heard it over the sound of the blood pounding in his ears.

He was determined to make up for his crazy, ass-grab moment in the car. Tonight he would woo D.J. with kisses alone. Kisses only. That was his objective. Kisses if it killed him. And after a relatively circumspect evening beside her in the glider, he might well be ready to die.

He gently broke contact with her mouth, but not before taking a little peck out of the lower lip. She answered with a flick of her tongue against him.

"Damn!" he whispered. "We're getting really good at this."

"You're the expert," she answered.

In the moonlight he could see that her skirt was hiked up and an expansive length of luscious thigh was visible. His hands itched to caress it, stroke it, taste it. He resisted. Deliberately he had not pulled her onto his lap. He was pretty sure if they had a repeat of the previous day's groping it would end either with him getting his face slapped or naked in her bed. Maybe both. Likely both.

The heat level between them had waxed and waned all night. It was amazing to him how easily the two of them fit together. It was almost as if she knew all of his favorite sweet spots. And he spent little time wandering in the wilderness for what torched her.

They would kiss passionately for a while and when they got to the brink where they needed to take things further, Scott would call a break for them to catch their breath and watch the combines.

"What are we doing?" she asked him, perhaps on the second or third occasion that they metaphorically went to their corners.

"Uh…well, we're necking, I think. That's what our parents' generation would have called it."

"Why?"

"Don't you like it?"

"Uh…yes, and…no."

Scott laughed. "That hits the nail on the head, doesn't it," he said. "I wanted to give us some time. Things have been moving really fast for us the last few days. It seems like a week ago that you didn't even like me."

She opened her mouth to deny it, but he stayed her words.

"I don't want to back off," he told her. "I really, really am interested in you. But I don't want to take it to the next level before we're ready. So…I thought necking might be nice."

It was.

They calmly, rationally set up the parameters of their exploration. Kissing only. Completely clothed. Not leaving the glider. Both agreeing that the word "stop" would mean exactly that coming from either of them. Then they gave themselves the freedom to give the game a go.

"I want to try every kiss I've ever heard of," he told her. "I want to do every one you've ever thought of."

By concentrating on the mere pleasure of one mouth on another, they discovered the whole gamut of reactions from aching passion to playful silliness.

Scott mostly managed to keep his hands to himself. Although more than once he found himself with a nice handful of plump, firm breast. That was against their rules, of course, but since her fingers kept accidentally straying to his lap, he thought it was, at least, equal.

They tried every style they could conjure up. Basic. Flirty. French. Total mouth. Travelers. Upper lip. Lower lip. Side-to-side. Reverse side-to-side. They even managed an athletically modified Spider-Man. Although the upside-down-on-the-glider was so awkward they were both laughing too much to get serious with it.

Ultimately, as the night wore on, they were lulled into repeated trials of the matchups that worked best for them. Scott loved the taste of her, the feel of her soft lips against his skin. He even liked the bite of her teeth in his flesh. He could have held her in his arms forever. Or he couldn't bear it another minute.

"Sweet, sweet D.J.," he said. "You need to go inside and I need to go downstairs."

"Do you have to?"

"Yes, yes, I think so."

"You…you could stay," she said, so quietly it was almost a breath.

In a moment of mental insanity he imagined himself laying over her naked across a bed and urging out all those sounds of pleasure that he knew were going to be inside her. Then he would ease himself into that tight wetness and bang her until they were both screaming for mercy.

He moaned aloud. "You know that I would like to, D.J." he said. "You know that I would really, really like to."

"Then why don't you?"

"I can't. Not tonight. It's too soon. This is too good."

"It's not too soon," she assured him in a voice that was almost a whimper. "I promise. It's not too soon."

He wanted to believe her. He wanted it badly. But he didn't. If they had sex tonight, tomorrow they would be weird together. Neither knew yet if they were having a hot sexy affair, or falling in love for a lifetime. Scott was not willing to shortchange himself on the latter by settling for the former. He'd made that mistake before. But it wasn't his affair with Eileen that came to mind. It was his one-night stand in South Padre. His whole life might have been different if...

He let the thought lie right there. That was then and that was her. This was now and this was D.J.

"Stay, please stay," she asked him.

"Nope, I can't," he said, easing himself back and taking a deep breath. "But I sure would like a rain check."

She didn't answer, but he knew how she must feel. She'd offered herself. Made herself vulnerable and had been rejected. That couldn't be good. But he hoped, really hoped, that he could make it up to her.

In the glimmer of light and shadows on the deck, he watched her compose herself. She pushed the wild, tousled hair into a semblance of order and tucked it behind her ears. She ran her hands across her blouse to make sure everything was in place. And she pulled down her skirt, hiding herself modestly from him once more.

"Sure," she said, a lot more casually than she probably felt. "A rain check."

He released his breath. He hadn't realized that he'd

been holding it. He couldn't linger. The temptation was too great. And he needed to keep it light. It was bad enough to end the evening with both of them wanting more. It would be a shame if they were to part in anger.

Sheer determination brought him to his feet. She stood, as well.

"Okay, bye," she said and held out her hand as if to shake.

He grasped it in his own. "Let me walk you to your door."

"It's five feet away."

"Sometimes the short walks are the best ones."

They took the few steps together, hand-in-hand like a couple of dopey sixth graders. He felt a little like a dopey sixth grader. He also felt a lot like a grown man who was deliberately denying the sexual cravings of his own body.

At the doorway she turned to him. "Good night."

Scott leaned forward to plant a tiny smooch on the peak of her nose.

He watched her brow furrow. "You mean after all that practice, that's the best you can do for a good-night kiss?"

Scott grinned, grateful that she, too, was trying to end the evening on a lighter note.

"Right now it is," he answered, feigning grave concern. "I've got to get back downstairs and phone my doctor. I could be having a medical emergency."

"What?"

"I'm pretty sure this erection you've given me has lasted for at least four hours and I haven't even taken any medication."

She was stunned for a moment before bursting into laughter.

He stepped away, but continued to hold her hand until the distance between them became too great.

"Good night, D.J. Dream about me, okay? I'm sure going to dream about you."

719.3 Natural Landscapes

The morning began way too early. That was to be expected when the night before had ended so late. It was after 3:00 a.m. when D.J. had finally settled into bed. And even then, she was too keyed up to sleep. The kissing had been…wonderful. Heaven. The most exciting, titillating and agonizingly frustrating date of her life.

He had told her to dream about him. And she did dream. In the fits and starts of her mostly sleepless night, dreams filtered through. But he was in none of them. It was all books. Rows of books. Carts of books. Mountains of books. She packed away title after title through the night. She packed them in big boxes. She packed them in little boxes. Boxes that were brown. And ones that were white. Boxes that were sturdy enough for heavy volumes and ones that were so flimsy they could hardly be lifted. Suddenly she realized that she'd forgotten Dew. That he'd somehow gotten sealed up in one of the boxes. Frantically she began calling his name and tearing into all the work that she'd accomplished. She had to find him. She had to find him.

The alarm went off.

D.J. sat up in bed, her heart pounding. She slammed down the ringer on the clock next to her and called out Dew's name twice before she remembered that he was still downstairs with Viv.

"Jeez!" she complained aloud.

She put on coffee, awakened herself in the shower and dressed for work. There was so much to get done. Today they would start the actual move. Scott had said he would help. And she knew that James would do what he could. But it was her job, her library, her idea. So most of it would be on her.

Half laziness and half practicality, she decided that the uniform of the day should be casual. Only '50s TV housewives did grunt work in pearls and heels. D.J. dug through the mess that was to soon be her closet and came up with a nice pair of jeans and a top that was more tee than blouse. She almost went for strappy sandals that would make the outfit look dressier. But better judgment prodded her to slip on sneakers. At least they were cute and they kind of matched.

She didn't want to be late for work, she wanted to be early. James was probably already in the stacks. She wolfed down her coffee with a piece of cheese toast, then brushed her teeth one more time before heading out the door.

On the deck stairs she deliberately kept her footfalls light. She didn't know if she was ready to see Scott yet this morning. And she liked imagining him all warm and snuggly in a tousled bed.

She could see that there was a light on in the kitchen as she passed. It really would be nice to see him. Talk to him. Share a cup of morning coffee with him. She could make the excuse of wanting to see Dew, but it would be obvious.

No, she told herself firmly. She needed to get to the library. He'd promised to come by and help. She would hold him to that promise. And the rain check. Was she going to let him cash in that rain check?

She felt herself blushing.

That would be stupid. It was amazingly stupid. She shouldn't even consider it. But she *had* offered. And it wouldn't be the right thing to renege. She began grinning to herself even as she recognized the significant flaws in her reasoning.

Scott had parked his van behind his mother's purple Mini. D.J. had to walk around the vehicle to get to her hatchback on the far side. She was fishing through the bottom of her purse when she stepped on something. She didn't have time to react before it reacted. In a blur of motion something wheat-colored lunged at her. It caught her ankle. More startled than hurt, she kicked at it. Almost simultaneously she recognized the attacker as a snake and the pain of the bite reached her brain.

D.J. screamed bloody murder.

She hopped twice on her good leg before falling onto the ground. The minute she hit she was suddenly terrified that there might be snakes everywhere. She tried to stand.

Suddenly Scott was there. He grasped her shoulders and was helping her up.

"What happened?"

"Sn-snake," she managed to get out, pointing in the direction of the grass.

He immediately dropped her. D.J.'s butt hit the ground again as he went running toward the attacker's escape route. Her concern for herself momentarily vanished as she watched him, naked except for blue boxer shorts, rushing toward the rattling sound that she could now distinctly hear.

"You're barefooted," she warned him.

Viv squatted down beside her. Dew went racing after Scott, barking dangerously.

"Get back!" she heard Scott order her dog.

Dew held his ground but didn't venture farther.

Scott turned. "It's okay," he hollered out as he came loping back toward her. "It's okay."

"It was a snake," D.J. said.

He nodded. "Prairie rattler," he told her as if that said everything. He turned to his mother. "Bring me a blanket and my cell phone. Car keys!"

As Viv hurried off, Scott squatted down beside D.J. He seemed very calm. It was weird, almost as if he were purposely slowing down his movements. He gave her a wan smile. "I'd say good morning, but I guess it's not."

"This really hurts," she told him. "That snake bit me!"

"I know," he said. "It was a rattlesnake. But you're going to be fine. I'm going to take you to Dr. Kim."

He got up and went around his van. D.J.'s brain was hardly functioning. Her foot and ankle felt as if they were on fire. Bending her knee she could examine the injury more closely. Two very distinct little wounds about an inch apart looked pretty innocuous. One was straight into her flesh. The other through the canvas of her sneaker. They were both small, but they really hurt.

She heard Scott sliding open the side door of the van and rifling around inside. He returned to her a moment later wearing a disreputable pair of running shoes.

He squatted down beside her. "Put your arms around my neck."

When she did, he slipped an arm under her knees and lifted her off the ground as if she weighed nothing. He carried her around to the vehicle's passenger-side door where he'd scooted the seat back as far as it would go and made a little nest of boxes. He stretched her bitten leg out straight upon the cardboard tower held together with duct tape, turning her slightly inward to give her more room before buckling her seat belt on.

"We want to keep your ankle elevated, but not higher than your heart," he told her.

She couldn't stop herself from a cry of complaint as pain shot through her as he peeled off her sneaker.

"Sorry," he said. "Your foot's beginning to swell. It's either jerk the shoe off now or cut it off later."

D.J. nodded, but didn't speak. She concentrated all her effort upon blinking back her tears and not howling like a crybaby.

"I'm going to try to immobilize your leg," he told her. "We want to keep the venom as localized as we can."

"Okay."

He used an Ace bandage and salvaged packaging materials to make her foot snugly unmoving in its cardboard splint.

"I saw the snake. It was a prairie rattlesnake, not a diamondback. They are both poisonous snakes, but the prairie rattler is a lot less dangerous."

"Okay."

He looked directly into her eyes. He seemed so unruffled, so in control. "I need for you to remain as calm and quiet as possible," he said. "This kind of thing is very scary and makes us all tend to panic. That raises the heart rate and gets the venom moving through the body much more quickly."

She nodded. "It's not the really dangerous snake. It's just the kind-of dangerous snake."

"Right."

"I don't think I like snakes."

"More people actually die from wasp and bee stings," he said.

"Well, I guess that's good to know."

Viv showed up with a blanket in hand.

Scott took it from her and began tucking it around D.J.

"I thought the blanket was for you," she said. "You know you're not wearing pants."

"I'm sure that's what the gossips will say," Scott teased. "He hangs out with the new librarian and can hardly keep his pants on."

It hurt too much to laugh, but she managed a half smile.

Scott leaned down outside and an instant later set a warm, black ball of fur into her lap.

"Dew," she said.

"Pet the dog," Scott told her. "It'll keep your blood pressure down."

D.J. looked down into the big dark eyes. "I'm going to be fine," she told him. But she wasn't sure who was reassuring who.

"I'm right behind you. As soon as I get dressed," Viv promised.

Clothing was apparently optional for the driver. Scott climbed behind the wheel. He started the engine and slowly backed up until he could turn around. As soon as he was headed forward he picked up his cell phone and pressed a couple of buttons. It took only a half minute before the call was answered. D.J. stroked Dew as she listened through the pauses to the one-sided conversation.

"Morning. This is Scott. I'm on the way to your clinic with a snakebite....No, it's D.J. Jarrow, the new librarian....Yes, I saw it myself. Prairie rattler....Brown with darker blotches. Definitely not a diamondback....I have some in the fridge at the store....Most of the box,

I think. Twelve, maybe fifteen vials.…Can I stop by on the way or should I circle back?"

Scott turned to D.J. "How you feeling? Are you nauseated? Chilled?"

"No. I feel okay, except for my leg."

"I think it's still pretty localized," he said into the phone.

"Less than ten minutes ago.…Okay. Will do. See you shortly."

He ended the call and set the phone in a holder on the dash.

"We're going to stop by the drugstore and get you some medicine," he told her. "And then we're meeting Dr. Kim at the clinic."

That sounded good to D.J. She hoped the medicine would stop the burning in her foot and ankle. In fact, everything below the knee was beginning to sting like fire.

"Did you hear the rattle before it bit you?" Scott asked her.

"Huh? Uh…maybe." D.J. tried to reconstruct the event in her mind. "No, I don't think so. I think I stepped on him."

"Oh, good. That's probably good."

"Why would it be good?"

"I think they say that if the snake is hungry or angry it secretes more venom," he said. "If you surprised him, he probably had less stored in his pit sacs than if he were out hunting."

"What was he doing there in the driveway?" she asked. "Are there snakes like that around everywhere?"

"They live out in the wheat," Scott answered. "They eat field mice and other rodents. We really don't see that much of them. But I'm sure the combines chased him out last night. He found what he thought was a safe place and was waiting it out until the day got warm enough to go back home. He was as surprised to see you as you were to see him."

Somehow that didn't make her leg feel any better.

They made it to Main Street, which was still mostly deserted. Scott pulled the van to park the wrong direction next to the sidewalk in front of the drugstore. The vehicle straddled three angle parking spaces and turned on the emergency flashers.

"I'll be right back," he promised as he got out.

D.J. hoped he wasn't kidding. The pain in her leg was transforming from mere hellish burn to hellish burn plus throbbing ache. She continued to pet Dew, but closed her eyes, unable to bear his sympathetic expression.

She opened them when a car pulled up to park directly nose to nose. D.J. recognized the man that she'd briefly met, but would have known him anyhow from the official county vehicle he was driving.

Dressed in a uniform of two different colors of brown and sporting a belt that holstered both a radio and a side arm, the policeman slowly walked up to the passenger side of the car. D.J. managed to roll down the window.

"Good morning, ma'am," he said in a deep voice that was both melodic and authoritarian. "What seems to be going on here?"

"A snake bit me," she answered.

He glanced inside the van, taking note of her foot propped up on the tower of boxes.

"Scott's getting medicine and taking me to the doctor."

"Did you identify the snake?"

"Prairie rattler," she answered. "I didn't really get a good look, but that's what Scott said it was."

The cop nodded as the man under discussion came charging out of the drugstore building. He hesitated only long enough to lock the front door.

"Does he know he's got no pants on?" the deputy asked her quietly.

"He was in a hurry," she defended.

"Hi, Karl," Scott called out. "A rattlesnake got D.J."

"So I hear."

"Can you escort us to the clinic?"

"Sure thing," the man agreed and headed back to his own car at a more hurried pace.

Scott stowed a bag in back of his seat before getting behind the wheel.

"How you doing?" he asked her.

"It really hurts," she answered, no longer willing to feign bravery.

"We're almost there."

The flashing lights on the deputy's car came on. He backed up enough to make a U-turn. And with the roar of a siren, they were back on the street, with Dew barking unhappily at the annoying sound.

753.1 Symbolism, Allegory, Myth & Legend

Scott's heart was pounding and it was not from the effort of carrying D.J. in through the clinic's emergency room door. He'd been coming out of the bathroom, still groggy from a sleepless night, when he'd heard her scream. He could not have testified about how he got from his room to her side—that was a blur. But from the moment he realized what had happened, he had deliberately focused on training, not instinct. First aid and CPR were certifications required for registered pharmacists and especially helpful for those, like Scott, who were in rural areas where emergency medical assistance was limited.

Thanks to Dr. Kim's practice and the half-dozen qualified nurses who lived in the community, it was rare that Scott's treatment skills were ever needed. But this morning he was very glad that he had them.

The nursing assistant directed Scott to lay D.J. on the examining table. They propped pillows behind her back to maintain her reclining position. The women looked at the bite and using a black marker drew a line at the limit of the current swelling. On the line she wrote the current time.

The nurse was friendly. "I'm going to need to start

an IV," she told D.J. "I'm not sure your puppy needs to
be around for that."

D.J. still held the dog in her arms. Scott had been
loath to take him from her, but when a room was going
for sterile, it was pretty clear that no pets were allowed.

"Don't worry about him," Scott told D.J. "I'll give
him to my mom as soon as she gets here."

He was surprised to discover Karl right behind him.

"I can do that," he said, taking the dog from Scott.

"Thanks."

Karl directed his next words to the nurse. "If you
need me to radio the ambulance or the helicopter, I'm
right outside the door."

She nodded her thanks.

"Ma'am," the deputy said, offering a tip of his hat
in D.J.'s direction. "Hope you're feeling better soon."

Without Dew to comfort her, Scott felt honored that
D.J. reached for his hand. From the moment this had
happened, all he'd wanted to do was take her in his
arms and hold her close. That wasn't going to happen.
Like the sexually unsatisfactory night before, there were
things in life that required specific timing. He had to
see her on the road to recovery before he could take the
time to hug her and tell her he loved her.

He loved her. That thought came as a surprise. But
he had no time to dwell on its validity.

Dr. Kim came around the corner and greeted them
both. He looked askance at Scott's wardrobe choice.

"There's scrubs out in the linen cabinet next to the
workstation," he said, more as an order than a suggestion. "I don't think having young, near-naked guys
running around does the reputation of my clinic any
good. And if one of my dear senior ladies in the wait-

ing room were to catch sight of you, well, some of them have heart issues."

Scott managed a smile. If the doctor thought D.J. was in deep trouble, he wouldn't care what anybody was wearing.

He quickly retrieved the comfortable blue cotton clothes. But he was unwilling to leave D.J. long enough to put them on. He carried them back to dress at her bedside. In truth, he'd completely forgotten that he was still in his underwear. He kicked off his shoes and hurriedly pulled on one leg and then hopped a couple of times as he put on the other. He tied them at the waist and put his running shoes back on.

"I was in such a hurry," he admitted to the nurse, who was eying him disapprovingly as he jerked the shirt over his head. "I didn't want to take the time to dress."

"Well, you did the right thing," Dr. Kim said. "Time is critical."

Scott nodded.

The man had a calming, fatherly presence that was undoubtedly an asset on the job. He whisked the curtain around them, turning the open examining area into a much smaller private space. He pushed up D.J.'s pant leg and examined the wound for a moment before measuring the distance from the distal vein to the edge of the swelling. He offered her a comforting smile.

"We'll need to draw some blood," he said to D.J. Then to the nurse he clarified. "I'll need a CBC with platelets, PT, PTT and Fibrinogen." He spoke to D.J. again. "When's the last time you had a tetanus shot?"

"I don't know," she answered.

"Well, then, we're going to give you another one."

D.J. didn't seem to care much about that. She was

flinching and biting her lip as the doctor moved her foot around, getting a good look from all directions.

"Do you think we can remove your jeans, or would you like the nurse to cut them off?" he asked.

D.J. never really came up with an answer. The nurse quickly undid the button and zipper and instructed her to plant her right foot flat on the table.

"Help us raise your bottom up," the nurse told her. "And we'll pull the jeans down over your hips."

The "we" in her scenario included Scott who was given the duty of right leg removal. It went fairly easily. Once over the hips, they skimmed down quickly.

The movement took a lot out of D.J. She lay back on the pillows, exhausted, her face pale.

Scott leaned close and whispered. "Cute panties." He hoped the teasing would add some color to her cheeks.

It worked. She blushed.

"I always wear nice ones in case I'm in an accident," she replied with a valiant attempt at sarcasm.

"So this must be your lucky day," he said.

"Or yours. I can't believe they let you help me undress."

Scott grinned. "I do admit that I've daydreamed about getting your pants off. But somehow it was never quite like this."

D.J. managed something near to a smile.

Dr. Kim cleared his throat. "Did you bring the Cro-Fab?" he asked. His tone was stern.

"It's in the van. I'll go get it."

As he flailed for the opening in the curtain, Dr. Kim spoke to D.J. reassuringly.

"We're going to have you back on your feet in no time," he told her. "We're going to start some anti-venom infusion and we're going to get you some pain medication for all that nasty burning sensation."

"Thank you," he heard her answer.

Stepping out of the door, Scott broke into a run. His van was still double-parked in the entry. With Karl standing right beside it, he was pretty sure he wasn't getting a ticket.

He retrieved his bag from behind the seats and gave his keys to the deputy.

"Could you move it for me?"

The man nodded.

Back inside, he spotted Dr. Kim washing up at the sink. The curtains were closed up around the area where he'd left D.J.

"Here's the CroFab. How's she doing?"

"She'll feel better after the pain meds kick in," he answered.

"What can I do?" Scott asked.

The doctor held up an IV bag of normal saline.

"Do you want to mix it," he asked.

"Sure."

"We're going to do four vials to start."

It was good to have something concrete to focus on. Scott washed and gloved and spread what he needed out on an empty counter. With a 30ml syringe he drew out the correct amount of saline from the bag and injected it into each vial of powdered anti-venom. Gently, turning the little bottles upside down and back up, he allowed the powder to suspend in the solution. When there were no loose particles of anti-venom visible, he used the syringe again to withdraw the liquid mixture and add it back to the bag.

When the IV was ready, he took the label from the

anti-venom and attached it to the bag. He carried it over to the curtained alcove and made his way inside.

The nurse and doctor were both there, but Scott's eyes were all for D.J. She lay back on the table and appeared to be sleeping. She'd changed into a hospital gown and was tucked in warmly with a white blanket. She was hooked up to monitors that kept track of her vital functions. And an oxygen tube stretched across her face.

The nurse doubled-checked the label against the orders and then against D.J.'s wristband before hanging the anti-venom on the stand.

The doctor spoke to Scott. "We're going to start at 50cc per to see how she tolerates it. If we don't get any anaphylactic reaction after the first ten minutes, we'll up the dose to 250ml."

"Sounds good," he said.

As he spoke, D.J. opened her eyes. "You're back," she whispered.

"I'm here," he assured her.

The doctor spoke to her, a bit more loudly this time, "Are you allergic to papaya or any of the papain proteins."

"Uh...no."

"Are you, or could you possibly be, pregnant?"

"No."

"That's good," Dr. Kim said.

"Yeah," D.J. said, groggily. "My boyfriend only likes necking."

Scott grinned at her.

"Are you the 'boyfriend'?" the nurse asked.

"I guess so."

She turned to the doctor. "I hope that's not a privileged piece of conversation is it, Dr. Kim? Suzy Granfeldt is in my Sunday School class and this is the kind of news the woman lives for."

Scott refused to be embarrassed. In truth, he was buoyed. If the caregivers were joking, then the situation was not as bad as it could have been.

The ten-minute trial passed with no untoward reaction. Dr. Kim sped up the delivery of the anti-venom.

"How's that pain medication?" Dr. Kim asked her.

"Better," she answered.

"It's okay if you want to take a little nap," he said. "This medicine is going to take some time to get inside you and you could probably use the rest."

"Okay," she agreed sleepily. Then her eyes popped open. "Scott?"

"Yeah, baby, I'm here." he told her, grasping her hand.

"Check on the library," she told him. "James will be all alone and he won't know what's happened to me."

"Sure, don't worry about it. I'll take care of James."

She sighed heavily in relief and then closed her eyes. A minute later, her mouth opened slightly and he knew she was sleeping. He watched her for several minutes, trying to get his mind around his feelings.

He was seeing only D.J. now. He knew that the whole resemblance to the girl from South Padre had confused his reaction to her. But it was the real person, not the remembered fantasy, who lay here sleeping. It was the real woman whose fear and pain cut into him like a self-inflicted wound.

He went outside to give his mother an update.

Viv was sitting on a bench beneath the overhang. She had the dog on the leash and seemed to be talking with the peppy fur ball.

"Is that the best conversation you can get around here?" he asked her.

She looked up and smiled at him. "He's a very good listener."

Scott chuckled.

"So how is D.J. doing?" his mother asked.

"Right now she's sleeping. I think it looks very positive so far," he answered. "Half of the snake bite went through her shoe. That kept it shallower on that side. And getting her infused in less than an hour, that's big."

He sat down next to her. Bent forward with his elbows on knees he wiped the tiredness out of his eyes. Then resting his jaw on his hands he let out a huge huff of air, as if he'd been holding his breath.

"It scared the crap out of me," he admitted.

"Of course it did," his mother agreed.

"Damn, it was that same helpless feeling I had when Dad was so sick," he said. "You go along thinking you have all the time in the world to say things and do things and share things and then suddenly you don't."

His mother's brow was furrowed. For a moment he was sorry he'd brought his father up. Dad always seemed like the elephant in the room these days. Still he attempted to explain.

"I will be forever grateful that we had the time we did," Scott told her. "I mean at the end. I'm so glad that I was able to talk to him when we both knew he was dying and that everything that ought to be said, got to be said. That was truly a gift."

Viv seemed even less pleased with that statement than the subject matter in general. Instead of disputing his words, however, she changed the subject.

"Fortunately, D.J. doesn't appear to be in danger of dying."

Scott nodded. "Rattlesnake bites are only rarely fatal. And even when they are, it's more often panic and a heart attack that does people in."

"Still, it is scary," she said. "I think most people have had an unhealthy fear of the creatures since the Garden of Eden."

Scott nodded. "And I should have warned her to keep an eye out for them after the cutting." He shook his head guiltily. "Wow, that scream D.J. let out. That certainly got our attention."

Viv chuckled. "Yes, now I know what people mean by bloodcurdling."

"It was definitely that," he said.

His mother reached over and patted his hand as if he were still a little boy. "I know you're beginning to have feelings for her." He didn't respond and Viv hesitated. "You *are* beginning to have feelings for her, aren't you?"

Scott shrugged. "Maybe. I think so."

His mother seemed to be waiting for more.

"I like being around her. She's got a good sense of humor. She's very smart and she's interesting."

"That seems promising."

He nodded. "But she reminds me of someone else and that makes it kind of weird."

"Really? Who does she remind you of?"

"A girl I met in college. Nobody you know."

Viv hesitated. "Well, I'm sure our D.J. is nothing like that other girl."

"No, I guess not."

"I think she's been lonely much of her life. Her parents mostly left her with nannies and babysitters until they were able to send her away. It was almost as if they didn't want children."

Scott nodded. D.J. had said as much herself. Then suddenly he realized that D.J. had also said she never talked about it.

"How do you know that about her?" he asked his mother.

Viv looked up, a little startled. "Oh...I don't know, I suppose she told me."

"I don't think so," he said.

"Well, maybe I heard it from someone else," his mother suggested.

"No," Scott answered, shaking his head. "D.J. doesn't talk about it."

"Someone like Suzy could have gotten it out of her."

He didn't believe that. D.J. was far too private to have things coaxed out of her. Suddenly, as clearly as if he could hear her voice, he remembered his sister's words.

"You hired the private detective to find out stuff about D.J."

Viv didn't bother to deny it. He hadn't even posed it as a question.

"If you're going to hire somebody on the internet, you'd certainly want to check them out."

"Mom, you vet people, you interview them, you contact their references, you *don't* have them investigated."

She shrugged with unconcern. "It's more than simply hiring for a job. It's inviting a new person into a tight-knit community. I think that you should see it as positive that I'm a bit more cautious than to trust my own judgment."

"It wasn't about bringing her into our 'tight-knit community,' it was about bringing her into our family," he said. "You *really did* hire her to fix me up."

"Well, you need somebody and I haven't got forever to wait."

"Unbelievable."

"Believe it. I found her. You like her. So are you going to complain about it now?"

Scott wanted to. But somehow he didn't.

"Mom, what's done is done," he said. "In the future, I would appreciate it if you would stay out of my personal life."

She smiled broadly at him. "I am completely done with that," she assured him. "From here on out, you are going to be totally on your own. I promise. Now, are you going to spend your day around here? Would you like for me to open the store?"

"I promised I would check on James," he answered.

"That's a very good idea," she said. "You go to the library and Mr. Dewey and I will see what is needed in the drugstore."

"Okay," he said. "I'll get Dr. Kim to call me with updates of how things are going."

795.6 Games of Chance

The front door to the library was open and inside the lights were on. Behind the circulation desk a short person sat up expectantly.

Scott cursed under his breath. He'd completely forgot about the little girl. But he supposed if an eight-year-old was going to be unattended, there were few better places to be than an empty library.

"Hi, Ashley."

"Hi. D.J. is not here. She hasn't shown up all morning."

"I know," he answered. "She's at Dr. Kim's clinic. She got bit by a snake."

"Oh, wow! A big snake?"

"Pretty big."

"Is she all right?"

"She's going to be fine," he told her. "Are you here by yourself or have you seen James?"

She looked warily toward the stacks and leaned forward to whisper. "I haven't seen him. But I hear him in there."

"Okay. I'll go back and check on him. I need you to do something for me."

She nodded enthusiastically.

"Call your mom at work. Tell her about D.J.'s snake-bite and that it's probably not great for you to hang out here with me and James. Tell her that my mom is at the drugstore and would probably love to have your company if it's okay for you to walk over there."

The little girl's brow furrowed. "Can I take my book?"

"Do you know how to check it out?"

"Uh-huh."

"Then check it out to yourself. And call your mom."
Ashley nodded.

Scott went looking for James. Typically, the guy was not easy to find. What he did find, however, was a bit surprising. James had been moving the books. Using the plan that D.J. had set out, he was temporarily storing each shelf grouping in the reading room. The sticky notes with their identifying future locations were visible atop each stack.

Scott was impressed. The guy had gotten a lot done and it wasn't even noon.

"James. James, are you here?"

"Yes." The answer came from the shadows.

"Did you hear me tell Ashley what happened to D.J.?"

"Yes."

"She probably won't be in to work for a few days."

"No."

Scott didn't really have any idea what to say beyond that.

"You've really gotten a lot done," he settled on finally.

"I don't like it," James said.

"But you're doing it anyway?"

"She wants it done. So I can do it," he answered.

It was a couple of simple declarative statements, but Scott realized there was a lot of power in them. James was willing to make changes he didn't want to make. He had no idea what D.J. had done to inspire James's loyalty, but he knew from where his own stemmed.

"You're right," he told the guy. "We can do it."

Scott fished the phone out of his pocket and called his mother. She picked up on the second ring.

"Hi, Mom. Everything okay there?"

"It all seems to be in order. No one waiting. No notes on the door and not many people around."

"Good, I'm sending Ashley Turpin over to you," he said. "Do you think you can keep her occupied until it's time for her to join her mother?"

"Certainly."

"I'm going to stay here and James and I are going to keep the work going on D.J.'s library rearrangement."

"Oh, what a nice idea. I'm sure she'll appreciate that."

"But we could use some help," he told her. "So if anyone shows up, finished with harvest and looking for something to do, send them over."

At the busiest time of the year, there were not a lot of extra hands to be had. But by midafternoon his mother showed up herself with Edna Kievener and Lola Philpot in tow. Mr. Dewey watched as the senior ladies and their eight-year-old mascot knuckled down in a team effort to remove the books.

It was a little after four when Dr. Kim called.

As soon as he said the doctor's name, all work around him stopped. Everyone stood there, listening, waiting.

"We've gained control of the advance of the venom. She's got some localized swelling and blistering, but no evidence of any significant coagulopathy. I think she's due to make a full recovery."

"That's great."

"I've sent her off in an ambulance to the hospital in Hays. I want them to keep an eye on her for the next day or two. It's precautionary."

"Is she awake?"

"Off and on. We're trying to keep her pain level low to counter the stress. She's mostly past our worries about that, but I gave her something to make her ambulance ride more comfortable."

"Should I go to see her in the hospital, then?"

"She probably won't get there until perhaps 6:30 or 7. Then she'll have to be checked in to her room. Visiting hours are over at eight. You might want to wait until tomorrow."

Scott had no intention of waiting.

They worked for another hour. They'd unloaded everything but the range closest to the windows.

He thanked everyone for their time. His mother took Ashley to the Brazier, and James assured him that he could lock up the building. Considering how secure he kept his rusty old bike, Scott had no doubts on that score.

He drove to his mother's house, took the shower that he'd missed that morning and put on real clothes. He was antsy to get on the road. Anxious to see her.

His mother was in the kitchen when he came out.

"I've packed you a sandwich to eat on the way," she told him. "And you should probably take this."

She indicated a familiar-looking, businesslike gray handbag.

"I found it in the driveway. Or more accurately, I guess I'd say that I found it all over the driveway. The contents were spilled out, but I think we got everything. I'm sure they'll be needing her insurance cards and such."

"Right. Good idea."

"It's a first step back into normal," she said. "When a woman wakes up in a strange place, she looks around for her purse."

"Got it," he answered as he headed out the door.

On the road he took a phone call from Amos. He was grateful for his friend's inquiry and passed on the doctor's update.

"I should have warned her about snakes coming in from the field," Scott said.

"Get off that train," Amos answered. "There is crap in life that we can't control. You can keep hashing over the past ad infinitum, but it's never going to change. It happened. It's over. We're moving on."

Scott hesitated on the other end of the line.

"Isn't this the pep talk I'm always giving to you," he said.

"Yeah, it is, as a matter of fact. And I'd say it's high time that you took some of your own advice."

"I will, if you will."

"I am," Amos answered. "I drove Jeannie home last night. We'd finished up and she invited me in for a beer."

"Oh, yeah?"

"We didn't stop square in the middle of the road, like some people I know. But I still managed to get a pretty nice kiss."

"My God. There is actually hope for you. Gotta hang up now. I need to call Suzy and get her to spread the news."

"You wouldn't dare," Amos said.

"How about you bribe me not to," Scott suggested.

"O…kay," Amos replied hesitantly.

"Could you show up at the library tomorrow to help James and I take down the shelving units?"

"Sure thing," he answered. "I wouldn't miss it for the world."

"We need all the hands we can get."

"Then you really should talk to Suzy," Amos said. "She'll get the word out faster than paid advertising."

Scott was hopeful. But he didn't have time to talk to Suzy yet. He arrived at the hospital, parked his car, grabbed D.J.'s handbag and carried it awkwardly at his side until he realized how much easier it was to sling it over his shoulder. He made a quick inquiry at the information desk, managed to find his way to her room.

She looked pale against the pillows and still seemed a bit groggy, but smiled when she saw him.

"Hello, you," she said.

He wanted to kiss her, but wasn't sure. Finally he settled on a peck on the forehead.

"You're looking happier," he said. "How do you feel?"

"A lot better than this morning," she answered. "Thank you, by the way."

"For what?"

"Rescuing me from the snake," she said.

"I believe the snake ran away on its own. And it was probably more scared of Dew than it was of me," he said. "And as for driving you to the clinic, the way you were hollering, I don't think I could have waited for an ambulance to show up."

"You did stop to get me the medicine."

Scott nodded. "Just wait until you get the bill. That anti-venom is seriously not cheap."

"So there's nothing to thank you for?"

"Well, I did bring your purse," he said, indicating the bag he was wearing.

"I thought it might be mine, but it looks good on you, as well," she teased.

Scott struck a pose, his brow feigning indecision. "I'm not sure it's the right color for this outfit."

She managed a little laugh then. He loved the sound of it.

South Padre Island (Eight years earlier)

She lay beside him. Speechless beyond sated. His arms held her tightly, as if he'd never let her go. She had wanted to find out what it was like, what sex was all about. She'd expected, hoped for, some fireworks. She had not anticipated having her whole world tilt sideways.

"I'm so greedy for you," he told her. "But I don't want this night to end."

She was exhausted. There was absolutely no way she could do any more. But she wasn't willing to let it go, either. It was just this one night, just this small piece of time out of time where she could pretend for a few hours that she was not the odd, unhappy girl, the socially stunted introvert, the unwanted and undated.

"Tired," was the only word she managed to get out.

"It's okay. You just rest. Sleep if you like, don't mind me."

Slowly he kissed his way down the length of her torso. When his tongue began to niggle the sensitive, intimate flesh she gained a surprising surge of new energy.

It was almost too much. She almost couldn't bear it.

But then she could. And then it was not enough. She had to have more. She wanted him inside of her again.

To make that happen, she tried doing unto him what he was doing to her. His response was positive.

"Oh, you are so damn good, incredibly damn good."

She loved the praise. She loved the power. But she also loved it when he shifted her on her side and spooned up behind her. It went on and on, long and slow, better and better. She wouldn't have believed that she could come again. But she did and it washed through her hot and silky, sinking into the deepest most hidden crevices of her longing. The struggling, the striving to connect with another person, now locked her into a state of bliss, of absolute fulfillment. They were a man and a woman, bonded together. A unit of home that she had sought all her life.

"I love you," she told him.

822.6 English Drama

Two full days of heavy pain medication had made D.J.'s brain very fuzzy. It had also given her far more dreams than she wanted to deal with. The creepy, crawly things and soup bowls full of spiders were bad enough. But she also had other dreams, where the fair-haired hero in blue boxer shorts was using his tongue on her as the ocean roared in the background. It was wonderful, incredible, magical. And then inevitably she would move her foot, the pain would shoot through her leg and she'd awaken, not with a sweet smile of satisfaction, but with the grimace of reality.

And if the drugs weren't bad enough, the lights and sounds of the hospital messed up her perception of time. Yes, the sun came through the windows and, yes, they turned off more lights at night, but waking and sleeping occurred so sporadically that she had a hard time keeping up with whether it was 10:00 a.m. or 5:00 p.m. Early evening or four in the morning?

She decided that was why patients kept their televisions on all the time. It gave them a solid, if mindnumbing, reference to the outside world.

Fortunately D.J. was lucky enough to have other references. The phone beside her rang surprisingly often for a newcomer to the neighborhood. Mostly the calls were from library patrons, concerned over her ordeal and offering well wishes for her quick recovery. There were also daily updates from Viv on the very busy life of her dog. Dew was apparently settling in nicely downstairs, although Viv assured her that he missed D.J. horribly.

"Mr. Dewey will notice that your car is in the driveway," she said. "And then he'll skip up the stairs and peer into the door as if he's trying to figure out where you are and why you haven't come for him."

D.J. smiled. "I'm sure that with all the attention that he gets from you, Dew is probably happier than he's ever been. I always hated leaving him alone all day."

"He enjoys the novelty of wandering through my life," Viv said. "But his first loyalty is to you and I don't want you to worry about that one little bit."

In all honestly, D.J. could admit to herself that she didn't. Dew was getting along great with Viv. It was wonderful the way they had bonded. And she loved the idea of the two of them wandering around Verdant, although she did suspect that Viv was not as vigilant about keeping him crated while driving around in the purple Mini. She forgave her for that.

Other calls were more formal. As if it were an expected courtesy to telephone the librarian in the hospital. Helen Rossiter assured her that "everyone speaks highly" of the hospital. And Claire Gleason told her that a few days of rest in the summer was a boon to the "thirtysomething complexion."

"I'm only twenty-nine," D.J. told her.

"Even better," she said.

Verdant had turned the corner on this year's harvest and as people went back to their regular lives, they took time to call and commiserate with her on the incident. Everyone who'd ever had a snakebite or had a family member who'd suffered one, or knew a friend who had a friend who used to know someone who had one, was eager to give her all the details.

There were also visits from the local florist. The room's long windowsill quickly became as colorful and fragrant as a flower garden. There were vases of gerbera daisies, giant arrangements of gladiolus, more than one bowl of native Kansas sunflowers and a hardy-looking dieffenbachia that D.J. decided was destined for a long life as part of the library.

Not one of these tributes was from Scott. She opened each card with that anticipation and could not quite stop herself from being ever so slightly disappointed.

Of course, he didn't owe her any gift, she reminded herself rationally. It was she who needed to be thanking him. And she was perfectly prepared to thank him, if and when he ever showed up again.

On the third morning of what she was beginning to think of as her Hays Hospital incarceration, she was told that she could go home. She would have to make an appointment for a follow-up with Dr. Kim, but she was encouraged to continue to rest, told what over-the-counter pain medications she could take and which she shouldn't, and given a prescription for physical therapy to get her right leg back in shape.

The nurse showed her how to wrap her own foot in the loose bandage. The puncture wound seemed incidental compared to the swelling around it. No shoe, if she had had one, would fit over the puffiness. She was fitted into an ankle boot as if she'd had a sports injury. Somehow she liked the idea of having kicked a lead soccer ball better than stepping upon a frightened snake.

Once dressed, she called Viv and asked her to come get her. Secretly she was hoping that Scott would show up. She could hardly even admit it to herself, but she missed him. She really, really missed him.

He had come by the night that she'd been admitted. He was so cute, teasing her and carrying her purse. She had wanted him to hold her, to simply melt in his arms. But of course, that was ridiculous. Yes, they'd had their little necking session. And yes, the emergency nature of the next morning had thrown them together unexpectedly. But there were still tremendous barriers to any kind of relationship between the two of them.

Scott undoubtedly had recognized that and was responding to it. They had gotten a little bit too comfortable with one another. A little too flirty. A little too close to intimacy. It was definitely time for both of them to take a step backward.

Still, she wanted to see him. She wanted to look at him. Laugh with him. Talk to him. She also wanted to hide in the wheat with him, to have him hold her tightly, to play necking games and, yes, to get herself flat on her back in a bed full of him.

She was in serious danger of getting her heart broken, but she couldn't seem to resist. And it seemed as if it no longer mattered that he was a player and a cheat. That he was unconscionable enough to prey on married women and judgmental enough to look down on a perfectly happy lesbian couple. That he would never offer the kind of complete, solid relationship that had once been her dream. She would be settling for little more than an habitual recurrence of the irresponsible sex fantasy she'd had that long-ago night at the beach. A more traditional, reasonable, pedestrian relationship seemed impossible for her to manage.

Maybe that was the answer, she told herself. Perhaps it was her inability to connect with a mate in any real way that led her to pine after the kind of man who was unattainable for the long term.

Against her better judgment, she retrieved the meager collection of cosmetics in her handbag and applied them to a pale complexion that did not appear "freshened" by all of her recent relaxation. She located her hairbrush and vigorously attempted to brush out any evidence of long-term bed head. By the time she was ready to go, she thought she looked pretty good.

So she was not only surprised but disappointed when it was Suzy that showed up to drive her home.

"I wanted to bring the bookmobile," she said, giggling girlishly at the plan. "I thought that would make you feel really special to be picked up in one of your own libraries! Amos completely nixed the idea. He said that it was too expensive to drive this distance and there would be no place for you to stretch your leg out. I know he's right, but I hate it when that happens."

"So are you back to work?" D.J. asked.

"Officially back tomorrow," she answered. "I figured it was not quite the thing to clock in and then drive to Hays to pick up a friend in the hospital."

D.J. smiled at her attempt at humor.

"Amos is back on his route today," she said. "This is his regular day for the stops at Washunga and Ponyvale. They're the farthest south we go and they finished up with harvest nearly a week ago. Since then folks have probably been standing, first on one leg and then the other, waiting for Amos to get there."

D.J. rode in a wheelchair out to the parking lot. An attendant helped her up and into Suzy's vehicle. And D.J. seriously did not hate stretching her leg out across the backseat of the Granfeldts' comfortable SUV.

It did make for somewhat awkward conversation,

driver in front, like a taxi or limo. But that didn't even slow Suzy down. She had a hundred stories that D.J. had missed. And had every intention of catching her up during the long, lonely highway toward home.

There was lots of gossip, big and little. D.J. listened with interest to all. But she was especially pleased to hear the latest on Amos and Jeannie.

"She is positively glowing," Suzy related. "I told her, you walk around looking that happy and everyone in Verdant will know what you're up to."

D.J. chuckled. But in the privacy of the backseat, she was blushing, as well. She seriously hoped that nothing about her feelings for Scott was detectable by small-town observers.

"And Amos," Suzy continued with a shake of her head. "I swear, that guy has not given anyone a second look for years. I thought he was completely past it."

"Apparently not."

"I guess people don't really get past it."

"I suppose that it's only human to want companionship," D.J. said.

"Is that what you and Scott are up to with him in his skivvies? A little companionship?"

D.J. blushed. "I was fully dressed and on my way to work. He's staying with his mother downstairs from me. Don't be starting any wild stories about us."

"Wild stories? Me? Not a chance," Suzy said. "I just loved being proved right."

"Huh?"

"I knew you two would make the perfect couple," she told him. "Now everybody in town agrees with me."

"We aren't really a couple," she explained. "We haven't even had a real date. We're just… I don't know what we are."

"I heard that he described himself as your boyfriend. Was he hallucinating?"

"I'm sure he was just caught up in the moment," D.J. told her. "He… We…well, it's…" She allowed her sentence to trail off, because she had no idea of its direction.

"Well, he must believe it," Suzy said. "With all that he's organized and accomplished the last few days, he must think he's honed in on the way to a librarian's heart."

"What do you mean?"

"He's moving the library. I don't mean he's moving it, but like he's moving it around like you wanted. That's why he hasn't come to see you all week, why he didn't come to pick you up. They're working like maniacs to get it all done before you get there." Suzy abruptly interrupted herself. "Oh shoot! I guess it was supposed to be a surprise."

D.J. was stunned. "It is a surprise."

"He knew how excited you were to get it done over the harvest," Suzy explained. "And then I guess the doctor kind of suggested that it would take some time to get you back to 100% and he didn't want you to have to wait."

D.J. tried to take it in. She'd been hoping he'd send flowers. Instead he'd given her library free labor. She tried to picture it. The change she'd imagined occurring while she slept off a snakebite.

"It's a big job," D.J. said. "There's no way he could have managed it in four days."

"Of course not, not by himself," she said. "Believe me, he's had help."

"Who helped? You and Amos, I guess."

"We're employees," Suzy pointed out. "What this required was volunteers."

"Who volunteered?"

"Okay, let me think who all I saw there before I left," she said, holding up her fingers as if intending to count them off. "Mike Russell was there. And Alvin Fremont. Leon Coaler, Earl Tacomb, Barnette Paske, Ed Morton…"

"I don't know any of those people," D.J. pointed out.

"I doubt many of them have darkened the library door in years," Suzy told her. "But they answered when they were called."

"Wow, I… Is there anybody that I know?"

"Well, there's my hubby. And several of the men from the Porter family that you probably met at Dutch's funeral. I put another call out on my way up. I suspect half the town is in there now."

"I can't believe it." D.J. was still shaking her head. "Is it just guys?"

"No, of course not. Guys mostly have the experience for the job. But there were plenty of women who showed up to help out. Nina and Mariana and Jeannie. Of course Stevie and Vern."

"Really? Did you ask them?"

"No, they probably heard about it and showed up to help."

"Scott doesn't like Vern."

"Well, duh," Suzy responded. "Actually, I think they get along pretty good, considering the circumstances."

"What circumstances? Being gay is not a circumstance that your neighbors should hold against you."

D.J. was nearly thrown out of her seat as Suzy swerved unexpectedly, staring wide-eyed into the rearview mirror.

"What's going on?"

"Sorry," Suzy answered. "I just couldn't believe it. You don't know? Everybody knows. How could you not know?"

"How could I not know what?" D.J. asked.

Suzy pulled the SUV off to the side of the road and put it in park. She unhooked her seat belt and turned around so she could look at D.J. directly.

"About Scott's divorce? What do you know about Scott's divorce?"

"Scott's divorce? Nothing. Except that it was an embarrassing public mess. He cheated on his wife."

Suzy shook her head. "He did not cheat on her. She cheated on him."

"She cheated on him?"

"For years, before and after they were married, maybe even as far back as high school she'd kept up the affair. Lying to his face and making an ass of him behind his back."

"Oh, wow."

"With Vern."

"What?"

Suzy nodded.

"This must have happened before Stevie."

"With Stevie," Suzy answered. "Stevie Rossiter is Scott's ex-wife."

908.1 History with Respect to Kinds of Persons

The worst thing about the whole perpendicular turn of the library shelving was that it simply could not be done piecemeal. Because the new shelving configuration was going to be sitting in the same space as the old one, every book had to be removed and every range of shelves broken down into its pieces. It was not until the floor was completely clear that they could begin repositioning. But of course, as soon as the floor was cleared, the obvious wear of the hardwood aisles was visible.

Scott had been momentarily discouraged. But his timing was perfect. Just as guys were leaving the fields, hyped up with the success of the harvest, word got out that the floors needed refinishing in the main stacks of the library. He quickly began to feel like Tom Sawyer. Every guy in town showed up with his own tools, his own level of expertise and an eagerness to get the job done.

They made quick work of sanding down the wood, cleaning everything up and applying a new stain. The most time-consuming aspect turned out to be waiting for it to dry.

None of that was hard or truly unexpected.

The one job Scott was least prepared to take on turned out to be mentoring James. With all the shelv ing piled up in metal pieces, there was no place for James to hide. He seemed to feel as exposed as if he were naked. And with the books all stacked up in the reading room and covered with drop cloths, there wasn't even anything to slam. Scott could see in the guy's eyes that he was close to a full-blown panic.

Scott took him into the break room, away from prying eyes.

"James, you can't freak out," he told him. "We need to get this done. It's for D.J. And you and I are the ones who are going to make it happen."

James was clearly nervous, shaking his hands in a repetitive way and unable to meet Scott's gaze.

"Okay, James, hang with me here," Scott said. "You're a smart guy. Smarter than a lot in this town. You know how to do a lot of stuff. What I need you to do now is troubleshoot."

"Troubleshoot," he repeated.

"Figure out what you can do, where you can go, to make yourself feel better."

"Shelves."

"There are no shelves right now. Try again."

He began nodding, but it was more like a tic than a positive response. Suddenly he seemed to catch sight of a book on a nearby table. He picked it up and loudly slammed it shut.

Almost as if the loud sound had quieted the static in his brain, he looked over at Scott, momentarily cleared.

"Bookmobile."

"Great idea."

James retreated to his haven on wheels for the duration of the invasion.

With the shelving down, it was truly amazing how much light poured in through the east-side windows.

"It looks wonderful!" Jeannie had positively gushed.

"And this is just the stacks," Suzy told her. "Think how good it's going to look once the reading room and the children's department are done."

Scott couldn't help but agree. He was glad that D.J. had decided to tackle the stacks first. They were the worst offenders and seeing the improvement would get more people fired up to help with the rest of the building.

The library's dark depression had lifted. And it was difficult now to even imagine how their grandfathers and great-grandfathers could have gotten the layout so wrong.

"It was back before we had *feng shui*," Earl Tacomb suggested.

Scott was genuinely surprised that Earl had even heard the term.

"But even from the dawn of time, people would have known the difference between blocking light and letting it shine in," Amos had pointed out.

Some of the men claimed to have always recognized that the shelves were going the wrong way. It was not as if the newcomer librarian had come upon a solution that wasn't already widely known. She had simply acted upon it.

Scott looked really askance at those statements. If it were so obvious to so many, then why generation after generation, had nobody bothered to mention it?

He didn't voice this skepticism aloud. Why alienate workers that he needed. And he really needed them. With the harvest completed and life settling back into normal, Scott had a real business to run. Paula was back on the job and his mom was helping out, but he was the only one with the license to fill prescriptions. So he found himself racing back and forth around the corner through much of the past few days.

Scott wanted to get this done for D.J. He wanted her to return to her library and find it to be all that she'd imagined. Maybe he couldn't make all her dreams come true, but he did think he could manage this one.

On Friday morning, he was not so sure. His mother called him at the library to tell him that D.J. was being released from the hospital and she needed a ride home.

Scott was torn. He wanted to go get her, but he also wanted to get the shelves installed and the books moved back on them before she saw the place. Amos and his bookmobile were expected on the route. Viv was needed at the drugstore.

"I'll go get her," Suzy volunteered.

"Can you drive really, really slow," Scott suggested. "That way we might have an outside chance of at least getting the shelves in place."

"Sure, better than that, I'll get you some more help over here. Have cell phone. Will travel."

Scott wasn't sure who else she might get to come and was genuinely surprised at the number of people who showed up at the door. Almost every businessman and woman in town.

"I put a sign on the front of the store," Otis Morton told him. "Closed to Help Out in the Library."

He was not the only one. Shops and offices all over town were shutting down for the day or sending what staff they could spare.

Wendal Rossiter showed up. So did Bryce Holland. Scott would have considered neither man as any kind of friend.

The Verdant High School shop class and their teacher, Sam Niles, arrived, boys and girls carrying wrenches and screwdrivers. And a bus full of residents of the Pine Tree Nursing Home shuffled in. The ones who could help, did help. And those that could not, sat on chairs lined up in the vestibule, cheering the workers on.

Each range of heavy-duty shelving had to be secured to the floor with a weight bearing capacity of 300 pounds per square foot. The T-shaped foundation of the units were screwed and then firmed up with a metal crossbar. Once that was in place, the individual units on the range were reconstructed piece by piece.

The first one was extremely slow going, but once everyone saw how it worked and what needed to be done, they were picking up the pace and naturally forming into specialized labor teams.

Scott was really getting stoked. It seemed like it was going to happen. He was proud of his community and he could hardly wait to see D.J.'s face, though he was still hoping that Suzy was driving slowly.

It was all going so smoothly, that it was almost destined to hit a snag. And they did.

The snag arrived in the person of Amelia Grundler home from her vacation, looking rested and refreshed and ready for battle. At her side was a sheepish, reluctant Karl Langley. And in her hand was a cease and desist order.

"The vandalism of this public building will cease!" she declared.

"Vandalism?" Scott shook his head. "We're renovating."

The woman eyed him as dismissively as if he were a kindergartener caught using crayons on the walls.

"No one in this room is authorized to make any physical changes to this building," she said. "None of you are employed by the library and I have serious doubts about who in this mob might be bonded and approved for doing refurbishment on a government structure."

"We didn't come in here and start taking things apart," Scott told her. "D.J. drew up the plans and we followed them."

"D.J. drew up the plans," Miss Grundler repeated in a snotty singsong tone. "Let me be clear, I do not blame her. Obviously the inexperience and ignorance of such a recent hire led her to believe that she could make substantive changes to the interior without the hearings and permits required by the county."

Everybody in the room began talking all at once.

Scott looked over at Karl. He shrugged and shook his head.

"Let me look at the order," Scott demanded.

Miss Grundler handed it over.

He glanced at the very official-looking judge's signature and then scanned anxiously through the legalese.

"It says, unequivocally, that due to the librarian's flouting of the county's policy and procedures, and her procurement of labor from uncertified workmen, the decision-making for all library activity will be temporarily handed to the employee with the longest seniority, to whom all power will be vested until the next *regular* meeting of the library board. That, as you may know, is in October."

Scott felt sick. He had tried to do something wonderful for D.J. and instead he'd brought down the wrath of Miss Grundler on her head. If Amelia maintained control until October, D.J. would probably be put on suspension. Only the board could fire her, but Miss

Grundler could make it difficult enough to make her leave voluntarily.

"Now," the woman announced to the entire room. "You must all vacate the premises. I have a *bonded* restoration crew on the way here from Salina. The library will close for the rest of the week while the shelving is returned to its traditional location. Then we will open up, as usual next Monday."

Scott couldn't give up without a fight. "Look around," he implored her. "Look at how much better the place looks. Look at all the people who are engaged in this. It's going to be good for the library. It's going to be good for the community. The judge up at the county seat probably never saw it as it was. And he's not here to see how it can be. But you can. This is where you've devoted much of your life. It has been the place where you've made your own career. Improving it is going to be as much a plus for you as it is for the rest of us."

"No." The woman's answer was short, cold and unyielding. "I am not allowing an outside interloper to change *my* library. All of you now, go home. Before I have to ask the deputy to escort you out."

The townspeople stood around stunned. There was a good deal of murmuring and grousing. Self-made men like Bryce Holland and successful women like Vern Milbank didn't typically take orders from low-level civil servants. And the senior citizens from Pine Tree were old enough and cranky enough to be extremely stubborn. But the community as a whole had grown accustomed to doing what Miss Grundler told them. She had been the dictator of the library for so many years, that no one dared to question her. No one dared to stand up against her. Slowly, angrily, unhappily they began to gather their things and head for the door.

A book slammed shut loudly in the shadows of the metal staircase behind the circulation desk and a voice that few had ever heard at that volume spoke up.

"Wait!"

Like a tableau everyone stood frozen in place for an instant. Then, as one, there was a shocked inhale of their collective breath as James emerged from his hiding place.

He was hunched over as if being beaten, his shoulder was raised on the right in an attempt to shield himself from the full attention of the room as he cautiously made his way across the floor. Although he was universally recognized, most had hardly caught a glimpse of him over the last few years. And no one had ever seen him step out in front of a crowd. He was more of a legend than a participant in the community. Still, eyes on the ground, he marched to the very center of conversation. Though he did stop on the far side of Karl, as if keeping the deputy between himself and Miss Grundler were the better part of valor.

"May I see the paper, please," he asked Scott.

He handed it over. James turned away from the eyes that were all upon him as he silently read what was written. Those around waited. The novelty of his appearance kept them in rapt attention for several moments. But as he apparently went over the words again and again and again, whispering began and complaint began to stir in the crowd.

"Oh, for heaven's sakes!" Nina Philpot blurted out. "Either say something or go back into hiding."

James turned. His pale face appeared even more wan than usual and he was trembling like a leaf, but his jaw was firm.

"So this injunction doesn't stop the work, it removes

D.J. from the decision and leaves the library board out of it until their autumn meeting."

The statement was directed at Scott. He was certainly no expert on legalese, but he had been one to read the document.

"Yes, I suppose that's the actual reading of it," he said. "It takes away D.J.'s choices about the running of the library, including the layout and whether it needs to be changed."

"And none of us can do anything about it," Karl added.

"At least until the fall."

The last threat came from Vern, who looked mad enough to spit nails as she shot Amelia a threatening look.

But Scott feared any chest pumping would be toothless. After such a public scolding and a probable suspension, D.J. would not be feeling particularly welcome. And even if she was willing to stay, Scott wasn't sure that even his mother would be able to convince the library board to go against Amelia again to keep D.J. beyond her probationary period.

Miss Grundler responded to Vern's bluster with narrow-eyed dismissal.

"The judge's order is completely valid," Karl told James. His voice was both certain and sympathetic. "As deputy sheriff you can be sure that I called the county to verify it."

James nodded. "It says that the management of the library will be temporarily vested in the employee with the most seniority."

"Tell us something we don't know," Harvey Hollar suggested snidely.

James flinched from the words, almost as if they had struck him. Then he answered quietly. "That...that person would be me."

912.7 Graphic Representations of Earth

The trip from Hays seemed to last forever. D.J. could hardly take it in. Just when she almost got her brain around the whole gift of the library move, she'd gotten distracted by the idea of Scott having been married to Stevie. And being the injured party instead of the cheat. And Stevie preferring Vern to Scott. Wow. That was big.

Throwing all her anti-gossiping principles to the wind, D.J. pressed Suzy for details.

"I don't know much more than what everybody knows," she admitted. "Those two started dating early, way early. Maybe like seventh or eighth grade. They never dated anyone else. Everybody assumed they'd get married right after high school. It didn't happen. Some people began to assume it would be right after college. Then Stephanie—we all called her Stephanie back then—came home and Scott went to pharmacy school. He came home some weekends. She went there some weekends. They didn't seem to be in any hurry. I figured they were at it like rabbits on every occasion. Hubby and I certainly were. But apparently the rabbit bits were saved for Vern."

Suzy giggled at her own little joke.

"So then Scott finally moves home and goes to work for his dad. Then she's got to decorate a house. And then she wants to buy cars. And then she wants a huge extravaganza with a dozen bridesmaids. In hindsight, of course you can see that they were all stalling tactics. But nobody got it then, especially not Scott. They had five hundred people attending the fanciest wedding Verdant has ever seen. And the marriage was totally over and she was living with Vern before the thank-you notes went out."

"Oh, that's awful." D.J. felt very sympathetic, but she attempted to hedge those emotions. "But wasn't he a player, too? Didn't he have kind of a reputation for seeing other women?"

"Scott?" Suzy shook her head. "Not that I ever heard about. He's always been a very straight arrow." She chuckled. "In the oldest sense of that term."

"Well I…I, uh, heard that he used to go off…like to spring break and…you know…play the field."

"Really?" Suzy sounded genuinely astounded. "Who said something like that?"

"Uh…I don't remember exactly."

"Well, if that happened, I never heard anything about it," Suzy said. "And I do try to keep my ear to the ground. What I recall about school breaks and such, he always came home to help out in the store. Now Le-anne, his sister, she was a wild child. She used to go off, I think. Got into some trouble now and then. She ended up married to a cop, so maybe all's well that ends well. But Scott, I don't think so. I can ask Amos. He won't tell me, but I'll be able to see the truth in his expression."

"No, no. That's okay."

When they finally arrived at the library, she parked out in front.

"Wait right here," Suzy told her. "I'll get somebody to help you."

D.J. had no patience for that. She managed to get her booted leg out the SUV door and hobbled up the sidewalk. At the beginning of the steps, she hesitated. D.J. was considering a walk around the building to the handicapped ramp in the back when the front doors burst open and Scott came galloping toward her taking the stairs two at a time. The look on his face was so young and so excited and so in love, that she thought he might grab her and kiss her. At the last minute, however, he seemed to think better of it and stopped.

"Hi."

"Hi, yourself."

"Suzy said she blew the surprise."

"I'm still surprised," D.J. said. "And I can't wait to see. Can you help me up?"

"I can carry you."

"Just give me your arm."

Side by side, step by step, they made their way up. Scott was talking rapidly, filling her in on the confrontation with Amelia. D.J. was stunned.

"Permits? I do not believe that shelf realignment requires permits. It's about rearranging the furniture, not doing construction."

Scott nodded. "Yeah, you probably could have won that in court, but who has time or energy or money to go to court."

"And James saved the day."

"Unbelievable, right?"

"Yes… Well, no, not really. James probably cares more about the library than anybody. Even way outside his comfort zone, he recognized his duty to rescue us."

They reached the top of the steps and walked across the porch. Scott held the door for D.J. as she stepped inside. A round of applause greeted her. But even more welcoming was the bright glow of natural light flooding between the bookshelves to the vestibule. D.J. knew that it was going to be better. She never imagined that it would be this beautiful.

Shocked, surprised, stunned, she slowly walked the length of the building, still on Scott's arm.

"It's fantastic. It looks wonderful. Thank you. Thank you all so much."

She was overwhelmed with all the people involved. She tried to express her gratitude to each one personally. There were a lot of "Oh, shucks" responses and some "Glad to do it," but some very thoughtful ones, too.

"It's our library," the old gentleman from Pine Tree told her. "It's about time we took some responsibility for the shape that it's in."

Suzy reminded everybody that the doctor said D.J. shouldn't spent much time on her feet. So a chair was set up for her in front of the circulation desk, where she could see what was going on, be in the middle of the action and still elevate her injured foot on a stepstool.

A few of the ranges were being put together, but books were already going on the installed shelves. All of her advance planning was coming into fruition as the nonlibrary trained volunteers were able to easily identify where each grouping of volumes should be shelved. And with all the help, they were going back up a lot more quickly than they had come down.

She asked about James, but nobody had seen him since he became the man in charge and ordered the work to continue. Karl had backed him up, as following the letter of the law. He had been an employee longer than Miss Grundler. And all the angry things she had to say about him didn't change that. The woman had stomped off furiously, though not seeming as much beaten as determined to regroup.

Amos returned from his bookmobile route in the late afternoon. He was impressed.

"I never believed it could get done today," he said. "I am totally blown away."

But not so blown away that he couldn't stow his gear and start helping out, as well. D.J. figured it didn't hurt that he was able to appoint himself as an assistant to Jeannie and start following her around like a faithful puppy.

And where faithful puppies were concerned, Viv showed up after closing the drugstore. She brought Dew inside with her. D.J. was excited to see him and he seemed likewise thrilled.

"You shouldn't bring him in here."

"He's on his leash."

"Yes, that's good, but only service dogs are allowed in libraries."

Viv winked at her. "He's been a lot of service to me. Besides, he's got a friend on the library board."

Edna Kievener pulled up a chair to sit beside her.

"I'm pretending to consult with you," she told D.J. "To give myself an excuse to sit down."

"I think being tired ought to be excuse enough."

The woman shook her head. "I don't want to be mistaken for one of those dear old souls from the nursing home whom we all expect to stay seated. Besides, Old Man Paske has been winking at me all afternoon. I that crazy lech is not careful I'm going to box his ears."

D.J. laughed. "I'm pretty sure nobody wants to se that happen," she said.

"Oh, I'm certain they do," Edna countered. "That' the kind of thing that passes for entertainment in thi town. But don't you worry, if the smelly coot can't take a hint, I'll have Mr. Dewey here bite his leg."

"Dew's not much of a biter," D.J. said.

"Oh, he seems like the kind of little fellow a woman could count on to protect her."

Claire Gleason also took a break to sit beside her and discuss what she'd heard about the proposed new bookmobile stops. She sounded impressed and pleased.

"I think we're all going to be excited about the expansion of service."

Ashley had a chance to pet Dew as she filled D.J. in on all the excitement that occurred in her absence. The typically silent, sluggish girl was almost effervescent in her enthusiasm.

"I've been helping Mrs. Sanderson in the drugstore, but mostly what I've been doing is taking Mr. Dewey for walks and playing with him on the sidewalk, 'cause he's not really supposed to be in the store. And I am totally sure now that I want a dog that's a little black terrier. Even if black is not my favorite color. Orange is my favorite color. Dogs don't usually come in orange anyway."

The little girl laughed delightedly. It was a great sound to hear.

As afternoon wove on into evening, more and more people stopped by. D.J. began to feel as if she were part of a reception line as new people came by to introduce themselves.

The community worked late. Everyone was keen on getting the job done. As the sun went down, several of the older residents including Viv, who were not so keen about driving at night, made an exit.

The Pine Tree residents cheerfully said their goodbyes, one declaring to D.J. that "watching all the work was the best fun I've had in months."

It was a quarter to seven when Stevie Rossiter showed up. She brought catered dinner donated from the Brazier. Julene Turpin came with her, both to pick up her daughter and to help serve the food.

Stevie dished a plate and brought it for D.J. She took the seat beside her.

"You know you look really good for somebody who just got out of the hospital. That's setting the standard way too high for the women of Verdant."

D.J. was pretty sure she was lying. Stevie was a natural beauty. Makeup free and bed-headed, she would outshine most of the women in the entire state of Kansas. But she thanked her for the compliment nonetheless.

"I found out today that you used to be married to Scott," D.J. told her.

Stevie's eyes widened. "You found out today?" she repeated. "And I thought my entire life story was being handed out in a pamphlet on the Newcomers Cart."

"I did hear about you and Vern very quickly," D.J. clarified. "But I didn't know Scott was part of the history."

"I'm surprised he didn't tell you himself," she said.

"He did tell me he was divorced," D.J. replied. "And I think he mentioned you a couple of times. But he called you Stephanie. I never made the connection."

"Ah," she said, nodding. "Stephanie was my *pretending to be a straight woman* name. Scott is about the only person who still uses it. Maybe because I pretended longest with him."

D.J. didn't know what to say to that, so she said nothing and offered what she hoped was a noncommittal smile.

"I hope this is not going to make things weird between us," Stevie said. "I really like you. Vern really likes you. We both think you and Scott will be great together."

"Oh, we're not really together," D.J. hedged quickly.

"Well, get that changed as quickly as you can," Stevie told her. "Scott is a great guy. What I did to him… what I did to Vern—heck, what I did to myself, was terrible, horrible, stupid." She sighed heavily and shook her head. "When we're young, sometimes we make those mistakes. It doesn't mean that we don't eventually deserve some happiness. My life has turned out to be really good. I think *you* would be really good for Scott. And I'm pretty sure he would be good for you."

783.2 Music for Single Voice

Viv had enjoyed herself the last few days. It had been fun helping out at the store, doing things she hadn't done in years. And the work at the library brought out an optimism and community enthusiasm that she'd almost forgotten. It was even better to have Mr. Dewey accompanying her. The little dog made friends wherever he went and his cheerfulness goaded smiles from the tired faces of the workers as easily as the senior citizens on their short respite from the nursing home.

But it was her friend, Edna, who really brought it all home to her.

"I like the looks of that," she said, indicating D.J. on Scott's arm.

Viv nodded.

"I've never seen a more smitten couple. They both look like they can hardly wait to rip their clothes off."

"Let's hope they wait until they get home," Viv teased.

"Ah…I remember those days."

Viv did, too.

"So no more time spent worrying about Scott," Edna told her. "Now you've got to see what you can learn to enjoy about freedom and independence."

Was that what she was supposed to do?

No. That was definitely not it. She had already decided. She wanted to be with John. There was nothing, nothing left for her here. That had been the entire plan. Once Scott was settled, she was free to…to do what John undoubtedly intended for her to do. There were no more tasks to be completed, no more lessons to be learned. She was free to go to him. And that *was* what he wanted, wasn't it?

Her certainty on the subject was wavering. There had been no more dreams. No more messages from the other side. He had not come to her again. That image of him, the young, strong image had become the one to linger in her memory, blotting out the persistent recall of his emaciated body lying cold against white sheets.

The youthful visage was like a gift, one that was so much easier to live with. But she'd decided that she didn't want to live. That's what she'd decided. Once Scott was settled, she was free to go.

She arrived back home questioning her own resolve. Was she losing her nerve? In the last few busy weeks had she inexplicably begun to think long-term? She had no long-term plan. Her plan was to be gone.

Edna was right. Scott and D.J. were far enough along that they were bound to find happiness together. If she waited longer, it was an artificial delay. Certainly today was not the best time, but there would never be a best time. If she put it off…

Viv refused to allow herself to finish the thought. She would not put it off. In fact, she would do it now.

She took Mr. Dewey off his leash, set her purse down on the kitchen counter and walked straight through to her husband's office. She pulled out the secreted cooler filled with bad cans and carried it to the kitchen. The dog followed close at her heels.

Carefully she unloaded the bulging canned goods into the sink. Several had already broken open.

"I was thinking," she told Mr. Dewey. "To fix a pot of stew. I have so many varied ingredients, a stew might work. But now I'm leaning toward a potpie. I used to make potpie for John and he loved it."

The dog continued to eye her curiously.

"Look at this cream of chicken," she said, and held up the misshapen can. Something brown was growing on the side of it. "Is that the scariest, nastiest-looking thing you have ever seen. Eww, totally disgusting."

She set it on the side.

"The good news about botulism," she said, "is that you can't taste a thing. I'm sure it's not the most pleasant way to die. But it's hardly the worst. Most people assume it's like food poisoning. That you get sick to your stomach and vomit yourself to death. That is absolutely wrong. It doesn't work that fast and if you're throwing up, you get rid of it and it doesn't sicken you at all."

A tin of carrots was so rounded on the bottom it wouldn't stand. She laid it next to the cream of chicken.

"Botulism bacteria attacks the nervous system and paralyses you," she explained. "They say the first thing you lose is the ability to speak. That seems like a plus. Even if I were to change my mind, I won't be able to call for help."

Viv moved to the counter across the kitchen. She dug through her utensil drawer until she found her pastry blender. Then she measured out the flour and expertly cut the shortening into it. Mr. Dewey stayed close beside her.

She began humming happily to herself. It had been a long time since she'd made a piecrust. *I should do this more often*, she thought to herself. And then laughed aloud at her own inability to hold a grasp of her actions.

Suicide was her positive step forward. She had considered it early on. She understood about those women throwing themselves upon a funeral pyre. Without John, her life was over. She wanted it to be over. And the wonderful thing about her plan was that no one would ever suspect what she had done. An old lady found dead in her bed would be a shock. But it was not as if she were taking a pistol out of the bedside table.

She rolled out the dough until it was thin enough to be flaky and large enough to be double the dish. She gently eased the bottom crust into place. Then let it rest as she put together the filling.

Peas and potatoes, carrots, tomatoes, white beans and sauerkraut. She laughed at the combination. Never in the history of potpies had such been brought together. She pulled her electric can opener out of its cubby and put it to work.

The first can spewed its contents halfway across the room.

Mr. Dewey barked at it.

"Let the fireworks begin!" Viv joked.

With several spews, a few fizzles and a share of drama-free openings, she managed to get all of her interesting potpie ingredients mixed together. She stirred it, but didn't cook it. She assumed that the less heat on the bacteria, the better.

"I feel like a witch," she told Mr. Dewey. "All it needs is an eye of newt and I could probably turn my Mini Cooper into a purple cabbage."

She poured the filling into the shell and then covered it with the top crust. She sealed the edges together and crimped them prettily, the way her mother had taught her a half century earlier. A few slits cut in the top would allow steam to escape. She looked at her work and smiled. It looked as nice as any she'd ever made.

"Who could imagine that? I've never even heard of a potpie with sauerkraut. It's too bad there's no time to leave the recipe in my will."

She laughed aloud at that small excuse for a joke.

"I suppose there really is time," she admitted. "It's six to twelve hours before the symptoms take effect. I could just write sauerkraut potpie on a slip of paper and stick it in my recipe box. Eventually D.J. or Leanne or somebody would find it. Right?"

Somehow that didn't seem like enough. It was a good hint, but she should probably scribble out the entire recipe. Of course, without her to recommend it, no one might ever even give it a shot.

"That's probably why I've never heard of it before," she told the dog. "All of the past consumers of it were probably busy committing suicide, as well."

She put her potpie in the hot oven and set the timer for thirty minutes.

"Now we have to clean up. Can't leave a shred of evidence."

She poured out and rinsed out all of the leftover "bad cans" and washed out the cooler for good measure. She cleaned up the kitchen, wiping down all the surfaces with anti-bacterial soap. She wanted botulism, but she certainly didn't want anyone else to get it. She flattened all the misshapen cans to disguise their issues and distributed them thoughout the recycling bin, so they would appear unsuspicious.

A flash of headlights let her know Scott and D.J. were home.

"Yes," she told Mr. Dewey. "This will be their home.

Oh, I know that Scott likes his new place, but once I'm gone it will make more sense to move in here. They can reopen the upper floor and make this the family house again." She glanced down at the little dog. "It will be perfect for you, I promise," she told him. "And wait until they fill it with little children for you to play with."

She liked the thought of that. The image of Scott and D.J. setting up their life here, recreating the happiness that she had shared with John.

There was a momentary pang of regret that neither of them would see it, but she pushed it away.

The oven timer rang like the toll of a bell. Viv looked around her kitchen with confidence that all her tracks had been adequately covered.

Her creation came out golden brown and smelling like heaven itself. She left it on the counter to cool as she set the table.

For this special occasion, she set a place for herself in the dining room, using her grandmother's revered and fragile bone china.

"Thanksgiving, Christmas and suicide," she quipped to the dog. She was amusing and enjoying herself.

The beautiful pie looked even better atop the white tablecloth, with a sterling silver serving spoon at the ready. She'd chilled a bottle of Chenin Blanc and poured herself a generous portion in a champagne flute for a bit more pizzazz. Lit candles, cloth napkin, it was all quite lovely. And quite lonely.

She went to the stairs pantry and found the dog treats. She put two on a dinner plate.

She smiled at her lovely dinner table. It was truly fit for the occasion. Unfortunately she was not at all hungry.

She'd eaten barbecue with everyone else when

she was still at the library. That had probably been
a bad idea.

Momentarily she thought she should sit down and
force herself to eat it. That was the best way to keep
second thoughts at bay. Still, she wanted her last meal
to be pleasant. There was nothing pleasant about eating when she wasn't hungry.

"How about we watch a movie," she suggested to
Mr. Dewey. "Then afterward we can enjoy a midnight
supper."

The dog did not reply, but he followed at her heels
as she went to the family room.

Viv flipped through the collection of DVDs until
she found the aging epic that she wanted. She held up
Titanic for Mr. Dewey's inspection.

"Kate Winslet. Leonardo DiCaprio. Everybody's favorite."

He seemed agreeable enough.

She put the disc in the player and settled in on the
couch, the ball of black fur snuggled up beside her.

Viv had seen the movie a half dozen times. There
was a lot to recommend it. Fabulous setting. Incredible
costumes. Thrilling drama. Viv liked the scene when
Rose jumped out of the lifeboat, more desperate to be
with Jack than to be saved. But the young people were
still trying to live, trying to survive. They were fighting desperately for a future together.

Viv felt too old for the fight and too tired to try to
swim. Her favorite character was Mrs. Straus, the wife
of a multimillionaire merchant who chose to stay onboard with her husband. Viv waited anxiously for the
brief scene of the two of them, side by side in their state-
room bed, holding each other, facing death warm in
each other's arms as the freezing water engulfed them.

Yes, love to the last, to the very last and together.

Viv retrieved a tissue to wipe the tears from her eyes. Deliberately she tried to ignore the admonitions of Unsinkable Molly Brown. Some lives were not worth living. Sometimes there was no reason to try to carry on.

She absently patted the companion beside her. He was not there. She looked down at the couch, the floor, she scanned the room. Mr. Dewey was not there. Surprising. He seemed to enjoy staying right by her side.

She heard something clatter in the dining room. Getting up, she walked in there.

"Mr. Dewey?"

The dog was inexplicably standing on the dining room table. He never got up on the furniture like that. There was a mess of food in the fur of his muzzle as he stood over the plate of chicken potpie.

For one long moment, Viv took in the scene in disbelief. The middle of her suicide meal was missing. With a little cry of horror, she grabbed the dog in her arms and tried to clean out his mouth.

"Why did you do it? You don't eat table scraps. You don't like people food!"

She glanced at the plate she'd set for him across from her own. The two doggie treats, his favorites, were left untouched.

"Why? Why?"

She carried him to kitchen and set him in the sink while she rifled like a crazy person through the cabinet. She finally found what she was looking for, a round box of ordinary table salt

She quickly poured a handful into her palm. Then holding Mr. Dewey tightly against her body, she forced the white crystals down his throat. He struggled against her, but he was small and she was large.

The poor little dog began hacking and gagging immediately.

"Why did you do it?" she asked him, as tears began coursing down her cheeks. "You don't like people food. Why would you do it?"

It was hardly a moment before he began vomiting in earnest. His whole body heaved reflexively as the bitter meal was forced out of him.

"Why did you do it?" she asked him again and again. "You don't like table scraps. You already had your dog food and your treats were right there on the plate. You never eat table food. And you never get on the table. If I'd thought there was any chance of you getting to that pie, I would have put it back in the oven."

Mr. Dewey was too sick to answer. He vomited again and again.

She was beginning to feel nauseated herself. Shocked and horrified at what might have happened to this small innocent creature who had only tried to be a friend to her.

They both heaved miserably for several minutes. In the aftermath, Viv was too exhausted to stand anymore, she slid down the cabinet door to sit on the kitchen floor.

Mr. Dewey was looking better. Moving around more like himself. He came up beside her, putting his front paws up on her knee and looking at her with love.

Viv looked back.

"You didn't want to be left, did you? You didn't want to have to be the one to carry on by yourself. But you see, it wouldn't make me happy for you to give up your life, just because I gave up mine."

Tears blinded her, as she rubbed the thick black fur at the little dog's neck.

"You have to go on. I want you to go on. I wouldn't

want to leave if I thought you weren't going to have your life."

After a long moment, she sighed and wiped away the tears.

"I'm sure my John felt exactly the same way," she said.

904.65 Collected Accounts of Historical Events

By the time the last book was shelved, the dinner was cleared and the volunteers had agreed on a schedule to begin work in the children's department, D.J. was exhausted.

The people began filing out. And James returned from his hiding place.

"Thank you for what you did," D.J. said as he slipped in between the nearby shelves.

"Okay."

"You really saved the day for me and for everyone who loves this library."

"Okay."

"Miss Grundler is not going to disappear. She's going to be back and she's going to be very mad at you."

"Okay."

"I wish we could throw water on her and she would melt, but that's not going to happen."

"Are you sure?"

D.J. laughed. And from within the depths of the shelving, she heard James laugh, too.

Across the room she spotted Scott saying his goodbyes as people filed out the door. Maybe no one else noticed that he shook Vern's hand and kissed Stevie on the cheek as if she were an old friend. But it was enough that D.J. did.

The library now cleaned and locked up, there were no questions asked about who was taking D.J. home. She hobbled her way to the back parking lot, but he swooped her up into his van and they drove through the mostly deserted streets of Verdant after dark.

"Thanks for letting me take you home," he said.

She shrugged. "Well, we are going to the same place."

"Not true," he answered. "I've got my house back."

"Really?"

"Yeah, the guys from the septic tank service finally got out there this week. They had to dig up a big chunk of the backyard, but they found the blockage and cleared it out."

"That's good."

"You won't believe what the guy told me," Scott said. "It's going to ruin your reputation."

"My reputation?"

"He told me the inlet was plugged up and to tell my girlfriend to stop flushing her tampons." Scott shook his head. "I swore to him up and down that no woman has been in there to flush anything since I've owned the house. He didn't believe me."

Had he really not had women in his house? Suzy didn't think so. She didn't think he was a player at all. After the revelation about Stevie, D.J. was no longer sure of anything. Something about tampons niggled at her brain, but she was so tired and so pleased with the sound of the girlfriend being herself she didn't bother to delve into it.

Scott parked the van next to her car.

D.J. opened her own door, but found herself slightly

hesitant to put her feet on to the ground where she'd last encountered a nasty bite. Ultimately, she didn't have to. Scott lifted her into his arms and carried her across the lawn.

"I can walk," she assured him.

"You don't have to," he said. "I've been wanting to hold you next to me for days. This seems like the perfect excuse."

He carried her up the stairs to her apartment, no small feat, she imagined, although he did it with an ease that belied the weight of a full-grown woman.

"I saw you talking to Stephanie today," he said.

His tone was really casual, but D.J. sensed that he was fishing. "Yeah, some girl talk," D.J. teased him. "Sharing secrets. Kissing and telling."

Scott reached the deck and set her down gently on her feet. He unlocked the door and turned on the light.

"Not every guy gets a good recommendation from the ex-wife," she added.

He nodded. "I'm sure she took the blame for everything," Scott says. "She always does. But I'm at fault, too."

"Oh?"

"Guilty of being an idiot," he answered.

She hobbled inside and down the hallway to the living room. He stopped her in the hallway and directed her to the bedroom instead.

"You need to get off your feet," he said.

"Is that your usual line for getting a woman into bed?"

"No, but if it works…" he answered, teasing. "Have you got pain meds?"

He glanced around the room, which was still in chaotic disarray.

"In my purse."

She handed him the bag and he rifled through it until he found the bottle.

"Sorry about the room," she said. "I still haven't really unpacked."

"Well, don't start now," he said. "*Rest* doesn't mean sorting out your apartment."

He put two pills in her hand and got a glass of water from the bathroom.

"You're going to feel a lot better in a few minutes," he promised.

Scott propped the pillows behind her back as she stretched her leg out. "Let's get this boot off," he said, as he began unstrapping the Velcro closures.

She sighed heavily once released from the stiffly boned air cast.

"Better?"

"Much."

"This thing is just to stabilize your leg and help with walking until you can wear shoes again. You probably shouldn't wear it all day."

She nodded. The hospital nurse had told her much the same thing. But she didn't want the conversation to turn to her snakebite recovery.

"So why were you an idiot with your ex? Because you didn't know she was gay?"

He hesitated thoughtfully. "I was an idiot all on my own. I *didn't* know she was gay. I knew there was something, even if I didn't know what it was."

"This is none of my business," D.J. stated. "But I'd like to know, if you feel comfortable in telling me."

Scott stretched out along the end of the bed, propping himself up with an elbow. "We started dating when we were just kids," he explained. "There is no way that

I blame myself for being attracted to her or thinking that she'd be perfect for me. She was smart and fun and pretty. We were great friends. Everybody thought we were so lucky to have each other. At first everything seemed fine. She liked holding hands and a quick kiss good-night, but when I began to want more than that, she didn't respond well."

D.J. tried to picture the mismatch of this hot guy and the gorgeous woman who could never be attracted to him.

"All the other guys were beginning to score with their regular girlfriends," he said. "Even giving a big discount for lying, I was not making much progress at all."

"Did you talk to her?"

He shook his head. "I thought Stephanie was perfect. The problem couldn't be hers. It had to be mine."

"Yours?"

"Yeah," he answered. "I was a fairly confident teenager, but it's an age of awkwardness. I thought my technique was bad. That I must be doing it wrong. I needed to know how."

"How?"

"So I tried to learn how to be better at it the same way I'd learned everything else. I studied. I read every book and magazine I could get my hands on."

"You're kidding?"

He raised a hand. "Scout's honor. I read *Playboy* and *GQ* and *Cosmo*."

"You read *Cosmo?*" she asked incredulously.

"Lots of good advice in *Cosmo*," he assured her. "All that necking stuff you liked, straight out of the *Lust Advisor*."

She laughed. "You really are a good kisser," she told him.

"I know. I've worked at it."

"But it didn't work with Stevie."

"Not so much. But I wouldn't give up. By the time we were in college, I pretty much pressured her into having sex with me."

"Not good," D.J. said.

"Bad, seriously bad," he corrected. "No matter what I did, no matter how hard I tried, she never truly enjoyed it, she only tolerated it."

"But again you didn't give up."

"I was sure that I was simply lousy in bed. I needed to learn how to satisfy her sexually." He shook his head. "My parents flipped when I got a B in Organic Chemistry. I couldn't tell them it was because I was too busy studying Female Orgasm."

D.J. laughed, she couldn't help herself.

"That's not the worst," he said. "I decided to get some hands-on training. I deliberately went out to find a hot, experienced woman that could teach me how it's really done."

"A prostitute?"

"No, I'm way too fastidious for that," he answered. 'I went out during spring break, you know, where all the girls go wild. I picked up the hottest, sexiest beach babe in all of South Padre Island."

D.J. felt her body stiffen all over.

"Nobody needs the details, but suffice to say, the woman blew out every brain cell in my head and left my body wrung out like a dishrag."

D.J. was staring at him, wondering. How many times had he been to Padre? How many women had he picked up?

"I'm telling you this, mostly to explain what happened afterward."

"What happened afterward?"

"I came home and had a talk with my dad. I told him about all the problems that I had with Stephanie and how…how great it was with this girl I met. How I felt as if, somehow I was a different person with her. A happier, more fulfilled person. I felt like…like I was in love with her. It was crazy. I didn't even know her. And yet, I had all these feelings for her."

D.J.'s brain had gone numb. She could hear every word he was saying, but couldn't quite take it in.

"Dad told me not to ignore those feelings. That what happened with her should prove to me that Stephanie and I were wrong for each other. He told me that the best thing for both of us was to break up. That I should wait for a woman who could make me feel the way I felt with the girl from South Padre."

Scott sat up.

"That's the only time that I can remember when I completely disregarded my father's advice," he said. "I was so consumed with my belief that Stephanie and I were perfect for each other, that I refused to hear all evidence to the contrary."

D.J. felt almost light-headed. She couldn't quite make the connection between what she was hearing and what she'd always known was true. It was as if the world had strangely tilted and she wasn't sure which way to right herself.

"I don't want to disregard my dad's advice anymore," he said. "D.J., I think you may be the woman that I've been waiting for. I realize that we don't really know each other that well. That we've hardly even dated. But I feel this connection to you. I feel like I've known you forever and that I've just found you again. Do you think we could…perhaps pursue this…this friendship further?"

She sat staring at him. He noted her expression.

"I've said it already in public and we know the gossips picked right up on it, but I would like to start seeing you, dating you, sleeping with you. I'd like to really be your boyfriend."

D.J. had to tell him. She couldn't let their relationship go one step further without revealing the truth. A long moment of silence passed between them as she tried to gather up her words.

"What am I doing?" he asked aloud. "I didn't mean for it all to come out that way. You got out of the hospital this afternoon and you're on pain medication. I shouldn't be pushing you. I need to let you get some sleep. We can discuss this tomorrow or the next day. When you're rested. Now what do you need? Pajamas?"

"Yeah, yeah, pajamas would be nice," she said.

She needed to be alone. She needed to be able to think.

Scott stood up and looked around the room at the mess of boxes.

"Maybe that box over there," she suggested, pointing to one next to the dresser.

Scott was sorting through her clothes as D.J. tried to organize her thoughts. Could that really be how it was? That Scott, who seemed to know everything about how to fine-tune a woman's body, had learned that in books? That he'd actually bought her fake veneer of sexual sophistication and he'd never recognized her for the silly, reckless virgin that she'd been. How would she confess to being his sexual siren? How could the past be revealed without messing up the present?

"Here we go," she heard him say.

As he turned, something caught on the jewelry box that she'd left on the edge of the dresser. With a crash it spilt out on the floor.

"Whoops," he said, tossing the pj's in her direction. He bent down and began refilling the box.

D.J.'s brow furrowed as she tried to think things through. How could she have gotten it all so wrong? She'd thought he was a player, but he wasn't. She'd thought he'd taken advantage of her naivety, but he hadn't even seen it. Their night together had been a terrible, youthful mistake. But it had kept her from ever settling for less. Now she could have everything. The brass ring was being offered, but in order to grasp it, she had to allow the prudish persona in which she'd clothed herself to fall away, revealing the vulnerable naked truth of herself.

Suddenly intruding upon her thoughts was a silence. It was a strange, ominous silence seeming to come out of nowhere that demanded her attention and filled the small bedroom.

D.J. looked across the room as, slowly, Scott rose to his feet. He turned to her, his eyes full of questions. It was then that she noticed what was in his hands. It was a broken piece of cheap, gold-colored jewelry. A bell band with a tiny, dangling pink heart.

South Padre Island (Eight years later)

She awakened to the sound of surf and the squeals of little girls. The book she'd been reading was still open on her lap, as if she hadn't been dozing beneath the shade of the beach umbrella.

D.J. yawned and stretched and looked over the expanse of sand in front of her. At the water's edge a tall, familiar guy with sandy-brown hair lurched, zombielike along the shore. His hands, frozen into claws, stretched out threateningly as the two children in wet swimsuits darted around him, provoking both giggles and shrieks. She watched as the girls got in closer and closer, able to touch the monster but somehow never getting caught. Then suddenly, without warning, the monster grabbed both of them around the waist. With a screaming girl under each arm, he ran, with grace atypical for the undead, toward D.J. and the seclusion of the umbrella.

She laughed as he dropped the two girls in her lap.

"Exhausted," he said as he dropped beside them on the blanket.

Like ever-energetic puppies, the girls immediately pounced upon his prone position, instigating "tickle wars." It was clear to D.J. that, as per usual, her husband was outnumbered and outclassed.

Sophie, age six, simply could not be tickled, but knew all the best spots to go for. Her little sister, Jaleh, got goosey at a mere finger pointed in her direction and could end up crying if she got too much.

D.J. let them torture Scott for a couple of minutes before she called a halt.

"Let Daddy rest," she told them. "You don't want to wear him out completely on only the second day at the beach."

Reluctantly the girls settled down. Sophie talked her father into a quieter activity, "toe math," where feet were utilized for counting, rather than fingers.

Jaleh, who after a long day of fun in the sun, was finally beginning to tire, took a seat in D.J.'s lap. She smelled of sea salt and suntan lotion. Resting her head on Mom's shoulder, D.J. expected her to be sleeping within minutes. But an intruder nixed that scenario.

The small dog suddenly burst in among them. He had as much silver in his coat as black, but his enthusiasm was youthful.

"Dewey!" Jaleh said, excitedly as she jumped up to play.

Sister and dog were joined by Sophie, who at least had the good manners to call out a greeting to the dog's owner.

"Hi, Grandma!"

D.J. shaded her eyes as she looked up at her mother-in-law. Viv, clad in a vivid lavender caftan and sporting a gigantic straw hat, looked perfectly decked out for a beach excursion.

Scott jumped to his feet. "Let me get another chair."

Viv tutted and shook her head. "Don't bother," she told him. "I'm here to collect the girls."

The children looked up expectantly.

"Gerald is taking us to dinner where they launch the pirate ship," she said. "I knew the girls would want to see that."

"Gerald?" Scott asked. "The old guy you met on the plane?"

"He wasn't that old," D.J. corrected him. "And he was very distinguished-looking, I thought."

"Yeah, okay," Scott conceded. "But why are you taking our children on your date?"

"It's not a date," Viv insisted firmly.

"Where have I heard that before?"

Viv gave a huff. "Well, the rule is love me, love my grandchildren."

She clapped her hands and urged the girls to bring the dog and come with her. They eagerly complied.

"We're going to have a sleepover in my room," she told them.

Sophie and Jaleh were thrilled.

"Is Gerald in on that?" Scott asked.

His mother wagged a warning finger at him.

"You don't have to babysit," D.J. told her. "You're on vacation, too."

Viv waved away her concern. "A vacation from retirement sounds like taking on a job. These two aren't a job, they are a pleasure."

After some noise, chaos, laughter and a bark or two, Scott and D.J. found themselves alone on the beach with a night on their own to look forward to.

"What do you think that was all about?" Scott asked. "Does she not want to be alone with this guy?"

D.J. shrugged. "Maybe," she said. "But I think she may have other motives, as well."

Scott raised an eyebrow. "What other motives?"

"Well, she's been making some veiled suggestions

about how nice it would be to have a grandson. And how much the girls would love to have a little brother."

"Oh, yeah? She hasn't said a word to me."

"She knows you'd tell her it's none of her business."

"Which it's not," Scott said. "But it is yours. What do you think? Is our family complete or are we missing somebody?"

D.J. shrugged. "I could go either way," she answered. "You know how I love babies. But we've finally got everyone out of diapers and on a regular sleeping schedule. Do we really want to start 2:00 a.m. feedings again?"

"And colic. Remember colic?"

"I still have flashbacks."

He chuckled.

"So how do you feel?"

"Another baby could be great," he said. "If you want to, I'm there. But our life is so good. We have a great marriage with two beautiful, healthy girls. We both have jobs that we love. Good friends. Wonderful family."

"We have the best sex in Kansas."

He laughed. "Really? You think we have the best sex in Kansas?"

"Well, I haven't had sex with everyone in the state, but I'm pretty sure ours has to be the best."

"I'm sure you're right," he answered, grinning.

"Even from this distance I can see your ego inflating."

"Best sex in Kansas," he repeated.

"Just remember, we're not in Kansas anymore. And here on South Padre, there are lots of guys running around that are almost half your age and with twice your hormones. So the competition is, shall we say, stiffer."

Scott howled with laughter. "You're incorrigible," he told her.

D.J. shrugged. "I'm a librarian, how could you expect anything else?"

He rose to his feet and offered a hand.

"Where're we going?"

"Some place a bit more private."

"Oh, yeah? And for what purpose?"

He grinned at her. "A South Padre tradition."

"Which is?"

"Shining a bit of sparkle on Mrs. Sanderson."

* * * * *

REQUEST YOUR
FREE BOOKS!

2 FREE NOVELS
FROM THE ROMANCE COLLECTION
PLUS 2 FREE GIFTS!

ES! Please send me 2 FREE novels from the Romance Collection and my 2 FREE gifts
fts are worth about $10). After receiving them, if I don't wish to receive any more books,
an return the shipping statement marked "cancel." If I don't cancel, I will receive 4 brand-
w novels every month and be billed just $6.24 per book in the U.S. or $6.74 per book in
nada. That's a savings of at least 22% off the cover price. It's quite a bargain! Shipping
d handling is just 50¢ per book in the U.S. and 75¢ per book in Canada.* I understand that
cepting the 2 free books and gifts places me under no obligation to buy anything. I can
vays return a shipment and cancel at any time. Even if I never buy another book, the two
e books and gifts are mine to keep forever.

194/394 MDN F4XY

me   (PLEASE PRINT)

dress   Apt. #

y   State/Prov   Zip/Postal Code

nature (if under 18, a parent or guardian must sign

Mail to the **Harlequin® Reader Service:**
IN U.S.A.: P.O. Box 1867, Buffalo, NY 14240-1867
IN CANADA: P.O. Box 609, Fort Erie, Ontario L2A 5X3

Want to try two free books from another line?
Call 1-800-873-8635 or visit www.ReaderService.com.

PAMELA
MORSI

31541	BITSY'S BAIT & BBQ	__ $7.99 U.S.	__ $9.99 CA
31540	THE COTTON QUEEN	__ $7.99 U.S.	__ $9.99 CA
31376	THE LOVESICK CURE	__ $7.99 U.S.	__ $9.99 CA

(limited q...

TOTAL AMOUNT
POSTAGE & HANDLING
($1.00 for 1 book, 50¢ for each a...
APPLICABLE TAXES*
TOTAL PAYABLE
(check or money ord...

To order, complete this form an...
order for the total above, payab...
3010 Walden Avenue, P.O. ...
In Canada: P.O. Box 636, Fo...

Name: _____
Address: _____
State/Prov.: _____ Zip/Postal Code: _____
Account Number (if applicable): _____
075 CSAS

*New York residents remit applicable sales taxes.
*Canadian residents remit applicable GST and provincial taxes.

31901055189692

H HARLEQUIN® MIRA®
www.Harlequin.com